Evil in Return

'A thoroughly engrossing read, with interesting characters and a well-paced plot. Add Mark Tartaglia and Sam Donovan to your list of must-read detectives' Peter Robinson

'DI Mark Tartaglia and DS Sam Donovan make a welcome return in Elena Forbes' *Evil in Return* . . . Switching between compelling characters' perspectives, Forbes keeps a tight rein on the tempo of this page-turning police procedural' *Time Out*

'It drew me in from the beginning. As Tartaglia probes deeper, the plot becomes even more intriguing . . . the identity of the killer kept me guessing . . . The book is tightly plotted and atmospheric – the creepiness of Brompton cemetery really comes across . . . It's an engrossing read and I would thoroughly recommend it' *shotsmag*

'Compelling . . . this is no ordinary serial story, but a novel in the vein of *The Secret History* . . . it's tautly written, with the race against time expertly handled' *Guardian*

Die With Me

'Hits the spot . . . tightly plotted, well written and convincing' *Daily Mail*

'The troubled Tartaglia is an interesting creation and the plot shifts and swerves in unexpected but pleasurable ways' *Observer*

'Forbes is good on plot, tension and lurking evil. The killer is clever and frighteningly normal' *The Times*

'A fast-moving novel, in which Forbes offers an original and compelling n

Elena Forbes has lived most of her life in London. Her first novel, *Die With Me*, was shortlisted for the CWA John Creasey New Blood Dagger, and was followed in 2009 by *Our Lady of Pain*.

EVIL IN RETURN

Elena Forbes

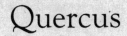

First published in Great Britain in 2010 by Quercus
This paperback edition published in 2011 by

Quercus
21 Bloomsbury Square
London
WC1A 2NS

ISBN 978 1 84916 259 3

10 9 8 7 6 5 4 3 2 1

Typeset by Ellipsis Books Limited, Glasgow
Printed and bound in Great Britain by Clays Ltd, St Ives plc

I and the public know
What all schoolchildren learn,
Those to whom evil is done
Do evil in return.

– W.H. Auden

For Kathryn Skoyles

He pushed open the door and went inside. It was a dark room, little more than a windowless tank, painted floor to ceiling matt black. The peculiar, tangy smell reminded him of the chemical labs at school and made him feel a little queasy. Hip-hop thudded from a player sitting on a chair in the middle of the floor, but there was no sign of anybody. He walked over and switched it off, his ears ringing in the silence. A red bulb hung from the centre of the low ceiling. It was swinging slowly from side to side as though it had been recently knocked and he followed its gyrations for a moment, wondering if the music had been enough to set it in motion. Cupboards ran along one wall with a stainless-steel sink unit. Above them, pegged to a wire, was a row of large black and white prints, each showing the same image. Superimposed against a blurred background of trees, two grinning faces floated in the centre, cheek to cheek, arms entwined like lovers. He gazed at the prints for a moment finding it difficult to see straight in the strange, shifting light. He felt dizzy, sort of pissed, although he'd had little to drink. He shook his head but it made no difference. The light was playing tricks with his eyes. The walls were billowing

1

gently like the sides of a tent in a breeze, and when he looked down the floor seemed to be moving. He fell to his knees, struggling to focus, and peered up at the photos, the images swimming in front of him. There was something about the faces ...

He heard a sound behind him. He looked around towards the open door, saw it close, heard the lock click softly into place. Then the light went out.

'Up there. On the left,' Mark Tartaglia shouted. Sam Sparro's 'Black and Gold' blasted through the Golf and he gesticulated violently towards the huge stone arch that framed the entrance to Brompton Cemetery. '*Left!*'

Sam Donovan swerved, slammed on the brakes, and pulled up sharply in front of the wrought-iron gates where a young uniformed constable was standing. She killed the music, leaned out of the window and flashed her ID. The policeman glanced at it, then peered at Donovan questioningly. Tartaglia caught the momentary hesitation before he handed back her ID. Donovan had noticed it too, he was sure. He had seen it before and knew how it irritated her. She was prettier than most, small and slim, with a neat-featured face and lovely large, grey eyes, hidden today behind Wayfarers. In her summer uniform of combats and T-shirt, with her brutally short brown hair, she looked more like a teenage boy than most people's idea of an experienced female detective. Whatever other people thought, it was never something that troubled him. He didn't care how she dressed or how young she looked. What mattered was that she was good at her job, he liked working with her and, more than that, he regarded her as a friend.

It was midday and sunshine streamed in through the car's front window. As Donovan exchanged words with the constable, Tartaglia turned his head out of the glare and took a final reluctant drag on his cigarette, savouring the moment before tossing it into the gutter. He removed his sunglasses, blew a small insect off one of the black lenses then slid them back on, yawning as he stretched his legs and flexed his shoulders. He had only just come back from a couple of weeks' holiday in southern Italy and was finding it difficult adjusting back into the normal work rhythm. Whether it was the heady warmth of the air or the fact that he had had yet another late night, he still felt half asleep, and the drone of cars from the Old Brompton Road was hypnotic. He watched lazily in the wing mirror as a group of passers-by paused by the entrance to gaze and point at the crime-scene tape that stretched in front of the gatehouse and the full width of the perimeter on either side. At least there were no journalists hanging around, although it wouldn't take them long to sniff out what had happened. A suspicious death in a central London cemetery made for good copy.

After signing them in, the constable waved them through the gate and they pulled up just inside behind a group of police and forensic vehicles. Donovan jumped out and as Tartaglia followed, he squinted into the bright sunshine and drew in a deep breath, inhaling the sweet scent of newly mown grass. The last time he had been to Brompton Cemetery had been a Saturday in early spring, when he had taken a short cut through it on foot with his cousin Gianni. They had been on their way to watch Chelsea play at home at Stamford Bridge, which was just on the far side of the boundary wall.

4

The weather had been overcast and drizzling, the atmosphere decidedly moody. It was difficult to recall now, in the heat of a summer's day and with the area peppered with the blue-suited figures of the forensic team.

'Look,' Donovan said, pointing at his feet. 'He thinks you're going to feed him.'

Tartaglia glanced down and saw a small grey squirrel sitting on its hind legs, looking up at him expectantly. He shook his head and held out his hands to show the squirrel they were empty.

'It's a positive zoo in here,' a cheerful voice said behind him. He turned to see Tracy Jamieson, the crime-scene manager, barely recognisable in her hooded suit and goggles. 'We've just unearthed a family of foxes from under one of the graves and there must be hundreds of rabbits and squirrels.'

'I must remember to bring peanuts next time,' he said. He took off his jacket, helped himself to a jumpsuit from the back of one of the vans, and began pulling it on over his trousers. He was already sweating heavily and hoped he wouldn't have to wear it for long. 'So, what have we got?'

'The victim's white, male, in his late thirties. He's been shot in the head. He's in one of the catacombs over there.' She pointed away along the drive towards a long avenue of neo-classical colonnades.

'Do we have an ID?'

'Name's Joseph Andrew Logan. His wallet and driver's licence were on him, and also about two hundred pounds in cash, so it doesn't look like robbery.'

Tartaglia turned to Donovan, who was struggling with a

suit several sizes too big. 'When you're done, go and find whoever's in charge. I want a map of the place. I want to know about opening and closing times and all means of access. And find out about security and cameras.'

'It's a South African bloke. Last time I saw him, he was in his office by the chapel,' Jamieson said. 'He was talking to one of the DIs from Kensington.'

'Where's the chapel?' Donovan asked, as she sat down on the bonnet of a nearby car and started to roll up one of the trouser legs.

'It's a round, domed building at the end of the drive. You can't miss it. Looks like a mini St Paul's.'

'Where's Arabella?' Tartaglia asked, spotting the battered, white Volvo estate that belonged to Dr Arabella Browne, the Home Office pathologist. It was parked next to one of the forensic vans and was easily recognisable by its Countryside Alliance bumper sticker. In the thick layer of dust on the back window, some wit had scrawled 'Also Comes In White'. He was pretty sure it had been there the last time he saw the car.

'Down in the crypt,' Jamieson said. 'She arrived about an hour ago but the photographers hadn't finished, so she had to wait. She wasn't best pleased.'

'Patience isn't her middle name.' He zipped up his suit and they started walking together along the drive towards the colonnades. 'You're sure the victim doesn't belong in the crypt?'

She shook her head. 'The last time anyone was buried in there was over a hundred years ago, and he wasn't in there yesterday afternoon, according to the bloke who runs the place.'

'He's in the habit of checking?'

'No, but some builders have been using the crypt for storage. Apparently they didn't notice anything out of the ordinary when they locked up yesterday.'

'Builders?' He sighed. 'So the crime scene's fucked.'

'Their stuff is all over the place, as are their footprints. We'll try and eliminate what's theirs but he wasn't killed in the crypt. There are no signs of a struggle or blood or anything.'

'What about out here?' he asked, gazing around at the dry, grassy expanse of land, which was the size of several football pitches. It was shaded by tall trees and densely packed with weathered graves and ornate mausoleums that looked at least a century old, many in a poor state of repair. Unless they got lucky, it might take days to search it thoroughly. The cemetery was well known as a gay cruising spot and he thought of the shadowy figures he had seen loitering in and around the colonnades when he had last been there. Was there a gay connection? It was too early to jump to conclusions, but if they could persuade people to talk, they might have some useful witnesses.

'So far nothing. We started with the area around the colonnades and we're working our way out.'

'What time did the builders lock up yesterday?'

'About four p.m., apparently.'

'They have it easy. What time was he found?'

'Just after eight this morning, when the gates opened. Someone was walking their dog and the dog ran off and pawed the door open. His owner had to go in after him. She said there was no padlock on the door and that the chain was just lying on the ground outside.'

'Maybe the builders left it unlocked.'

'They say not. The padlock's missing, by the way.'

Tartaglia left Jamieson at the inner cordon and walked up the drive to the colonnades. Built of yellow stone, they ran for a good hundred feet on either side of the road, with a raised, covered walkway above and catacombs below. In the middle of each section, stairs led down to a pair of large, arched double doors. One set was chained and padlocked, but on the opposite side, one of the doors was slightly ajar and he saw light within. He went down the steps, noticing how the soft sandstone walls and mouldings around the doors were pitted and crumbling. The decay seemed symptomatic of the whole place. The doors were painted black, with ornamental grilles and two large, curling snakes for handles. He pushed the right-hand door and went inside.

The air in the burial chamber was noticeably cooler and heavy with damp. Lying immediately below the colonnade, the ceiling was oppressively low. Shelves were set into the brick walls, stacked with ancient coffins. In many places the wood had disintegrated, revealing the lead linings glinting in the light from the portable lamps. A huge green bell sat upright in a dusty corner with the bronze figure of an angel attached to the back, and a large roll of blue polythene sheeting lay on the floor beside it, along with a roll of wire, a hammer and a Tesco's bag containing the remains of somebody's lunch.

Dr Browne, looking like a short, squat snowman in her hooded suit, was in the next-door room, kneeling down beside the body and muttering into a recorder. The dead man sat stiff as a doll on the ground, his back leaning against a

8

wrought-iron railing, his legs stretched out in front of him in a 'V', feet bare, arms rigid at his sides. He appeared to be of medium height and build and was dressed in a well-worn denim jacket, faded jeans and a dark-coloured T-shirt. His face was in Browne's shadow. Tartaglia moved closer and crouched down to get a better look. The man was clean-shaven but his face was streaked with earth and what looked like dried blood. A dirty black hole marked the middle of his forehead like an inkblot, the edges tattooed with gunshot residue. The gun had been fired at point blank range.

'Just the one shot?' he asked, as Browne finished her sentence and paused the recorder.

She glanced over at him and gave a curt nod of recognition. 'Far as I can see. Exit wound's clean. No sign of the bullet.'

'Tracy said he wasn't killed down here.'

She nodded. 'I can't check the *livor mortis* until I undress him, but there's no blood spatter or anything. I'll be able to give you more when I examine him properly later on. Now forensics have done their stuff, I want him bagged up and out of here as quickly as possible.'

'Someone's sure worked him over,' Tartaglia said, noting the heavy swelling around the man's nose, eyes and mouth. He also picked up the sour reek of vomit and urine. He peered down at the man's hands, which looked unmarked as far as he could tell, the nails cut short and clean. Not a vagrant, it seemed. 'What about defence wounds?'

'Nothing obvious, but he's got ligature marks on both wrists and ankles. They look ante-mortem. Maybe he wasn't able to defend himself.'

With a gloved finger, Tartaglia eased back each sleeve of the man's jacket in turn. The watch on his left wrist was a simple black Swatch. The marks made by the ligatures were clearly visible. The killer had used something fine, with a sharp edge that had cut into the skin like a blunt knife; plastic cable ties, maybe.

'Have you found the bindings?'

'No.'

'What about his shoes?'

'Double negative.'

The shoes might have easily dropped off when the body was shifted after death, but the lack of ligatures was puzzling. They must have been deliberately removed, although it wasn't obvious why.

'What's all that on his jeans?' he asked, noticing a large, dark, oily-looking patch that spread across the man's lap.

'Blood, I think. I can't tell where it's coming from until I get his clothes off.'

Still gazing at the man on the ground, he got to his feet. The killing had all the hallmarks of a professional hit, although, unless there was some intended irony, the choice of dumpsite was puzzling. The victim would be around twelve to thirteen stone, at a rough guess: a fair weight, even for someone strong, to lug all the way down into the crypt. He wondered why the killer had bothered when there must have been many more easily accessible hiding places outside in the graveyard. But he had learnt not to over-analyse. Time would tell, and sometimes there was no explanation.

The stale, dank air caught in his throat and he coughed. 'How long's he been dead?'

She sat back on her heels and fixed him with watery eyes. 'Mark, you know how I hate that question.'

'And you know I have to ask. Just a general indication will do for now. He's stiff as a board, so I assume we're not talking that long, although it's quite a bit cooler down here than outside.'

'The temperature is lower, but not enough to make a meaningful difference, and it's heating up a fair bit as the sun moves round. I certainly wouldn't keep my good claret in here.'

'So?'

Browne gave a wheezy sigh. 'Rigor's fully established, as you say. No signs of it passing off just yet either. My guess is he's been dead anything from twelve to twenty-four hours, thirty-six at the very outside. I hope that helps. You know what I say . . .'

He nodded. 'Yes, yes. When was he last seen, when was he found, etcetera, etcetera. He apparently wasn't here late afternoon yesterday, which means we're probably looking at closer to twelve hours than twenty-four. I can't see anyone shifting him down here in that position, can you?'

'Well nigh impossible, I'd say. As I said, I'll check the *livor mortis* later.'

'But how the hell did they get him here without being noticed?'

Browne shrugged as though it was none of her concern. The space felt suddenly claustrophobic and he decided the rest could wait until the post mortem.

'Anything else?' He started to move towards the exit.

'Well, his hair and clothes are wet.'

'It's pretty damp down here.'

'It's more than that.'

'Maybe someone tried to wash him off.'

'If so, they didn't do a very good job. He positively reeks.'

'I noticed. So when do you want me?'

'I'll try and squeeze it in this evening. Hope you've nothing special planned.'

'Nothing that can't wait,' he said, thinking regretfully of the two pretty New Zealanders who had just moved in next door and who had asked him to drop by that night for a drink and a barbeque. 'See you later, then.' Anything to get out into the sunshine and breathe some fresh summer's air.

'Try to stay awake this time.'

He smiled. 'I'll make a special effort.'

Outside, the light was blinding. Tartaglia put on his sunglasses and started to walk towards the cemetery office, finding relief in the cool line of shadow cast by the colonnade. Almost immediately, Donovan appeared round the corner of the chapel, marching briskly towards him. They met in the huge circle of graveyard in front of the chapel.

'I've got the map you wanted,' she said, holding up a rolled sheet of paper. As she stretched it out on one of the tombs, weighting it down with a few fragments of stone from the ground, he looked around, noting the high wall, overlooked by the back of a terrace of tall houses that marked the eastern boundary. On the western side the wall was lower; the overground railway was just beyond, he remembered. He looked down at the map, reminding himself of the general layout, the position of the various buildings and

ELENA FORBES

paths and the location of the two gates, one on Old Brompton
Road to the north and one on Fulham Road to the south.
There seemed to be no other exits.

He shielded his eyes with his hand and looked up at
Donovan, catching his reflection momentarily in her
Wayfarers. 'It's looking like a professional hit, single shot to
the head, point blank range. He's been tied up at some point
and he was probably killed somewhere out here then dumped
in the crypt. What time do the gates shut?'

'Eight p.m. at this time of year.'

'If the builders locked up around four, that gives the killer
four hours when the cemetery is still open. But this place is
crawling with people during the day, it's far too risky. My
gut feeling is that whatever went on, happened after hours,
when it was dark. So – based on Arabella's guesstimate for
time of death – we're talking about last night. What's the
locking-up procedure?'

'An outside security firm is responsible for opening up in
the morning and securing the gates at night. It's basically a
couple of men in a van. I have the name of the company.'

'I want a check on all personnel on duty and their routine
over the last couple of weeks. What's security like?'

'What you'd expect. It's a cemetery. The Parks Police patrol
two to three times a week during daylight hours, but there's
nobody at night. The guy who looks after the place lives in
a flat over the north gate and says he'd hear if anyone tried
to break in. There are CCTV cameras on both the Fulham
Road and Brompton Road entrances, linked to a remote
recorder. The memory's good for fifteen days and I've sent
someone for the hard drive.'

He nodded. 'What else?'

'The railings on either side of the gates are about twenty feet high, but people have been known to climb them. You know . . .' She gave a meaningful shrug. 'Beats me . . .'

'Yes, quite. They must be desperate.' He looked down at the map. 'Is there any other way in?'

'You've got houses all along here and here, apart from the entrance gate,' she said, indicating the eastern and southern perimeters.

'Couldn't someone climb over the back wall from one of the houses?'

'Too high. I've checked.'

'What about from the railway?'

'The tracks are right below and there's a very big drop. There are a couple of access doors that lead down to the railway, but they've both been checked. They're jammed shut and there's no sign of either of them having being opened in donkey's years.'

'What about the offices and the chapel?'

'All locked and alarmed at night.'

While puzzling it over, he saw Tracy Jamieson half jogging, half running towards them.

'What is it?' he called out.

'We've got something,' she said, as she came over to them. 'God, this heat . . . These fucking suits . . . I can't cope.' She fanned her face, which was now bright pink, and wiped a stray wisp of dark hair from her glistening forehead. 'The main gates on Fulham Road . . . they're open every day, but the pedestrian gates on either side . . . they keep them padlocked. Always. They're still chained, but one of the padlocks looked newer than the other . . . so we checked the keys in the office. The one the keeper has . . . for the right-hand gate . . . it doesn't fit.'

'So, somebody's changed the padlock,' Tartaglia said. Jamieson nodded. 'At least we now know how he got in,' he continued. 'Although it doesn't explain much else.'

He thought of the missing padlock from the crypt door and the chain left casually lying on the ground where it would be seen. Either the killer had been disturbed before he had a chance to replace it or, more likely, he had meant for the body to be found and had left the chain to draw attention to the crypt.

'When was the pedestrian gate last used?'

'Ages ago,' she said, still drawing deep breaths. 'Months, at least, according to the keeper.'

Tartaglia looked at Donovan. 'Thought you said there's a camera on that gate?'

'That's what I was told.'

'Well, hopefully it should show us what happened – *if* it's working.' He had lost count of the number of times they had been let down by a vital camera being out of action, or there being no tape in an old-fashioned, non-digital recorder.

Jamieson shook her head. 'It's working, all right. That's not the problem. It's one of those fish-eye things. Pretty ancient piece of kit. Looks a bit like a smoke alarm. Anyway, it's up on the wall of the South Lodge, about fifteen feet off the ground. Covers the whole gate and path inside.'

'And . . . ?' Tartaglia prompted.

'Well, I thought it looked a bit odd. So I sent one of the lads up to check. You can barely see from below, but the lens has been totally covered. Someone's sprayed it with black paint.'

2

Tartaglia parked the Ducati by the railings above the canal and dismounted. As he took off his helmet he felt the warm evening breeze on his face. He wiped the sweat off his forehead, ruffled his flattened hair with his fingers and gazed momentarily down over the still water. The sun was slowly sinking over Browning's Pool, the light washing the neo-classical villas on either side of the canal and reflecting off the windows of the little café perched on top of the next bridge. The ribbon of tree-lined water stretched out straight in front of him, disappearing into the dark hole of the Maida Hill Tunnel. He found himself thinking back to just over six months before, remembering the murdered young girl whose body had been pulled out of the water only a few steps away from where he was standing. Today was the first time he had been back to that stretch of the canal and he felt a pang of sadness, sharp as a blade. How quickly life moved on.

He chained his helmet to the motorbike and walked along the railings towards the gate that led down to the towpath. The address on Joseph Logan's driving licence was nearly two years out of date. He had moved several times since and it had taken the whole afternoon to establish that he had been living for the past two months on a narrow-boat on Regent's Canal, near Little Venice. A wide area of road, pavement and towpath around the berth of Logan's narrow-boat had been cordoned off to enable a thorough search of his living-quarters. Members of Tartaglia's team, helped by uniformed officers from the local station, were also busy knocking on doors of other boats and of houses in the vicinity. Apart from valuable background information on Logan, the priority was to establish when he had last been seen and if he had had any visitors in the past couple of days.

Ignoring the various locals who had gathered to watch proceedings on either side of the tape and at the railings on the opposite bank, Tartaglia was signed in by the uniformed gatekeeper and made his way along the towpath to Logan's boat. It was moored in front of a large Victorian church that faced the canal, in the middle of a line of other narrow-boats of varying sizes, styles and colours. Logan's was about sixty feet long, painted in dull, blistered panels of black and maroon, with a series of decorative lines and swirls in faded gold encircling the name *Dragonfly*. He had never understood the appeal of narrow-boats. This stretch of the Maida Canal was probably one of the most sought-after moorings in the city, yet he would hate to live parked on a dirty, smelly strip of brown water, his windows overlooked from the streets on both sides as well as by the boats moored opposite. He valued his privacy more than most things. He wondered what Logan had been doing there and what had made him move from his previous address in the country.

The entrance was at the stern, via a small deck that was cluttered with pot plants and a couple of ancient-looking folding metal chairs and a table. As Tartaglia bent down to climb in through the open doors, he saw DC Jane Downes at the bottom of the cabin steps, peering up at him short-sightedly through thick-lensed, owlish blue glasses. Short, naturally blonde hair with a heavy fringe framed her face, emphasising the roundness of her cheeks and a large nose. A full rucksack was slung over one shoulder and she cradled a heavy-looking archive box in her sturdy arms.

'Are you done?' he asked, lowering himself into the tiny kitchen area of the cabin.

'Ah, it's you, sir. Couldn't tell for a moment against the light. I've still got a bit more to pack up.'

'Where's Nick?'

'With Karen, talking to some of the boat owners. I was just taking this lot to the car. Thought I'd go through it back at the office. You can barely move in here and I don't like being watched. They think it's a ruddy spectator sport.' She jerked her head in the direction of the porthole. The cluster of people gathered beyond the railings on the opposite bank were clearly visible.

The internal space of the boat was not more than about seven feet wide, with inward-sloping panelled walls that reminded him of an old-fashioned railway carriage. The kitchen was screened off from the rest of the cabin and had a quaint, country feel, with pine units and open shelving, which was filled with a colourful jumble of crockery, mugs and kilner jars. Amongst a pile of dirty dishes in the sink, he noticed the remnants of a bowl of cereal and milk that looked relatively recent.

'Have you checked the fridge?' he asked.

'Yes. He hasn't been gone long. All well within the sell-by date, and I found a till receipt for some food and bits and pieces in the bin, timed at six-ten in the evening the day before yesterday. The shop's just around the corner. Dave's gone over there now to see if they remember him. It's a Sainsbury, so they should have CCTV.'

For a moment Tartaglia thought of the fuzzy footage recovered from Brompton Cemetery, which he had watched only an hour before. The first part showed a dark-clad figure with a backpack, clearly male and of athletic build, his head covered by a Batman mask and balaclava. He was using bolt cutters on the padlock of the pedestrian gate. The next showed him fifteen feet up on the roof of the South Lodge, wiping out the security camera with a can of spray paint. As nobody at the cemetery ever bothered to check the footage unless specifically requested, it had gone unnoticed. How the man had got up there was unclear, but the procedure had taken a matter of minutes, captured on the remote hard drive three days before, at one thirty-four in the morning. At that time, Logan was still alive, unaware of what lay in store for him.

Tartaglia's head brushed the gently curving ceiling as he moved past Downes into the tunnel-like sitting room. The porthole windows were closed and, in spite of the doors at the end being open, the air was stale. He could tell from the smell that Logan had been a heavy smoker. There was no sign of central heating and the only source of warmth seemed to be an old-fashioned enamel stove in the far corner. He imagined it must get pretty cold and damp in winter. For the second time that day he started to feel claustrophobic, not helped by the fact that the cabin was painted a deep pink. A couple of armchairs covered in bright patchwork throws were placed to one side, opposite a flat-screen TV. Beside them was a small bookcase, overflowing with paperbacks which revealed a healthy interest in dieting, self-help and chick-lit. A jug stuffed full of imitation red and pink roses sat on the top. The whole feel of the place was feminine and he assumed Logan must have a partner.

He turned to Downes. 'Does anyone else live here?'

She shook her head. 'There's barely enough gear for one man, let alone two, and there's certainly no sign of a woman. I checked with MISPER, but nobody's reported him missing.'

'So he lived alone, on somebody else's boat, by the looks of things. Find out who owns it and what Logan was doing here. What sort of state was this place in when you got here?'

'More or less like it is now, although there were a few empty beer bottles out on the deck, and an ashtray with a load of butts and what looks like the remains of a joint.'

'No signs of a struggle?'

'No, and the doors were double-locked from the outside. I've sent the bottles off to be printed and I've bagged up the rest in case we need it.'

'How did you get in? There weren't any keys on his body.'

'He kept a set under one of the flowerpots out on the deck. The guy on the next boat told me where to look.'

'Jesus. Doesn't anybody worry about security?'

She shrugged. 'He says Logan kept mislaying his key.'

'So anyone could have known where it was kept. You sure nobody's been in here?'

'Impossible to tell. As you can see, Logan wasn't very tidy.'

'What's all this?' He pointed at a folding table under one of the portholes, which was being used as a desk. An anglepoise lamp was clamped to one side and papers spread out messily over the surface, next to an overflowing in-tray.

'I had a quick look. It's mainly newspaper clippings and stuff printed off the internet. I'll come back for it once I've loaded this lot into the car.'

Tartaglia noticed a small printer tucked away on the floor under the table, but no sign of a phone or fax. 'Have you found his mobile?'

'Hasn't turned up. There's no landline, so he must have had one. Maybe I'll find a bill hiding in all the papers.'

'What about a computer?'

'He had a laptop. It's gone off for analysis.'

'What's the progress on tracing the next of kin?'

'Nothing yet. Maybe one of the neighbours will be able to help, or something will turn up on the computer.'

'OK. Go and find Nick, will you? I want to hear how he's been getting on.'

He left her to carry the box upstairs and went into the bedroom in the prow. Painted a sunny yellow, it was tiny and functional; somewhere to sleep, not a place where you would want to spend much time. A small double bed was built along one side under a window, a pair of crumpled black jeans dumped on the floor beside it, along with underpants, a T-shirt and an old leather jacket. It looked as though Logan had barely bothered to undress before climbing into bed. The duvet was rucked up and the pillows were stacked against the wall as though Logan had been reading. A half-drunk mug of something cold and grey sat on the floor, next to a well-thumbed paperback copy of Richard Dawkins' *The God Delusion* and an ashtray containing the butts of several roll-ups. Either Logan had been interrupted or he couldn't be bothered to clear up. Some drawers under the bed contained a small, untidy collection of casual clothing and underwear, all of which would fit easily into a single suitcase. There was nothing new, nothing expensive or flashy. Underneath the tangle of clothes he unearthed a handful of relatively tame porn magazines. Assuming they belonged to Logan, it seemed that he was straight.

Tartaglia picked up the jeans, then the jacket, and felt in the pockets. He pulled out a tissue and a battered Old Holborn tin with a flower painted in silver paint on the front and the initials JAL. It contained tobacco, papers, a zip lighter and a small lump of cannabis resin. He left it all on the bed for Downes and went over to a cupboard in the corner. Inside was a small shower cubicle and WC. The shell-framed mirror above the basin was cracked and it all looked in need of a good clean. One toothbrush, one disposable razor, shaving gel, shampoo, soap and a bottle of inexpensive aftershave, barely used. Nothing else. The small medicine cupboard was bare, apart from some paracetamol and a pack of Rennies. The way someone lived, their things, the choices they made, said a lot about their character. From what he could tell so far, Logan really was living out of a suitcase.

As he turned to leave, he saw the thin, dark-haired form of DC Nick Minderedes in the doorway. 'You looking for me?'

'Yes. Any joy with the neighbours?'

'Most of them are still out at work. The ones we've spoken to say they barely exchanged more than a few words with

Mr Logan. They say he kept himself to himself and wasn't very friendly.'

'Well, try harder. I don't care what they think of him. You can't move in a place like this without someone seeing what you're up to, whether you like it or not. Somebody, somewhere along here, must know something.'

'There's one that sounds promising. The woman in the boat two along, down towards the tunnel, says she knew him, not that she'd tell me much. She wants to speak to you.'

'Me?'

'Yes.'

'Can't you deal with it?' he said, checking his watch. It was nearly seven-thirty. He ought to be making tracks for the post mortem, where Sam Donovan was holding the fort.

'Says she will only speak to the man in charge. She saw you arrive and asked one of the uniforms who you were. I tried to tell her I'd do just as well, but she was having none of it. As I said, she seems to know Logan quite well. Calls him Joe and she's quite upset.'

As Alex Fleming turned the corner, he heard the hoot of horns and saw blue flashing lights down by the canal. He crossed the road, stopped on the bridge and peered over the high railings, trying to see what was going on. A police car was parked at right angles in the middle of the road alongside the water, with another pulled up further along. Part of the road appeared to be blocked off and a couple of uniformed officers were redirecting the oncoming traffic away down a side street. The walk from the tube had taken no more than a few minutes, but he was hot and out of breath. His shirt was sticking to his back and his head throbbed. He felt the sudden familiar pressure in his sinuses, followed almost instantly by a warm trickle of blood over his lip. It ran down his throat and he tilted his head forwards, staring down through the railings at the canal below and pinching the bridge of his nose hard, as he rummaged in his pockets for something to staunch the flow. He found an old scrunched-up paper napkin and held it tight to his nose, as he tried to see what was going on down below. A few people were gathered by the railings, looking down over the water. They seemed to be watching something and he wondered if somebody had fallen in. Joe's boat was almost immediately below where they were standing and the area around it appeared to be taped off. Squinting hard, he thought he saw signs of movement inside. He wondered if it was Joe, if he was OK.

The bleeding stopped almost as suddenly as it had begun. He crossed the bridge and walked quickly along the pavement until he came to the line of police tape where the people stood.

'What's going on?' Alex asked a young woman with long brown hair, who had also just joined the group. She was pushing a buggy with a small child asleep inside and was talking to a middle-aged man.

'No idea,' she said, distractedly. 'Just got here myself. It's a ruddy nuisance, whatever it is. They won't let us through and they're saying we're going to have to go all the way round.'

'Do you have any idea?' he asked the man next to her.

'Not sure, but they're taking stuff off that boat. See that

woman over there?' He pointed to a dumpy blonde-haired woman in baggy blue trousers, who was loading a box into the boot of a nearby car. 'I think she's police.'

'Police?'

'Maybe it's drugs,' the woman said.

'I'll bet someone's gone in the canal,' another man said, joining them. 'Just a mouthful of that water's enough to kill you.' He had a small brown and white dog in tow, which was yapping and tugging impatiently at its lead.

The woman shook her head. 'There's no ambulance. Gotta be something else.'

'I reckon it's terrorists,' the first man said.

Alex saw further movement inside Joe's boat. Without waiting for the woman's reply, he went over to a young uniformed constable who was standing by the tape, guarding one of the gates that led down to the canal.

'What's going on?'

'I'm not able to say, sir.' He was sweating heavily, as though he had been there for a while.

'But something's happened, hasn't it? Has somebody fallen in?'

'No. Nobody's fallen in. That's as much as I can tell you.'

Over the constable's shoulder, he saw two men emerge from the front of Joe's boat. They both had black hair and were deeply tanned. One was tall and muscular, casually dressed in what looked like leather motorbike trousers and a T-shirt, the other was shorter and slighter and wore a suit. More plainclothes police, he assumed. No sign of Joe. The two men exchanged a few words on the towpath, then parted, the taller one striding away in the direction of one of the other boats, the shorter one starting along the path towards them. He remembered what he and Joe had talked about the other night and he felt a surge of alarm. Had Joe said something after all?

He turned to the constable. 'That boat over there. The one they're all looking at. It belongs to a mate of mine.' As soon as he said it, he wished he'd kept his mouth shut. He remembered Joe's words: *Not the police* . . .

'A mate of yours, sir?'

'Is he in some kind of trouble?'

'What trouble would that be, sir?'

'How do I know?' He shrugged then glanced down at his watch, barely aware of what it said. 'Anyway, I'd better be off. I'm running late.' He turned to go.

'One minute, sir. Wait just there.' The plainclothes policeman was coming up the steps from the canal and the constable called over to him. 'This gentleman says he knows Mr Logan.'

The man closed the gate behind him and came over to Alex. 'Is that right?' He was a few inches shorter than Alex, slim and wiry, with smooth black hair and dark eyes. His suit was well cut and his open-necked mint-green shirt was clearly chosen to set off his tan. He gave Alex a tight, thin-lipped smile. 'So you're a friend of Mr Logan's?'

'I don't know him well,' Alex said hastily. 'He's not a close friend or anything. We just have the odd bevy in the pub from time to time, that's all.' He made it sound casual, hoping his anxiety didn't show. If he kept it simple, hopefully they'd let him go. 'What's happened?'

'I'll come to that in a minute, sir,' the man said, still

smiling as he felt in his breast pocket and handed a business card to Alex. Below the Metropolitan Police logo was the name, DC Nick Minderedes. Alex folded his arms tightly around himself, wondering what Joe had done. Had he gone to the police after all? Was that what this was all about?

'Are you all right?' Minderedes asked, looking at him in a way that made him feel even more uncomfortable.

'Yes. Why?'

'It's just you've got blood on your face and shirt.'

'Oh. Oh that.' He realised he was still clutching the blood-stained napkin. He balled it in his fist. 'I'm fine. I've just had a nosebleed, that's all. It's the heat.' He wiped his top lip with the back of his hand. He felt the sweat pricking his face, running down his neck and back. He must look a sight.

Still studying him, Minderedes took out a notebook and pen. 'Perhaps you could start by giving me your name?'

'Why do you want my name? I just want to know what's happened, that's all.'

'Routine, sir, I'm afraid.'

'This doesn't seem very routine. Why won't you tell me what's going on? Has something happened to Joe?'

'Can you just let me have your name for the record? My governor will give me grief if I don't do it by the book.'

Alex took a deep breath and nodded. He should never have stopped in the first place, should never have asked any stupid questions. 'My name's Tim. Tim Wade.' It was the first name that came to mind, probably because he and Joe had been talking about Tim only the other day.

'And your contact details?'

Not wanting to give Tim's real details, Alex gave the address of an old family friend who lived nearby. It sounded plausible and it was all he could think of. It seemed to satisfy Minderedes, who noted it down without question.

'We'll need to get a statement from you. Someone will be in touch to make an appointment. Do you have a phone number so we can contact you?'

He reeled off a number that he hoped sounded genuine and prayed they wouldn't try calling it until he was well gone.

'Do you know Mr Logan's number, by any chance?'

'No. I never spoke to him on the phone.'

'When did you last see Mr Logan?'

'About a week or so ago. Why?'

'Where was this?'

'In the pub.'

'Which pub?'

'I can't remember the name but it's further along the canal. On the water. That way.' He waved his hand vaguely in the general direction. He had had a drink there once with Joe, so it was partly true.

Minderedes made another note. 'Did Mr Logan go there regularly, do you know?'

'No idea, but that's where I usually saw him.'

'And you haven't seen him since?'

'No.'

Minderedes held his gaze for a moment, lips slightly parted as if he had something more to say. Alex's heart was thumping. He wanted to fill the gap with words but he couldn't risk blurting something out. He thought he was going to burst, then Minderedes snapped his notebook shut and slipped it away in his pocket.

'OK, sir. That about wraps it up. Thanks for your help. Just as a matter of routine, do you have any ID on you?'

Alex patted his pockets as if feeling for his wallet, then shook his head. He could feel it tight in the back pocket of his jeans, but hopefully the tail of his shirt covered the bulge. He didn't know much about the law but he was sure they had no right to search him. He took a deep breath. 'Sorry. Guess you'll just have to take my word for it. Now, please can you tell me what's happened? Is Joe OK?'

Minderedes puckered his lips as though he had tasted something sour. 'No. I'm afraid your friend is not OK. He's had an accident.'

'An accident? What do you mean?'

'I'm very sorry to tell you, Mr Logan is dead.'

3

Maggie Thomas's boat was even more brightly coloured than Logan's and was decorated like the inside of a pasha's tent. But the windows were open wide, a vase of fresh flowers stood on the kitchen counter next to an unopened bottle of red wine, and the air was full of the smell of garlic, tomato and thyme from a pan simmering on the stove. It was a combination he was familiar with from childhood, coming as he did from a family of good Italian cooks. He sat down on a kelim-covered armchair in the sitting area and watched as she washed a bunch of parsley that she had cut from one of the many pots on the roof of her boat.

'I understand you knew Mr Logan,' he said gently. When she had greeted him it was clear that she had been crying. Without turning around, she nodded and started to chop the parsley. 'Don't know why I'm so upset, really, I didn't know him that well. I mean, he hasn't been here long. It's just that it's a bit of a shock. I really liked him, you know. It's such a waste.'

She stopped chopping, put the knife down and turned to face him, wiping her hands quickly on a tea towel. She was striking-looking, deeply tanned, with streaky dark blonde hair pulled back in a loose ponytail and a lovely wide, generous mouth. He wondered what she would look like if she smiled. She might easily have passed for mid-forties, except that her hands and the laugh lines around her brown eyes gave her away. For some reason, she looked familiar to him, but he couldn't put his finger on why.

He took out a small notebook and pen from his back pocket. 'Anything you can tell me about him would be a help. Do you know who owns the boat he was living on?'

'Yes. It belongs to Sally Mathews. She's a friend of mine.'

'Where is she?'

'Gone to LA for a few months. Got a little part in a film and she's going to stay and see if she can pick up some more work. She let Joe have the boat until she gets back.'

'She's a friend of Mr Logan's, then, or more than that?'

'Just friends,' she said firmly. 'I think they were at drama school together.'

'I'll need her number, if you have it.'

'Of course.' She came and sat down opposite him in a large, comfortable-looking armchair, tucking her feet up on the seat, her toes just visible beneath the hem of her flowing, gypsy skirt. Even though she was a good decade or so older than Logan, she was still a fine-looking woman and he wondered if there had been something between them. It would explain why she was so upset over the death of somebody she claimed not to know particularly well.

'So Mr Logan's an actor?'

'Yes. Or at least he used to be. Like me. That's what we had in common, why we hit it off.'

An actress. Maybe that was why she looked so familiar,

although he still couldn't place her. 'I see. What do you mean, "used to be"?'

'Well, from what he told me, he did a bit of theatre, some telly and radio, but nothing mainstream. He wasn't bad looking and he had a nice voice, but there are a lot of guys like that. No USP. It's tough if you don't get a break. There's bugger all you can do if nobody wants you except sit at home and twiddle your thumbs and wait for the phone to ring. Even if you've got the skin of a rhino, it does your head in. I was lucky, I got into location work.'

'What's that?' he asked, curious to know a little more about her.

'I run an agency for film and TV. Say a location manager on some telly programme wants a big house in Hampstead for a shoot, or a Gothic country mansion, they come to me. I've got hundreds of great properties on my books. I started about fifteen years ago as a sideline when work was slow. Now it's more or less all I do.'

'What about Mr Logan? If he wasn't getting much work as an actor, how did he keep himself busy, pay the bills?'

She arched her dark brows in surprise. 'Joe? Don't you know?'

'Know what?'

'He wrote that book, *Indian Summer*. You must have heard of it, it won some big prize, the – what's it called?' She clicked her fingers in the air, then shook her head. 'My memory's terrible. Anyway, it's selling like hot cakes, or so he said.'

He made a note. 'Unfortunately, I don't get much time to read.'

'Me neither. I lent my copy to a friend, otherwise I'd show it you. Anyway, it was a big success. I think Joe was a bit flummoxed by it all. Before that, I think he had a job as a teacher at some posh boarding school.'

'We're trying to trace Mr Logan's movements over the past few days. When did you last see him?'

'Only yesterday. That's why this is all so sudden. One minute he's here, full of the joys of summer, then bang, he's gone.' She sighed heavily and hugged her knees.

'What time was this?'

'Just before five, I think.'

'How sure are you?'

'Positive.'

This brought forward Logan's death to within the last twenty-four hours. He made a note, then asked, 'Do you have any idea where he was going?'

She shook her head. 'I was coming home and I met him on the towpath. He was on his way out and he was whistling. He seemed pretty cheerful. He had his bike with him so I assumed he wasn't just going down to the shops.'

'He had a bike?'

'Yes. That's how he got around. He didn't have a car and he said he hated buses and the tube, they made him feel claustrophobic.'

'Where did he keep the bike?'

'Chained to the railings or on the roof of the boat. But it's not there now. I checked.'

'Can you describe it?'

'Sorry, I'm the wrong person to ask. It was just a bike to me, nothing special about it. I can't even remember what colour it was. Anyway, we had a brief chat. You know ... about the weather and stuff. They say the hot spell's going to break in a day or so, although I hope they're wrong.'

'Do you remember anything else?'

She frowned. 'Well, his hair was wet, so he must have just had a shower. And he'd shaved. I noticed because he often didn't bother for days.'

'Do you remember what he was wearing?'

She thought for a moment, then shook her head. 'Just that he looked nice. And smelt nice. Don't know if it was soap or aftershave, but he'd made an effort for a change. He usually looked pretty grungy.'

'Have you ever seen him with anyone?'

'He was with some bloke the day before yesterday.'

'What time?'

'Early evening. Half-six, maybe. I was going out and they were sitting on the little deck of Sally's boat – Joe's boat, I should say – having a drink.'

'What did the man look like?'

'About Joe's age, I suppose. Nice-looking fellow actually, with lovely dark red hair. Real auburn, if you know what I mean.'

'What sort of height?'

'Couldn't tell as he was sitting down, but he looked lean and fit and he had nice broad shoulders.'

'Have you ever seen him before?'

'Only once. In the Bargeman's Rest a couple of weeks ago.'

'Is that a pub?'

She nodded. 'Just along the canal, heading west. It overlooks the water and it's where we all go when the weather's nice. Joe and the red-haired fellow were having a drink and a smoke. I was with a friend of mine and they seemed quite engrossed over something, so I didn't stop to say hello.'

Tartaglia made a note to check the pub. 'You don't know the man's name?'

'No, but I'd say they knew each other quite well.'

'Why's that?'

'Body language. You can tell. They were relaxed together and they were having a really good old chinwag.'

'You only saw the man twice.'

She shrugged. 'Call me nosy, but I couldn't help being curious. Joe never talked about his friends, you see, apart from Sally. It was as if the subject was off limits, which of course made me curious. Maybe you should ask Sally if she knows this bloke. Anyway, she was the one told me to keep an eye on Joe, said that he'd suffered a bit from depression in the past. He hadn't lived in London for ages and it can be tough if you don't know anybody, particularly if you spend all day on your own wrapped up in some fantasy world in your head. So I had him over for the odd drink, just to get him off the boat. I even cooked him supper one evening. He brought a decent bottle of wine and a bunch of flowers. He wasn't a cheapskate.'

'What did you talk about?' he asked, still wondering about the nature of her relationship with Logan.

'This and that, nothing special, really . . . about the book, of course, and all the fuss there's been. I think he really hated all the attention. His publisher was trying to get him to do a lot of promotional stuff but he didn't want to do it. They couldn't make him, could they, but they were putting

a lot of pressure on him. I asked him what he was going to
do next and he said he was working on another story but
he didn't seem to want to talk about it. I think he may have
had writer's block or something. Writing a bestseller must
be pretty paralysing, don't you think? I mean, what do you
do for an encore?'

'Did he ever mention his family?'

'No. No, he didn't. He didn't volunteer and I didn't want
to pry. He really wasn't happy talking about himself and he
didn't much like living here, I can tell you.'

'Why's that?'

'Well, it's a bit like living in a goldfish bowl, isn't it?' She
gestured towards a window, which gave a clear view of another
boat moored opposite on the far side of the canal as well as
the towpath, public pavement and road beyond. 'We're all
on top of one another, aren't we? You can't hide anything,
even if you keep your curtains shut all the time. It doesn't
bother me, I'm used to it, but Joe said he hated it.'

'Why didn't he move somewhere else?'

'He'd promised Sally to look after the boat until she got
back and I imagine he was getting a pretty good deal on the
rent. Even so, I was sure he wouldn't last. It really wound
him up, everyone trying to get to know him, making small
talk every time he left the boat for a pint of milk, keeping
an eye on his comings and goings. He had some pretty funny
names for a few of the people along here, I can tell you. I
told him it was just because he was new but he wouldn't
listen.'

Tartaglia frowned. 'He thought someone was spying on
him?'

37

She waved the idea away with her hand. 'Oh no, not like that. Nothing sinister. They're just a load of old busybodies, nothing much going on in their lives, that's all.'

Tartaglia sympathised, but he started to wonder if Joe Logan just wanted some privacy or if there was more to it than that. It would be worth doing a full background check on all of the boat occupants.

'Was he gay, do you think?'

She giggled and shook her head. 'Joe? No. Although I wouldn't say he was particularly confident with women. He was shy. Hidden depths to unlock, if you know what I mean. If I'd been ten years younger . . . well, who knows . . .' Her eyes lit up and she gave him such a dazzling, mischievous smile, it took him by surprise. He wanted to say that her age didn't matter, she was lovely the way she was, but he didn't want to appear crass. He also wondered afresh if maybe there was more to her relationship with Logan than she was letting on. If so, in such a close-knit community, they would soon find out.

'So the only person you ever saw him with was this red-haired man?'

Still smiling, she raised an eyebrow. 'Well, there was the girl. I suppose you'll want to know about her.'

'The girl?' Tartaglia looked at her questioningly. He had the feeling that she was teasing him, deliberately keeping the best until last. 'You mean a girlfriend?'

'Oh, I wouldn't go that far, I only saw her a few times. He said she was some sort of journalist and she was interviewing him for one of the Sunday papers, but they went for a walk together at least once. I watched them go, and when they came back an hour or so later they were deep in conversation, walking quite close together. At one point Joe put his arm out and touched her shoulder for a moment. It was quite tentative, but it was intimate. I'd say he was keen on her. Definitely.'

'What about her?'

'I'm sure she was well aware of the effect she was having.'

'When was all this?'

She paused for a moment. 'The first time I saw her was about six weeks ago, I think, soon after Joe arrived. The last was on Friday.'

'You're sure about the day?'

She nodded. 'I'd been to the dentist and my mouth was still numb. I was walking along the towpath and as I passed Joe's boat I looked in, just to see if he was at home. I'm not sure where he was, but she was in the kitchen doing something at the counter. She may have just been making a cup of coffee but she looked quite at home.'

'You think there was something going on between them?'

She put her head to one side thoughtfully. 'Difficult to tell.'

'But you sensed a spark?'

She nodded. 'Certainly on his side, as I said. Only thing is, I'd say she was in a different league, poor chap, although maybe the fact that he was a best-selling author was enough to take her fancy. You know how some women are, and men, poor sods, are so easily flattered.' She gave Tartaglia a meaningful look. 'I asked him to come round for supper this coming weekend but he said he might be going away. He didn't say where, but I wondered if it had something to do with her. He'd never mentioned going away before.'

'What did this girl look like? Can you describe her?'

'Really pretty. *Naturally* pretty, and fresh, like the most gorgeous, wide-eyed, eighteen-year-old. And she knew it, by God. You could just tell.'

'You're saying she was in her teens?'

'Oh no. That's just the impression she gave, like one of those actresses who always play ingénues even though they're a good ten years older than the part. I'd say she was quite a bit older than she looked.'

'What sort of age are we talking?'

'Late twenties, early thirties maybe. She's certainly been around the block a fair few times. She was very confident, very sure of herself. She held Joe in the palm of her hand and she knew it.'

He sensed her disapproval and smiled. 'I'm afraid I'm going to need more of a physical description.'

'Yes, of course. Sorry. It's just that I find people quite fascinating, and whatever I think of her character she's certainly something different. She's about my height, I'd say. Five-four, maybe five-five, but more straight up and down, girlish, you know. Greyish-blue eyes, I think, although I could be wrong, and lovely long, dark brown hair, a really rich dark brown. My hair used to be that colour until it went grey and I decided it was easier to have it blonde.'

For a moment, he struggled to picture Maggie with dark hair, then it came to him. The chocolate commercials: the silly little romantic soap that had gone on for several years, played out between a man, a faceless cipher as far as he was concerned, and a lovely dark-haired woman, all over a box of chocolates. He'd watched them as a young teenager and fancied her rotten, although she must have been nearly twice his age at the time. He'd seen her in other things too, but it was the chocolate commercials that had stuck in his mind. How funny that, after all those years, he was sitting here with her now.

The small brass carriage clock on the side table started to chime. He looked over and saw that it was eight o'clock.

'Would you be able to do an e-fit of her, do you think?' he asked, hurriedly getting to his feet and tucking his notebook and pen away.

Smiling, she hugged her knees tightly to her ample chest. 'I can do better than that as a matter of fact. I'm afraid again I was curious, maybe even a little jealous, if I'm totally honest. Certainly interested, anyway. So, with a bit of subterfuge, I got him to tell me her name and then I googled her. She used to have a column in one of the dailies. Her name's Anna Paget.'

4

Tartaglia folded his arms and met DCI Carolyn Steele's eye. 'Cause of death was a single contact shot to the head.'

'What sort of weapon?' Her accent was a flat generic southern with no noticeable regional quirks.

'They think some sort of nine-millimetre semi-automatic pistol, although without the bullet it's impossible to be more precise. The head X-rays were clear. No fragments left inside, so ballistics have absolutely nothing to go on.'

It was well past midnight and Tartaglia had only just returned from Joe Logan's post mortem. They were in Steele's cramped, threadbare office back at headquarters in Barnes. The DCI sat hunched deep in her chair, stockinged feet up on the edge of her desk, swivelling slowly from side to side and sucking thoughtfully on the end of a pen. For a woman who hadn't been home since early morning the previous day she looked remarkably untouched, still in the same pristine, fitted white blouse and dark grey pinstriped trousers. She had a broad, handsome face, her skin pale even in summer, as though she rarely saw daylight, and chin-length, layered black hair that emphasised her pallor.

'What about outside in the graveyard?' she asked.

'They're still working it, but so far there's no sign of any blood anywhere. It's looking like he was killed elsewhere. One of his wrists was fractured and his hands and feet show quite deep restraint marks and bruising, as though he'd struggled hard against whatever was used to tie him up. He'd also been punched in the face before he died and his nose is broken. But there are no defence wounds, which is odd. No obvious needle marks either. He was fit and healthy, by all accounts, and certainly no weakling. It's not clear how he was overpowered.'

'Maybe the tox results will come up with something.'

'Perhaps the gun was enough to make him cooperate. And there's something else. The poor bugger was castrated.'

'Castrated?'

'Yes. Arabella found his dick stuffed down his mouth.'

Steele blinked and exhaled loudly. 'Jesus wept. They've got too much bloody imagination these days. So, we're looking at something really unusual, then. Last time I had a body mutilated like that were those gay murders three years ago in Soho.'

'This is different,' he said, remembering the case she was referring to. 'This wasn't a frenzied attack. If anything, it seems pretty cold-blooded. Mercifully Logan was dead when it happened.'

'I thought you said his trousers had blood on them?'

'Arabella said there'd still be quite a bit of leakage even after death.'

'So he's shot, *then* castrated.' She rubbed her eyes and shook her head, then slid open one of the filing drawers and pulled out a full bottle of Laphroaig and a couple of plastic cups.

Without a word, she poured out two decent measures. 'Here.' She thrust one of the cups towards Tartaglia as though he had asked for it. 'Sorry there's no ice.'

He took it without question, trying to hide his surprise. She was not a heavy drinker, as far as he knew, and in the six months or so they had worked together she had never offered him anything stronger than a cup of tea or coffee; nor had he ever seen her have a drink with anyone else in the office. Occasionally she would join them in the pub after work and buy a round, but her preferred tipple was diet coke or slimline tonic with ice and lime. The idea of her keeping a bottle of good single malt stashed away in her desk drawer was intriguing.

'Sláinte.' He tipped his cup to her and leaned back against the wall, enjoying the smoky taste of the whisky. The air conditioning in the building was on the blink again and she had opened the seventies picture window as far as it would go. The gentle, dusty breeze felt good on his face, bringing with it the smell of dry grass and earth from the common nearby. The usually busy road below was silent and he heard the bark of a fox somewhere nearby.

Steele took a gulp of whisky, coughed as though unused to it, and set the cup down on the desk, eyes watering. 'That's better,' she said, hoarsely, clearing her throat. She rocked back in her chair and looked up at him. 'So where are we at? What do you make of things so far?'

Tartaglia massaged his chin, suddenly aware of the thick growth of stubble and wishing he had had time for a quick shave. He hoped she hadn't noticed.

'The CCTV footage from the cemetery has gone off for

analysis, but from what I saw we're looking for a pretty athletic man and, given the logistics, it's possible more than one person's involved. The forensic team have been all over the roof but nothing interesting has turned up. The bloke on the tape was wearing gloves, so I didn't expect any prints, but they say it also looks as if the roof has been swept.'

She nodded. 'So we're dealing with someone organised, who plans ahead. But what's it all about?'

He shrugged. 'When I heard Logan had been castrated, my first thought was that the motive was sexual, particularly given the connection with Brompton Cemetery and all the shenanigans that go on there. Like you, I thought of the Soho murders, but so far there's no reason to think Logan was gay.'

'You're sure?'

'Nothing yet to indicate it. At the moment the only possible gay connection is the choice of dumpsite. The killer clearly knows the area but a lot of people use the cemetery who aren't gay. Problem is, we don't know where or how Logan met the killer. The last sighting we have of him is around five in the afternoon, pushing his bike along the towpath on his way out to meet someone.'

'So why the castration, do we think?'

He grimaced. 'Could be all sorts of reasons. Even if he isn't gay, it could still be sexual – a mark of contempt, or punishment. Maybe someone was trying to make an example of him as a warning to others. He was certainly left where he'd be found, and the choice of the crypt is striking though I haven't a clue what it means.'

'You're thinking it's drugs or gang related, some form of organised crime?'

'It would tie in with the method of killing. From the little we know, Logan was a writer and a teacher, though he'd been an actor. We don't yet know what else he was involved in, but if he was dealing it wasn't from the boat. The neighbours would have picked up on it, plus we found no physical evidence.'

'Hopefully his papers or bank records will reveal something.'

He nodded. 'Maybe it's a simple crime of passion, maybe he was messing around with someone else's wife or girlfriend, someone who has a gun.' He paused, then decided to go further. 'But it was all carefully planned. Logan was taken somewhere, beaten up and executed. Whoever did it stood right in front of him as they delivered the coup de grâce. They looked him in the eye. Whatever the motive, it's got to be personal.'

He watched Steele's face for a reaction, but there was none. According to the office rumour mill, Steele's direct superior, Superintendent Clive Cornish, had put forward the wild theory that Logan had been picked off the street at random by some gun-toting whacko. Cornish had come up through the ranks in uniform and had no hands-on experience of murder investigations in his career; he was best known for his expensive suits and smooth political skills. Tartaglia had no idea if Cornish had actually expressed this view, although from what he knew of him, it rang true. Nor had he any clue what Steele's opinion of Cornish was; as with everything else, she played her hand close to her chest and he had never felt sufficiently at ease with her to express his views freely. But he wanted to hit the theory on the head right away. If not, they would lose precious time and resources on what he was positive was a non-starter.

She rubbed her bottom lip thoughtfully with her finger and he caught the flicker of a smile. He wondered if she, too, was thinking of Cornish. 'No,' she said, with a quick nod of the head. 'Whatever happened, it certainly wasn't opportunistic.'

'But there's one thing that doesn't add up,' he added, relieved that she seemed to agree with him. 'The killer chooses to dump the body in a disused crypt in central London, right in the middle of about forty acres of public land. Apart from anything, it's taking one hell of a risk. A pro wouldn't go to so much trouble.'

Steele nodded slowly. 'Unless it was part of the contract, for some reason. What about Logan's phone?'

'Still hasn't turned up, but one of his neighbours gave us the number and we've traced it back to the provider. It's switched off, so it could be anywhere, but we should have all the details and a cell site analysis of his calls by tomorrow morning, plus the lab will report back on his computer.'

She turned towards the window, eyes half closed as though she was picturing something far away. He wondered if she was having personal problems, or if it was just the stress of the job, but he knew better than to ask. She never brought her private life into work. Even her office gave nothing away, with no photos or personal items of any sort on show. Apart from the fact that she was single and lived alone in a basement flat in West Hampstead, a detail that had come to light accidentally in a previous investigation, he realised how little he knew about her. She was only a couple of years older than he was and she wasn't un-attractive, far from it in fact, but she had an aura about her that said 'keep off'. It was a self-protective mechanism he had come across a lot with policewomen in what was still very much a male-dominated world, but with Steele there was more to it, he felt, and he was curious.

He followed her gaze through the window. Immediately opposite, a terrace of low-built Victorian houses backed onto the road that led from Barnes village green to the common and mainline station. The odd light was still on here and there, revealing sleepy little snapshots of domestic life. In one house, he saw the flicker of a television; in another, he watched a dark-haired woman in a pink dressing gown make her way slowly up the stairs with a mug of something in one hand and a black cat draped over her shoulder. The sight brought on a sudden wave of tiredness and he stifled a yawn. The day's adrenaline high had evap-orated and he wished that he could be back in his flat, about to crawl into bed. But the immediate prospect of that was a remote one.

After a moment, Steele gave another hearty sigh and turned back to him, fingers steepled under her chin, fixing him with her strange green eyes. Her mouth softened unexpect-edly into a smile. 'I agree with everything you've said, Mark. It looks like a cut and shunt. Maybe someone's messing us around.'

Her unexpected warmth surprised him. She wasn't usually so easy to convince. If it had been anyone else, he would have been tempted to say that she was flirting with him, or at least trying to win him over, but Steele wasn't that sort of woman, and she'd taken no more than a mouthful of whisky. Something else must be behind it and he felt instantly wary.

'It's personal,' she continued distantly, still gazing at him, seemingly unaware of her body language. 'The answer's buried somewhere in Joe Logan's life, if only we can find it.'

There was a rap on the open door and he turned to see Minderedes.

'Sorry to interrupt. But someone's using Logan's phone.'

5

'If I catch you nodding off, you're for the high-jump, lassie,' a deep Scottish voice said immediately behind Donovan.

She started, but didn't turn around. Along with a waft of coffee, she had caught a trace of DS Justin Chang's familiar aftershave. She shook her head. 'I know it's you, Justin, and Mark doesn't talk like that anyway. I've had about two hours' sleep, so don't blame me if I'm a bit dopey.' She carried on tapping at her keyboard, inputting a witness statement from the previous evening.

'I've got you a coffee,' he said, in his normal voice. She looked around. The expensive aftershave was an incongruous touch in someone who usually dressed like a student. Today, though, he was wearing a suit, although it looked as though it had seen better days. His tie was loosely knotted and the top button of his collar was undone. But in spite of the fact that he too had been up most of the night, his expression was irritatingly cheerful.

'Here.' He handed her a cup from a paper bag, which came from The Food Gallery, her favourite deli in the High Street, where they made the best coffee in Barnes. 'I told them to put an extra shot in it. Thought you'd need something to keep you on your toes.'

'Thanks. I need all the help I can get today. What do I owe you?'

He waved her away. 'Don't worry about it.'

Too tired to argue, she shook her head and removed the lid to take a sip. But the coffee was piping hot and she put it down to let it cool. Chang had joined the murder team less than two months before and had taken to bringing her coffee most mornings, so far refusing to let her pay him back, or return the favour. In the small, open-plan office, with its central bank of desks, nothing went unnoticed for long. Jane Downes, who was sharper-eyed than most, had already made a couple of teasing remarks about special treatment. Luckily Downes was away from her desk and the other members of the team were either busy on their computers or the phone. But Donovan decided that she was going to have to say something to Chang.

He removed his jacket, threw it over the back of his chair and sat down at his desk, which was next to hers, rubbing his hands briskly. He opened the bag and took out another coffee, a smoked salmon and cream cheese bagel, an apple and a large chocolate brownie, which he laid out in a row in front of him.

'Breakfast,' he said, tugging his tie undone and dropping it casually into a drawer.

'You mean lunch.'

He gave her a broad smile. 'Dinner, actually, if you really want to know. By the time I realised I hadn't eaten last night, it was already morning and I was too tired to do anything about it. Is it always like this?'

She nodded. 'It's always crazy at the beginning of a major new case. The DCI before Carolyn Steele kept a sleeping bag in his office for overnight stints.'

'Rather him than me,' he said. 'I like my home comforts.'

'Well you'd better get used to it. At least there's the overtime to think of.'

'What about my social life?'

'You're not allowed one. Didn't they tell you?'

'Just as well I don't have one then.' He took a large bite of the bagel.

'You'll have me feeling sorry for you in a minute. Where've you been?'

'On a wild goose chase trying to follow up on a man Nick interviewed yesterday. Wasted most of the morning.'

As he spoke, Tartaglia entered the room and came over to Donovan.

'Karen just called in,' she said, looking up at him. 'She's on her way back from NatWest now. She's been through Logan's bank accounts for the last year and so far it all looks kosher – no big deposits, except via his agent, no other sources of income, no large outgoings or cash withdrawals or anything out of the ordinary. He was also pretty frugal on the expenditure side. Apparently he had a very healthy current-account balance and an even fatter deposit account.'

'So much for impoverished writers.' He sat down on the corner of her desk and folded his arms. He looked tired and was badly in need of a shave. She wondered if he had made it home the previous night. 'I guess it demolishes one theory,' he said, rubbing his eyes. 'Unless Logan had another bank account tucked away somewhere, it looks as though we can rule out gambling or extortion.' He looked over at Jane Downes, who had just come into the room. 'Any luck tracing Logan's next of kin?'

'Not yet,' she said, sitting down at her desk opposite Donovan. 'But one of his neighbours has ID'd the body.'

'What about the victim profile?'

'Coming along slowly. I've spoken to Actor's Equity and Spotlight and I finally managed to track down his acting agent, but he wasn't very helpful. Apart from being very sorry to hear what had happened and a load of stuff about Logan being a decent bloke, seems he hadn't spoken to Logan for several years. He had nothing to do with the publication of the book. I'm waiting for the headmaster from St Thomas's to call me back. Hopefully, he'll be able to fill in some of the gaps.'

As she spoke, Minderedes entered the room and Tartaglia stood up. 'Come over here for a minute,' he said, beckoning everyone over. 'Nick's been chasing down Logan's phone. I want you all to hear what he's got.'

'Where shall I start?' Minderedes asked, as they gathered around.

'Go from last night.'

'OK. As you know, Logan's iPhone was missing and switched off. About midnight last night, someone turned it on again. The provider contacted us immediately. We eventually traced it all the way from Covent Garden to a B&B in Victoria. Just after four this morning, we raided a room and unearthed a spotty little git called Chester. He's on holiday from Seattle with his parents and younger brother and claims to have found it in the gents at a Pizza Hut near

Leicester Square at around eleven-thirty. He was using it to text his girlfriend back home.'

'They were up late,' Downes said.

'Jetlag, apparently, and they'd been to see a show. The little bugger got the fright of his life when we burst in, which serves him right for not turning it in. The long and short of it is he seems to be telling the truth, which means the killer must have deliberately left it there to play silly buggers with us. The place was full. No cameras in the gents, of course. We'll appeal for witnesses but it's unlikely anyone noticed the phone being left.'

'It's gone off for testing,' Tartaglia added. 'But I expect it will have been wiped clean before it was dumped. Let's go back to Logan's calls.'

'OK. We now have a log of everything going back over the last six months, including transcripts of any voicemails still on the service provider's server. The call volume is pretty low. Doesn't seem like he had many friends, or at least didn't like talking to them. But in the days just before he died, three numbers come up more than once, both incoming and outgoing, and all three callers left voicemails. The first is a woman called Jana Ryan.'

'Logan's publisher, judging from the transcript,' Tartaglia added.

'She called twice and left a message each time, asking Logan to call. There's no record of his returning the call. Next is a man named Alex. In the week Logan died, he called four times and left two voicemails, one three days before Logan died, another on the day of Logan's death asking Logan to return the call, which he did. Each time they talked for several minutes. The last call was timed at four thirty-three in the afternoon. Judging from the cell-site analysis, Logan was calling from on or near the boat, which corroborates what we've been told about his movements that day. Alex was somewhere close to the main mast in Kentish Town. We're trying to trace him through his mobile, but so far no luck. It's a pay-as-you-go and it appears to be switched off. The last caller is a woman named Anna. She rang and left a message two days before Logan's death, saying she had some further questions. Logan called her back. They talked for a couple of minutes and it seems they arranged to meet. The evening of Logan's death, she leaves two voicemails, one at seven forty-five saying she's in the bar waiting for him, and another at eight-twenty, saying she's going home and asking him to call. She thought he'd stood her up and she sounded quite pissed off. Both calls were made within a half-mile radius of the mast at Earl's Court.'

'We think she's a journalist called Anna Paget,' Tartaglia said. 'According to one witness, she was interviewing Logan for some newspaper. We're trying to trace her now.'

'We'll be checking every number on the phone list, but these three callers are a priority.'

'Any news on the laptop, Dave?' Tartaglia asked, looking over at Wightman, who was sitting opposite and was the youngest member of the team. He was short and stocky, with thick blond hair and glasses. He had a degree in computer science and was usually tasked with anything related.

'They're sending over a copy of the hard drive within the hour,' Wightman said.

'Good. What about you, Jane?' he said, turning to Downes. 'How are you doing with Logan's papers?'

'I've been through his files and what was in his in-tray. It's mainly bills, bank statements, that sort of thing, plus some fan mail that had been forwarded from his previous address. Nothing particularly interesting. There was also a whole load of stuff printed off the internet about Thailand and Malaysia. Looks like he may have been planning a trip, although I couldn't find a booking confirmation or an e-ticket or anything. But I did find this.' She held up a sheet of paper. From what Donovan could see, it looked like an email, with a paragraph of tightly spaced, strange-looking black type below the address. 'This was sent to Logan's Mac account just over a week ago,' Downes said. 'The address is a bit odd for starters: alice_in_wonderland91@hotmail.com. And it gets even weirder.' She started to read:

and laughed conspiratorially as they stumbled down the steep spiral stairs together. The candlelight flickered on the bare crumbling brickwork and the gauzy spiders' webs. She heard footsteps and voices from the others just behind. At the bottom was a heavy wrought-iron gate, decorated with an ornate coat of arms. The metal was badly rusted and part of the shield fell away as she touched it. She was sure there were rats in such a place and she held on even more tightly to his arm. He was still laughing and the sound echoed around the small subterranean chamber. She suddenly wanted to whisper. A drop of icy water fell onto her bare shoulders and looking at her intently, he slowly wiped it away with his finger. The floor below was flooded with an inch or so of water and she got her feet wet as she stepped down. A giant key sat in the lock invitingly. She held up the guttering church candle and peered through the bars of the gate into the gloomy darkness beyond. A small stone altar lay immediately in front and on either side were rows of ancient coffins. The ones at the bottom sat in the water. She wondered if they would float if the water rose some more. 'Have some more wine, my pretty,' he said, filling her glass to the brim. 'I like the way it

'It stops there, in mid sentence. There's no beginning or end. No greeting, or anything.' Downes looked from one face to another and shrugged. 'Given where Logan's body was found, I thought it was worth mentioning.'

'He was a writer,' Minderedes said.

'Are you saying he had second sight?' Downes replied sharply. 'It mentions a crypt.'

Minderedes shook his head sceptically. 'Looks like a piece from a book. Must be something he wrote.'

'And emailed himself?'

'Sounds like part of a Gothic novel,' Donovan added.

'More like Hammer Horror,' Chang muttered under his breath.

'Whatever it is, I can tell you it's not describing the crypt at Brompton Cemetery,' Tartaglia said. 'Although, I agree it's a coincidence and worth looking into. Was there anything else like this amongst his things?'

'No.'

Tartaglia turned to Wightman. 'Get onto the techies and tell them I want the email traced, plus copies of any other emails from the same source. Anyone else have something?'

Chang raised his hand. 'I've just come back from Maida Vale. I was following up on a witness statement Nick took yesterday, a man called Tim Wade, who was hanging around the boat and said he was a friend of Logan's. Anyway, the phone number and address he gave are false. The number belongs to a traffic warden in Doncaster, who's never heard of a Tim Wade, and there's nobody of that name living at or anywhere near the address he gave.'

'I remember him,' Minderedes said. 'He had blood on his face and shirt. He said he'd had a nosebleed.'

'What did he look like?' Tartaglia asked.

Minderedes narrowed his eyes. 'Tallish bloke, about six feet, medium build, red hair. Brown eyes, I think. He was wearing jeans, a baggy blue and white striped shirt and trainers. He was very keen to know what was going on and what had happened to Logan, even though he said he didn't know him that well. He seemed quite edgy, couldn't stand still, and he was sweating heavily. I thought it was the heat. It all seemed a bit odd but there wasn't a lot I could do.'

'If the phone number and address are false, I'm betting the name is too.' Tartaglia turned to Chang. 'A red-haired man was seen having a drink with Logan on the boat three nights ago, the night before Logan was murdered. Get onto the council and pull all the local CCTV footage for yesterday. There are a couple of cameras along the canal and check the tube stations. If that doesn't get us anywhere, I want the buses checked as well. We've got to find him.'

Just as he finished speaking, DS Sharon Fuller, the office manager, poked her head around the door. 'Sorry to interrupt, sir. I can't get hold of Anna Paget, but I've set up an appointment for you with Jana Ryan. She's Logan's editor. She's expecting you at her office in an hour.'

6

The offices of Stormont Publishing were located in a pair of eighteenth-century terraced houses in Bloomsbury. Tartaglia and Donovan were shown into a high-ceilinged room on the ground floor overlooking the street. The two sash windows were wide open, letting in a breeze as well as the heavy drone of traffic from the busy road outside. The room was furnished with a long, modern white table and matching chairs, with glass shelving units on either side of the marble fireplace that displayed a range of hard-cover and paperback books. Several of the authors were familiar to Tartaglia, including Tom Niccol, a fellow Scot and former Detective Chief Superintendent he had once worked for, who had turned his hand to thrillers on retirement. Tartaglia was about to take down a copy of Niccol's latest novel when the door opened and a sturdily built, dark-haired woman, dressed in a bright, geometric-patterned shift dress, entered the room.

'I'm Jana Ryan, Joe's editor,' she said, closing the door behind her.

Tartaglia introduced himself and Donovan, and Ryan motioned for them to sit down. 'I'll close the windows,' she said, as a bus rumbled past. 'If it gets too hot for you, you'd better say.'

'You know why we're here?' Tartaglia asked, as she came over to the table and sat down.

She nodded. 'We're all in shock. Can't really believe it. Can you tell me what happened?' She spoke quietly, with a light American accent; East Coast he thought, although possibly diluted by living in the UK for a long time.

'There'll be a press conference later this morning. I'm sorry but I can't say anything until then.'

'But he was murdered?' She held his gaze. Her heavy, black-framed glasses gave her an earnest, academic look, but there was warmth in her eyes and genuine feeling.

Tartaglia nodded. 'I'm afraid so.'

'I saw something in the paper this morning about a man's body being found in Brompton Cemetery. A name wasn't mentioned, but I wondered if it was Joe.'

'Yes, it's Mr Logan.'

She shook her head slowly as though she couldn't believe what had happened. 'Do you have any idea who—'

'Not so far, which is why we're here. We need to find out everything we can about him.'

'What was he doing in London?' Jana Ryan asked, looking at him questioningly.

Tartaglia frowned. 'He was living here. You didn't know?'

'No. Last I heard, he was teaching at some school down in Somerset or Dorset.'

'He left just after Easter. For the last couple of months he's been staying on a houseboat in Little Venice.'

Ryan grimaced. 'That's really odd. I had lunch with him

only a few weeks ago, and he didn't say anything about being in London. I guess he didn't want us to know he was here.'

'I understand you'd been trying to get hold of him.'

She nodded. 'Yes. He was avoiding me, if you want the truth.'

'Why was that?'

Looking from Tartaglia to Donovan, she leaned forward and folded her hands neatly in front of her on the table. 'Have you read his novel *Indian Summer*?'

'I'm sorry, no,' Tartaglia replied. Since leaving university and starting work, reading had become a luxury, confined mainly to holidays. But he was surprised to see Donovan also shake her head. She was rarely without a book in her bag and often swapped titles with a couple of the other women in the office. There had even been talk about forming a book group, although he wasn't sure what had come of it.

'It doesn't matter,' Ryan said. 'Let me put it in context. It's a work of literary merit, but also one of those rare birds that crosses the genres and has popular appeal. It won a prestigious prize but Joe refused point blank to come to the awards ceremony. He made some excuse about being ill, but I knew it was because he didn't want to come. In the end I had to collect the award for him. He positively loathed the limelight.'

'I understand a journalist called Anna Paget was interviewing him.'

She shook her head. 'I doubt it. I'll ask his publicist, but last thing I heard Joe wouldn't speak to anybody, and I mean *anybody*.'

'I'd appreciate it if you'd check before we leave.'

'Sure,' she said with a shrug.

'When did you last talk to him?'

'Not since our lunch. After the awards dinner Radio 4 were chasing us, offering Joe a slot on *Front Row* with Mark Lawson, and I hoped we might be able to twist his arm somehow. His publicist had had no luck, so I tried calling and left a couple of messages, but he didn't return any of my calls either.'

'Why was he so reluctant?'

'Most writers hate being involved in publicity. They're very comfortable putting words on paper, but talking about it is another thing. Doing interviews and book signings also takes up a lot of time.'

'Why did you keep badgering him then, if he didn't want to do it?' Donovan asked.

Ryan leaned back in her chair and gave a heavy sigh. 'Unfortunately it's part of the job these days, particularly if you find yourself winning a prize and with a bestseller on your hands. I understood it was difficult for Joe. He wrote his book, took several years to do it from what he told me, and he felt that should be enough. The book should stand or fall on its own merits as if it was totally independent of him.'

'What's wrong with that?'

'We badly needed his support to promote it. People are interested, they want to know about the writer, particularly when it's someone who's come from nowhere and had such unexpected success.'

'And you want to sell books,' Tartaglia said.

She smiled. 'Naturally, although it's not just about the money, at least not for me. Very few of our writers make it to the bestseller lists. Most of the time it's about covering our costs and hopefully making a small margin, but when you hit the jackpot, well, of course it's fantastically satisfying for everybody involved. It gave us all such a buzz and it wasn't purely the sales numbers.'

The pressure on Logan to perform must have been huge, Tartaglia thought. He remembered what Maggie Thomas had told him about Logan's aversion to publicity. Whilst he could see both sides of the coin, his sympathies leaned towards Logan. If it had taken him years to write his novel, it must have meant a great deal to him; it must have been something incredibly personal. Clearly he had never envisaged the book being such a success and perhaps that wasn't part of the bargain as far as he was concerned.

'You worked closely with him?' he asked.

'We had a few meetings, but we mainly communicated by email or phone. He said it was difficult coming to London. I have to say he wasn't the easiest writer to edit; he absolutely hated making even the smallest changes. He found the whole process incredibly painful and I was sorry for that, but there was nothing I could do.'

'How well did you know Joe? I mean, how much do you know about his personal life?'

'Not a great deal, I have to say. I know he wasn't married, and I don't remember his ever mentioning a partner. The protagonist in *Indian Summer* is straight, so I sort of assumed Joe was too, but I never thought much beyond that. On the few occasions we met, we talked about the book. He wasn't at all chatty or forthcoming about himself. He really gave little away. I'm afraid I simply put that down to his being a man.'

Tartaglia smiled. 'How did you discover him? Did he approach you?'

'No. We don't look at unsolicited work. Like most publishers these days, we just haven't got the people or the time. We use agents as filters. A draft of the novel came in via someone I've known for a long time, whose judgement I respect. She said I just had to read it, that it was right up my street. Even so, things were hectic as usual and it took me almost a week to get around to it. I remember she'd been chasing me, saying that others were interested, and I ended up reading it in the car driving down to Wiltshire to watch my son play in a rugby match. My partner was driving, I should add. Anyway, I was hooked from the first page. I just couldn't put it down and I sat in the school's car park, with the heater on, trying to finish it. In the end, I missed the whole match and the tea afterwards. What was even worse, my son scored two tries and his school won. He practically killed me, although he knows what I'm like.'

She smiled wistfully, looking down at the table for a moment, then back at Tartaglia. 'You know, Joe's novel was the most exciting thing I'd read in a long time. We may not have seen eye to eye over everything, but I'm very sorry indeed he's dead. He had real talent.'

'We'll need his agent's name and number.'

She nodded. 'She's in the US at the moment. I spoke to her on the phone only yesterday when I couldn't get hold of Joe. After I heard what had happened, I rang this morning and left a voicemail. She'll be devastated. I'm sure she'll be in touch as soon as she wakes up and gets the message.'

'What's the book about?' Donovan asked.

'It's about a group of men who were buddies at university. Fifteen years later they're brought together again when one of them dies. Basically, his death opens a can of worms. I don't want to give away too much of the plot because you should read it, but it's about the destructive power of guilt and envy, about being in the wrong place at the wrong time and the choices we make.'

'Is the novel autobiographical in any way?' Tartaglia asked, thinking that it didn't sound like his cup of tea.

Ryan put her head to one side and made a moue. 'Most first novels have some autobiographical element, and in some superficial ways Joe was quite a lot like Jonah, the main character.' She paused for a moment, as though thinking it all over, before adding: 'But Jonah commits suicide at the end of the book, or so it seems. He's a deeply unhappy, dissatisfied man. I certainly never saw Joe as someone standing on the edge of a precipice, either metaphorically or in reality.'

'Do you think the book could have a bearing on Mr Logan's murder?'

Ryan looked surprised. 'I don't see how. I mean, it's hardly news.'

'I understand he'd started another book.'

'Yes. He mentioned it when we had lunch, but he didn't tell me a great deal about it.'

'Could the second book have anything to do with what happened to him? It may seem silly but we need to explore every angle.'

Ryan pursed her lips thoughtfully. 'I don't know what to say. He didn't give me the impression the idea was *hot* in any way. If anything, he seemed a little woolly about the story line, as though he hadn't really worked it out just yet. We hadn't even talked about a contract and he was a long way from having anything he wanted to show me, from what I could tell.'

'Thank you.' Tartaglia unfolded a copy of the email found amongst Logan's papers and slid it across to her. 'Do you recognise this paragraph?'

She read the text, then passed it back, frowning. 'I've never seen it before.'

'So it's not from *Indian Summer*?'

'Absolutely not.'

'What about his next book?' Donovan asked.

Ryan shook her head. 'I doubt it. It's not his style.' She waved her hand dismissively.

'How can you be so sure?' Tartaglia asked.

'One minute. I'll show you what I mean.' She got up and went over to one of the bookshelves, standing hand on hip as she scanned the wall of titles. 'Here we are,' she said, stretching on tip-toe to take a copy down from one of the shelves. She came back to the table, handed it to Tartaglia and sat down again. 'This will give you an idea of Joe's writing. You can keep it, if you like. It's certainly a good read, if nothing else.'

It was a fat paperback, the title *Indian Summer* highlighted against a sepia-toned photograph of an old house and garden.

He frowned. 'It says here it's written by someone called Andrew Miller.'

Ryan nodded. 'Andrew was Joe's second name and Miller's his mother's maiden name.'

'He used a pseudonym. Why?'

'I wouldn't read too much into it. Lots of writers do it. He said he wanted to keep his acting and writing identities separate.'

Tartaglia skimmed the blurb. It was more or less as Ryan had described, with nothing that immediately suggested a possible connection with the case. He then switched his attention to the back. On the inside of the cover he found a small, black and white snapshot of Logan. Taken somewhere outdoors, Logan was seated on a wooden bench, squinting into the sunlight, his arm resting lightly along the back, with a cigarette between his fingers. He had a pleasant face, if a little weak, but there was something appealing and humorous about his expression, as though he found the whole thing amusing and wasn't taking it too seriously. It wasn't the pose of a vain man, Tartaglia thought, nor was his choice of photograph for his book jacket. He found himself thinking back to the body he had seen lying on the gurney in the morgue. Even cleaned up, the face bore little resemblance to the man in the photograph; as often happened, death had robbed him of any humanity.

'We had quite a battle to get a photograph out of him,' Ryan said. 'In the end, I think he got a friend to take it.'

'That's strange. He was an actor. He should be used to putting himself in the public eye. If nothing else, you'd think he'd use a professional studio shot.'

'As I said, I imagine he wanted to draw a line between the two careers.'

'Is it a good likeness?' They needed something to release to the press in the hope that someone might remember seeing Logan the night he died.

'Yes. It captures what he was like, pretty much.'

'We'll need a copy of the jPeg.'

She nodded.

He read the few lines of biography underneath the photo but they gave nothing new away, other than that Logan had been born and raised in Crewe, in Cheshire. At least that might help with tracing the next of kin.

He tapped the cover. 'Doesn't tell you much about him, does it?'

'That's the way he wanted it. Lots of authors are like that, I have to say.'

Still not satisfied, Tartaglia turned the book over and started to read aloud some of the newspaper quotes that filled the back cover.

'*"Claustrophobic and haunting first novel . . . "*, *"Compelling and disturbing . . . "*, *"A gripping and absorbing read that keeps you guessing until the end . . . "*, *"Deep and intense, with an evocative sense of place . . . "*, *"An extraordinary debut . . . "*, *"Peter's Friends meets* The Secret History *. . ."'*

He looked up at Ryan again. 'Do you write these your-selves?'

Ryan smiled. 'No. They're all genuine quotes. As you can see, it was very well reviewed and deservedly so, in my opinion.'

'Why's it called *Indian Summer*?' Donovan asked.

As she spoke, Tartaglia felt the vibration of his phone in his pocket and pulled it out. He saw a text message from Minderedes: Found journalist Anna. Call when u r done. Nick.

'Writers can be funny about titles,' Ryan was saying. 'Joe must have changed it at least five times . . .'

Not waiting for her to finish, he scraped back his chair and got to his feet. 'I'm sorry. I've got to go.' He handed Ryan a business card. 'Sergeant Donovan will need to speak to Logan's publicist and we'll also need his agent's details. If you think of anything else, please give us a call.'

7

'Please answer the question, Miss Paget,' Tartaglia said irritably.

Anna Paget fixed him with a look that was diamond hard. 'Why won't you tell me what happened to Joe?'

As she spoke, he saw the flash of a tongue stud. She had what his grandmother would have described as a gin-soaked voice, surprisingly low and ragged at the edges, with a vague London twang. Not unpleasant to listen to, he thought, in another context. 'I've explained why,' he said.

'Surely you can at least tell me how he died. The papers said he was shot. Was it an accident?'

'Answer the question, Miss Paget. What happened that night?'

They were seated in the rear alcove of Kazbar, a Moroccan café bar just off the Earl's Court Road, Tartaglia and Minderedes perched opposite Anna on a pair of uncomfortably low velvet stools. Her laptop lay open on the coffee table, along with some papers and a half-drunk diet coke. She had a deadline to meet and was trying to finish off a piece. To save time, she had asked that they meet at the bar and, even though it seemed an odd choice, Tartaglia –

wanting to put her at her ease – had agreed. The bar was no more than a five-minute walk from where Logan's body had been found. As a rule, he didn't believe in coincidences, but he didn't know what to make of it. At least there was little chance of their being overheard, the only other clientele being an elderly man engrossed in a copy of the *Spectator*, and a trio of women drinking coffee, their conversation deadened by the background thud of Led Zeppelin. An old-fashioned fan, better suited to some far-flung colonial outpost, circled lazily above his head, barely stirring the air. Even though he hadn't been there long and had removed his jacket, his shirt was clinging to his back. What with the music and the heat, he was finding it difficult to think straight, let alone follow what Anna was saying. He hoped the interview wouldn't take long.

She held his gaze as though she hoped he would weaken. Then she gave a petulant shrug and retreated back into the depths of the ancient brown leather sofa, crossing her slim, bare legs and folding her arms defensively. 'I waited here – exactly where I'm sitting now – for three quarters of an hour. But he didn't show. Simple as that.'

After Maggie Thomas's description he had been half expecting to meet Anne Hathaway, although he seemed to remember Anne Hathaway had brown eyes. The reality was less conventional, but more arresting. Anna was wearing frayed denim shorts that barely covered her bottom and a skin-tight black vest that left nothing to the imagination. He took in the mess of long dark hair, the broad, upturned nose and wide-apart, heavy-lidded blue-grey eyes. Sitting there, lolling back amongst the cushions, playing irritably with a loose thread from her vest, she could almost pass for a teenager. Until he looked into her eyes. What he glimpsed, a hardness and an unexpected hostility, took him aback. He wondered what lay behind it, and whether Maggie Thomas had been right about Anna's relationship with Logan – that Logan had fallen for her.

'So you left?'

'I was pretty pissed off, but what else could I do? I thought he'd stood me up.'

'Where did you go?'

'Home. My flat's around the corner.'

'Can anyone corroborate that?'

'No. I live on my own.'

'What time were you supposed to meet Mr Logan here?'

'Seven-thirty.'

'You're sure?'

'Of course I'm sure. Why?'

'We need to establish a timeline.'

The last person to see Logan alive had been Maggie Thomas, when she met him coming along the towpath with his bicycle just before five o'clock. If he had been on his way to meet Anna, maybe that explained why, according to Maggie, he had made an effort with his appearance. But the journey from Maida Vale to Kazbar in Earl's Court would take about half an hour or so by bike. There were roughly two and a half hours unaccounted for. He must have been going some-where else first. 'Do you have any idea what he was doing before he was supposed to meet you?'

'No.'

'Why had you arranged to meet?' Minderedes asked,

looking up from his notebook. 'Hadn't you finished inter-viewing him?'

She gave him a weary look. 'I had some more questions.'

'Why didn't you go to his boat as before?' Tartaglia asked.

'Is it important?'

'I'm just curious. Why the change of venue?'

'No big deal. He suggested coming my way for a change, but I didn't want him in my flat so I suggested here.'

'Why not your flat?'

'It's too small to entertain. Anyway, I like to keep my busi-ness and personal lives separate.'

She spoke emphatically. Although not convinced after what Maggie had told him, he accepted the statement at face value for the moment. First, he wanted to establish the basic chronology of what had happened between her and Logan. He also needed to get her to loosen up and lower her guard.

'So when was the last time you saw Mr Logan?'

'About a week ago.'

'Which day?'

'Friday, I think.'

'I'll need you to be more precise.'

With a theatrical sigh, she pulled out a BlackBerry from her bag, tabbed through it. 'Friday, as I said. I had a lunch meeting that day and I went over to see him straight after-wards. I got there about three, before you ask.'

'So, what did you talk about?'

'About him. About his life. That's why I was there.'

'What time did you leave?'

'Around seven, I guess. I was going out, so I went home to change.'

Again, she spoke matter-of-factly. He found her lack of emotion curious, wondering if it really was genuine. She uncrossed her legs and stretched forwards to pick up her coke. As she lowered her gaze and took a long, slow sip, he studied her for a moment, noting the curve of her slender shoulders, the sheen on her skin, the small tattoo just above her ankle, wondering how to get through to her. Unless Logan was sexually abnormal, he must certainly have found her attractive. Had there been a mutual connection, or had she merely been using Logan? From the little he had seen of her, his money was on the latter. If so, he pitied Logan.

'You seem very unmoved by what's happened. Don't you care?'

She glanced up at him and he caught a wariness in her eyes, as though she hadn't anticipated the question. 'What do you want me to do? Burst into tears? I'm not a hypocrite.'

'But he was murdered. It was a violent death. Surely that must mean something to you?'

She put down her glass and carefully folded her arms. 'Look, I'm very sorry Joe's dead but he wasn't a close friend or anything.'

'You're sure about that?'

She held his gaze. 'Yes.'

He didn't believe her but he had nothing to confront her with except Maggie Thomas's suspicions. She had slipped off her flip-flops and was tapping her bare foot on the floor impatiently. She reminded him of a spoilt child, used to getting her way, and it angered him. He took a deep breath.

'OK. Let's go back to the beginning. How did you first meet

74

Mr Logan? How did you persuade him to let you interview him?'

'I tried the usual channels first, but when that didn't work, I wrote him a letter care of his publisher.'

'Just a letter?'

'And copies of a few interviews and articles I'd done, plus some general background info on me. I didn't know if they'd pass it on, or if he would read it, but about a month later, he called me. He said he wanted to meet and talk first. He wanted to suss me out, see if we got on, before he'd let me interview him.'

'Which paper was it for?'

She mentioned the name of one of the big Sunday spreads.

'Did they commission this interview?' he asked.

'No. It was my idea. I used to do a regular interview slot for the *Standard* so it's what I'm known for, although I'm freelance now and do other things too.'

'I'm told Logan hated publicity and refused to give any interviews. What made him choose you?'

She shrugged. 'Haven't a clue.'

A lock of dark hair fell across her face and she flicked it away as though swatting a fly. She was being disingenuous and he remembered what Maggie had said about her: *She held Joe in the palm of her hand and she knew it.*

'I'd like to see a copy of what you sent.'

'I wrote the letter by hand. I can give you copies of what I printed out but it really won't tell you anything.'

'I'd still like to see what you sent.'

It might mean nothing, but her manner aroused his curiosity. He was determined to see what Logan had seen, try and figure out what had made him agree to meet her when he had turned everybody else down. How had she hooked him? What had she said or shown him? If nothing else, it might reveal something about Logan. Maybe a simple photograph had done the trick, slipped in with her package of articles and references. Anything to get a foot in the door. If so, he couldn't blame her, but it highlighted Logan's vulnerability. He wondered what Logan had done with the letter, if he had kept it, and he made a mental note to get Jane Downes to have a thorough look again through Logan's papers.

'So, when was your first meeting?'

'About a month ago. Maybe five weeks.' She consulted the BlackBerry for a moment, then gave him the date and time.

'And what did you do?' he asked, as Minderedes noted down the details.

'We met in a pub and had a few drinks and chatted. About general stuff. Life, travel, music, you know. At the end of it, he said he felt comfortable with me and that I could interview him. We arranged a time to meet the following week.'

'Why were you so interested in him? Why did you go to so much trouble to get an interview with him? He was hardly an A-list celebrity.'

Anna stared at him as if he were mad. 'Because of the book, of course. Because I absolutely loved *Indian Summer*. If you bothered to read it, you'd understand. I wanted to get under his skin.'

'And did you?'

She sighed. 'Maybe not as much as I'd have liked, but it still makes a great story. Failed actor and jobbing teacher –

a pretty sympathetic character, the way I paint it – struggles for years, then writes debut novel and hits the jackpot.'

'You saw him how many times in total?'

'After the first meeting, just three times. That's all.'

'How did you spend your time with him?'

'We mostly stayed on the boat. It was a real dump, but he seemed to feel comfortable there, he didn't like going out much. I wondered if he was a bit agoraphobic.'

'You were with him for how long?'

'A few hours each time. It was difficult to get him to focus so we'd just chat for a bit, have a drink or two, listen to some music. I went along with whatever he wanted. I needed to get him to relax so he'd open up. When his mind wasn't on it, lots of stuff came out, about his childhood, about his time at school, little glimpses of what made him tick as a man, which is what interested me. I felt a bit like a therapist. I don't think he'd talked to anyone in a long while.'

'Did he mention his family or his friends?'

'Only in passing.'

'What about his love life?'

'From what I gathered, there hadn't been anyone around for a while. He said that writing was a solitary business and that he wasn't easy to be with when he was working. He said he was pretty hopeless at relationships.'

He looked at her closely but there was nothing in her expression to indicate that she was lying. It still didn't explain what had gone on between her and Logan. 'Did you go out with him anywhere?' he asked, thinking back to what Maggie had told him and wanting to see what Anna would say.

'Once we went for a walk along the canal. It was a lovely sunny day and I hated being stuck inside. I told him he needed some fresh air. I'd arranged for a photographer mate of mine to come and take some shots of him. I thought it would be nicer if it was somewhere along the canal and not in that manky old boat.'

'I'll need the photographer's name.'

'He cancelled. He had to do a shoot at the last minute, so Joe and I ended up having a drink at a place he knew.'

'We'll still need the photographer's name and details.'

With a shrug, she reeled off a name and mobile number from her BlackBerry.

'And what about the pub? Where is it?'

'I can't remember what it's called, but it's right on the canal, past all the big houses. About a five-minute walk.'

'This was when?'

'Last week, as I told you. The last time I saw him.'

Minderedes looked up from his notes. 'Do you normally spend so much time with someone you're interviewing?'

She gave him a blank stare, as though she didn't appreciate the question. 'No. Usually their publicist provides me with the background stuff, then it's just a quick drink or a lunch and off they go, with maybe a follow-up over the phone to check some details.'

'Why was it different this time?' Tartaglia asked.

'I'd had such a tough time getting to meet Joe, I wanted to take it slowly, not scare him off. After the first session I wasn't totally happy, but I thought I probably had enough to be going on with. Then he called me and said he wanted me to come over, said there were some other things he wanted to talk about. Bottom line is he was lonely. He just wanted some company, that's all.'

Lonely. It was a word that had already come to mind, although there were a lot of people who were happy in their own company, who liked a solitary life. 'How would you describe your relationship with Mr Logan?'

'I told you, this was work,' she said sharply.

'We have a witness who describes the two of you as being close.'

She shook her head. 'Whatever someone's told you, they're wrong. *Nothing* happened between me and Joe.'

'Maybe he felt differently.'

Tartaglia saw the colour rise to her cheeks. Guilt or anger? He wasn't sure. Maybe she did feel something after all. 'You're making way too much of this,' she said, with a fierce look. 'Sure I spent time with Joe, I had to. He wasn't the easiest person to talk to and he'd never given an interview before.'

'But somehow *you* managed to get him to talk. You obviously have a special touch.'

Her mouth tensed. 'From an interviewer's point of view, he was a bloody nightmare. If you want the honest truth, he was like a passive-aggressive clam.'

'That's a pretty odd way to describe him.'

'What can I say? He was really cynical about the whole publishing process, being expected to perform like a fucking dancing bear – his words, not mine – with all the probing and pressure and stuff. Have you read his book?' She looked at him in an accusatorial way.

'Not yet.'

'Well, you ought to. You might understand him better.'

He nodded. The book would have to be read, if nothing else to tick the box, and he had already made up his mind to ask Donovan to do it. She was a quick reader as well as a good judge of character. They would also need to look at whatever Logan had been writing just before he died. Anna was watching him, abstractedly twisting her long hair into a rope and coiling it up on the top of her head. It struck him that whatever had gone on between them, she had probably spent more time with Logan than anyone else had in the last few weeks, or even months, of his life. Yet something was missing.

'You seem to know him very well,' he said, thoughtfully.

'I have an instinctive feel for people. It's why I do what I do.' She let her hair drop and clamped her mouth shut as though slamming a door.

'What else can you tell me?'

'What do you mean?'

He leaned forwards towards her and spread his hands. 'Look, given what's happened, there must be something that came out of your conversations that I should know.'

'I don't think so.'

'There has to be something, even if it seems trivial.'

There was a beat before she answered. 'No. Most of the time we talked about the past. Look, I've told you everything I know. Now I really must be getting on. If I don't go home and email my copy, my editor's going to crucify me.'

Frustrated, he ran his fingers through his hair and stared at her for a moment. She had every right to walk out the door and no doubt she knew it, but he couldn't let her go that easily. Instinct was telling him she was keeping something from him.

Maybe it was information about Joe Logan – it was even possible that she didn't understand the value of what she knew. Or maybe it was just the simple fact that she had slept with him. That she'd used him. He wasn't there to make moral judgements. All that mattered was whether or not it had any bearing on the murder, but he had no idea how he was going to get it out of her.

'What can you tell me about his second book?' he asked abruptly.

Her eyes widened a fraction. 'His second book?'

'Yes. I understand he was working on another book. You must have discussed it.'

'Naturally it was one of my questions. I mean, how do you follow something like *Indian Summer*? I thought it must be pretty difficult as a first-time writer to live up to something like that.' She frowned and put her head to one side. 'Why are you so interested in all of this? What the hell does it matter?'

'Please answer the question. What did he say?'

'He said he'd started something but he wasn't ready to talk about it.'

'What, not even to you?'

'He was really cagey, like it was something precious he was guarding, something sensitive.'

'So, he didn't trust you?'

She hesitated and bit her lip, staring hard at him before replying. 'In the end, I got it out of him. I suppose I can tell you. I mean now he's dead, he's hardly going to write it, is he?'

'Go on.'

She sighed. 'He was writing some sort of a thriller. OK?'

'A thriller?' He couldn't help sounding surprised.

'Yes. About a man, an English teacher, like Joe, whose best friend is involved in some sort of a conspiracy or cover-up. Then the friend gets bumped off and the teacher has to find out what really happened and clear his friend's name. It all sounded a bit of a cliché . . .'

'What sort of conspiracy?' he said, trying not to sound too interested.

'Search me. As I said, he wouldn't tell me. Worried I'd steal his idea, maybe.'

Hopefully, Logan's laptop would give them everything they needed. Not wanting to arouse her curiosity any further, he changed the subject. 'Did you tape your conversations?'

'He wouldn't let me. He said he didn't like hearing the sound of his voice. He said it put him off.'

'But he was an actor. Didn't you find that a bit strange?'

'Sure. There were a lot of strange things about him.' She shifted in her seat still holding his gaze. 'What's going on? What are you not telling me?'

'I told you before, I can't give you any more details.'

'There's a personal motive. That's what you're saying, right? That's why you're so interested in his private life, in what he said and did in the last few weeks. That's why you're grilling me.' She gave a husky laugh and leaned back against the cushions.

What could he say? There was nothing more to be gained from talking to her and he stood up, Minderedes following suit. 'I can't say anything ahead of the press briefing, but if you want to attend it, I'm sure it can be arranged.'

Anna remained seated, smiling and looking up at him expectantly, as though she hoped he'd sit down again. 'That would be useful, yes. But I'd rather get it from you, the horse's mouth, as they say. Promise I won't reveal my source. Is it something to do with the new book he's writing?'

He shook his head and handed her a business card. 'We'll need copies of whatever notes you've got, plus any drafts of the interview. If you think of anything else, give me a call.'

Her eyes flicked to the card in her hand, then back at Tartaglia. She got to her feet. 'Look, it'd be really good if I could put something in my piece about what happened to Joe. Just a line or two. I've answered all your questions. Surely you can tell me *some*thing?'

He held up his hand. Others might be mollified by the sudden softening of her tone but it had no effect on him. 'I'm afraid you're the one jumping to conclusions. You were one of only a few people to see Mr Logan in the weeks before he died and you spent quite a lot of time together. Naturally, we need to speak to you and get some background info on him, but I can assure you it's just routine.'

'Routine?' Her smile widened. 'Pull the other one. It's got bells.'

Outside in the street, the dusty pavement reflected the heat of the day like an open oven door. Pausing in the deep shadow of the bar's awning, Tartaglia wiped his brow and turned to Minderedes. 'Wait until she's gone then go back inside and find out who was in charge the night Joe Logan died. See if they have CCTV. I want to know exactly when Anna Paget arrived and when she left that night. She seems to be a regular here. Find out everything they know about her. After that, pay a visit to the newspaper she works for and do the same.'

Minderedes grinned. 'My pleasure. What a foxy little—'

'What an attitude, you mean.'

'And some. She thawed a bit at the end though, didn't she?'

'Because she wanted something.' He gave Minderedes a penetrating look. It wasn't the first time his usually acute judgement had been blurred by a pretty face, which was fine so long as he kept it out of the workplace, particularly away from anyone concerned with a case. But Minderedes had crossed the boundary before and had missed being suspended by the skin of his teeth. He hoped the man had learned his lesson, but somehow he doubted it. Minderedes generally acted as though he had nine lives. 'Don't go getting any ideas.'

Minderedes held up his hands in surrender. 'I know better than that, boss. You know that.'

'I hope so, for your sake. You know the consequences.'

'I was just looking. No harm in that.'

'So long as your brain's still working.'

'At least she's not the sort you forget in a hurry.'

'It can work both ways,' he said sharply.

If Minderedes didn't wipe that stupid smile off his face PDQ, he'd do it for him. Whether it was the heat, lack of sleep or Anna herself, Tartaglia felt irritable and on edge. To make things worse, he had the nagging feeling that he had let her off the hook, although he had no idea how. 'Wait in the car until she leaves. Don't on any account let her see you.' In spite of Minderedes' protestations, the less he had to do with her, the better. He didn't trust either of them, nor did he want to alert Anna to the fact that they were checking up on her.

Minderedes nodded. 'Cool. So what do you think, sir? You think she's lying?'

'I honestly don't know. But I mean to find out.'

8

'I still can't believe it,' Tim Wade said, shaking his head slowly as he struggled to uncurl his baby daughter's fingers from his ear. 'When I picked up the paper this evening, I thought it had to be a mistake.'

Alex nodded. 'I was supposed to be seeing him last night. I pitched up at his boat as we'd arranged but the police were swarming all over it. They wouldn't tell me what had happened, just that he'd had an accident.'

'Some accident. The papers said he'd been shot.'

The child started to whimper and Tim shifted her into his other arm, bouncing her gently up and down as he wiped a streak of dribble from the shoulder of his jacket.

It was just after seven in the evening and they were sitting in Tim's cosy study on the ground floor of his house in Kennington. All the way there, Alex had wondered if he had made a mistake in calling Tim and asking if he could come over, but sitting now in the reassuring comfort and normality of Tim's world, he felt better about it. After what had happened, he had to talk to someone and Tim was one of the few people who would understand.

Tim had only just got home from work and was still in

his sober suit and tie. It had been six months or so since Alex had last seen him, but he seemed to have aged ten years in that time. How life had changed. For a moment the vision of Tim as a golden, vital youth reared up in his mind like a ghost: head boy, sporting icon of his year, good at everything he turned his hand to, enjoying the rapturous admiration of men and women alike. Alex had envied him. Following in his father's footsteps, Tim had scaled the heights of the Bar with equal ease, yet here he was, sweating heavily, his once trim body blurred and thickened, at the beck and call of a one-year-old monster. Married life, Alex thought to himself with a shudder. There but for the grace of God . . .

The little girl gave a series of blood-curdling shrieks, grabbing at Tim's spectacles until he removed them, then tearing at his thinning brown hair. He threw a despairing glance at his friend.

'Don't look at me,' Alex said, shrinking deeper into the soft leather of the old armchair. 'Babies aren't my thing, as you know.'

Tim got to his feet with a sigh, rocking the child backwards and forwards in his arms. 'One day you'll have to give up your Peter Pan existence and join the real world.'

'Is that what you call it?' Alex smiled. 'Not if I can help it. Not if this is what I've got to look forward to.'

'It's not normally like this.'

'Really?'

'I'd go mad if it was, but she's teething. We've been up all night with her and the au pair's off sick and I don't know how Milly's going to cope. I've got a big case starting in Oxford the day after tomorrow.'

The child started yelping as though jabbed by something sharp, and her face turned a violent pink.

'Are you sure she's OK?'

'I think she's hungry. Let me see if Milly's ready to take her now.'

Tim left the room with the baby and Alex heard him calling to Milly, wherever she had hidden herself. Sensibly out of earshot, no doubt. When he'd arrived, she was breast-feeding an even smaller infant in the kitchen. In a voluminous white nightdress, her hair like a haystack, it wasn't clear if Milly had just got up or was going to bed. He just prayed that she would take pity on them and keep the children out of earshot for a while.

Evening sunlight slanted in through the sash window, dazzling him as he shifted in his seat. The room was stuffy and his head was starting to spin. If he wasn't careful, he'd have another nosebleed. He watched motes of dust spinning in the shaft of light, feeling on edge and filled with a sense of disquiet that had been gnawing at him since learning of Joe's death. He got up, opened the window as wide as it would go, and gazed at the small back garden with its untidy strip of lawn, ramshackle shed and overgrown flowerbeds. A wooden table and chairs sat under a large tree at the end of the garden. It would be cooler out there and a smoke might help calm his nerves. Tim wouldn't tolerate his smoking inside, but he couldn't risk their being overheard by someone in one of the nearby houses or gardens. He drew the curtains against the light, leaving a gap for air, and switched on a lamp.

After a cursory glance along the familiar regiment of

framed photos on Tim's desk, he spotted a late edition of the *Evening Standard* lying open on the rug by the fireplace, amidst a collection of toys and wooden bricks. The headline **BESTSELLING WRITER MURDERED IN WEST LONDON CEMETERY** was blazoned across the front page. He had already seen an earlier edition, but he picked it up anyway and scanned the pages, hoping for some more news. Coverage had been expanded, and there was a small paragraph about Joe's book and its extraordinary success, along with a quote from his publisher talking about his talents as a writer, their shock at his premature death and the loss to the literary world. The rest of the report focused, as before, on the police investigation, with a police spokesman trying to calm speculation that the murder was linked in some way to the gay community. Other than that, there was nothing new and he threw the paper aside.

Tim reappeared moments later. He had taken off his jacket and tie, rolled up his shirtsleeves and put on a pair of black velvet slippers embroidered with gold lion's heads. Tim's father had worn slippers almost exactly the same, Alex remembered. He had often gone to stay in the school holidays at Tim's parents' converted mill house near Basingstoke. Unlike his own much more modest home, it was luxurious, filled with antiques, and had a huge garden with a tennis court and an outdoor swimming pool. At the time, owning such a house seemed the pinnacle of achievement. Like clockwork, Tim's father would arrive home on the train from Waterloo and the first thing he would do was get changed and put on his slippers. Like father, like son, it seemed.

'Hopefully we'll get some peace for a bit,' Tim said. 'I'm

absolutely knackered. I've been in court all day and I've got a shed-load of work to do tonight, but first I need a drink. I'm sure you could use one too.'

'Thanks.'

'There's wine, beer, whisky, brandy, vodka, maybe some tequila . . .' He rubbed his hands together briskly.

'What are you having?'

'Vodka and tonic.'

'That's fine for me too.'

Tim left the room again, reappearing shortly afterwards with some bottles of tonic and a bowl of ice. He kicked the door closed behind him and went over to the small table by the window where he started to mix their drinks. 'How's the acting?' he asked, his back to Alex.

Alex hesitated. It was a loaded question. Apart from a couple of small things for Radio 4, he hadn't had a job in over six months, certainly nothing that would count with Tim. Short of playing Hamlet at the National Theatre, it was impossible to satisfy him. In so many ways, Tim made him feel like a child. Although very different in character, Tim often echoed Alex's father, the cliché of the driven, self-made man, who had pulled himself up from humble origins and wanted to give his son the best education that money could buy. And for what? So that Alex could fritter it all away in a pointless and wasteful existence? Tim was more measured in his comments, but he too thought Alex should have given up acting long ago and found a proper job and he made no bones about saying so, particularly after a few drinks. They had known each other for so long and, like family, Tim felt entitled to express himself freely.

For some reason Alex put up with it. In spite of everything, or perhaps because of everything, he still liked Tim. The fact that their lives were now so different didn't signify.

Joe had been a lot less tolerant. 'You're too fucking senti-mental, Alex,' Joe had said. 'Free yourself. Forget the past. Get rid of your ghosts and start living in the present.' Maybe that was what had made Joe write that book. Perhaps it had been a form of exorcism.

'Got anything interesting in the pipeline?' Tim added, when Alex didn't reply.

'A bit here and there.' He heard the satisfying plink of ice followed by a soft fizz.

'You were really good in that Guy Ritchie film. I watched it again the other night when I couldn't sleep. But it must have come out about ten years ago. It's a shame nothing big came of it.'

Alex made no comment. Tim was right. It had been one of his best film parts to date, too long ago now to count for much with casting directors.

Tim glanced over his shoulder. 'Lemon?'

'Please.'

'Still working in that restaurant?'

'It pays the bills. Means I don't have to worry when things are slow.'

'Well, I suppose that's something, and you *are* one of the managers. How long have you been there?'

'Just over a year.' It was more like two, but he doubted Tim was counting.

'Here you go.' Tim came over to the sofa and passed him a full tumbler before flopping down in the chair opposite and resting his feet heavily on a small stool. He smacked his lips and took a slug of vodka and tonic. 'Well, they're lucky to have you. You must be worth your weight in gold.'

Alex took a couple of mouthfuls; the mixture was reassuringly strong. Tim knew how to mix a drink and he was always generous with his booze. Alex set the glass down on the edge of the nearest bookcase and sank back against the cushions. 'I keep asking myself, why would anyone want to kill Joe?'

Tim sighed heavily and rubbed his eyes. 'I know it's upsetting, but I wouldn't dwell on it too much. This is London, after all. I expect he was just unlucky, in the wrong place at the wrong time.'

'But what was he doing wandering around a cemetery?'

'Research for another stupid book, I wouldn't be surprised. Maybe he was meeting a source.'

'In a cemetery? He was a novelist, not a journalist. I don't think he had sources, and from what he told me he wasn't into research.'

As he gazed at Tim's tired, genial face, snippets of things Joe had talked about that last night came to mind: living on the canal; imagining what it must be like in winter; the awful, nosy neighbours; the new book he was struggling with; his publisher; his mother and her new husband, whom he disliked, and Ashleigh Grange. He tried to make sense of the stream of consciousness, put it in a vague order, hoping to spark some sort of clarity, but nothing came. They had had several beers and a smoke of some good, strong stuff Joe had produced, and then some wine. After that he had crashed out. It was all a bit of a blur. He shook his head.

'Joe hated cemeteries. He said they made him feel depressed.'

'I thought he liked wandering around them. Don't you remember that time we went to see Siegfried Sassoon's grave in that little village near Bath? It was pissing down with rain and we got soaked. Wasn't it Joe who insisted we went to look at it when the rest of us wanted to stay in the pub and have a few more pints?'

'I remember the rain, but I thought you were the one who was so keen on going out to find it.'

Tim shook his head dismissively. 'I tell you, it was Joe. Anyway, you said the police were at his boat. What were they doing?'

'Looked like they were searching it. I wonder what they were after . . .'

'It's standard practice. If there's no obvious suspect or motive, they'll be going through his things with a fine-tooth comb. They'll want to find out everything they can about his life and his movements leading up to his death. They'll be wanting to speak to you at some point, you know. You saw him so recently.'

'I expect so,' Alex said noncommittally. On his way to Tim's after the lunchtime shift, he had switched on his phone and picked up a voicemail from a female detective asking him to get in touch. She had said she wanted to talk to him about Joe and about some calls he had made to Joe's phone earlier in the week. He assumed they had heard the voicemails he had left as well. Luckily they were pretty innocuous, but the police were certainly moving quickly. He had turned his phone off immediately afterwards. He had no intention of calling her back until he had had time to think things through and had worked out what to say, but he decided it was better not to mention any of this to Tim. He could be very black and white when it came to the law. He also didn't dare mention that in his panicked state by the canal, he had given them Tim's name instead of his own. He wouldn't understand.

'Have you spoken to Paul or Danny?'

Tim shook his head. 'Haven't seen either of them since Fi's wedding. There was such a crowd and we didn't get a chance to talk. We meant to meet up afterwards, but you know what it's like. Can't see everyone. Not sure I even have their current numbers.'

There was silence for a moment. They had all been so close at university. He was surprised that Tim, of all people, had lost touch. He had been the glue that had held them all together, a combination of sheer force of personality and the fact that everything he touched seemed to turn to gold. They had all been in awe of him, happy to bask in his glory, perhaps in the naive hope that it would rub off on them too. The wedding had also been the last time Alex had seen Paul Khan and Danny Black. Although he had spoken to them both, it was the polite conversation of people who no longer had anything but the past in common. Paul was now a successful lawyer in a big City firm, with a loft apartment in Hoxton, an expensive car and a string of increasingly young girlfriends. He had become a cliché of superficial success, but it wasn't enough. Even after all these years, he was still trying to prove something, trying to distance himself from his immigrant roots and become part of the establishment, still comically and pathetically insecure compared to Tim. Next thing, Joe had said, he'd be running for Parliament. Joe had dismissed Paul as someone without imagination, which for Joe was the ultimate put-down, and Alex found himself reluctantly agreeing. The seeds had always been there, but maybe when they were young it hadn't mattered. As for Danny, he was still doing something on the fringes of the film business, with fingers in several pies, although from what Alex had heard from others, things weren't going so well. Danny had been so pissed at the wedding it had been impossible to get much out of him. Joe hadn't gone, he remembered. He had made some excuse but it was clear he wasn't interested. Things had moved on, he had said, for all of them. Joe, Tim, Alex, Paul and Danny. 'The Famous Five', as they had once, on a drug-and-drink-fuelled high, styled themselves, or the 'Fucking Five' as someone – some narked woman, no doubt – had written a few days later in the dirt on Paul's car outside the law library, along with the words 'fuck off'.

Alex studied Tim's face for any sign that his thoughts were running in the same direction, but Tim seemed absorbed by the glass in his hand and it was impossible to tell what he was thinking. The elephant in the room, the subtext that neither of them dared to refer to. They had been doing it for years. He felt a hypocrite.

'It all seems a long time ago, doesn't it?'

Tim gave him a penetrating look. 'What do you mean?'

'University.' He chickened out as usual.

Tim nodded. 'But at least you still kept in touch with Joe. How was he when you last saw him? Happy?'

'Yes. I think he was. Finally. Although he hated the publicity mill, it was good for him to have some recognition.'

'You two were always very close.'

'I thought you were too.'

Tim shrugged. 'We were once. But work ... and being married ... having a family ... It all gets in the way.'

And Tim's desire to distance himself from that time, Alex thought. Although Joe had never said anything, he had sensed the slow, quiet rejection and been stung by it. It was probably at the root of his recent bitterness about Tim. As for Tim, he had created a buffer zone of success and respectability, but it could easily be blown away. Maybe that was what he feared. He wondered how Tim would react when he heard what Joe had told him.

'When did you last see Joe?' Alex asked, wondering how to bring it up.

'It must have been at least a year ago, then he turned up out of the blue at my Chambers a couple of weeks ago. You know what he was like. Never thought to ring ahead. I was in court, so he hung around for a bit until my clerk turfed him out. After that he phoned a couple of times, but I was rushed off my feet and I didn't get around to returning the calls. I feel bad about it now.'

'You don't know what he was after?'

'I assumed he wanted to borrow some money, like the last time.' There was no disapproval in Tim's tone; it was just a simple statement of fact.

'It can't have been money he was after. He made a packet out of the book.'

'Well, sod that. If you ask me, he doesn't deserve a penny.'

Tim took a deep draught and stared down at his glass as if lost in it. It wasn't really the money that Tim resented, Alex suspected. More the fact that Joe had used some of their common experiences for his own ends. It was all too close for comfort.

'I hadn't seen him for a while either,' Alex said. 'Then he called me. It must have been about the same time he came to see you. He'd had a couple of funny emails and he wondered who'd sent them, if it was one of us.'

Tim looked up at him over the edge of his tumbler. 'One of us? What sort of thing?'

'They were really odd, like they were part of a book, or something, but with no beginning or ending, just a paragraph cut off mid sentence, written in some sort of funny Gothic print.'

'From Joe's book, you mean?'

'No. The first one talked about an old country house, set in woods. It was all pretty bland.'

'He showed it to you?'

'Not the first. I think he deleted it. But I saw the second one. It was weird. It described some people going down into a crypt, with candles, laughing, music playing . . .'

Tim's expression hardened. 'What else?'

'That's about it, but he was quite worked up about it.'

'He always over-dramatised.'

'Maybe.'

Tim held Alex's gaze. 'I assume you didn't send them?'

'That's what Joe wanted to know, but no, it wasn't me.'

'Well, it wasn't me either. It must be Paul or Danny having a laugh.'

'Joe didn't think so. For starters, he said he hadn't spoken to either of them for a long while and neither of them had his email address.'

'It's pretty easy to find out. They could ask any one of his friends, or they probably rang his publisher and made up some story.'

'But why? What's the point?'

'Envy, maybe. You said the book's a success and he made lots of money. Maybe someone's jealous and wanted to rattle his cage, make him feel a bit less full of himself.'

The bitterness in Tim's tone took Alex aback. That Tim, who seemed to have achieved everything he wanted, might actually be jealous, was an odd thought. Maybe he had sent the emails after all, although bitterness aside, it wouldn't be in character. If not Tim, it had to be either Paul or Danny. Paul had a devious side, but of the two, his money was on Danny. The weasel, as they'd called him. He pictured his long-nosed, freckled face, the small, beady brown eyes behind the tinted John Lennon glasses. He had always been a bit of a joker, but the humour was razor-sharp and usually at someone else's expense. He certainly liked to push things to the wire when he could.

'Who do you mean?' he asked, watching Tim closely, still undecided.

Tim drained his glass and put it down forcefully on the corner of the desk. 'I don't know. I can't believe either Danny or Paul would be so petty.'

'Well, if it's not one of us, there's a simple explanation. Someone's talked.'

'I hope to God not.' Tim stood up abruptly and moved over

to the window. He pulled open the shutters and gazed out for a moment, as though searching for something. Then he turned around, frowning, and jammed his hands deep in his pockets.

'Is it blackmail? Is that what you're saying?'

'Blackmail?'

'Was someone trying to blackmail Joe?'

Maybe the dope had dulled his brain, but thinking back to that evening he was sure Joe hadn't said anything about blackmail. 'I don't think so. There were just the two emails. No threats. No demands. As far as I know, there was no follow-up.'

'You're sure?'

'Positive.'

Tim looked relieved. 'Well, that's something.'

'But now he's dead and in a cemetery too. It's a bit of a coincidence.'

'A coincidence?' Tim shook his head. 'I'm not with you. Loads of people visit the Brompton Cemetery, as I found out pretty graphically in a case I did recently. It's an interesting place during daylight and as safe as anywhere. All sorts of famous people are buried there, you know.'

'As I said, you're the one obsessed with graveyards, not Joe. What are you getting at?'

'My point is, Joe being there doesn't have to mean anything.'

'But it's hardly close to where he lived.'

'Maybe he was going to watch Chelsea and something happened.'

Alex gave him a withering look. 'The season's over.'

'OK. Maybe he was meeting someone or just going for a walk.'

'But why there?' The question hung in the air for a moment before he continued, 'Do you think . . .' He stopped and shook his head. He knew what Tim would say.

'What is it?'

He studied Tim for a moment, feeling suddenly foolish.

'Spit it out.'

For a moment he didn't answer, then he took a deep breath. 'Well, I wondered if I should go to the police.'

Tim stared at him. 'Jesus Christ. Have you gone stark raving mad?'

'Isn't finding Joe's killer more important than anything else?'

'Whoa, hang on a sec. Now you're getting as paranoid as Joe. Maybe he wrote the emails himself.'

'Joe? Why would he?'

'Perhaps it was a wind-up. Perhaps he wanted attention.'

'I told you, I saw one of them. And I saw how shaken he was.'

'He was an actor.'

'I tell you, he wasn't faking.'

'OK. But I don't see why you're trying to link the emails to what happened to him. Someone's just having a bit of fun, that's all.'

'Fun? I still think—'

Tim held up his hand. 'Let's look at this logically. What are the possibilities? If it's one of us, it's a joke, although not a very amusing one, I agree. I don't believe for a minute any of us would resort to blackmail.'

'And if it's not one of us?'

He frowned. 'Well, I still don't believe it but, for argument's sake, if someone has inadvertently let something slip, then maybe we are talking blackmail.'

'I swear Joe never mentioned the idea.'

'Perhaps he didn't want to worry you. He may have just been sounding you out. See what you'd say. Anyway, if blackmail was the intention, why kill him? What's the point? You'd be killing the golden goose.'

He could see from the stubborn set of Tim's mouth that there was no point arguing. Anyway, it was what he wanted to hear. His head told him Tim was talking sense – hell, none of them wanted to dig up the past unnecessarily. The link was pretty tenuous. He should ignore the stupid whisperings of his heart.

Tim was looming over him, searching his face for a reaction. Again Alex wondered if maybe Tim was behind the emails. He drained his glass and got to his feet. 'So, you really don't think the police should know?'

'No, I don't. I'm speaking here as a friend rather than in a legal capacity, of course.' He smiled and put his arm around Alex, giving his shoulder a friendly squeeze as he walked him to the door.

'I'll remind you of that when I get arrested for withholding vital information.'

'Now you're being silly. Listen, the police are bound to find the emails when they go through what's on Joe's computer. It's one of the first things they'll do. Let them worry about what to make of them. What they don't need is you sending them up a blind alley. OK?'

9

Tartaglia sat at his desk in his shoebox of an office. Logan's laptop was still with the experts, being analysed, but a copy of the hard drive had been couriered over for them to check. Wightman and Downes were busy going through the contents of Mail, Address Book and iPhoto, but Tartaglia wanted to look through Logan's other files himself. He had borrowed an Apple laptop, which lay open on the desk in front of him, and he plugged the memory stick Wightman had given him into the drive and opened the folder marked Joe Logan.

Inside he found two folders – one labelled Personal and the other Work – and a long list of individual items. He trawled through a miscellany of jPegs, podcasts and internet downloads that Logan hadn't bothered to file or delete, but found no common theme or anything of particular interest. He clicked open the Personal folder and scanned the long list of documents, most of which were several years old. Logan had been as haphazard with his files as with his housekeeping and, again, had made no attempt to organise them by category. He sorted them by date order and opened the most recent file, which had been created three weeks before Logan's death.

It was a letter, addressed to the Reverend Tom Sutton, Headmaster of St Thomas's, the school where Logan had been employed, thanking him for the 'very kind offer' of a permanent job in the English Department to start that autumn. Tartaglia wondered if Logan was being polite or if he had actually intended to go back to teaching in spite of the success of his book. Logan said that he wanted to think things over and, in the final paragraph, he mentioned that he would be coming to the school to pick up some things in the next couple of weeks and that he would drop by to see the headmaster, whom he addressed as Tom, and give him his answer then. Wondering if Logan had found time for the trip before he was killed, Tartaglia made a note to check it immediately. If Logan's things were still at the school, it would explain why they had found so little on the boat.

Nearly an hour later, after ploughing through a series of letters to bank managers, insurance companies and the like and finding nothing of any interest, he decided to hand over the task of going through the rest to Wightman. He turned his attention to the Work folder, which contained a few documents mainly relating to publicity, as well as another folder entitled Books. Inside were individual chapters and drafts of *Indian Summer*, character notes, various attempts at a blurb for the jacket, and several jPegs showing versions of the UK cover. He scanned them all but found nothing relating to a second book. He had already spoken again to Jana Ryan and questioned her about Logan's second book but she had been unable to add anything to her earlier comments. It looked as if the only person Logan had talked to about the new book had been Anna Paget.

Frustrated, he picked up the phone and was about to dial Wightman's extension, when Wightman appeared in the doorway.

'I was just about to buzz you,' Tartaglia said.

'I must be telepathic, sir. Thought you'd be interested in this.' He passed Tartaglia a sheet of paper. It was an email from Logan to Anna Paget at her work address, dated two months before.

Hi Anna, thanks for your letter and kind words. The material you enclosed is certainly interesting. As you say, there's a connection that may be worth exploring. I'd love to see the article you mentioned. Let's meet up and have a drink and see where we go with this. I'm in London for a few months, staying on a friend's boat in Maida Vale. I'm working on another book so short on time, but if you don't mind coming this way, there are a couple of half-decent pubs in the area. Give me a bell and let me know what you'd like to do.

He added his address and mobile number and signed himself 'Joe'.

'Interesting,' Tartaglia said, looking up. 'I wonder what he means by "connection". He also mentions another book but I can't find anything that looks like one on the drive you gave me. That's why I was calling you. Are you sure we have everything from Logan's laptop?'

'That's what they told me.'

'Then you'd better get on to them. Tell them we think there's a file missing.'

'Is there a title, or a description of what we're looking for?'

'It's his second novel, that's all we know. Get them to try and recover anything that's been recently deleted off that computer. What about the email from Alice in Wonderland?'

'No joy. The address is untraceable.'

Tartaglia shook his head wearily. 'We've got to find that book.'

'I'll get onto it right away.'

As he left the room, Minderedes came in. 'I've found out a bit more about Anna Paget, Boss. The barman at Kazbar was very helpful.'

'And?'

'She's single, as far as he knows, lives around the corner from the café and likes to work there most mornings and sometimes afternoons, depending on how noisy it gets. Doesn't smoke, doesn't drink, likes skinny lattés with cinnamon and San Pellegrino with lime—'

'I get the picture. Anything important?'

'After you left, I waited until she'd gone, then I went back inside. The barman was there the night before last when she was supposed to meet Logan. There's no CCTV but he more or less confirmed what she said. He couldn't remember exactly when she arrived but said it was before eight and that she left not more than an hour later. She was alone. She sat on the sofa where she was today, had a large glass of orange juice, which she didn't finish, and was on her BlackBerry most of the time.'

'He's observant.'

'I think he has the hots for her. He also said the bar wasn't full. He said she seemed really pissed off when her friend didn't show. She made some comment to him about not being used to being stood up.'

'You surprise me. What about the newspaper?'

'I spoke to her editor and he also confirmed what she said. She's freelance and the idea for the interview was her own, although they're clearly very excited about it, particularly now Logan's dead.'

'Aren't people something?'

Minderedes nodded. 'Anyway, he's worked with her for a couple of years and spoke highly of her.'

'Well, that gets us nowhere. Has she sent over anything yet?'

'No. Nothing so far.'

'Call her and tell her I want all the stuff she said she'd send round. I want it now, no excuses. Whatever she sent Logan worked like magic, according to an email we found on his computer.'

'Why does it matter?'

'Because I'm curious, that's why. Any problems, send someone round for the originals and we'll let her have them back in due course.'

As Minderedes turned to go, Jane Downes appeared behind him in the doorway. 'I've managed to locate Logan's mum, sir. His dad's dead and she's remarried and living in Portsmouth. Someone from her local station's broken the news and she's coming up to London tonight. She's insisting on seeing Logan's body, poor woman. Apparently he was her only child.'

10

'Number twenty-five,' Chang said, pulling over on a yellow line and peering up at the tall, gloomy, redbrick house. 'There's a light on, so someone's home.'

'Thanks. I can see.'

'Shall I come with you?'

'No. You stay here and keep watch. Be ready to back me up if there's any trouble.'

'Whatever you say.'

He took it better than expected. She bit her lip as she got out of the car and walked away down the street. She could handle things on her own but she knew she was being mean-spirited. By rights it should have been Chang's show. He was the one who had eventually traced the red-haired man that Minderedes had spoken to by the canal. The man had been captured on CCTV footage at Warwick Avenue tube station where, after leaving Minderedes, he had caught a train to Kensal Green. Luckily for them he had used an oyster card, which made things easy. It had been bought online nearly six months before and topped up several times since. It had given them the details of his many journeys over that period, as well as his real name, Alex Fleming, and an address in one of the backstreets of Kilburn. It was all too much like Big Brother, for her liking, but at least it suited their purposes. They assumed he must be the Alex who had called Logan's phone several times and left a couple of voicemails in the days before he died.

Chang was keen, like anyone in a new job, and Donovan couldn't blame him for it. She was also never at her most patient when she was tired, but he had been getting on her nerves all day with his eagerness to please, asking questions that, although legitimate, interrupted her train of thought. If she couldn't have silence, at least some physical space would do for a while. Deep down she knew that her irritation was not really to do with him, just part of a general, creeping sense of dissatisfaction that had been affecting her for a while, although she had no idea what was at the root of it. Chang was just the unlucky recipient.

Like many of the houses in the road, number twenty-five had been divided into flats, with satellite dishes sprouting from every floor. The front garden had been concreted over and an old Fiat Panda and a Triumph motorbike occupied the space, along with a motley collection of rubbish bins. She climbed the steps to the front door. There were no names on any of the bells and she was about to press the bottom one when she heard a loud rap on the glass of the ground-floor bay window that overlooked the front door. An elderly lady, half hidden behind a swathe of net curtains, stared out at her suspiciously. Donovan mouthed the word 'police' and held up her ID card to the glass. The woman gave it a cursory glance then disappeared back into the room. Moments later the front door opened and she stood proprietorially in the entrance, leaning heavily on a stick, her other hand curled around the doorframe.

'What do you want?' she said loudly, as though she was hard of hearing. She was tiny, even shorter than Donovan, with straight, chin-length white hair, clipped back on either side with hairpins, and thick glasses, which magnified a sharp pair of watery eyes.

'I'm looking for this man.' Donovan held up the e-fit image that Minderedes had put together. 'He apparently lives here.'

'You want upstairs,' the woman said in a clear, precise voice, pointing. 'But I haven't seen him for a while.'

'Which floor?'

'First,' she shouted. 'But he's not there now.'

'There's someone at home,' Donovan said, gazing up at the first-floor window, where she could see a light. She also heard music coming from above. The woman stared at her as if she didn't understand the question. 'Who lives up there?' Donovan mouthed the words slowly and pointed upwards.

'There's three of them and sometimes more, if you get my drift. But I told you he's not there any longer.'

'You're sure?'

'I may be deaf but I'm not blind. Alex left a few months ago.'

'You knew Alex, then?'

'As much as you get to know anyone these days. He was a nice young man, unlike some I could mention. Used to bring the post in for me, help me with my shopping bags.'

'Do you know where he's gone?'

The woman shook her head.

'I need to find him. Any ideas?'

The woman seemed to consider the matter, then said, 'You'd best ask Kate. She's the boss up there, from what I can tell, although she's a rude, unhelpful cow. Hasn't got time for anyone but herself. I'd like to see how she copes when she's eighty-five . . .'

'Is she in now?'

'That's her horrible rust bucket out front, blocking my view, so she can't be far. Doesn't know what her legs are for, that one.'

'I'd better go and speak to her. May I come in?'

She shrugged and shuffled aside to let Donovan pass, muttering, 'She'll know where he is, mark you me.'

Donovan looked around at her. 'Are you saying she's his girlfriend?'

The woman sniffed. 'Who's to say? She'd certainly eat him for breakfast given half the chance, although I imagine he has more sense.'

Donovan thanked her and followed the strains of Simply Red up the narrow stairs to the first floor. She knocked on the door several times before she eventually saw a shadow under the crack and heard the rattle of a security chain. The door opened a few inches and a plump-faced young woman in a pink dressing gown peered out at her, her hair wound up in a towel turban.

'Who are you?'

'I'm with the police.' Donovan held up her warrant card to the gap. 'Are you Kate?'

The woman squinted at the card short-sightedly, then looked back at Donovan. 'I prefer to be called Katherine. How did you get in? Did someone leave the front door open again?'

'No. The lady downstairs let me in.'

'That old cat.'

'I'd like to talk to you. May I come in for a few minutes?'

There was an audible sigh. 'Look, I've just got home from work and I'm in the middle of washing my hair. What do you want?'

'I'm trying to find a man called Alex Fleming. I understand you know him.'

Alex walked to Stockwell Tube Station and caught the Victoria line, heading north. Most people in the carriage seemed to be going into town for the evening. He felt strangely detached, still mulling over in his head everything Tim had said, trying again to remember how the conversation with Joe had gone. They had talked at some length about the emails, but he was sure the word blackmail hadn't come up at any point. Maybe Tim was right. Perhaps Joe hadn't wanted to worry him, but there had been no sense that Joe was keeping something unpleasant from him. Maybe it hadn't dawned on him that blackmail was on the cards, or maybe it had and he had discounted the idea. Like Tim, Joe had been against going to the police, but then he hadn't foreseen his own murder.

At Oxford Circus he followed a crowd of chattering Japanese students out of the carriage and up the escalator, making his way to the Bakerloo line where he caught a train a few minutes later in the direction of Kensal Green, where he lived. He had been planning on going straight home, getting a takeaway and watching a DVD, hoping that his flatmate, Paddy, was working late as usual. But as the train pulled into Warwick Avenue, he changed his mind, got up from his seat and jumped out, nearly knocking over a woman's bag of groceries as he dashed for the doors.

Within minutes, he stood on the little bridge, looking down along the canal in the direction of Joe's boat. No flashing lights, no police, no gawping passers-by. Everything was back to normal. He crossed over and followed the pavement along the canal until he came to Joe's boat, where he stopped in front of the railings. A thick double streamer of blue and white police tape barred the entrance onto the boat from the towpath. The two small half doors that opened into the cabin were boarded up and padlocked, with an official-looking paper stuck to the front. The curtains were pulled back, but the interior was dark and in the slanting evening light he couldn't make out anything inside.

The table and chairs were still out on the deck and for a moment he pictured the two of them sitting there, Joe with his eyes half shut, a roll-up between his fingers, bare feet up on the edge of the boat. He remembered the warmth of the air, the quiet, and the colour of the sky as they watched the light fade over the water. They had stayed there for a good hour or so, until the temperature dropped and they went inside. Then Joe had heated up a couple of frozen pizzas and put an old REM CD on the player. They had sat at the little table Joe used as a desk, Joe sweeping the pile of papers onto the floor as if they didn't matter and lighting a large pink scented candle that belonged to the owner of the boat. It suddenly came to him that Joe had talked about going to Thailand for a few months and had asked him to go with him. He had even offered to pay his air fare. Alex swallowed hard. So much had changed in a matter of days.

'Hey, you.'

He started. It was a woman's voice, high-pitched and pene-trating. He turned and looked along the canal in the general direction and saw a slim, blonde-haired woman standing on the roof of one of the boats further along. She was waving at him.

'Yes, you. Can I have a word?'

His first thought was that he had done something wrong, an instinctive reaction that went back to childhood. He looked around but there was nobody else in sight. He squinted hard, trying to see her more clearly, and she waved again. She def-initely meant him. Tanned, and wearing a white, short-sleeved T-shirt and faded jeans, she stood in the sun amidst a colourful sea of potted plants and flowers, her hair pulled back in a ponytail. At least she was nothing to do with the police. Wondering what she wanted, he followed the railings until he came to her boat.

'Sorry to make you jump. You're a friend of Joe's, aren't you?' She climbed nimbly down onto the deck, with a pair of kitchen scissors and a large bunch of what looked like basil in her hand. 'Have you heard what's happened?'

'You mean about Joe?'

She nodded.

'Yeah, I know, thank you.'

'I just wanted to make sure. I thought maybe ... Well, I saw you with him the other day, and before that, in the garden of the Bargeman's Rest. It must be a real shock. Have you just found out?'

'I was here yesterday. I was supposed to be seeing him, but the police had the area sealed off. I sort of panicked. I still can't quite get my head around it. That's why I came back.'

She squinted at him, hand shielding her eyes. 'My name's Maggie.'

He remembered her now from the other evening. Joe had been quite rude about some of the neighbours who had trailed past his boat – 'prying, pain in the arse time-wasters' he had called them – but he had pointed her out as she walked past them on the towpath and waved. He had said something about having had supper with her and that she was OK, which was about the most praise Joe gave anyone new.

'I'm Alex.'

'Look, do you fancy a quick drink? I was about to have one myself.'

He hesitated.

'Do come,' she said, smiling, her head slightly to one side. 'I won't bite. It would be nice to talk to someone who knew Joe. I really liked him, you know.'

Again he hesitated. He wasn't sure that he wanted to talk about Joe at all, let alone with someone who barely knew him. But if she and Joe had had dinner recently, she might be able to shed some more light on what had been going on with Joe. If nothing else, she seemed harmless and it wasn't as if he had anything better to do. 'OK,' he said, nodding slowly. 'Thanks.'

'The gate's just along there.' She gestured along the towpath with the scissors. 'Although, silly me, you know that already.'

Five minutes later they were sitting at a pretty wrought-iron table on her front deck, surrounded by more plants in brightly painted pots. The tabletop was a weathered piece of greyish-white marble, which had seen better days. But the base, which had been painted pea-green, had once been part of an old-fashioned, pedal-operated sewing machine, the word Singer still just visible across the front.

'My granny used to have one of those,' he said, taking a sip of cold white wine and pointing at the table. 'Where did you find it?'

'It came off a skip. It beggars belief what some people throw away. My mum had one too. Made all our clothes on it and taught me and my sister how to sew, but nobody bothers these days, do they? Who has the time? Anyway, it's cheaper to go to Primark.'

He nodded. Even sewing on a button was a stretch. He hoped she wouldn't notice the safety pin that was holding his shirt together halfway down. 'Another amazing sunset,' he said after a moment, feeling awkward.

'It's beautiful, isn't it? The light's wonderful all year round. Something to do with the water, I think. It's why I carry on living here, even though the boat's smaller than most studio flats and the damp and cold's shocking in winter.'

'Well, I think it's great.' A narrow-boat would do him fine, he thought. Apart from the fussy, feminine décor, he had felt at home in the cramped space of Joe's boat, with its little deck outside. It was cosy, with everything to hand. Perfect for one person. Many of the boats along the canal looked tatty, but he imagined a berth in such a location must cost an arm and a leg, probably way beyond his means.

'Have you ever taken a boat trip down the canal?'

He shook his head.

'I don't mean one of these.' She waved her wine glass dismissively in the general direction of the canal and the lines of narrow-boats. 'Most of them don't go anywhere. But see there, where the canal opens out? You can pick up a water taxi, just by the floating café. It will take you all the way to Camden Passage, if you want. It's a great way to see parts of London. Some of it's really seedy, but you go past these incredible mansions with huge columns and billiard-table lawns. They don't look as if they belong in central London at all. Then, of course, there's the zoo. There's a special stop if you want to get out. You should try it one day, if you have time, particularly when the weather's like this. I've lived in London most of my life but I love being a tourist when I get the chance.'

He gazed along the canal, watching as a couple of tourists stopped by the railings above to take photographs. The light was beginning to fade and the flash went off several times. He realised the camera was pointed directly at him and Maggie. Not wanting to be part of the view, he shielded his face with his hand. In the distance, silhouetted against the sky, was the little bridge that he had crossed earlier and, beyond it, a large open stretch of pearly water, with an island in the middle. 'What's the name of that bit of water past the bridge?'

'Browning's Pool, after the poet Robert Browning.'

'That's right.' He remembered now Joe telling him that. For some unknown reason, Joe had liked Browning, along with some obscure and nearly forgotten poets. It was typical of Joe, he thought. He had always gone his own way, never caring about what other people thought or following a trend.

'Browning had a house overlooking the water,' Maggie said. 'It must have been a lovely spot in those days.'

'Is it still there?'

'No. I think it was either bombed or pulled down after the war. There's just a blue plaque on an ugly seventies building. Difficult to imagine how it must have all looked, particularly now with that hideous Paddington Basin development clogging up the horizon. Don't you sometimes wish you could just go back in time and see how things used to be?'

'It may have looked a lot better, but just imagine the smell.'

She laughed and took a sip of wine. They sat in silence for a couple of minutes, gazing at the water, then she raised her glass. 'To Joe.'

He raised his. 'Wherever he is, poor sod.'

'Did you know him well?' she asked, after a few moments.

'We met at university. We were both studying English and drama, and we hit it off more or less from the first day. We shared a house for the last two years of our degree. We didn't always see eye to eye, but it didn't matter. After we left, we were doing different things, and when he started teaching he more or less moved out of London. We wouldn't see each other for months sometimes. Then we'd meet up and it was as if no time had passed.'

'You must have been good friends.'

'We were.' Avoiding her gaze, he drained his glass.

'I'm very sorry.'

He swallowed hard. 'Thank you. I just wish I knew what had happened. I mean, I just don't understand what he was doing in Brompton Cemetery or how he could have got himself shot.' He sighed and looked up at her, not knowing what to say next.

She frowned and pursed her lips, as though undecided about something, then said, 'There's something I ought to tell you. I don't think Joe was killed there, you know. From what I heard, his body was only left there after he died.'

'How do you know that? I saw nothing in the papers.'

Still looking at him, she put down her glass. 'The police were here yesterday and again this morning. They wouldn't say anything of course, but I overheard one of them on his phone. He'd interviewed me yesterday and I recognised his voice.'

'What did he look like?' He pictured Minderedes, with his small, sharp, brown eyes.

'Tallish, well-built, dark-haired, very good-looking.' She gave him a sideways smile.

'Was he called Minderedes?' he asked, doubtful that Minderedes could be described as 'tallish' or 'very good-looking', although a certain sort of strutting, macho self-confidence went a long way with women, he had learned.

'No, he had an Italian name, although his accent was Scots. I've got his card somewhere downstairs. He was a nice bloke, actually, quite sympathetic, all things considered. Anyway, he was standing on the pavement up there, by the railings, right by that signpost.' She pointed to a spot no more than a few metres away from where they were sitting. 'The others were still on Joe's boat so I guess he came over here to get a bit of privacy. He was talking pretty quietly, facing the canal. I had the doors and windows open as I was doing some ironing, but I don't think he saw me. Maybe it was the direction of the wind, or maybe he didn't care, but I managed to hear quite a bit of what he said. There was something about a press conference, and someone making a serious mistake if they didn't release certain information immediately.'

'What information?'

'I'm not sure. He was arguing with the person at the other end and he said, "It's important they know he wasn't killed there", or something along those lines.'

'They?'

'I think he meant the public, or the press. The gist was that if someone had seen something suspicious somewhere else, they wouldn't think to report it. From the way he spoke, I'd say he was talking to a superior, but he sounded mighty fed up.'

'You're sure about this?'

'Positive. He didn't mention Joe by name, but who else could it be? And it makes sense, don't you think? I looked at the paper again and watched the six o'clock news. They talked about Joe's body being found in Brompton Cemetery, but they don't actually say he died there. The devil's always in the detail, isn't it? I wonder what else they're keeping back.'

'You think he was killed on the boat?'

She shrugged. 'I don't know. I'm sorry.'

He saw the concern in her eyes, but he didn't know what to say. Even though she didn't strike him as a gossip and she seemed genuinely affected by what had happened, it was difficult hearing her talk about it all. Her words had alarmed him in a way he couldn't explain to her. If Joe hadn't been killed in the cemetery, but had been put there deliberately, then the link between the emails and his death was stronger than he'd thought. He ought to speak to Tim again, although he knew he would tell him he was reading far too much into things.

She finished the last sip of her wine and leaned forwards, gently touching his arm. 'Are you OK?'

He nodded.

'I'm sorry. Perhaps I shouldn't have said anything.'

He sighed, barely trusting himself to speak. 'I'm glad you did. I need to know what happened, whatever the truth.'

'Look, do you have time for another glass?' she asked, noticing that his was empty. 'It's so lovely out here.'

He stretched and inhaled the warm evening air. His head was buzzing. He felt too stirred up to make the journey home just yet and some more alcohol would be a good thing. 'Thanks. I'd like that very much.'

Donovan climbed back wearily into the passenger seat beside Chang.

'You've been a while,' he said, starting the engine. 'Any luck?' He put the car into gear and they pulled away.

'Alex used to room in the first-floor flat but he left a few months ago. I spoke to one of his former flatmates, a grumpy woman called Kate, or Katherine as she prefers to be called. According to the woman downstairs, she and Alex were friends and possibly more than that, but Kate said she hadn't seen him or spoken to him since he left. She tried to make out she didn't know him very well but I'm pretty sure she's lying.'

'What are we going to do?'

'After I spoke to her, I went back downstairs and managed to get the landlord's number from the woman on the ground floor. I'm hoping he's still got Alex's details, a bank account, or forwarding address, or something. I'd like you to follow it up.' She thrust a piece of paper at him with the name and number, which he took and tucked away in his pocket.

'Anything else?'

'Short of tapping Kate's phone, or putting a tail on her, both of which will take time to set up and neither of which Steele will authorise, I'm sure, there's not a great deal we can do.'

They stopped at a traffic light and he glanced over at her. 'You look tired. Fancy a drink?'

She shook her head. 'We'd better go back to the office. I've got a zillion and one things to catch up on, plus I do have another lead if the landlord doesn't come up trumps.'

'Which is?'

'Well, the woman on the ground floor told me our Alex is an actor, like Joe Logan. If nothing else, we ought to be able to trace him through Spotlight.'

11

Alex unlocked the door to his flat, listening for the sound of the TV in the living room above that would indicate that Paddy was home. But the flat was silent and in darkness. He breathed a sigh of relief. He had the flat to himself, thank Christ. Paddy was in the throes of a new infatuation and he hadn't seen him for days. While Alex was still asleep, he would creep home at crack of dawn to shower and change for the office, the only evidence that he had briefly been back being a wet towel and sopping bathmat dumped on the floor in the bathroom, or a carton of milk left out on the kitchen counter in haste. Long may it last, Alex thought to himself, although from what he knew of Paddy, such things usually ran their course in a few weeks.

He went up to the small living room, turned on the light and opened the window for some air, letting out a bluebottle that was buzzing at the glass. The hum of the traffic below filled the room but it didn't bother him. He had other things on his mind. He put his phone on to charge, switched on the TV for background noise and went into the kitchen to find something to drink. The small fridge, as usual, was empty of food or anything worth drinking; neither he nor Paddy ever bothered to shop ahead. The cupboards were equally bare and he was on the point of giving up and going to bed when he remembered a bottle of Geneva gin in the freezer that had been there since he moved in. Paddy had been given it by some Dutch client and no doubt forgotten its existence. He poured himself a tumbler full and took it back into the sitting room, where he flopped down onto the sofa in front of an episode of *CSI*. A forensic scientist with long blonde hair and huge tits was examining the body of a young man. The 'vic', as she called him, dressed in jeans and a T-shirt, was flopped over a pool table, the cue still in his hands, eyes staring vacantly into the camera. Blood trickled like honey from a bullet wound in the centre of his forehead. Were bullet wounds always so tidy? Alex took a gulp of ice-cold gin, swilling the viscous liquid around his mouth and letting it coat his tongue. It slipped down his throat and he felt an instant cloud of warmth rise in his chest.

He had ended up spending several hours with Maggie. They had downed a good deal of wine and she had cooked him dinner, some sort of stew, he vaguely recalled. He also vaguely recalled thinking that she had wanted him to stay, although maybe he had imagined it. He wished now that he had paid more attention. Even though she was quite a bit older than he was, she was an attractive woman, with a nice way about her and a good sense of humour. But the moment, if it ever had been there, was lost. His mind had been on Joe. She had talked a great deal about him, about conversations they had had, about what sort of person she thought he had been, about what a waste it was that he was dead. He had let it all wash over him like a warm gust of air, only half paying attention. Somewhere in the conversation she had mentioned a journalist called Anna, whom she said Joe had been keen on. If it were true, it was strange that Joe had never mentioned Anna, but then Joe had kept a lot of things to himself. The news that Joe hadn't been killed in Brompton Cemetery, that his body had been dumped there later, was still sinking in. He needed to find out more, try to understand exactly what had happened.

He was sweating heavily. He knocked back some more gin and held the frosted glass to his forehead. He closed his eyes, still aware of the flickering light in the room as he pictured the water of the canal, with the moon above it, and Joe's dark, empty boat. He felt his muscles relax, felt himself slide towards sleep. Joe's voice burbled in his head, conversational in tone but the words indistinct, little more than the background buzz of a radio. He thought he heard the name Ashleigh. He saw the full moon rise above water, the cool, shimmering blackness beneath, so deep it appeared to have no bottom, and the girl, her hair fanning out through his fingers like silk, her bare skin bleached the colour of chalk in the strange, silver light. He heard the gurgling trill of her laughter, mocking him, enticing him, carrying high above the music. He felt the water treacle-thick between his legs as he kicked out towards her. She disappeared like an otter, bobbing up elsewhere to giggle at him. Then he remembered the touch of cold, dead flesh . . .

With a start, he opened his eyes and shuddered. He could still see her there and he shook his head vigorously, trying to rid himself of the smell and feel of her. The pressure was building in his head again, the clenching pain knotting his gut. It was all mud stirred up from the depths of a river, the stuff of nightmares. The glare of the room, with its dull, workmanlike furnishings, was reassuring. He gazed around unfocusedly, then noticed the red flashing light of Paddy's landline phone sitting on the shelf unit, indicating voice-mail messages. He had been so distracted by everything that had happened, he hadn't thought to check. He struggled up from the sofa and went over to the handset. The small screen showed four messages. Sleepily, he tabbed through the menu and pressed play. The first two were for Paddy, nothing impor-tant, but the next made him pay attention.

'Hi, this is a message for Alex. My name's Anna Paget. I'm a journalist and I was interviewing your friend Joe Logan.' The voice was husky, the tone breezy and a little flat, as though she was in a hurry and just making a routine call. 'I'm really sorry about what's happened. I'd so like to talk to you, if it's at all possible. Can you give me a bell?' She left a couple of numbers. Alex played the message a second and a third time until he got the numbers down correctly. He wasn't sure he wanted to talk to her about Joe, but after what Maggie had said about her maybe he might learn some-thing.

He played the last message and heard a breathy, girlish voice that he recognised almost instantly.

'Alex, sweetheart, are you there? It's me. It's Katherine.' There was a brief pause. 'If you're there, Alex, pick up.' Again another pause. 'I guess you're out somewhere. I've tried your mobile and then the restaurant, but they said you weren't working tonight. I need to speak to you. It's really, really urgent.' Another pause was followed by a deep sigh. 'Please call me, Alex. It doesn't matter what time. I've had the police round here. Don't know how they got this address but they're looking for you for some reason. They wouldn't say what it's about and of course I didn't tell them where you are, but I hope you haven't been a naughty boy.'

12

'Mark, we're here.' Tartaglia felt someone gently shake his shoulder.

He half opened his eyes, looked around, and saw Donovan beside him, in the driver's seat. He gazed blearily around him. They were pulled up in the middle of the street outside his flat, engine idling. He shook his head. 'Jeez. Thought I was home in bed.'

'Not yet. Good thing you didn't try riding the Ducati. You've been out for the count ever since we left the car park.'

He rubbed his face vigorously, flexed his shoulders and yawned. 'No question of it. Would've called a taxi if you hadn't kindly offered.' He stretched and yawned again, and stared out of the window for a moment. Someone was playing dance music loudly close by. It was late, but now that he was awake he needed something to eat and it would be good to have some company. 'You know, I feel better for a quick kip,' he said, yawning again. 'I'm famished. What about you?'

'I was just going to have a bowl of cereal and go straight to bed. Justin's picking me up at six-thirty. We're seeing the headmaster of St Thomas's at nine.'

'How's it going with Justin?'

'Fine.'

She sounded unenthusiastic and he wondered why. Chang had been fast-tracked and had joined the team at the same rank as Donovan, although she wasn't the sort to care about such things, and from what he'd seen Chang was easy-going, not the sort to create waves.

'He's a smart guy,' he said, thinking of the hassle of getting Chang transferred in and his more than impressive CV. 'We're lucky to have him.'

'Yes.' Again the tone was flat.

'You OK?'

'Just tired, that's all.'

He nodded, deciding for the moment to take what she said at face value. 'I know it's late, but do you want to come in? May as well cook for two as one.'

'Aren't you knackered?'

'I'll revive in a bit. I *must* eat something before I sleep and it would be good to talk. I've barely seen you all day.'

'OK. If you're sure.'

He smiled. 'Positive.'

At that hour, the street was lined on both sides with cars. Eventually she found a parking space a couple of streets away and they walked back together. It was a quiet, tree-lined area, close to the busy Shepherd's Bush Road. The houses were Edwardian and wider than usual, with neat front gardens and hedges. Some had been divided into flats, but many were still family homes. Already most of the inhabitants were in bed, but as they turned the corner and neared his house, the music grew louder again along with the babble of voices.

'Your next-door neighbours seem to be having a party,' she said, as they walked up the short tiled path to the front door.

'Yes. It usually goes on all weekend.' He fumbled in his pocket for his keys.

'I thought you had an old lady living next door with a nasty, yappy little dog. It gave me a fright more than once.'

'Poor thing was deaf and blind,' he said, finally finding the right key and letting them into the small communal hall, which he shared with the upstairs flat. 'Somebody took pity on it and put it out of its misery. Rosa's gone to live with her daughter in Portugal and they've rented out the house to a group of New Zealanders for the summer. They're in their twenties and they're basically in London to have fun. It's a revolving cast, but from what I can tell there's a hard core of about fifteen of them, plus friends camping on the floor. One poor sod was even sleeping in the garden shed for a while.'

'They're clearly big on hospitality.'

'Yes. Reminds me of my student days.' He picked up a couple of letters from the floor, unlocked the door to his flat and ushered her into the sitting room. The air was stuffy from the heat of the day and he drew back the wooden shutters and opened the large sash window as wide as it would go, letting in a pleasant breeze as well as the music.

'Doesn't it drive you mad?'

'What?'

'The noise. I'd find it difficult to think or read with all that going on.'

He shrugged. 'I just tune it out and they're really quite nice. Anyway, I'm not here enough for it to bother me.'

'What about the woman upstairs? I thought she was quite pernickety.'

'She's away at the moment, luckily.'

He went around the room switching on various lights. Even in the heat of summer, it was a pleasant place to come home to with bare white walls, wood flooring and a few pieces of modern furniture, mainly Italian, which he had spent time choosing when he had bought the flat several years before. He knew that many found his home too Spartan, particularly women, Donovan included. But it was the way he liked it and luckily he just had himself to please. The only decoration was a large black and white photograph from the early nineteen sixties of a young woman walking past a sun-drenched bar in a run-down quarter of Rome, which he had bought from a photographer friend of his father's. The woman was lovely, in a natural, unconscious sort of way, frowning into the sun as she brushed a long lock of black hair from her face, unaware that she had been caught on camera. He often wondered what had happened to her, what sort of life she had led, where she was now. She looked so young and fresh in the photograph but she must be old enough to be his mother. His family had come originally from a little village near Rome and settled in the UK at the turn of the last century. He had been born and brought up in Edinburgh, but he still considered himself Italian and he particularly liked the image because it reminded him of his roots.

He took off his jacket, hung it over the back of a chair and turned to Donovan, rubbing his hands enthusiastically. 'So, what do you fancy eating?'

'I don't mind. What is there?'

'Can't remember. You'd better come and take a look.'

She followed him down the narrow passage that led from the sitting room to the kitchen extension at the back. Like the rest of the flat, the space was modern, all stainless steel and wood, with a large, round glass table in one corner. Lights were on in the next-door garden and a large crowd of people were gathered on the other side of the dividing wall. Even with the windows shut, he could smell the smoke of a barbeque and it made him even hungrier.

He opened the freezer door and peered inside at the stack of cartons, which came from the Food Gallery, the best deli in Barnes.

'That's rich,' Donovan said, peering over his shoulder. 'You always make fun of me for my microwave dinners. Have you given up cooking?'

'No. This is just for emergencies like tonight. What will it be? There's Lamb Casserole, Malayan Chicken Curry, Green Thai Chicken, Lemon and Ginger Chicken, or Moussaka. Take your pick. There's also some pesto my sister Nicoletta made last week. She gave me a couple of jars to bring back from holiday.' He looked around at her. 'We could have spaghetti al pesto, if you like.'

She frowned. 'I thought you were diving with your cousin Alessandro?'

'I was. I stayed with him in Milan then we drove down to Sicily together. But on the way home I spent a couple of nights with Nicoletta and the family. She and John have rented a house for two weeks on the coast, just south of Rome.'

She was looking at him enquiringly. 'How was it?'

He shrugged, wondering why she was so interested. He saw a lot of his sister Nicoletta, her husband John and their two children, who lived in north London – too much he felt sometimes. He hadn't been that keen on the idea of spending a few days of his precious holiday with them, but Nicoletta had made it clear he had no option. For the sake of peace he had gone along with it, as he usually did. He had no problem with the children, or with John, an intelligent, mild, self-effacing man, whom he genuinely liked irrespective of the family connection. But Nicoletta knew no boundaries, particularly where he, her younger, unmarried brother, was concerned. He went to their house for lunch most Sundays, which was more than enough to satisfy familial duty, he felt. Donovan had met them on a number of occasions, although he had made it clear to Nicoletta that there was nothing going on between them. 'What a shame,' his sister had said pointedly more than once, as though she didn't believe him and wanted to find out more, but he had refused to be drawn.

'It was OK,' he said. 'She was trying to fix me up with one of her friends, as usual.'

'And?'

He met her eye. However attractive some of Nicoletta's friends were, it wasn't bait worth taking. He would rather stay celibate. 'And nothing. So, what do you want to eat?'

'Whatever's quickest and easiest.'

'Spaghetti, then,' he said, taking a small glass jar from the fridge. He peered inside, wondering what else to offer her. 'I might even run to some rocket salad, if you're lucky. Do you want a beer or a glass of wine? Or would you rather have something soft?'

'Wine please, if it's not too much trouble.'

'No trouble at all. If you want red, help yourself to that bottle on the counter. I only opened it yesterday so it ought to be OK. Otherwise there's some white in the fridge.'

'Red's fine.'

'Pour me one while you're at it. Wine glasses are over there.' He gestured towards the row of shelves above the counter, which held a variety of plates, crockery and glasses. 'I'll put the water on.'

She removed the rubber stopper and poured two glasses, passing one to Tartaglia. 'Anything I can do to help?'

He shook his head. 'Go sit down and put your feet up. I'll bring it in when it's done.'

It wasn't long before he had almost everything ready, carrying in forks, plates, a chunk of Parmesan with a small grater, and a large bowl of dressed salad, which he put down on the coffee table in the sitting room.

'The pasta will be ready in a few minutes. Why don't you put on some music?'

'Too much competition from next door. Besides, the music's not bad, actually. They just played Dizzee Rascal.'

He gave her a pained look, before returning to the kitchen. His taste in music was relatively eclectic, but it stopped well short of commercial rap. The water was boiling hard. He stirred the spaghetti, looped out a strand and tested it. Almost done. He was pleased Donovan had decided to come in. Of late, he had felt as though some sort of an invisible barrier had sprung up between them, although he didn't know why or what to do about it. He assumed something must be going on in her personal life, but as she didn't appear to want to talk about it he had let it go until now. At the back of his mind, though, was another thought. 'She's keen on you, Marco,' Nicoletta had once said. 'Why don't you . . .' But he had stopped her. He had no desire to discuss anything personal with his sister. Whether it was Nicoletta's overactive imagination, or Donovan actually was keen on him, he wasn't sure. But he had little desire to find out. What would he say, when his own feelings towards her were unresolved, blown erratically here and there depending on his mood and whatever else he had going on in his life? At times he found her attractive, even to the point of thinking he should do something about it. More than once he had been sorely tempted, but something had always got in the way and the moment had been lost. Afterwards, he found himself grateful for the interruption. Whatever way he looked at it, it didn't feel right. There was too much at stake. Occasionally, he felt a stab of what he assumed was jealousy when he thought she was seeing someone else, but he knew it wasn't logical and felt doubly confused. Whatever lay beneath it all, it wasn't sufficiently strong or pressing to risk what was more valuable to him than anything: her friendship. Some things were best left up in the air.

He tried the spaghetti again. Finding it perfectly *al dente*, he drained it, poured it into a large terracotta bowl and added the pesto, stirring it around and around until it was evenly mixed then sampled a small forkful. It was delicious, the flavour of the basil more concentrated and peppery than any the UK could ever produce. He also liked the way Nicoletta always used a hint of chilli to add depth. He added a little more pesto until it was exactly the way he wanted it, then carried the bowl into the living room and put it down with everything else on the coffee table.

'Ah, I love basil,' Donovan said, breathing in the pungent aroma.

'Me too. You can just smell the sun.'

They helped themselves and sat down, Donovan on the sofa, Tartaglia opposite, pulling up a black leather chair.

'So, what do you think so far?' she asked, when they had both nearly finished.

He looked at her questioningly. 'Do you really want to talk about the case?' He had been hoping that with the benefit of some wine and food, she might be tempted to open up about whatever was niggling her.

'Yes, if you don't mind. I find it baffling.'

'You're not the only one.'

'Well?'

He finished the last few mouthfuls and put down his plate, relaxing back into his chair. If she didn't want to talk about herself, he knew better than to push. 'OK. The gap in the timeline bothers me for starters. Logan just walks out into a sunny summer's evening with his bicycle and is never seen alive again. He isn't due to meet Anna Paget until seven-thirty, so where was he going? That's two and a half hours unaccounted for. Who was he meeting? There was nothing in his diary. How and where did he encounter his killer?'

'It could be something really simple. Maybe he was going to do some shopping, or stopped off at a bookshop, or had a cup of coffee or a drink, on the way to meeting Anna. I always have a book or my iPod in my bag in case I've time to kill.'

He shrugged. 'Anything's possible. His photo's all over the papers so maybe someone will remember him.'

'Perhaps he met the killer by chance.'

He shook his head. 'Whatever happened, it was deliberate, even if it didn't look that way to Logan. Don't forget the camera in Brompton Cemetery was disabled two days before, which was probably when the padlock on the gate was substituted. It was all carefully planned.'

'Then maybe the killer followed him from the boat.'

'That's more likely, but we know Logan left the boat of his own accord. So how and where was he abducted, if that's what happened? Or did he go willingly? Was it someone he knew? We've got to trace his movements somehow and fill in that gap.'

She finished her spaghetti and helped herself to some salad. 'Someone must have seen something,' she said, pushing the bowl towards Tartaglia.

'I'm sure they did, but Clive Cornish, or whoever was responsible in the press office, decided not to make it clear at the press briefing that Logan wasn't killed at Brompton Cemetery. The impression left is that he was yet another bad-luck victim of gun crime, so the public switch off and don't make any connection to something they may have seen.'

'We can't give all the details at this stage.'

'No, but we should have made it clear that he was killed somewhere else. Apart from the usual loonies inspired by a near full moon and the Gothic location, no decent witnesses have come forward saying they saw anything suspicious.'

'Why wasn't it spelled out?'

'According to Carolyn – and, as usual, I'm not sure where

she stands on this – the powers that be took the view that if we let on that Logan was only dumped in the cemetery later, the killer might cover his tracks.'

'You disagree?'

'I thought it was a price worth paying. At the moment, we have no idea where to start looking. It's possible they'll release the information tomorrow, but we've wasted twenty-four hours. No doubt the killer's gone to ground. In the meantime, things are no clearer than at the start.'

'Come on. We've made some progress.'

He shook his head. 'Nothing that narrows the field in any material way. We still have no clue why Logan was killed or who might have done it. We've spoken to everyone along that stretch of the canal, bar two people who are away. Nobody saw anything and nobody remembered him at the pub, the Bargeman's Rest, either.'

She finished eating and put down her plate, stretching back against the cushions. 'That's London for you. It must be a popular place at this time of year, with lots of tourists coming and going.'

He nodded. 'And it seems Logan didn't get out much. The cell-site analysis of his calls shows that he spent most of the week before he died in and around his boat. He made or received a total of twenty-odd calls that week, of which half are personal. Yet so far nothing interesting has emerged. Apart from Maggie Thomas, the only people Logan saw were the mysterious Alex Fleming and Anna Paget.'

He got to his feet and began to clear away their empty plates. She got up to help him and followed him into the kitchen.

'Why don't you leave it for the morning?' she said, as he started to load the plates and glasses into the dishwasher.

'I'd rather get it over and done with. I can't relax with it hanging over me.'

'Can I do anything?'

He shook his head and started washing the pan and bowls in the sink. 'This won't take long.'

She leaned back against the cupboards, watching him. 'Maybe Superintendent Cornish was right,' she said after a moment. 'Maybe we have a nutter on the loose.'

He laughed. 'Clive Cornish right? That would be a first.'

He saw a glimmer of a smile, the first that evening. Cornish was worth something, after all. 'OK,' she said. 'Maybe not. Perhaps the killer's someone local, maybe one of the neighbours.'

He gave her a quizzical look.

'Say there's someone from Logan's past, who hates him,' she continued. 'Logan then turns up living on the same canal, or nearby, and they decide to bump him off.'

'That's the stuff of cheap fiction,' he said, stacking the pans and bowls on the drainer and drying his hands on a tea towel. 'You know I don't believe in coincidences. If there was a connection between Logan and any of his neighbours, it will eventually come out. Whoever did this would know that.'

She said nothing and he could tell she disagreed. He gave the counter a quick wipe, then turned back to her. 'Coffee or tea?'

'Tea, please,' she said, distractedly. 'Anything herbal if you have it.'

'Fresh mint?'

'Please.'

He switched on the kettle, unlocked the kitchen door and went out into the back garden, returning within a minute with a bunch of leaves. The smell of mint was strong as he tore the stems and put them into a large white teapot.

'Maybe it's simple,' she said. 'Maybe Logan just rubbed someone up the wrong way.'

He shook his head. 'You don't honestly believe that either. Logan had only been living there a couple of months, that's all, and this isn't about some petty little quarrel. Whoever did it beat him up, put a bullet in his head at point blank range and cut off his dick. Either they were making an example of him or they hated his guts. They then went to a great deal of trouble as well as personal risk to dump him in the cemetery. It was planned and premeditated down to the last detail. We were meant to find him in that crypt, although what it's all about escapes me.'

The kettle pinged and he filled the teapot. 'Don't get me wrong,' he said, glancing over at her. 'People do terrible things for the most trivial of reasons. Maybe Logan really did piss off one of his neighbours, who just happens to be a violent psychopath. The background checks will show if any of them have form of any sort. If there's a connection to Logan in some way we'll find it, but the way I see it, there has to be a bigger reason for it all than a chance meeting or a neighbourly spat.' He took two mugs from the shelf and poured out the tea, passing her hers.

'What's your gut telling you, then?' she said.

Cradling his mug in his hand, he leaned back against the

139

wall, facing her. Although it was late and she said she was tired, her eyes were bright and she had a good colour in her cheeks. 'If you want to know, I'm stumped. Logan was a one-time actor and teacher turned best-selling novelist, not some dirty little pusher or gangland heavy. Did the two worlds collide somehow? That's the big question.'

'Maybe he had a secret life.'

'If he was mixing with the wrong people, we'll soon know. But nothing's turned up. So far, he's squeaky clean. The missing second book's another mystery, although it seems to be common knowledge that Logan kept a key to the boat underneath a flowerpot on the front deck. It would have been child's play for someone to get inside, find his laptop and delete the file. The password was written on a yellow sticky above the table where he worked.'

'It would have been simpler just to take the laptop.'

'Maybe they didn't want to draw attention to what they were doing.'

'They could have made it look like a break-in.'

He sighed, tired of talking about the case. 'You're right. It's yet another thing that doesn't add up. I just hope that if someone tampered with Logan's laptop, we'll be able to recover whatever was there before. But if he was killed because of something he knew, something he was going to put in his next novel, what the hell was it? He wasn't an investigative journalist who stumbled on something big. Even the way he was killed and dumped doesn't add up. To give Carolyn her due, she described the whole thing as a cut and shunt and that's exactly what it is. None of it makes sense. You know what we need more than anything?'

ELENA FORBES

'What's that?'

'A bit of luck.'

'If anyone's lucky, it's you. Have you thought of talking to a profiler?'

'It's too early. You know how difficult they are to get hold of, how much red tape there is. Anyway, there's not enough to go on to warrant it, plus I'm sure Carolyn wouldn't sanction it, let alone our blessed superintendent. He thinks profilers are akin to psychics or witch-doctors.'

'I meant off the record, just for a chat. Who's the one you spoke to a few months ago . . . about the Watson case . . . you know . . . what was her name?' She clicked her fingers, trying to remember.

'Angela Harper?'

'I think so. She spoke to you off the record, didn't she? She was pretty user-friendly, I seem to remember.'

He frowned. He wasn't thinking straight. 'You're right, as always, Sam. Why the hell didn't I think of it? I know Angela will tell me it's too early, but if nothing else it may help me get my thoughts in order. I'll call her first thing tomorrow.' Unable to stop himself, he yawned.

She put her mug down on the counter. 'I'm keeping you up. I'd better go.'

'I'm fine.'

'No, I really must go. You're making me tired just to look at you.'

He picked up a hint of reluctance, as though perhaps she wanted him to persuade her to stay. Not sure what to do, he followed her to the front door and opened it for her, wondering if maybe, after all, she wanted to talk. Or was it something more? If only he didn't feel so tired . . .

As she turned to go, he caught her gently by the arm. 'Sam?'

'Yes?'

He couldn't tell anything from her tone. Silhouetted against the light from the street, her face was in shadow and he couldn't read her expression. He decided to let it go. 'Shall I walk you to your car?'

She shook her head. 'I'll be fine.'

'Good luck tomorrow, then.'

'Thanks. I'll call you.'

He watched her walk down the path. A minute or so later, he heard her start the engine and she drove away. As he closed the door and went back into his flat, part of him wished he wasn't going to bed on his own.

13

'I understand that Joe Logan was with you for about six months,' Donovan said.

'Yes, just the two terms. He left at Easter.' The Reverend Tom Sutton leaned back into the cushioned depths of his chair, elbows on the armrests, fingers steepled in front of him.

'Did you get to know him at all while he was here?'

Sutton shook his head. 'We have a large teaching staff and, although I was part of the initial interview process, I personally didn't spend much time with him. By all accounts, he was a good teacher, well-liked by his peers and the pupils, and from what I saw of him he seemed a very nice man, God rest his soul.'

Donovan and Chang were seated in Sutton's huge, vaulted study in a wing of the main school building of St Thomas's. The room was thickly carpeted and panelled, the walls hung with oil portraits of previous headmasters in heavy gilded frames. Taking its cue from the ruined abbey in the grounds, which had been destroyed during the dissolution of the monasteries, the architecture of the building was high Victorian, all honeyed stone, finials and Gothic windows. It reminded Donovan of the Houses of Parliament, somehow fitting for a man of the cloth, although Sutton was surprisingly young and informally dressed. With his short, blond hair, chinos and button-down, striped shirt, he looked more like a fresh-faced, newly ordained priest than a seasoned headmaster.

'Why was he here as a supply teacher?' Chang asked, pen poised over his notepad.

'A member of staff went on maternity leave.'

'We found a copy of a letter he wrote to you on his laptop,' Donovan said. 'I understand you'd offered him a permanent job?'

'Yes, the lady decided she only wanted to return part-time so we then offered him the job, but he declined.'

'I thought he hadn't made up his mind, or that's what he said in the letter?'

'That's right. He declined the first time, but my head of department then had the idea of trying to combine the post with the slot of writer-in-residence. Creative writing's an increasingly popular option in the sixth form.'

'I can imagine, particularly with a best-selling author offering tuition. The parents and governors would have been pleased.'

Sutton inclined his head.

'Was it because of his writing that he left?'

'I really don't know. I got the impression he had just made up his mind to go at the end of his contract. Perhaps he just wanted a change, or somewhere a little less isolated. From what I hear, he'd taken jobs all over the country.'

'Were they all residential posts?'

'I think so. He wasn't married, so I suppose he had that

flexibility. Sometimes when people get used to that sort of life, they find it difficult or boring to settle in any one place.'

Donovan nodded, although privately wondering why Logan had exchanged such a job in an idyllic location for a pokey narrow-boat on a stretch of urban canal. She thought back to her conversation with Tartaglia the previous night. Maybe Logan had been hiding from something – or someone. If so, how had they found him?

'Who's in charge of English?' Chang asked.

'A woman called Susan Hamlyn. You really should talk to her, but she's away on holiday now with her family. I think they've gone camping in Greece. Term ended last week and I'm afraid most of the teaching staff have already left for the summer.'

'Do you know if Mr Logan was working on another book while he was here?' Donovan asked.

'Again, Susan would have been the one to speak to, or Ed Burton. He teaches Latin and ancient Greek. Joe was rooming with him, so he might know.'

'I understand Mr Logan left some belongings here.'

'Yes. After you called yesterday, I spoke to Ed. He's expecting you and he'll be able to let you have whatever's there. Apparently, there's a trunk and a suitcase. His cottage is down the drive past the theatre block. It's about a five-minute walk.'

'Well, we'd better get going,' Donovan said, standing up to leave. There was nothing more to learn from Sutton and she was keen to find out what Logan had left behind. She thanked Sutton for his time. He gave them directions and showed them out.

Although the air was fresh and sweet, the dew on the

ground was quickly evaporating. It was going to be another hot day. Trees, immaculate lawns and playing fields, bathed in the morning sunshine, stretched as far as the eye could see; woods were visible in the hazy distance, and there wasn't a road or town in sight. Donovan glanced briefly back at the cathedral-like building behind them and the ruins of the mediaeval abbey beyond. It was a far cry from the crowded and cramped London grammar where she and her sister had gone to school.

'I wouldn't mind working here,' she said, as they crossed the broad sweep of drive and headed down a path signposted 'Theatre'.

'You really fancy teaching?' Chang looked surprised.

'A place like this, who wouldn't? Both my parents were teachers, so it's in the blood, although it was positively the last thing on my mind when I left university. Same goes for my sister, Claire. She's a solicitor. I never thought either of us had the patience, let alone the dedication, but now I don't know. There's a part of me that could do with something a bit slower-paced.'

'You serious?'

'I am. Think of the peace and quiet, plus there's a lot to be said for a full night's sleep.'

'You're just saying that because you're tired.'

'Maybe, but it takes its toll.'

'It wouldn't be like this in term time.'

'No, probably not.' Looking about, the place did feel empty with nobody around, as though its heart and soul were missing. The only sound came from a tractor mower that was ploughing steadily up and down cutting the grass in front of an old-fashioned, white-painted cricket pavilion. It must all feel very different with children running around.

'I'd have hated boarding, being sent away from home,' she said. 'My parents would never have been able to afford it anyway, but I suppose for the lucky few it must be an incredible experience.'

'You make it sound like Hogwarts.'

'Well, isn't it? Just without the magic? It must be great fun, if you don't get homesick.'

Chang said nothing.

'What I don't get is why Logan didn't take the job,' she continued after a moment. 'I mean, it must be a perfect billet for a writer. I know the school day doesn't finish when lessons are over, you've got to mark essays and stuff, but it's hardly full on, twenty-four seven, like what we do. And then there are the holidays, with endless time to write.'

'I'm sure teaching posts like this don't grow on trees,' Chang responded.

'Exactly. Why give it up? His editor said he took years to write the first book, and I can't think of a nicer place to hole up for a while to write number two.'

After a couple of detours, they eventually found Ed Burton's cottage. It was one of a pair, built of brick and flint, semi-detached, and on the edge of the campus close to one of the entrance gates. Burton must have seen them coming down the hill because he was waiting at the top of the small flight of steps that led to the two cottages. He was dressed in jeans and a checked short-sleeved shirt, and was tall and thin, with a pronounced Adam's apple and a slight stoop. He towered over them both as he shook their hands.

'Joe's stuff is all here, ready for you,' he said, ducking as he led them inside. 'This is it.' He indicated a large black suitcase and an old-fashioned trunk that were sitting by the door in the tiny hall. 'I had a friend coming to stay, so I had to move them out of his room. I put them in the cupboard under the stairs. I didn't know what else to do with them.' He spoke apologetically, as though it were an unfriendly thing to do to a dead man's possessions.

'Do you know what's in them?'

'No idea, but I expect some of it will be his winter clothes. The suitcase isn't locked, so you can take a look if you like, but as you can see, the trunk's padlocked. It weighs a ton, so I imagine it's full of his books. He had a fair number when he was living here.'

'We'll get them both back to the office and look at it all there,' Donovan said. 'We found some keys among his things, so we may not have to force the lock.'

They followed Burton into a small sitting room at the front where a sofa and two armchairs were grouped around a fireplace. Even though it was high summer, the room smelled strongly of wood smoke. Apart from bookshelves on either side of the chimney breast, there was little space for anything else and it felt crowded with the three of them there. Donovan wondered if Logan had spent most of his time in his bedroom.

'Do you know if he left anything behind to do with his computer?' Chang asked, as they sat down.

'What do you mean?'

'A separate hard drive or memory stick, maybe?'

Burton shook his head. 'I doubt it. As far as I know, he took all that sort of thing with him.'

'So he didn't leave anything specifically with you, for safe-keeping?'

Burton looked puzzled. 'Other than the suitcase and trunk, no.'

'Any notebooks or other writing materials?' Donovan asked. 'It's just that we seem to be missing some of his files.'

'As I said, if he left anything like that behind, it'll be in the trunk. He cleared out his room thoroughly when he left.'

'OK, thanks. We'll check when we get back to the office. Did he talk to you about his writing at all?'

'Sometimes. We'd have the odd jar in the pub together. And of course I have a copy of *Indian Summer*, which he signed, but I haven't got around to reading it, I'm afraid.'

'I meant the second book.'

Burton shook his head, again frowning. 'He was working on something, but he didn't really talk about it. I got the impression he was a bit sensitive about it. Writers can be, can't they?'

'Yes,' she said, reassuringly. 'Did he mention what it was about?'

'No. I suppose he didn't want to give away his idea or expose it to the air.'

'But he was definitely working on something?'

Burton nodded. 'Sometimes we'd be in the middle of a conversation and he'd break off to scribble down a note, so I guess even when he wasn't actually writing, he was carrying it around in his head.'

'With his living here, you must have seen quite a lot of him,' Chang said.

'During the week, yes, although we were both busy with

our schoolwork. My girlfriend lives in Exeter, so I was away most weekends. On the odd occasion when she came here, we were usually tied up doing things together.'

'But you liked Mr Logan?'

'Yes, I did. He was a quiet bloke, a bit reserved, and he kept himself to himself most of the time. He wasn't the tidiest, but I've shared with a lot worse and he was pleasant enough to have around. I was very sorry to hear what's happened.'

'Apart from you, did he spend time with anyone else while he was teaching here?'

'He'd go out for the odd drink with other members of staff, but there was nobody in particular he saw.'

'Do you think he was lonely?' Donovan asked.

'No. He wasn't unfriendly either. I don't want to give that impression. I'd just say he was self-contained, happy in his own company, if you get my meaning. Maybe he was different with people he knew well. When he was here, teaching took up a lot of his time. The writing had to fit around it and there was little time for anything else.'

'What about phone calls? Was there anyone particular you remember him speaking to?'

'I can't say. There's no phone in the cottage. Any calls would have been on his mobile, although the reception's pretty poor.'

'What about the internet?'

'The main school building has wi-fi. I remember Joe using his laptop in the common room quite a lot. It's what we all do.'

'Thank you for your help.' Donovan said, getting up from

her seat. 'Would you mind if I take a quick look at his room before we go?'

'Be my guest. It's right up the stairs, the one on the left.'

She climbed the steep, narrow staircase to what had once been Logan's room. It was small, painted institutional cream, with cheap green carpet and woodchip wallpaper. But the two windows set into the eaves gave it a light, airy feel. It must have been a pleasant place to work. A divan bed was pushed up against one wall, covered with an Indian throw, there was a pine wardrobe in a corner and small bookcase beside a desk and chair under the far window. The room looked freshly cleaned and, as far as she could see, there were no obvious hiding places. As Burton had said, all traces of Logan himself had long since gone, but if this was where he had lived for six months, he had been a lucky man. She still struggled to understand why he had left.

She was standing at the window admiring the view of the countryside and hills beyond and enjoying the silence, when Chang called out from below:

'Find anything, Sam?'

Reluctantly, she went back out onto the landing. Chang was standing with Burton in the hall.

'Justin, can you go and fetch the car?' She started down the stairs towards them. 'I hope you won't mind giving us a hand with the trunk, Mr Burton. Justin won't be able to get it into the boot on his own and I don't think I'm up to lifting even one corner.'

'No problem,' Burton said, as Chang disappeared out the door. 'While you're waiting, I'll put the kettle on. I'm sure we could all do with a cup of tea.'

14

The glass door of the restaurant swung open and a girl with long dark hair and huge sunglasses strode in. She wore a short white T-shirt-type dress with a wide, hip-hugging belt, and carried a leather satchel slung over one shoulder. The girl came straight up to the bar where Alex was going through the lunch bookings and leaned across the counter. 'I'm looking for Alex Fleming,' she said in a husky voice.

He put down his pen. 'I'm Alex. You must be Anna. I thought you said you were coming earlier.'

'Sorry. I got held up.' She smiled and hurriedly held out a small, cool hand, then slid onto a stool opposite. 'I tried calling your mobile, but there was no answer.'

'It's on the blink.' He had switched it off to avoid any calls from the police.

'Can we talk now?'

He checked his watch. The first reservation wasn't for another three quarters of an hour. He glanced quickly through the arch into the restaurant beyond. The tables looked more or less ready, the waiters just adding the finishing touches. 'I guess I can spare you fifteen minutes, if that's any good.'

'Perfect.' She smiled again and removed her glasses, folding the arms and placing them carefully on the counter in front of her. Without them, she looked older and more confident, less like a young girl who has borrowed her big sister's clothing. He realised she must be somewhere in her late twenties, early thirties at a push. She was also extraordinarily pretty, although not at all what he would have said was Joe's type. But perhaps that had changed, like so many other things.

She felt in her satchel and pulled out a small recorder. 'Do you mind?'

He shook his head.

'Good. Makes my life easier. I'm crap at taking notes, always miss something.' She stood the recorder on the counter and pressed play. 'Ready?'

'I suppose so. You said you were doing an article on Joe.'

'That's right.' She gave the name of one of the Sunday papers. 'It started off as a straight interview, but given what's happened, I wanted to broaden it, put in some background and bring in more of his fabulous book. Which is where you come in. I understand you were at university together.'

He nodded, a little surprised. 'He mentioned me, then?'

'Yes. How did you two meet?'

He sighed. His main reason for returning her call had been curiosity, especially after what Maggie had told him. He didn't really want to talk about Joe at all. He also wondered how much Joe had told her. For someone who so fiercely guarded his privacy, it was surprising that Joe had agreed to talk to her at all, but Alex realised that if he wanted to get anything out of her he would have to appear to be cooperating. He reached down to the small fridge under the counter and pulled out an already open bottle of white wine. He pulled out the stopper. 'Would you like a drink?'

'No thanks, but don't let me stop you. I guess it's not easy for you to have to talk about Joe, is it?'

'No.' He poured himself a glass and took a large sip. For some reason, she made him nervous, as though *he* was the one under the spotlight. 'What was the question?'

'I asked when you and Joe first met.'

'It was in the very first week. We were both studying English and Drama.'

'He told me you roomed together.'

'We were in hall together for the first year, then we shared a flat in the second.'

'And the final year?' She cupped her chin in her hand and gazed at him with large grey-blue eyes. Her eyelashes were long and thick and gave her eyes a languid quality. She really was mouth-wateringly lovely and he wondered just how far Joe had got with her – if he had dared. The sleeve of her T-shirt slipped down over her shoulder exposing a large part of her breast.

'Some friends rented a cottage in the countryside and we moved in with them,' he said, trying not to stare.

Automatically, she shrugged the sleeve back into place. 'Where was it?'

'It was a twenty-minute drive outside Bristol, near Bath.'

'Like in the book?'

'A bit like that, yes.'

'Tell me about it. The place I mean.'

'Nothing much to tell. Paul, one of our friends, had this uncle who had bought a big, nearly derelict estate. He was a developer and he was going to turn it into a hotel with a golf course and stuff. He wasn't having much luck with the planners, so he let us have one of the cottages while he was waiting. It was part of the stable block.'

'Sounds lovely.'

'It wasn't. It was a pit, if you really want to know, freezing cold and damp and riddled with mice. I woke up one morning and found one curled up asleep on my pillow.'

She laughed. 'I'd have liked that. I love mice. It must have been great in the summer, at least.'

He nodded reluctantly, wondering where this was going.

'So Joe got his inspiration from that place?'

'Partly.'

'Did he always want to be a writer?'

Alex shook his head. 'I was actually quite surprised when he told me he was writing a novel. I mean, he'd never talked about wanting to write, but then I guess he was always reading loads of books and stuff, and the acting and teaching's all just an extension of the same thing.'

'It's a pretty dark book, though, isn't it?' Her gaze was intense and he looked away.

'I suppose so.'

'It's never clear if Jonah's death is an accident or suicide. Was Joe a depressive at all?'

'Definitely not.'

'Where did all that come from then? All that guilt, all that angst?'

'I don't know. From his imagination, I suppose.'

'He seemed lonely to me.'

'I wouldn't say so,' he said stubbornly. 'Didn't you ask him about it?'

She gave a dismissive little shake of her head. 'I tried, but he wouldn't give much away. I thought you, knowing him so well, could give me some perspective.'

'You're reading too much into it all. It's just a story.'

She pursed her lips. 'Mmm . . . Don't you think you're being a bit naive?'

'Naive?'

'Yes.'

He stared at her. Even though the air-conditioning was blowing above his head, he felt sweat break out on his top lip. He wiped it away with the back of his hand. 'How do you mean?'

'Well, on one level it's just a story as you say, but there are loads of parallels, aren't there? Did he base any of the characters on you?'

'Me?'

'Yes. Which one of them is you?'

'It wasn't like that.'

'Really?'

'It's just a book, for God's sake.'

'But the place, the situation—'

'Obviously Joe used elements for the book but it wasn't in any way autobiographical.' He said it as forcefully as he could without raising his voice, aware that one of the waitresses had come into the bar and was busy straightening the few tables and chairs just behind where Anna was seated.

'I see,' she said in a tone of disbelief. He wondered if she'd been like this with Joe. According to Maggie they had spent quite a lot of time together. How much had he told her? 'So the house wasn't like the house in *Indian Summer* . . . Is that what you're saying?'

'Yes. Now, can we talk about something else?'

'What's it called?' she asked, as if he hadn't spoken. 'The place where the house was, I mean. It'd be quite nice to get some pictures of it. If nothing else, it must be a great location, if it's anything like the one in the book.'

Even though he was avoiding her eye, he could feel that she was watching him. 'It's not. I told you his novel wasn't based on real life. The house in the novel doesn't exist outside Joe's imagination and I'm sure if you'd asked him, he'd have told you that too.' Without thinking, he drained his glass in one and put it down forcefully on the counter between them.

She held up her hands. 'Take it easy. OK?'

'I'm fine.'

'I'm sorry if you're a bit sensitive about it . . .'

'I'm not. I just don't want you getting the wrong idea, that's all.'

'OK, I won't.' She gave him a disarming smile and leaned back on her stool as though the interrogation was over. 'Do you know anything about the second book he was writing?'

'No. We didn't discuss it.'

'Are you sure? I mean he finished writing *Indian Summer* a couple of years ago. He must have told you what he was working on after that?'

'Look, we'd lost touch. He'd been out of London for quite a while. We only met up again recently.'

'From what he told me, it was sort of a thriller. The police seem very interested in it, you know.'

'Really?' he snapped, wondering if she was trying to wind him up.

'Don't you know anything about it at all?'

'I said no.'

'Do you think it could have anything to do with Joe's death?' She let the question hang.

He met her gaze. 'What do you mean?'

She shrugged, still smiling. 'Well, as I said, the police seem very interested in it. Make of it what you want.'

He shook his head stubbornly. 'I can't help you. I'm sure you know a lot more about it than I do.' He wanted to say 'more about Joe than I do', but it didn't seem worth it. From the little he had seen, she would have prised Joe open like an oyster and Joe would have let her. She knew a lot more than she was letting on. But how much? 'The second book, you say it's some sort of thriller . . .'

A phone was ringing. She held up her hand in front of his face. 'One sec.' Grabbing her BlackBerry out of her bag, she checked the screen, then answered it. 'Hi, Ted, what's up? I'm in the middle of interviewing someone . . .' Her voice tailed off. She was silent for a few moments, listening. He watched her expression change, surprise being the only thing he could read, then much more quietly, the words barely audible over the background music, she said: 'Jesus. I hear you. Don't worry, I'll be there as soon as I can.' She killed the call and looked up at Alex. 'Gotta go, sorry.' He saw excitement now in her eyes.

She rummaged hurriedly in her bag for a card, practically flinging it across the counter at him as she jumped off the stool and looped her bag over her shoulder. 'Thanks for your help. Would love to speak some more. I'll call you.' Before he had a chance to say anything, she picked up her sunglasses and marched out of the restaurant.

As Chang drove out through the gates of St Thomas's, Donovan slid the passenger seat as far back as it would go and stretched out her legs. It was nice being driven for a change and Chang was a good driver; she could relax and take her eye off the road for a while. She was feeling more awake now than on the journey down to Dorset when, apart from a brief stop for coffee and bacon sandwiches, she had dozed most of the way. She reached down into her rucksack and took out the copy of Logan's novel, which she had brought with her. There would be no other time to read it in the near future and she didn't feel in the mood to talk. Anyway, Chang seemed happy listening to some current affairs programme on Radio 4. She skimmed the blurb, then the long list of quotes from various newspapers on the back. At first glance it wasn't exactly her cup of tea, but at least Logan's editor had promised a good read. The photograph of Logan on the back caught her eye and she studied it for a minute. He looked relaxed, squinting good-humouredly into the sunlight, a cigarette between his fingers. She thought she recognised the place where it had been taken, on the little bench outside the cottage, to the right of the front door. A perfect spot to sit and smoke a cigarette. She wondered who had taken it, if it had been Ed or someone else. Without further ado, she opened the book and started the first chapter.

She hadn't been reading long when she heard her phone ringing. She pulled it out of her bag and saw Tartaglia's name on the screen.

'We've just started back,' she said, turning down the radio. 'We found a trunk and a suitcase belonging to Logan at the school but—'

'Tell Justin to step on it,' he cut in. 'I need you both back here asap. There's been another murder.'

15

Tartaglia watched as the sheeted form of the victim was loaded into the back of a mortuary van. 'Thanks for the call,' he said, turning to Arabella Browne.

'My pleasure, Mark.' She unzipped her protective suit. 'Single shot to the head, ligature marks, castrated. Naturally, I thought of you.'

'I'm touched.'

They were standing by her Volvo estate, in the narrow cobbled street outside the Hammersmith Blades Rowing Club on the northern bank of the Thames. The boathouse was two storeys high, built of blistered white clapboard. The large wooden doors on the ground floor were open and he could see racks of boats inside. A set of steep, rickety-looking stairs led up to a gallery on the first floor, where there was another door and a couple of picture windows dating from the seventies. The road ran parallel to the Thames and a section had been cordoned off, with the area immediately in front of the boathouse designated as a car park for members of the forensic team. It was already full when he and Minderedes arrived and he had left Minderedes to find a parking space further away.

'Where was he?'

'In the clubroom upstairs. He was sitting on the floor behind the bar with his knees bent. Rigor's well established and we've had a job straightening him out.' Holding tightly onto the side of the car, Browne wriggled awkwardly out of her suit, removed her overshoes and bundled it all into a plastic bag, which she dumped in the boot. With a wheezy, asthmatic cough, she swung the lid closed. 'Bloody hayfever. Hate this time of year.'

'If he was castrated, did you – er—'

'Find his penis in his mouth? His jaw's locked. I didn't want to force it open here, so you'll have to wait until the post mortem. But everything else looks the same to me, if that's what you're worried about.'

He nodded, reassured. The specific details of Logan's injuries had not been released to the press and castrations were rare. With everything taken together, unless it was sheer fluke or a deliberate copycat, it was looking strongly like the crime had the same signature.

'One other thing,' Browne said, ambling with him around to the driver's door. 'This one's also wet, or at least his upper body is.'

'You mean water?'

'Far as I can tell.' She got into her car, switched on the ignition and rolled down the window. 'It's more obvious than the last one, although maybe he didn't have time to dry out. He also stinks of urine. I'll leave you to work out what it all means. See you later.' She put the car into gear and bumped off slowly down the road towards the cordon.

'You must be Mark Tartaglia,' a female voice said just behind him.

He turned to find a slim young woman in a fitted grey trouser suit staring at him. 'I'm Kate Gerachty. I'm with DCI Grainger's team. I understand we're going to be working together on this.' As well as a northern Irish accent, he picked up a certain sharpness of tone.

'Yes. I'm Mark.'

She offered a limp hand to shake that was quickly withdrawn. She looked to be somewhere in her mid-thirties, with straight, reddish-blonde hair tied back in a very tight ponytail, not a hair out of place, and a wide, full mouth which would have been attractive if it weren't for her sour expression. Grainger's team in Hendon had initially received the call and had been working the crime scene since the early hours of the morning. He knew all the other DIs based at the Peel Centre in Hendon, which was home to the majority of the teams in the Homicide West division, but hadn't come across Gerachty before. He assumed her arrival had been announced while he was on holiday and wondered if she was new to homicide or had transferred in from another division elsewhere, or possibly from outside the Met.

From the little Steele had told him, it had taken considerable bargaining for him to be allowed in on the case, on spec, at such an early stage. He was curious to know exactly how she had wangled it with Clive Cornish. Steele seemed to have powers of persuasion with Cornish that nobody else had. At least some luck had finally come his way. If it weren't for Arabella Browne, it might have been a matter of days, if not more, before a possible connection was made, by which time Grainger's team would have fully owned the case, making things far more difficult for everybody.

'I'll just be shadowing your investigation,' he said with a smile, meeting a pair of chilly blue eyes.

'We do all the donkeywork until you prove a link, you mean. Then we hand it all over to you on a plate.'

For the sake of diplomacy he decided to ignore the comment. 'This is Nick Minderedes. He's a DC on my team,' he said, as Minderedes joined them. 'He'll be taking notes while you give us the guided tour. I understand the body was found upstairs.'

'Right. Let's get this over and done with, then I can get back to work. Forensics have finished with the clubhouse, so we can take a look up there now.'

She started briskly up the steps to the first-floor gallery, Tartaglia and Minderedes following. She was wearing clumpy black shoes that squeaked as she walked, but she had a nice, tight little arse just visible below her short jacket. He caught Minderedes' eye and shook his head. Minderedes stifled a smile and held up his hands in mock surrender.

'Do we have an ID?' Tartaglia asked, as they got to the top.

She turned to face him, back to the door. 'Paul Nasir Khan, aged thirty-eight according to his driver's licence. It's registered to an address in EC2. Our people are over there now.'

'His wallet was on him?'

'Yes.'

'What about his phone?'

'He had a work BlackBerry, but there's no sign of it. Maybe he left it somewhere at home or at work.'

'Or the killer took it,' he said, thinking of what had happened to Logan's phone. No doubt Khan's would turn up in a public place too, another little provocative diversion. He wondered whether to share what he knew with Gerachty, if nothing else to save her time, but he decided to wait and see how the rest of the meeting panned out.

'It's backed up on the office network so it doesn't matter.'

'Did he have a computer?'

'A company laptop. It's at his office and we're fetching it now.'

'When you go through his emails, if there's anything strange or out of the ordinary, let me know.'

She met his gaze. 'What do you mean by strange?'

'I'll let you have a copy of the two emails our victim received and you'll get the idea. What about next of kin?'

'There's a girlfriend or partner in his flat. She hasn't seen him since he left for work early yesterday morning. He's a lawyer, apparently.'

'I'll need to speak to her.'

She gave a curt nod of acknowledgment and pushed open the door. The room was large and sparsely furnished. It had a barn-like feel, with a high, pitched roof and a floor of varnished pine. Sunshine flooded in through two pairs of tall French windows at the back, overlooking the river. The walls were painted white and decorated with old-fashioned wooden oars and rowing photographs, some of which were sepia-toned and dated back to the early part of the last century. The majority of the photos were more recent and showed men's and women's eights on the water at a number of regattas and championships, as well as victorious team members posing with medals and silver cups.

'Where was the body found?'

'Over there behind the bar, I think.' She waved her hand towards the long, L-shaped bar in the corner.

'Where exactly?'

'On the floor, so I'm told. I've only just got here myself.'

'Really? Then you've missed the party,' Tartaglia said, failing to stifle his surprise. The initial priority at a crime scene was always on the forensic investigation, but wherever possible he liked to get a feel for the place with the body *in situ* before it was disturbed. He wanted to see things as close as he could to the way the murderer had left them. Every little detail was important and, although it would all be captured on camera, in his mind it was no substitute to walking the scene. It generally went against correct forensic procedure but he knew he wasn't alone in this respect, certainly not among experienced detectives. He guessed that Gerachty was new to homicide.

He strode over to the bar and leaned over it. There was a small patch of congealed blood on the floor in the corner by the wall, with a smear of blood and something sticky-looking on the glass door of one of the under-counter fridges. The space was narrow, which would explain why, if the victim had been put in a sitting position, his legs had been bent. But why had the killer left him that way? The image of Logan sitting on the dusty floor of the crypt with his legs outstretched, flashed through his mind. Was it the same hand? If so, why had the killer hidden the body away behind the bar? Had he been disturbed?

Gerachty stood still in the middle of the room watching his every move, hands in her pockets. 'Find anything?'

'I'd like to see the video footage and photos as soon as possible,' he said, rejoining her.

'I can let you have copies.'

'He wasn't killed here, I understand.'

'That's the easy part. No blood to speak of, no bullets, no signs of a struggle.'

'In reverse order, surely,' Minderedes chipped in.

She blanked him. 'He definitely wasn't killed here or anywhere in the vicinity, that's for sure.'

'Any idea how the killer brought the body in?' Tartaglia asked.

'Has to be up the stairs at the front. It's the only way in. The main door was unlocked and one of those back windows was also open, but there's no way out from there except onto the terrace outside.'

'What about the alarm?' He had seen an old alarm box on the wall at the front.

'There isn't one – at least not one that's working.'

'Who has keys?'

'Quite a few people, from what I can tell. We're obviously checking now to see if anyone's missing their key.'

Minderedes walked over to the main door and swung it to and fro on its hinges for a moment. 'No sign of it being forced,' he said. 'The lock's nothing special, no problem getting a key copied, and easy to pick as well, if you know what you're about. Wouldn't take more than a few seconds.'

'I'm pretty sure that's what he'd have done,' Tartaglia said.

'You think it's a waste of time our checking the keyholders?' Gerachty said sharply.

He shrugged. 'Look, I'm not here to tell you what to do.'

'I'm glad that's clear.'

He sighed. 'Obviously, you must check every angle. But if it *is* the same killer, he's highly organised. He knows what he's doing, and stealing someone's key and having it copied is risky, plus it gives us a link back to him. I think it's much more likely he picked the lock.'

'*If* it's the same killer.'

'I'm assuming it is.'

'Well, I'll be keeping an open mind on that, if it's all the same to you. And if you've got a profile, I'd like to see it.'

'There's no profile yet.' It was the truth, but he could tell from her expression that she didn't believe him. Too bad. He had no intention of sharing his fragmented, somewhat incoherent thoughts about the Logan case with her. It was not her concern. He was due to meet Angela Harper, the profiler, early that evening for an off-the-record chat. Whatever might come out of their conversation was also for him alone at this stage. Anyway, if Browne was right and the two murders were connected, the new case wouldn't be Gerachty's for long.

'So, what is it exactly that makes you think the two murders may be linked?' she asked. He could see he had sparked her interest. Against his better judgement, he decided to give her the bare bones. If nothing else, it might soften her attitude a little.

'Because of what Dr Browne found.'

'Which is?'

'Both victims are white, male, almost the same age, and both died from a single shot to the head. Both have pre-mortem ligature marks on their ankles and wrists, both were castrated, both killed elsewhere and their bodies dumped on the floor in a sitting position . . .' As he ticked the points off with his fingers he watched her face for a reaction, but all he got was a blank stare like that of a bored child in school. If it really was her first homicide, maybe she didn't appreciate the importance of such parallels. Both bodies were wet, Browne had said, although he didn't feel the need to mention it to Gerachty, if she hadn't found out for herself. Nor was he sure what it meant.

'Appearances can be deceptive,' she said primly.

He shook his head. 'It's the same MO, the same signature, the same killer, from what I can see. What more do you want?'

'I'm paid to keep an open mind. I'm just doing my job, you know.'

'Right. And I'm just doing mine.'

She folded her arms tightly. 'But what's clear to me is you've already made up your mind.'

'Look, it doesn't matter what I think, and I don't need to convince you, either. I've been told to see if there's a link and that's what I'm doing. I expect your full cooperation. If you have any issues with that, you'd better say so and we'll take it up with Superintendent Cornish. If it is the same killer, the sooner we all know the better. We want justice for the victims, don't we? That's what's important.'

She coloured and bit her lip. 'Just don't go getting in the way. If you need to speak to anybody to do with the case, and I mean *anybody*, I want to know. And I want to be kept up to speed on what you're doing. OK?'

'I have no problem with that,' he said, although he had no intention of letting her block anything he wanted to do.

EVIL IN RETURN

'Until I'm told otherwise, this is *our* investigation.'

'I'm aware of that,' he said wearily. He turned and gazed around the room, scanning for a camera. 'Is there CCTV anywhere?'

'No. According to the membership secretary, there's nothing worth taking.'

'Apart from the boats,' Minderedes said, coming over to where they were standing.

'You'd look pretty silly going along the high street with one of those, wouldn't you?' she replied. 'Not much of a re-sale market down the local, I'd have thought.'

'I was only joking.'

She raised her eyebrows. 'They're mainly worried about vandals and silly pranks by rival rowing clubs, not burglars. They seem to think security's up to scratch enough to cope with that.'

'Who found him?' Tartaglia asked.

'We had an anonymous tip-off. A woman dialled 999 from a local payphone. She actually asked first for an ambulance and said the body was still warm. The call was logged around eleven-thirty last night. It's one of the shed-load of things we're trying to follow up at the moment.'

'Warm? That's interesting. So he hadn't been dead long.'

'The woman said she wasn't sure if he was alive or dead.'

'He'd been shot in the head. How could she miss that?'

Gerachty shrugged. 'You can listen to the recording, if you like, although it won't tell you much other than that the woman sounds pretty upset; hysterical, I'd say.'

'Was she young, old . . . ?

'Young, well-spoken, English, but no particular accent, as

170

far as I could tell. It sounded real to me, like she was in shock or something. Her voice was slurred and she was very emotional.'

'Maybe she was drunk. It was late. I wonder what she was doing here.'

'Whatever. She said, "I fell over him." She said it over and over again, like maybe she'd hurt him, or something. I tell you she wasn't making sense. She also said she'd got blood on her hands.'

'Just like Lady Macbeth,' Minderedes said.

Again she ignored him.

'Apart from behind the bar, did you find any blood anywhere else?' Tartaglia asked, still wondering what the woman had been doing there at that hour.

She looked at him quizzically. 'Forensics found a couple of prints smeared in blood around the light switch by the door.'

'Well, that suggests something, don't you think?'

'You tell me. You're the hot-shot detective, or so I'm told.'

He grimaced, now understanding her hostility. On top of her worry about losing the case someone had poisoned the water, but there was no time to try and put the record straight.

'OK. She goes behind the bar to get a drink, but she doesn't see the body right away because the lights are off. She falls over the body and only then goes to switch on the lights. Perhaps they were out for some reason. Can you try them, Nick?'

Minderedes went over to the panel on the wall by the door and switched on each set of lights in turn. They all appeared to be working.

'Maybe when she came in she decided not to switch them on for some reason,' Tartaglia said. 'It was almost full moon last night, there'd have been plenty of light coming in through those big windows. Do you know who was here yesterday?'

'Just a few members and guests after the evening training session. Apparently the last person left around ten and the barman locked up.'

'He's sure about that?'

'So he says, and one of the members left with him. We're taking statements from everyone who was here – that's fifteen people, including the barman and the secretary. The club-house is pretty dead during the week from a social point of view. The secretary and the barman were the only ones here last night with keys. The secretary apparently had a train to catch and left early.'

'OK. So, they lock up around ten, and one and a half hours later the body's found. It's a short time frame.' Gerachty looked as though she wanted to say something but thought better of it. 'Maybe the killer was still here, hidden somewhere,' he continued. He looked around the room again, but there were no obvious hiding places. 'What's through there?' He pointed to a door in the far corner at the back of the room.

'The toilets.'

He walked over to the door and opened it. He went into the gents, then the ladies, checking the cubicles, but there was nothing out of the ordinary.

'Forensics have been all over everything up here,' she said defensively, as he came back into the main room.

'What's downstairs?'

'Just boats, showers and changing rooms.'

'Any direct access from up here?'

'No. As I said before, the only way in is from outside at the front, up the steps.'

'Just checking. Which of the windows was open?'

'I don't know. It will say on the report.'

He stopped himself from saying something sharp and went over to examine the windows, deciding after a moment that it was probably the right-hand one, judging by the volume of print powder on the frame and handle. He opened it and glanced out. The terrace faced almost due south and ran the length of the building. The tide was low, exposing wide, muddy stretches of shore on both sides, dotted with seagulls. The turreted green outline of Hammersmith Bridge was just visible past the river bend, beyond the trees and playing fields of St Paul's Boys' School on the opposite bank. It was no more than half a mile from his office. The sun was hot on his face and he imagined that, day or night, it must be a lovely place to sit and enjoy a drink.

'I wonder what she was doing here,' he said, almost to himself, coming back into the room and looking outside again. 'I'll bet she opened the window. I'll also bet she had someone with her.'

'Don't you think you're letting your imagination run away with you?'

'Imagination's got nothing to do with it. It's about psychology.'

She made a small noise, as though she didn't agree. 'Well, there was no other voice on the recording. If she'd had a man with her, surely he'd have made the call for her? She was very upset.'

He turned to face her. 'Tell me, then. Why would a woman come here alone at that hour?'

She shrugged. 'It's one of the many little mysteries we're dealing with here. Maybe she left something behind.'

He shook his head. 'I don't think so. It's much more likely she was with someone and they left the lights off so as not to draw attention to themselves.'

'More romantic that way,' Minderedes said, with a teasing look at Gerachty.

'There's that, too. They open the window onto the terrace for some air, or maybe to admire the view, she goes to the bar to get a drink and stumbles over the body. They panic and go, leaving the main door open. Unless the killer left the door unlocked, one of them must have had a key. My guess is it's either the secretary or the barman, and she was probably here last night too. It's vital you find her. She, or whoever was with her, may have seen something.'

Again Gerachty coloured to the roots of her hair. 'We're already onto it, thanks, and I don't need you to tell me how to do my job.'

'You've taken statements from both the secretary and the barman and checked what time they came home last night?'

She clenched her fists at her side. 'Not yet, but we will. We'll obviously try and match up the voice and the prints to people who were here last night and the rest of the members, if need be.'

'I'd treat it as a priority.'

'Thanks, but I don't have to justify what we're doing to you. Now, if there's nothing else you need, I'd best be getting on, *if* you don't mind.' She turned to go.

174

'Hang on a sec,' he said, locking eyes with her. 'Is there anything else I should know?' He didn't expect a revelation, but he needed to put down a marker, in case she was deliberately keeping something back.

'I've answered all your questions, haven't I?'

'Yes. But is there anything else?'

'We've covered everything.'

He nodded, unable to read from her expression whether she was telling the truth or not. If she was hiding something important from him, he'd make her regret it. 'Let me know how you get on with finding that woman,' he said. 'Meanwhile, I'm just going to take a quick recce around the rest of the place. Nick will go with you to exchange details. I'll also need Mr Khan's address and stuff. I want to speak to the girlfriend right away.'

'Fucking uptight bitch,' Minderedes said, as he manoeuvred the Nissan forcefully through a group of press photographers who were waiting at the outer cordon like sharks around a fishing boat. 'What the hell's eating her?'

Tartaglia sighed. 'Don't let it get to you. My guess is she's new to homicide. She doesn't know how it works.'

'She's just a fucking paper-pusher, that's all. She hasn't a clue.'

Tartaglia smiled at the strength of his reaction, wondering what exactly Gerachty had said to him when they were alone. 'She's right about one thing, though. If the two cases are linked, which I'm pretty sure they are – my money's always on Arabella – then she's doing all the spadework for no glory. I'd feel mighty pissed off in her shoes.'

'She should have bloody well kept it to herself.'

'I agree. She's got a lot to learn, in more ways than one.' He would have struggled to keep a lid on his frustration in a similar situation, but he knew enough about the game to handle things differently, nor would he have made the same basic errors.

As they pulled up at the traffic lights at the Hogarth Roundabout, heading back into town on the A4, Minderedes glanced quickly over at him.

'Sir, if the two deaths are linked, do you think Super-intendent Cornish will want to keep the investigations separate, like with the Jubilee murders?'

'That was different,' he said, after a moment. 'Homicide South were also involved with two of the killings, so Clive Cornish didn't have the final call. At least this is all happening on our patch. He may be a right pillock in many ways, but if it looks like it's the same killer, even he has the nous to bring the cases under one roof.'

'Ours, you mean?'

Tartaglia shrugged. 'I bloody well hope so. As usual, this is all about politics, and by all accounts Grainger's yesterday's man.'

'And DCI Steele's the super's blue-eyed girl.'

'Green, you mean. She's got green eyes.'

'I hadn't noticed.'

'Take my word for it,' he said, surprised that Minderedes' usually keen observational skills for such things didn't extend to Steele. Maybe he regarded her as so impenetrable that she didn't merit the same attention as other women. He was never one to waste his efforts on a lost cause. 'Anyway, it seems she can do no wrong with Cornish, which is lucky for us. If only we can make some more headway with the Logan case, then I think we'll get our hands on this one. We've got to find the link.'

16

The address Gerachty had given them for Paul Khan, the murder victim, was in a converted Victorian warehouse in Tabernacle Street, between Old Street and City Road. The area was within walking distance of the City law firm where Khan had worked. Originally a light-industrial district for furniture making, it had come a long way since Tartaglia had last been there ten years before: as well as expensive loft conversions, restaurants, bars and galleries had mushroomed all over the place in former factory buildings and warehouses. He told Minderedes to wait outside in the street, went into the building and rang the bell beside Khan's name. Within moments it was answered by a member of Grainger's team, who told him to take the lift to the fourth floor.

A thin, wiry woman, with short, dark hair and acne-scarred skin was waiting for him in the lift lobby and introduced herself as Linda Barber, the Family Liaison Officer.

'DI Gerachty said you'd be coming straight over,' she said. 'But I'm afraid you've had a wasted journey. Khan's girl-friend, Lauren, is asleep. She had to be sedated, poor little thing. She looks like she's barely out of school and she doesn't know what's hit her.'

Tartaglia followed Barber into the huge open-plan living room, where he was hit by the unexpected but welcome chill of air-conditioning. Floor to ceiling windows ran the length of the room, which was at the top of the building, giving a good view of the City skyline and the Gherkin in the distance. A kitchen and bar area were at the back behind a glass partition, and he assumed that the large gallery above was the sleeping area. A massive plasma screen hung on one wall, showing an old episode of *Columbo*.

'Did you manage to find out anything from Lauren?' he asked, as Barber went over to one of the sofas where she had been sitting, and muted the sound of the TV.

'Enough to be getting on with for the moment. She says she came over here last night at about seven-thirty, expecting him to be back by eight. Apparently he'd given her a key, although from what she said, they haven't known each other long. Lauren's a model, she told me. They met at some party to do with one of his clients. Anyways, they were going out for dinner with friends somewhere and he'd told her not to be late. When he didn't appear, she tried his mobile, but that was switched off, so she rang his office. They said he'd gone to a client meeting in the West End at four-thirty and wasn't expected back. She stayed here all night waiting for him and when he still hadn't come home this morning, she called her dad and he called the police. Her mum's on a train down from Leicester as we speak.'

'You don't know when Lauren's likely to wake up?'

She shook her head. 'The doctor's only just been and gone. My guess is she'll be out for several hours at least. I have instructions to call DI Gerachty soon as she comes to.'

'What about his next of kin? Have they been contacted?'

'All we know is they live somewhere in Harrow, but Lauren's never met them. We're trying to trace them through the HR department at his office.'

Frustrated, he sighed. There was nothing to be done until later. 'OK. Thanks. I'm just going to take a look around. Where is she? I don't want to disturb her.'

'In the spare room, right at the end. She got quite worked up at the idea of sleeping in his bed, and anyway I thought it was easier in case she's still here when we start going through his things. But don't worry, you can come and go as you please. A bomb wouldn't wake her just now.'

He walked around the room, giving it a cursory check, but there was little to read from it other than that Khan was clearly not short of a bob or two. His main interest seemed to be fast cars. Four large, framed photographs of recent Formula 1 grand prix cars were grouped together on one wall, with a shiny red model of a Testarossa, mounted on a granite plinth, on the bookcase below. The furniture was modern and expensive, with a couple of huge, brightly coloured abstracts on the other walls that might have come from one of the local galleries. He wondered if Khan had bought them himself or if they had been chosen for him as part of the designer look. The steel and wood Italian kitchen was also new and, from what he could tell, rarely used, with a state-of-the-art Gaggia coffee machine sitting on the black granite counter still in its clear plastic wrapping. Khan had obviously had the best money could buy, but maybe it was just like ticking a box. There was little else to note, other than a small, well-equipped gym in a room at the far end which he would have given his eye-teeth for, and a bed the size of a football pitch.

He was about to go when Khan's phone rang. It was on the table next to where Barber was sitting, again glued to *Columbo*.

'Let it ring,' he said, as she muted the sound and stretched for the phone. 'Is there an answer machine?'

She nodded. 'It's one of those built-in thingummies.'

He counted three more rings, then heard the answer machine kick in and what he assumed was Khan's voice over the phone's loudspeaker telling the caller to leave a message. At the end there was a pause, followed by the sound of someone clearing their throat. 'Hey Paul, it's Danny. Where the fuck are you? Bin calling your mobile but it's dead as a friggin' dodo. Your message seriously freaked me out, man. We need to fuckin' talk . . .' He sounded like a Scouser, and judging from his slurred, hyped-up tone, he was either drunk or high on something. Tartaglia reached over and picked up the phone.

'Hello, Danny. You want to speak to Paul?'

'The fuck's this?'

'My name's Mark.'

'Don't fuckin' care what your name is. Put Paul on.'

'Paul's not here, Danny . . .' The line went dead.

The phone still in his hand, he turned to Barber. 'Is this thing backed up?'

'Not yet. But they're sending someone over soon.'

'Has anyone called before?'

'Yes, about an hour ago, but they hung up as soon as I answered.'

He tabbed through the menu until he came to the answer system. There were four stored messages. He pressed play.

'Paul, it's Tim. I got your voicemail. I think we'd all better meet and sort this out. If you get hold of Danny, I'll call Alex. I'm in Oxford at the moment, but can do the weekend. Unless you can think of anywhere better, can we come to yours? It's pandemonium here.' The voice was deep and authoritative, the message timed at one thirty-five the previous day. Alex. The name was common enough, but it still gave Tartaglia pause. So far, they had failed to trace Alex Fleming, who seemed to have disappeared into thin air. They had also checked Paul Khan's name against Logan's contacts on his computer, but there was no match. Wondering if he was reading too much into things, he played the rest of the messages. Apart from two, where the caller hung up after listening to the recorded message, the only other was the one from Danny he had just heard. Gerachty would be pulling the phone records as a matter of course so there was nothing more for him to do.

He was about to pass Barber the phone, when it started to ring again. He decided to answer it. 'Paul Khan's telephone.'

There was a pause, then a woman spoke: 'Is Paul there, please?' The voice was soft, well-spoken, and sounded middle-aged, with a hint of a Pakistani accent.

'Who's speaking?'

'It's his mother. Is everything all right?'

'Is there anyone there with you, Mrs Khan?'

'Yes. My husband's here, why do you ask?'

He heard the alarm in her voice and took a deep breath.

'My name's Mark Tartaglia,' he said. 'I'm with the Metropolitan Police.'

It was nearly three in the afternoon and the lunchtime crowd was beginning to thin out. Alex was in the middle of sorting out a problem with someone's bill when one of the waiters came up to the bar and leaned across.

'Alex, there's a friend of yours over there.' He jerked his head in the direction of the long window. 'He says he needs a word when you have a sec.' Alex glanced in that direction and saw Danny hunched over one of the small tables, staring into space. He hadn't noticed him come in and wondered how long he had been sitting there. 'I told him you're busy, but he says he'll wait.'

'Thanks. I just need to finish this.'

'He also wants a large glass of white wine. He said anything will do. Shall I get it?'

'No, I'll take care of it. Tell him I'll be over as soon as I can.'

It didn't take a minute to reverse the incorrect wine entry on the customer's bill but Alex took his time, peering at the computer screen as though he was deep in some complicated transaction while he thought things through. As far as he knew Danny was still living not far away, somewhere up Ladbroke Grove, but he had never before troubled himself to venture into the restaurant. There could only be one reason why he had come and Alex felt wary. Talking to Tim about what had happened was one thing; Danny was a different kettle of fish, plus the restaurant was busy and not the right place for such a conversation. Also, at the back of his mind was still the thought that Danny had sent the emails. Had he come to wind him up? He should find out what he knew then get rid of him as quickly as possible. He printed out a fresh copy of the bill and handed it to one of the waiters to take back to the customer, then poured a large glass of Sauvignon Blanc and took it over to where Danny was sitting, his head jerking in time to some imaginary beat.

'How are you, mate?' he said, putting the glass down in front of Danny, who was drumming his fingers hard on the table. Danny stopped nodding and looked up. His eyes were hidden behind wraparound dark glasses and Alex couldn't read his expression, but he could tell from his mouth he looked tense.

'Not good, man.'

'You heard about Joe?'

'Yeah. Sorry.' He bowed his head, then reached out and patted Alex's sleeve. 'You all right?'

'As much as I can be.'

Danny nodded as though he understood. He was wearing his usual uniform of Converses, black jeans, and a black T-shirt with some obscure logo on the front. His hair was longer than the last time Alex had seen him and he had grown a funny little beard that made him look a bit like a Hobbit. He took a large slug of wine as though very thirsty. He said something, but he spoke quickly and the words were lost against the background noise from the room.

'What's that?' Alex asked.

'Sit down, will you?' Danny said, practically shouting. 'I'll fuckin' crick my neck if I carry on looking at you up there.'

Alex slid into the seat opposite. 'OK, keep your hair on. But I can't stop long, I'm working.'

'Right. I had these messages from Paul and I can't get hold of him. Thought maybe you'd know something about it, or where he is. You talked to him at all?'

'Not recently. What did he say?'

'He said someone's trying to stir up stuff about Ashleigh Grange.'

'Really?' He hadn't expected anything like this. 'He said that?'

Danny nodded.

Maybe Joe had spoken to Paul before he died; maybe that had shaken Paul up, unlike Tim. Alex leaned across the table towards him and folded his hands. 'What exactly did he mean?'

'I dunno.'

'Was it about an email?'

'He just said we needed to talk. It got me real worried.'

'You're sure he didn't say anything about an email?'

Danny gazed at him for a moment. 'Maybe he did.'

'He'd *had* an email? Was that it? Or had he been speaking to Joe?'

'I'm not sure.'

'What else did he say?'

'That was about it.' Danny started to tap his fingers again on the table.

'But you're sure he mentioned Ashleigh Grange?'

'Yeah. That's what got me going.'

He stared at Danny, wondering if he was telling the truth and if his memory could be relied upon. It was odd his coming there, even odder his not being able to speak to Paul when he wanted. Maybe it was all part of the scam and he was the one behind the emails to Joe. He didn't look all there behind the shades, but that was nothing new. It had been happening for a long while, most noticeably in the last couple of years, Danny's slow drift down into a spiral of self-destruction. His periods of detachment from the real world – Joe's tongue-in-cheek euphemism for it – were becoming the norm, sobriety a thing past. And what lay behind it? Fuck only knew. He came from a stable background, his father was a local councillor in his home town and relatively well off. Was it a sense of failure, maybe? The hope, enthusiasm and promise he had shown at university had gradually been eroded by a mix of bad luck and poor judgement, as well as a general preference for the easy route.

At university, although never a leading light, he had more or less kept up with Tim and Paul academically, but that was long past. Time had divided all of them, and in Danny's case the crack that had slowly opened up over the years had become an unbridgeable chasm. In his moments of lucidity, how could the present-day comparisons and thoughts of what might have been escape him? But whatever he felt inside, outwardly he showed no bitterness. Whilst always in awe of Tim, he had stayed particularly close to Paul. Maybe he and Danny were in this together, Alex thought. Maybe it was their little joke to wind the others up, although in very bad taste now that Joe was dead. But why would Paul bother? He seemed to have everything he wanted.

'Look, Danny,' he said, attempting a friendly smile. 'Paul must have said something else. Surely you can remember?'

Danny looked at him in a dazed way. 'Listen, man. His

words aren't important. It was his tone . . . I tell you, he sounded really, really rattled and that's not like Paul.'

Alex sighed, still not convinced. 'No, you're right, but I—'

'Sorry to interrupt, Alex,' one of the waiters said, coming over to their table and bending down close to his ear. 'But the bloke on table twenty-seven's still going on about his bill. Can you come and talk to him?'

'Sure.' Alex got to his feet. 'Carry on with your wine, Danny. I'll be back in a minute.'

17

As soon as he got back to the office in Barnes, Tartaglia went looking for Steele. She was at her desk, ploughing through a pile of papers, eating an egg-mayonnaise sandwich. He wondered if she had skipped lunch or was merely hungry. Unlike most of the women in the office, who seemed to be on a permanent diet, she had a healthy appetite and didn't seem to care what she ate or when. It also had no impact on her broad-shouldered, athletic figure.

She looked up. 'There you are, Mark. I've just had Jim Grainger on the phone, saying that you've been roughing up one of his DIs.'

'I wouldn't put it quite like that.'

'He said you were very aggressive. I told you to go easy, not throw your weight around.'

'I didn't. But the woman wouldn't listen.' He explained what had happened at the boathouse.

Steele finished the last bite of her sandwich and wiped her mouth and fingers quickly with a paper napkin. 'OK. She sounds wet behind the ears and I'll give you the benefit of the doubt. And if they screw up, it sounds like it will fall on us to clear up the mess. If Jim starts sounding off again, I'll let him have it with both barrels.'

'Just tell him we got off on the wrong foot.'

She waved him away with her hand. 'Rumour has it he's put in for early retirement. He's feeling a bit sensitive about life at the moment. Doesn't want to go out with egg on his face. Now tell me why you think the two murders are linked.'

He explained what Arabella Browne had found, as well as the circumstantial evidence of the missing phone and the position of the body, then filled her in on his trip to Paul Khan's apartment.

'You think it's the same hand?'

'I'm sure of it. The post mortem's sometime this evening.'

'OK. I'll need Arabella's summary report before I can speak to Clive. In the meantime, we've got more than enough to keep us busy. Let Grainger's team clear the ground for us and you stick to the Logan murder. So long as they cooperate and share information, it's no skin off our nose.'

'Yeah, so long as they do.'

'If you encounter any problems, let me know and I'll sort it. Now, what's happening about finding the elusive Alex Fleming?'

'Still no joy. We're trying to get an address for him through his agent. We thought it was faster at this point than trying his bank. The address they had on file is an old one and the man who handles him is out of the office at the moment. We've left messages and they say he'll get back to us at some point later today.'

'Someone must know where to get hold of him.'

'His agent seems our best bet. In the meantime, there's one

other thing Arabella mentioned. If you remember, Logan's body was damp when she found it.' Steele nodded. 'Well, this one was even wetter, although she says it was only the upper body. Both bodies had restraint marks and one of Logan's wrists was fractured, as though he'd struggled hard. Both bodies smelled strongly of urine. The best explanation is that they were both tortured.'

'Waterboarding, you mean?'

'Something like that.'

She gazed at him thoughtfully, head slightly to one side. 'If you're right, it changes everything.'

He nodded. 'It isn't just about punishment or revenge. Both men had something the killer wanted. There's got to be a connection.'

'What the hell are we going to do?' Alex asked. A copy of the late edition of the *Evening Standard* belonging to one of the waitresses lay folded in front of him. The headline **ANOTHER LONDON SHOOTING** danced before his eyes. He was standing behind the bar, phone clamped to his ear, trying to block out the voices of a group of diners who were sitting just through the arch. A fresh peal of laughter drowned Tim's reply.

Alex crouched down. 'Say that again?'

'I said, what do you mean?' Tim was in the car, talking over the loudspeaker, and his voice sounded distant over the background drone of the traffic outside.

'Danny was really worried.'

'I thought you said he didn't say very much.'

'He never says very much, but I tell you, he was worried. He said that on the message Paul left him he was worried too.

He said that someone was trying to stir up stuff about Ashleigh Grange. It all ties in with what happened to Joe.'

'Why did you let Danny go?'

'I didn't have a choice. One minute he was there, next he'd buggered off. He didn't even pay for his drink.'

'Where on earth are you?' Tim said gruffly.

'Still at work.'

'I think we should talk about this later. Why don't you come over?'

'I can't. The guy who was supposed to be on duty's rung in sick and I have to cover. I'll be here until late. I think we should go to the police.'

'And say what, exactly?'

Alex hesitated, suddenly unsure. What would they say? That they'd known both Joe and Paul, that someone was sending funny emails? What else could they say without it all spewing out, and if it did, did it matter . . . He was getting to the point when he almost didn't care.

'We could tell them about the emails.'

'I told you before, they'll find out by themselves. There's no point our getting involved.'

'Maybe they won't make the connection. First Joe, now Paul. There's got to be a connection, hasn't there?'

There was a pause before Tim replied. 'Maybe, maybe not.'

'There has to be. Will it stop here? Or will it be Danny or me or you next?'

'You're being melodramatic. As I said before, it's just a silly prank gone wrong.'

'Not any longer, it's not. It's not a joke. Who's doing this, Tim? Why?' He heard his voice rise to a wimpish whine.

'What phone are you calling on?'

'One of the restaurant lines. I switched my mobile off. The police keep ringing me.'

'Honestly, Alex, I wouldn't call from a public place, if I were you. And I wouldn't use your mobile.'

'Great. So what do you suggest?'

'Go and get one of those pay-as-you-go phones until this all dies down.'

'Dies down? Unfortunate choice of words.'

'And don't use your oyster card either. They can use it to trace you.'

'When you spoke to Paul—'

'I didn't speak to Paul. We kept playing phone tag. I never managed to get hold of him.'

'Tell me again what Paul said about the email he had had.'

'There's nothing much to tell. All he said in his message was that he'd had a funny email and did I know anything about it. He was quite guarded, and contrary to what Danny said he sounded more intrigued than rattled. Naturally it made me think of the one you told me Joe had received, but I may have got the wrong end of the stick.'

Tim's tone lacked a sense of urgency. Didn't it mean anything to him? Now Alex wondered again if Tim was behind the emails.

'But he mentioned Ashleigh Grange to Danny. It says in the paper that Paul was shot. There was a whole load of stuff about gun crime. It's just like with Joe.'

'Look, I doubt they have the full picture just yet. It could just be a terrible coincidence.'

'And what if it isn't? What are we going to do? I still think one of us should speak to the police.' A noise behind him made him turn around. One of the waitresses was putting a drinks order on the clipboard and gave him a funny look. He wondered how much she had overheard. He walked away to the other end of the bar, out of earshot. 'I think we should all sit down and talk this through sensibly first,' Tim was saying. 'We may be jumping to conclusions. I'll try and get hold of Danny. Do you remember the name of his company?'

'I heard it was going down the pan.'

'Me too, or at least that's what Paul said when I saw him at Fi and Bill's wedding. He'd sunk quite a sum of money into it and sounded pretty worried.'

'What about Fi? She must have an address or something for Danny.'

'Good idea, I'll try her. I'm on my way back to London now so let's meet up and work out what to do. Call me at home tomorrow, first thing. In the meantime, Alex, for God's sake don't do anything stupid.'

18

After his talk with DCI Steele, Tartaglia went along the corridor to his office, where he found Sam Donovan kneeling on the carpet beside Logan's suitcase and trunk. The usually tidy room looked like a charity shop, with piles of books and clothing stacked everywhere on the floor. He was amazed to see how much stuff could come out of a single trunk and one suitcase. It looked as though Donovan would be a while before she had finished checking and logging everything and he wondered if he would be able to get any work done in such chaos.

'How are you doing?' he asked, trying to hide his impatience as he picked his way across the floor to his desk.

She was patting down a heavy winter coat to see if anything was hidden in the pockets or seams. 'Nothing interesting, so far. Just a load of winter clothes, that's all. There were some papers and personal stuff in the trunk that I've put on your desk for you to look at when you have a moment.'

He squatted down and ran his eye over the piles of books. They were mainly biographies and paperback classics, all looking well worn. They gave no insight into Logan's more recent interests. 'Have you found anything that might have some bearing on the second book?'

'No.' She folded up the coat and put it on the floor with the rest of Logan's things. 'I found some old scripts, but nothing like a book, and not even a memory stick.'

'What's this?' he asked, picking up a scrapbook from off the top of one of the piles.

'Just press clippings and stuff from his acting days. Nothing to do with his writing.'

He flicked quickly through it, but the cuttings were old and, as Donovan had said, all related to Logan's acting career. The two thick lever arch files underneath contained bank statements going back several years, plus income statements, haphazardly filed, with wodges of stapled receipts, presumably for Logan's tax returns. He put them back and sat down at his desk. An old cigar box sat on the top of the things Donovan had left for him to look at. It was secured by a couple of old rubber bands, which snapped when he tried to peel them off. Inside he found a quartz paperweight in the shape of a frog, an old fountain pen, a penknife with a horn handle, and a couple of postcards of paintings by Turner, which were blank and dog-eared. The corners were studded with small holes as though they had been fixed to a pin board at some point and it reminded him of the board above his desk in his university digs that he had covered in post-cards and photos. He picked up the frog and turned it over slowly in his hand, feeling its cold, smooth surface, wondering if Logan had once done the same. It was a motley collection of objects, with no apparent significance, and gave no better understanding of the man. But at least they had more of a personal flavour than the possessions retrieved from the boat.

At the bottom of the box was a large folder full of photographs. He spread them out on his desk like a pack of cards, and gazed at the black and white ten-by-eight professional shots of a younger, leaner Logan in his acting days, and snapshots from school and university. Amongst them he found a photo of a blonde-haired woman with a small boy on her knee. The woman's hair and clothing were dated and he assumed it was a picture of Logan with his mother. He remembered that Logan had been an only child. Another photograph caught his eye. In it, Logan looked to be in his late teens or early twenties. Dressed in jeans and a T-shirt, he was standing at a bar with his arm clasped around a man with thick, reddish-brown hair. They were grinning, and each had a pint in his hand, raised to the camera. Tartaglia wondered if the other man was Alex Fleming. If so, he had known Logan a long time. He put it aside to show Minderedes. He had just pulled out a photograph of a line of snow-covered cars parked in front of a terrace of Georgian houses, when Donovan looked over his shoulder.

'That's Windsor Terrace. It's in Bristol.'

'You know it?'

'Claire had a flat there when she was at university.'

'I'd forgotten she went to Bristol.'

She nodded. 'So did Joe Logan, according to the bio on his book jacket. But he was a few years older than she is, so I doubt she knew him. I'll ask her later.' She picked up a pile of clothing from the floor and transferred it back to the suitcase.

'How are you getting on with his book?'

'I've only just started. I tried reading it in the car coming back from Dorset this morning, but I started to feel sick, so I had to stop.'

'Don't blame you. I can't read in a car either.'

'I'm usually fine, but Justin was driving rather fast and there wasn't a single decent, straight stretch of road until we hit the M3.'

As he tucked the photographs back in the folder, he noticed an envelope at the bottom of the box. It had been addressed to Logan at St Thomas's school. Inside was a letter written in a large, childish hand:

Dear Joe

Thanks for your note. Here's a copy of the article you mentioned. As you can tell, it's a subject close to my heart. I'd love to hear what you think and if you want any more info, let me know. It would be good to talk and I'll give you a call in the next few days. I can also put you in touch with Jennifer, if you like. I'm sure she'd be happy to speak to you and I promise to respect your need for privacy.

Anna

Clipped to the back of the letter was a computer printout of an article from one of the dailies dated earlier that year, with a small headshot of Anna Paget, uncharacteristically smiling. He gazed at the letter for a moment, not sure what to make of it. He was sure she had only mentioned writing to Logan once.

'What's that?' Donovan asked, looking over from the pile of books she was cataloguing.

'Take a look.' He stretched over and passed her the letter.

'What's bothering you about it?' she asked, after reading the letter.

'I don't know. Something she said doesn't add up.'

'Does it matter?' she said, handing him back the papers.

He shrugged. 'Maybe not. It may just be an innocent mistake. It just bothers me that she got a detail wrong.'

He unclipped the article and started to read:

MISSING PEOPLE

With renewed calls for a national database,
Anna Paget asks what are we doing
to keep track of them?

When Kirstie Jenson's remains were discovered last week in a shallow grave beside the busy A4, near Marlborough, Wiltshire, it ended an 11-year wait for her parents, John and Diane Jenson. They no longer need to listen out for the phone, or the sound of her key in the door, or scan each crowded street for her face. That nightmare is over. Although their worst fears have come true, at least they finally know where their daughter has been all this time.

The promising undergraduate was last seen getting into a car with an unknown man outside a nightclub in Swindon town centre on 31st October 1999. She would still be missing now if it hadn't been for some heavy rain, and a local man who pulled over by the roadside to relieve himself. In the last eleven years, countless people have whizzed back and forth past that spot, unaware of what lay so close. It's a sobering thought. In our daily journeys to and from work, or school, our trips to the shops, to the pub, or out for a meal, how many of us unwittingly pass by the remains of the missing?

Every year, in the UK, nearly a quarter of a million people are reported missing. Almost all are found within a year, with three-quarters in the first 48 hours. But according to research, the longer someone is gone, the more likely they are never to be found. Yet only a handful of cases trigger the sort of newspaper headlines and publicity that could help trace them. The rest just slip between the cracks. What's even worse, more than half of the 2,000 or so who disappear for good each year are assumed to be dead. That's over 10,000 people who have died unaccounted for since Kirstie Jenson got into the wrong car. Where are they all? And what are we doing to find them?

Missing people range from the very young to the very old and the reasons why they disappear are many. This means that there is no single easy approach to finding them. It also blurs the focus of what needs to be done to improve the current situation. To make matters worse, not all people who disappear are reported to the police. But looking at the research, one thing is striking. Roughly two thirds of those reported missing each year are under 18, with twice as many girls as boys. Even if they haven't been abducted, what chance of long-term survival do these children have, once they are off the radar? And what about the family and friends who are left behind in limbo? What are we doing for them?

Jennifer Collins's only daughter Laura left home one morning 5 years ago on her way to school, never to be seen again. 'Each waking hour is torment, but I've never given up hope,' she says. 'Her bedroom's just as she left it, ready for her if she ever comes home.' She describes her life as being on hold. Her marriage broke up a year after her daughter went missing, then she lost her job and had a breakdown. 'I live every day as it comes, just waiting in case there's news. I know it's unlikely to be good, but I still hope. The worst thing is not knowing what happened to Laura.'

For a lucky few, there is a happy ending. Sabine Dardenne and Laeticia Delheze were both rescued from the clutches of the Belgian paedophile and murderer, Marc Dutroux. Jaycee Lee Dugard, in the US, was discovered alive eighteen years after she was abducted from a school bus stop. Such cases give hope to every desperate parent of a missing child. Although John and Diane Jenson will never see Kirstie again, they are lucky compared to some. At least they finally know what happened. For the majority, there will never be that closure. However, a lot could be done to increase the odds . . .

Tartaglia sighed. He had read enough and stuffed the papers back into the envelope. The call for a national database wasn't new, and with over fifty police forces in the UK and no centralised system, it was justified. But as always, a shortage of funds coupled with the lack of a clear-cut message or a high-profile lobby group won out over logic in the political debate. From his early days in CID, he remembered the case of a young Asian girl who failed to come home from school one day. She came from a tight-knit Muslim family and, according to everyone they spoke to, was not the sort of person to go missing and cause her parents worry. After making enquiries, the general assumption was that she had had a row with her parents and walked out. Echoing the Fred and Rosemary West cases, he later discovered that two other girls of a similar age had disappeared without trace in the same area of west London. But by that time it was too late, and short of pulling down each house or digging up every back garden in the area, there was nothing they could do. The disappearances weren't broadcast as it was thought best not to panic the public. As far as he was aware, none of the girls had ever been found. Things had improved over the years, but as Anna said, the missing still slipped 'between the cracks'.

'Interesting piece?' Donovan asked, as he put the envelope back on the pile.

He nodded. There was genuine feeling in the writing and, whatever else he thought of Anna, she had gone up several notches in his estimation. 'What's particularly interesting,' he said, 'is that Joe Logan circled the first paragraph as well as highlighting the line, "How many of us unwittingly pass by the remains of the missing?"'

'You think he was going to write about the subject?'

'He was certainly curious about it. At least I now think I know how she got him to agree to an interview.'

His phone started to ring. He picked up and heard Gerachty's voice at the other end.

'I thought you'd like to know, I've just been interviewing the anonymous caller,' she said, not bothering with any greeting or preamble. 'Her name's Mandy Wilson and she's a new member of the rowing club. She was one of three women there last night and she caved in pretty quick when we told her we had the voice recording and prints. It turns out she's been having an affair with Craig Sykes, the club secretary,' she continued, rattling through it at top speed, in a flat tone of voice, as though ticking a box. 'Instead of going home to his wife and kids after the practice session, he took her out for a curry. When they'd finished, they decided to go back to the club for a nightcap, or something. Anyway, when they got there, they found the door was closed but unlocked. They thought the barman had forgotten to lock up. Reading between the lines, they were pretty pissed, or at least she was. She had quite a hangover today, looked positively green. If the killer was still there, he must have heard them coming.'

'Did they notice anything else that was odd?' he asked, when she finished the account.

'Apart from the door being unlocked, no. Like you said, they didn't turn on the lights as they didn't want anyone knowing they were there. She said she and Craig went out onto the balcony to look at the view, then they decided they fancied something more to drink. She volunteered to go and get it, which is when she tripped over the body. At first, she thought it was one of the other members who'd had a skinful and gone to sleep behind the bar. It was so dark, she couldn't see anything much. She remembers noticing that the fridge lights were out, which she thought was a little odd. I don't know what bit of Paul Khan she touched, but she said he felt warm.'

'Did she scream?'

'Not so as anyone outside in the street would hear, or at

least I think that's what she said. You can check her statement if you want. Anyway, she swears she thought Khan was still alive. She then called Craig, who was still out on the balcony admiring the view, and he came over. He tried to turn on the lights by the door, but she said they didn't work. He then used his phone to shed a bit of light on the scene and that's when they realised the man on the floor was in a bad way. She says he had blood on his face and it was then she saw she had blood on her hands from where she'd touched him. That totally freaked her out, although they both insist they still had no idea Khan was dead. They thought he'd just been beaten up and was unconscious. What's really odd is she said she suddenly got the idea that there was someone else in the room with them.'

'Where?'

'She didn't know for sure and she couldn't see much, but it gave her the creeps. When she told Craig, he wanted to get out of there as quickly as possible.'

'So much for the macho lover.'

'They don't exist,' Gerachty said sharply. 'When I asked her why she made the call and not Craig, she said he was desperate not to be involved. I get the impression he was more worried about that than the man on the floor. He insisted she make the call while he skedaddled off home to his wife. I don't think Mandy'll be seeing him again in a hurry.'

'I don't blame her.'

Gerachty gave an affirmative sniff. 'And before you ask, I can't find anyone who says they turned the lights off at the mains, so it must have been the killer.'

'Who turned them back on?'

'The emergency staff. The fuses were tripped, that's all. I'm having forensics go over the toilets again, just in case the killer was hiding in there when Mandy and Craig arrived.'

'Sounds good to me.' If nothing else, Gerachty was efficient when pointed in the right direction. Maybe, in time, she would learn the rest. 'Have you had a chance to look at Paul Khan's emails?'

'We've only just got hold of his work laptop. They didn't want to give it to us, they said there's all sorts of highly sensitive stuff on it, client confidentiality and all that crap. In the end we had to threaten them with a court order and they backed down. Tell me again exactly what it is you're looking for?'

'I'll send something over to you now. You'll get the picture when you see it. Have you pulled his phone records?'

'I should have them soon.'

'When you do, can you get a copy over to us asap so we can cross-reference them with Logan's?'

'Sure. I understand you're coming to the post mortem.'

'That's right.'

'Well, I'll see you over there, then.' There was a pause before she added a muffled: 'And thanks for earlier.' Before he had time to say anything, she hung up.

As he tucked away his phone, he smiled. It was the closest thing to an apology he was likely to get.

He rang through to Wightman, and told him to forward Gerachty a copy of the strange email that Logan had received. Minderedes had left the envelope Anna Paget had given them with the photocopied pieces she had originally sent Logan.

He looked inside but all he found was a selection of interviews with actors, pop stars and a couple of politicians. The article about missing people wasn't there, nor was the draft he had requested of her interview with Logan. She had already left two messages for him that day asking for an update, both of which he had ignored. He decided it was time to call her. He punched in her number and she picked up almost immediately, as though she had been waiting for the call.

'Anna Paget.'

'It's Mark Tartaglia. I need to talk to you about the things you sent to Joe Logan.'

Anna Paget sighed. 'Look, I haven't finished the article yet. That's why I haven't sent it over to you. I've been tied up with other things, plus with everything that's happened it's needed some major re-jigging. I'd also like to put in some stuff about the investigation as well.' She was looking at him enquiringly.

They were sitting at a table in a small room behind the front desk at Kensington Police Station, a fifteen-minute ride by motorbike from the office. Anna had tried to suggest that they meet somewhere less formal, but he had insisted. Formal was how he wanted it. If there was air-conditioning, it wasn't working and he had been forced to open the small, barred window. It let in the smell of fried food from the canteen but no draught. He had taken off his jacket and loosened his tie, but he was still sweating. By contrast, she seemed unaware of the heat, but then she wore little more than a belted T-shirt and sandals.

'What sort of thing are you talking about?' Tartaglia asked.

'The readers will want to know what's going on, some theory as to why he was killed and what you're doing to find the killer.'

'Is that all?'

'Our crime desk seems to be in the dark for a change and your press office has been less than helpful.'

'I'm sorry about that, but you'll get as much out of them as from me.'

'Look, surely you can tell me something?' she said, widening her eyes. 'I mean, there's been another murder, hasn't there? Down by the river. They said the man was shot.'

'Shootings in London happen, as you know.'

'Is it anything to do with what happened to Joe, do you think? Are we talking serial killers?'

He slapped his hand hard on the table. 'Jesus! Do you people always just think about the next headline?'

She sat back in her chair, as though stung by the remark. 'I'm sorry. I really didn't mean it to come out that way. I just wanted to know if there's a link.'

'I know nothing about the other murder. It's being handled by a different team.'

'Oh,' she said, frowning. 'Another team? So there's no connection? I'd heard—'

'It seems not,' he said firmly, wondering what had been said. No doubt her paper's crime desk had caught wind of something. However hard they tried, it was difficult to stop the off-the-record little chats and snippets of information. He would have to speak to Gerachty right away and make sure she stopped any leaks at her end. 'Now, can we get back to your piece? I'd like to see a draft of whatever you've done so far. I don't care if it's not finished, I still want to see it.'

She shrugged. 'I still don't understand why. I mean, it's not going to tell you who killed the poor sod.'

'Every little piece of information helps, and in the few weeks before his death you spent more time with him than anyone else. Plus you have an outsider's objectivity. It may shed some light.'

She seemed disappointed. 'So you're in the dark. You still have no idea who did it.'

'It's early days.'

'Which means you haven't a clue. Poor Joe. I really hope you find whoever did it. Now if that's all . . .'

As she stood up, Tartaglia put out his hand. 'It's not all. Please sit down. How many times did you write to Joe Logan?'

'Just the once, as I told you.'

'You're sure?'

'Well, I sent him a letter and a package of stuff I'd written. I sent it to his publisher, as I didn't have his address, and they forwarded it on to where he was living. I told you all this before.'

'Then what happened?'

'He wrote back asking some questions, mainly about me and what I'd done.'

'Do you have that letter?'

'No. Maybe I sent him a note, or maybe I called him, I'm not sure. It's no big deal, is it? Anyway, soon after that he called me and we met up. I told you the rest.'

He shook his head and pushed a copy of her article on missing people across the table to her. 'You sent him this, with another note.' He caught the brief flicker of surprise in her eyes. Maybe she had genuinely forgotten what she had sent, or maybe she hadn't expected Logan to keep it. He suspected the latter. 'Did you mark the article, or did Logan?'

'He must have done.'

'Do you have any idea why he ringed the first paragraph or why he underlined that sentence?'

'None at all.'

'It clearly interested him. You didn't discuss it when you met him?'

'We may have done, but if we did, it was only in passing and I don't remember.'

'Who's Gareth?'

'You obviously haven't read the article properly. He runs a missing persons' charity and I quote from him several times. All the statistics come from him too and I thought Joe might like to speak to him.'

'Was this anything to do with the second book?'

She looked at him strangely, as though she was trying to work something out in her mind. 'Are you still going on about that? I told you all I know.'

'OK. Then explain why you chose this particular article to send to him.'

'Because it's topical.'

It didn't ring true. He remembered Logan's email to Anna and his talk of a connection. Judging by the dates, he must have written it after receiving the second note and the 'Missing' article. 'There's more to it than that, surely? In the note you say that it's "close to your heart". What did you mean?'

'I really don't want to talk about it.'

'I'm afraid you must.'

'It's personal. It's nothing to do with what happened to Joe.'

'I'll make that decision.'

He held her gaze until she finally nodded. 'If you really want to know, I'll tell you ... not that you'll find it that interesting. But can we go somewhere else? It's so stuffy in here and I could do with a cold drink and some fresh air.'

He checked his watch. He was expecting a call from Browne's office to say that she was ready to do the post mortem, but last he had heard she was running late. He had already had to postpone his drink with Angela Harper. 'OK. There's a place we can go and get a drink. It's only a minute's walk from here.'

'Thank you,' she said, standing up and picking up her satchel. 'I feel like I'm a suspect or something, sitting here.'

Although she wasn't a suspect, he was pleased that she felt some discomfort. He was sure she had lied to him, and was probably still lying, although he had no idea why.

19

The wide strip of paved garden at the front of the Scarsdale Arms was awash with multi-coloured flowers in tubs and hanging baskets. The sun had moved off the front, but it was packed and all of the tables outside were already taken. Nobody looked as if they would be moving soon and although he was dying for a smoke, they would have to go inside.

'What can I get you to drink?' he asked, as they went into the gloomy wood-panelled interior.

'Diet coke, please, with a slice.' She sat down at a table in an empty corner of the room.

He went up to the bar and bought her coke, plus a soda with lemon for himself. As he carried it back to the table, he couldn't help noticing in the dim light how attractive she was with her slim, bare legs crossed and mass of long dark hair. Again he wondered what had gone on between her and Logan.

'Right,' he said, sitting down opposite. 'I'm afraid I haven't got long. Tell me why the subject of missing people is so close to your heart.'

'Before we start, can I just ask you something?' She was looking at him seriously, head a little to one side.

'What is it?'

'Why do you do what you do? I mean, it's a pretty odd way to make a living.'

'Because somebody has to,' he said, a little surprised. He had assumed she was going to ask about the investigation.

'Yes, but why you?'

'You want the personal angle? Because somebody needs to find out the truth. It's vital, both for the person whose life has been stolen and for the family.'

'You really believe that?'

'Yes.'

She gave him a dazzling smile. 'So, you're one of the good guys. Like an avenging angel.'

'No. As I said, it's about the truth.'

'Do you believe in justice?'

'What, as an abstract concept?'

'No. Do you think the system works?'

He could see the headline already and he didn't like it. He had reservations about a lot of things that he had to deal with in doing his job, the justice system being one of them. Sometimes, through no fault of the system, the guilty still escaped true justice, if there was such a thing. But he had no intention of giving her material for another article, let alone finding himself quoted.

'We do the best we can. Now, I think you've had your question.'

'This is off the record, if that's what you're worried about. I just want to know for myself. Do you think you deliver justice to the victims and their families?' She spoke as though it meant something to her and as she gazed at him, she looked like a young girl, whose illusions about life were still intact. Was there genuine passion or idealism inside the cynical hack? Maybe this was the side that Joe Logan had seen, that had won him over.

'We're only part of the process, but hopefully more often than not.'

She smiled again, this time more thoughtfully and shifted back into her seat. 'OK. I get what you're saying. Thank you for being so honest. Just one last little thing, I'm just curious by nature . . .'

'What is it?'

'Do you think of yourself as Italian or Scottish? I mean, you look so Italian but . . .'

She was looking at him expectantly. Again her interest appeared to be genuine. 'Italian, I suppose, although I was born and brought up in Edinburgh. But my whole family's Italian. My father's side originally came from a little town called Picinisco in Lazio, near Rome. Now that's enough about me. It's your turn. Why's the subject of missing people something you care about so much?'

She sipped her coke, looking at him for a moment before she put the glass down. 'It's not something I generally talk about, but maybe if I tell you you'll understand and leave me alone.'

'No promises,' he said, taking a mouthful of soda.

'I first met Jennie a couple of years ago.'

'Jennie?'

'Jennifer Collins. I quote her in the article. Her daughter Laura's missing.'

'Yes, I remember, now.'

'I was doing a piece on these people who win prizes, you know, they enter loads of competitions and win fridges and cars and holidays. Some people do it more or less as a full-time occupation and Jennie's been pretty successful. She's even won a prize for winning prizes, can you believe.'

'I thought she'd had all sorts of personal problems after her daughter disappeared?'

She nodded. 'She had a breakdown and she still suffers from depression and takes endless pills. I suppose doing the competitions keeps her busy and she can do it from home. She's mentally too fragile to get a proper job and physically she can't cope. She had a car accident a couple of years ago and she's now in a wheelchair, so she can't get around that easily. Some people have all the luck, don't they? She's been totally destroyed by what happened. Anyway, I interviewed her and it came out about Laura. I filed it away in my head, as one does, and when Kirstie Jenson's remains were found, I decided to write something. We're really crap in this country at dealing with the whole issue of missing people and some-thing needs to be done.'

'Things have got a lot better.'

She shook her head. 'I still think it's a disgrace. A body turns up in, say, Yorkshire, but unless there's ID, there's no easy way of linking it to the kid who disappeared ten years before in Cornwall. You only have to look at how things are in the US, with the FBI running the show, to see how back-ward we are.'

'You make the point very well in your piece,' he said, 'but I still don't understand why your interest is personal.'

She sighed and looked away. 'I had a pretty dysfunctional

childhood. I never knew my father, and my mother died when I was really young. I don't want to go into the details, but in the end I decided the best thing was to run away.'

She spoke matter-of-factly and he was struck by her lack of self-pity. He wondered what it had cost her to be so detached. 'You were in care?'

'Sort of.'

'I don't know what to say.'

'There isn't anything to say. I was just one of the statistics. If you read my article you'll know that the largest category of people who go missing are young girls. If they're repeat runaways, nobody's interested. They're just written off.'

'How old were you?'

'Fifteen. I hitchhiked my way to London, slept rough for a bit, then I met someone who gave me a break. Thanks to him I didn't end up buried under someone's patio or left to rot in a rubbish bag by the roadside. That's why, when I read about all these girls, speak to their parents and stuff, it really gets to me. I realise how bloody lucky I am. Maybe I have nine lives, but it could easily have been me if Brian hadn't rescued me.'

'Brian?'

'He was in the music business. He was much older, of course, but it didn't bother me.'

'For Christ's sake, you were fifteen,' he said, unable to hide his disgust.

'In heels and make-up I could pass for older. Anyway, I was almost legal.'

'Come on, that's not the point. Surely there must have been someone else you could have turned to?'

She met his gaze. 'No. There was nobody.'

Coming from a close-knit, family-orientated Catholic background it was difficult for him to imagine such total emptiness, although he knew it existed. He wasn't at all religious but sometimes religion could fill the void. Maybe he didn't need it because it was there. He shook his head at his lack of sensitivity. 'I'm sorry.'

'Don't be. It's just the way it was and I knew what I was doing. Brian used to say I was fifteen going on thirty, that I was the adult, not him. In many ways he was right, he was just like a big, soppy child. He had this massive place up in Hampstead full of really cool stuff and he looked after me. It was the first time anyone had ever done that. He was like the dad I never had.'

'The *dad*?' He stared at her horrified, wondering just how dysfunctional her childhood had been.

She nodded. 'Sort of. He used to take me out shopping and to restaurants and clubs. I was supposed to call him Dad or Uncle Brian when we were out. Occasionally, if I was tired or bored, I'd call him Brian, just to wind him up and make him take me home. It makes me laugh even now. He'd get in such a strop . . .'

'I'm amazed you can laugh about it. He should have been slung in jail.'

She shook her head. 'I know what it looks like from the outside, but there are lots that deserve it more than him. He could be a right shit when it came to business, but he was a kind, soft-hearted, decent man to me and he looked after me. He was the one who encouraged my writing.'

'Really?' Just like Happy Families, he wanted to say. Maybe

putting such a positive spin on everything was part of her survival technique, but she seemed sharper and more observant than most, not the type to delude herself. He wondered if, deep down, she felt anger or bitterness for what had happened to her.

'As you can imagine, I never had much of a formal education, but even when I was little, I always loved reading, whatever I could get my hands on, whether it was yesterday's paper or the cereal packet. Then I started writing. First it was just a journal, with my thoughts and things, then it grew. Brian used to have these pop stars and people hanging around the house all the time – it was like one big party. I used to chat to them, ask them questions and stuff and write it all down. They treated me like a kid sister and they didn't mind talking to me – when they weren't totalled, that is. I suppose nowadays I'd write a blog and someone would turn it into a bestseller. Diary of Wild Child. It would be good, wouldn't it?' Catching his eye, she smiled. 'Most of them were really quite ordinary, sweet guys. Anyway, I started doing interviews for one of Brian's mates who had a music paper, and one thing led to another.'

'What about Brian?'

She sighed. 'He had a heart attack. It was a couple of years ago. He wasn't even sixty, poor sod. Too much rock 'n' roll, I suppose, plus he was in bed with a couple of beautiful Russian hookers at the time. Personally, I hope I die alone in my bed, but I guess it's the way Brian would have wanted to go if he could have chosen, so I'm happy for him. I'd moved out long before then, but I was still sad when I heard. He was a great bloke and I owe him a lot.'

'So he was in his forties when you and he—'

'Hooked up?' Meeting his eye, she smiled, and said, 'A bit younger. About your age.'

'There's still a word for it,' he said forcefully, draining his glass. He tried not to imagine what she must have looked like. It was all getting a bit close to home, even though he'd never fancied any fifteen-year-old girl, at least not since he was that age. 'I now understand where you're coming from, but why did your article touch such a chord with Joe Logan?'

'He never actually said. My guess is that he knew someone who disappeared one day and didn't come back. He seemed really moved by it. Loss is one of the main themes in his book, loss of innocence, loss of youth, loss of friends, which is why I thought he might be interested in the first place. Joe was one of those people who was permanently searching for an answer, but of course he never found it.'

'You say you're curious. Didn't you ask him what happened?'

She shifted in her chair and folded her arms, as though suddenly cold. 'I'm always curious. It's part of the job. But as I told you before, he hated discussing anything intensely personal. He'd scuttle back into his little hole the minute you got close. Have you read his book yet?'

'I haven't had time.'

'I thought you liked to get the full picture.'

'The factual picture, not the fictional one.'

'There's a lot of him in that book, but we've been over all that before, haven't we?'

He heard the muffled sound of his phone ringing in his jacket pocket and reached for it. Arabella Browne's name was on the screen. 'Excuse me,' he said, standing up quickly and walking over towards the door to take the call. He couldn't risk Anna overhearing a word.

'Where are you?' Browne said gruffly. 'Sounds like you're in a bar.'

'I'm interviewing someone.'

'That's what you lot always say. What's wrong with a decent interview room?'

'Too hot.'

'Well, get your handsome hide over here now or we'll start without you. This new lady detective of Grainger's is champing at the bit and I was up till three this morning. I want to be done by midnight, if that's OK by you.'

As Donovan put her key in the lock, she heard the sound of the TV blaring from the front room. Her sister Claire was still up. She let herself in, dumped her bag in the hall and put her head around the door of the sitting room. Claire was lying on the sofa, feet up on one of the arms, still in her work suit. She was watching *Newsnight* and had a glass of wine in her hand. The remains of a bowl of Frosties sat on the floor beside her.

'I thought you'd be in bed,' she said, as Claire looked up and muted the telly.

'I've only just got in myself. You look knackered. Hard day?'

Donovan nodded and sat down on the arm of the sofa. 'I've just been in the pub with Justin and Dave and a few of the others, but I've left them to it. I had a couple of J20s and some soup and decided to call it a day. I need my bed.'

'I'm not surprised. You were out even earlier than me this morning. Remind me, where were you off to?'

'A school in Dorset. We had to pick up some things belonging to the murder victim, Joe Logan. Sadly, we didn't find what we were looking for, but some of it was interesting. If you have a sec, I wanted to ask you about Logan. I found out he went to Bristol.'

'Go and get yourself a drink and I'll turn this thing off. There's a bottle of red open on the kitchen table.'

She went down the narrow corridor to the kitchen, which was at the back of the house, and helped herself to a large glass of red. The house was in the middle of a low-built Victorian terrace, only a couple of streets away from the river in Hammersmith. It had just enough space for the two of them, although neither of them spent much time there except at weekends. With both of them working long hours, keeping it tidy was the main problem. She took a wine glass out of the cupboard. How Logan had managed with so few personal possessions amazed her. If she had to pack all her stuff away, it would probably fill several containers.

Going through all of Logan's things, looking at his clothes, his books and other personal items, had added some colour to the voice that came through so clearly in his novel. She had been surprised to find how much she had been enjoying it until car-sickness kicked in on the journey back from Dorset. As well as a simple, forthright style, he had a keen sense of observation and irony, and the main characters came alive on the page. But the emotion that came through the clearest was guilt. It seemed very real. Everybody they had talked to had played down the autobiographical side of it, but having read it now, she was less sure. The modern-day part, starting with the funeral and focusing on the complex relationship between the five friends, had more than a ring of truth, as did the flashbacks to the time they were all at university together. Logan had changed the name of the university town, but it was easily recognisable as Bristol. It made her wonder how much else was true.

She took her wine back into the sitting room and sank down into an armchair.

'I suppose you're working?' Claire asked.

She nodded. 'It's all go at the moment, although we seem to be making some progress. It turns out the murder victim was at Bristol. I wondered if you knew him. He's a couple of years older than you but I was hoping your paths might have crossed. He read English and Drama.'

'The name doesn't ring a bell. Sorry. Why so interested in where he went to university?'

'I've been reading his book *Indian Summer*. Part of it is set in Bristol when he was a student. It seems very real.'

'Any good?'

'Yes. It's actually quite intriguing.'

'Perhaps I should borrow it when you finish. How old was he?'

'Thirty-eight.'

'It's just possible we overlapped, but the university buildings are spread out all over the place and the English and Drama departments are nowhere near the Law faculty. Unless we had friends in common, I probably wouldn't ever have come across him.'

'We don't know who his friends were, that's one of the problems. It's something we need to find out. I'm particularly interested because of the book.'

'You should contact the university. I'm sure there's a website for alumni. You could try putting an ad in and see if anyone remembers him.'

20

It was nearly one in the morning by the time Alex left the restaurant. He was exhausted, barely able to stand by the end of the shift. On the plus side, the restaurant had been more or less full all evening and working flat out had helped take his mind off things. All he could think about was Joe and Paul and the few words he had exchanged with Danny earlier on. The conversation with Tim had been less than satisfying. It was all very well for Tim to tell him not to panic. Had Tim sent the emails? But if so, what was the point? Tim never did anything that wasn't carefully thought through from start to finish and the rationale wasn't clear. It was more likely to be Danny and he hoped Tim had been able to get hold of him. In his most paranoid moments that night – on his own in the men's, accompanied by some vodka that he had stashed away – Alex wondered if either Tim or Danny was capable of murder, deciding to silence the rest of them after all those years. Tim stood to gain the most by getting rid of them all. No more skeletons in the cupboard to rattle at an inconvenient moment while he made his way up the greasy pole. But he'd known Tim for most of his life and the thought was so unpleasant, so unrealistic, he forced it from his mind. Whoever it was, it dawned on him that he wasn't safe either, possibly none of them were.

Wrapped in the cocoon of his thoughts, the journey home from the restaurant on the tube passed without notice. He almost forgot to get out at Kensal Green. From the station, he cut through the backstreets and turned down Chamberlayne Road towards home. He was about to cross the road, when a car raced around the corner, causing another car to swerve, and skidded to a halt in the middle of the next block of shops. Two men jumped out. One remained by the car, while the other ran up to a door and rang a bell. The car was unmarked, but he was sure it was the police. It also looked like they had gone to Paddy's flat, which was over a drycleaner's, recognisable even from a distance by its striped awning. Alex stopped in the shadow of a bus shelter and watched. After banging on Paddy's door, the man stepped back and stood looking up at the first-floor window. Under the orange glow from the street lamp, his face was clearly visible and Alex recognised him. It was Minderedes. The lights upstairs were off. Either Paddy was in bed and refusing to come to the door or, more likely, he was out again for the night. The two men stood craning their heads upwards, as though they didn't believe the flat was empty. Unless they broke down the door, they were in for a long wait. Paddy wouldn't be back until morning.

Hunching his shoulders, hands in his pockets, he turned and walked back towards the tube, not daring to look around, any moment expecting to hear the thud of footsteps behind him. He had to find somewhere safe for the night. He didn't trust using his phone and went back into the tube station where he found a call box in working order. Although it was late, Tim was an insomniac at the best of times, and even more so when he had a big case on the boil. Alex was sure he would still be working, poring over papers in his study.

He dialled Tim's number, which he knew by heart, and Tim picked up immediately.

'It's Alex. We've got to talk.'

'Are you drunk? Do you know what time this is?'

'I'm not drunk and don't pretend you were asleep.'

'I'm working. What is it you want?'

Alex explained what had just happened. 'Thanks to you telling me not to talk to the police, I now seem to be the chief suspect.'

'You mustn't speak to them.'

'So you keep saying. I need somewhere to stay, at least for tonight, until I work out what to do.'

'Well, you can't stay here. Why don't you go and find a hotel?'

'I haven't got any money on me, I obviously can't go home to get some, and I don't want to use a credit card. They might trace me.'

Tim sighed. 'You think you're bloody Jason Bourne now, do you?'

'Look, they found me somehow. I just need a bit of time, that's all, and we've got to talk. Did you manage to get hold of Danny?'

'Yes. He's coming over here tomorrow morning.'

'Good. That's another reason for you to put me up. It's either that, or I hand myself in.'

*

224

'Are you going to be OK?' Tartaglia asked, coming back into the room.

'I'm fine now, thanks,' Gerachty said in a matter-of-fact voice. 'Don't know what came over me.'

He wasn't deceived. She looked uncharacteristically shaky and washed out beneath what was left of her make-up. 'Are you sure?' he asked, even though he could see that his concern wasn't welcome.

'Positive, although my head hurts. I think I must have banged it on a chair when I fell.'

They were in Browne's office in the basement of the Westminster building, Gerachty sitting in Browne's battered old chair sipping some brandy that the pathologist kept in her drawer for such emergencies. The post mortem on Paul Khan was still going on in a room along the corridor, but Browne had nearly finished and he had thought it safe to leave and see how Gerachty was doing.

He and Gerachty had been watching the proceedings from behind the glass wall, Gerachty sitting beside him ramrod straight, as though at a parade. They could hear Browne's comments to her assistant over the two-way speaker system, and could make comments of their own if they chose to. Gerachty had said nothing, which he thought a little strange, and the preliminaries had just finished, when he heard a sound and saw Gerachty slip to the floor at his feet. Most people he had come across felt queasy at their first post mortem, some threw up, and some, like Gerachty, fainted. He had seen even the biggest, toughest, ex-rugby-playing constable reduced to a mass of jelly on the lino with the first cut or buzz of the saw, and everyone accepted it as par for the course. But Gerachty seemed to mind more than most.

'I guess you think I'm a right prat now,' she said bitterly.

He shook his head, wishing that she wouldn't be so hard on herself. 'It happens to the best of us, honest.'

'What, even you?'

'Yes. Even me.'

'You're just saying that.'

'The first few times, I didn't faint, but I well and truly puked. Didn't matter whether I'd had anything to eat or not and you can imagine the jokes that went around. Someone even stuck one of those airline sick bags to my computer with my name written on it. Trust me, it's ten times worse if you're a bloke.'

She gave him a hard look, as if she didn't see the difference. 'I really thought I was going to be OK, but the smell when we arrived . . . Jesus, it turned my stomach. Then I was sitting there trying not to think about what was going on in front of me and suddenly the room starts to swim. Next thing I know, well, you're carrying me in here.' She pursed her lips. 'I didn't . . .'

He smiled, wondering what she was worrying about. 'You didn't do anything. You were out cold and light as a feather, so don't worry.'

'Did anyone—'

'Nobody saw what happened except me and I promise I won't tell a soul.'

She looked relieved. 'Thanks.' She took a slug of brandy. 'I suppose you know it's my first post mortem.'

'Yes.'

'It's also my first homicide.'

'I gathered that too.'

'I was in vice before.' She held the glass up to him. 'Cheers. This brandy's not at all bad, you know. It's making me feel a whole lot better.'

'That's what it's for.' He realised, looking at the bottle sitting on Browne's desk, that she'd had quite a bit of it since he'd left her on her own, but at least it was softening the edges nicely. 'Arabella's just wrapping things up now, so I can see you home, if you like.'

'I'll be fine. If we're done here I'll go and find a cab.'

'I'll come upstairs with you, then.'

As she got to her feet, she was still a little shaky and he supported her with his hand and picked up her bag for her. 'Thanks. I can take it from here.' She turned to the little mirror on the wall and smoothed down her hair. 'Well, now I've no secrets any longer, I can honestly say you're not at all as bad as I was led to believe.' She caught his eye in the mirror, then rubbed a smudge of lipstick from the corner of her mouth.

'I'm delighted to hear it. And what exactly were you led to believe?'

She waved him away with her hand. 'Oh, you really don't want to know.'

'Yes I do.'

She smiled and tucked a stray strand of hair behind her ear. 'You won't hold it against me?'

'I promise.'

She turned to face him. 'Well, just that you're one cocky bastard, that you think you're God's gift, that you have DCI

Steele in the palm of your hand, that she's sleeping with the Chief Super and . . .'

'Is that all? I'm surprised they didn't tell you I'm sleeping my way to the top too.'

'They left that bit out, but I can see it now,' she said, walking a little unsteadily out the door into the corridor.

He followed. 'You should know not to listen to office gossip. It's rarely accurate.'

'You're right. They're clearly badly informed and I'll ditch my source. It's obviously a case of very sour grapes.' They were half way up the stairs, when she stopped on the landing and turned to look at him. 'I'm really bitter to be losing this case, you know.'

'It hasn't happened yet. It's not a done deal.'

'No, but it will be. The writing's on the wall. The post mortem's the clincher, even I can see that, and it's the most logical thing to do, if logic comes into it, which it should.' She started slowly up the stairs again. 'I don't mind so much, now I've met you. I know you'll do a good job.'

'Thanks.'

Again she stopped. This time she held out her hand. 'Truce?'

He shook it and nodded. 'Truce. Now, let's go and find you a cab.'

21

The next morning, Tartaglia yawned and drew back the bedroom shutters. Momentarily dazzled by the brightness, he gazed up at the sky. It was a bright, limpid blue, with not a cloud to be seen. He had only had a few hours' sleep and his head felt thick, as though he had taken a sleeping pill. Most Saturday mornings he would go for a run, but it was already nearly seven. The morning briefing was at eight and he needed to pick up some papers before his meeting with Angela Harper. He showered, made a pot of strong coffee and heated up a little milk. When it was ready, he filled a large breakfast cup, opened the back door and went outside. All was quiet next door, which wasn't surprising, given that the music hadn't stopped until about three that morning. He had got home from the post mortem just after two and had fallen asleep almost straight away. He was amazed that none of the neighbours had complained. Maybe, like him, they had more important things to worry about.

The air was still cool and fresh and he sat down at the small garden table, put his bare feet up on another chair and lit a cigarette. He leant back, his face full in the sun, closed his eyes and listened to the sound of the birds. He was dozing, imagining himself by the sea again in southern Italy, sand between his toes, the water lapping at his feet, when he was jolted by a noise just over the wall in the next-door garden. It sounded like someone yawning, followed by a series of heavy, drawn-out sighs, as though they were stretching. He opened his eyes and saw the face of a young woman with curly, butter-blonde hair peering through a gap in the trellis that ran along the top of the wall.

'Hiya,' she said sleepily, followed by another yawn. 'Thought I could smell someone smoking. Can you spare a ciggie?'

'Sure.' He didn't recognise her but that meant nothing. He got to his feet, suddenly aware of the fact that he had nothing more than a small towel around his middle. It was one of those funny things about smoking, he thought, as he handed her the Marlboros and his lighter. You could be sitting almost anywhere, enjoying a cigarette, and a total stranger would come along and think nothing of asking for one. And often, before you knew it, they were telling you their life story. He had heard from his sister that walking a dog had the same effect.

'Good party?' he asked, as she fumbled with the lighter, fingers trembling.

'Not bad. Haven't had a Red for years. Everyone smokes Lights these days.'

'Lights have no taste.'

'I suppose, but I get dizzy on these things, they're *so* strong. At least it'll get me going, and I sure need it.' She finally lit one and, eyes narrowed, took a deep draught then handed him back the pack and lighter. 'That's better. We ran out last night and I haven't the energy to go to the shops.

I'm Christy, by the way.' She held out her hand. 'I'm a friend of Becs and Janelle. I'm just staying for a few days.'

'I'm Mark. I live here. You've got some stuff in your hair.'

Frowning, she combed her fingers through it and pulled out a collection of dried grass and leaves. She smiled. 'I fell asleep. Most people had gone, at least the ones that were going, and I was lying on the ground looking up at the stars and listening to the music. Next thing I know it's morning and the birds are making a right din. I'm thinking it's all a bit bright and I should go inside, then I smell your cigarette. It was a great wake-up call. Thank goodness it's Sunday and I don't have to go to work.'

'It's Saturday.'

She shrugged. 'Same thing.'

'Well, sadly I have to work and I'd better be getting on.'

'Is that coffee?' she asked, as he picked up his half-drunk cup, which was probably cold.

'Yes.'

'Do you have any more? My head's really killing me. I was thinking of making some but there's no milk – someone drank it all last night – and no coffee either, come to that.'

She looked so helpless and wrecked he decided to take pity on her. 'OK. You're welcome to what's left, although it's probably cold.'

'No worries. Anything's better than nothing.'

He went into the kitchen and poured out what was left of the coffee and milk into another large cup. When he took it outside, she was leaning limply on the wall with her face turned to the sun, eyes screwed shut.

'Here you go.'

'Ah thanks. You're a star.'

As she took the cup, he heard his mobile ringing in the kitchen. 'Just leave it on the wall when you're done,' he said.

'Thanks again,' she called out behind him as he sprinted inside. He picked up on the last ring just before it went through to voicemail and heard Geraghty's voice.

'Are you in the office?' As usual, she got straight to the point, not bothering with a greeting. She sounded surprisingly bright and brisk.

'No, but I'm on my way.'

'It's funny. I had you down as a morning person. Early bird catches the worm and all that.'

'Usually I am. I'll be there in about fifteen minutes.'

'Glad to hear it, because I've got a present for you and you'll need your full faculties. I'm emailing it over to you now. It's going to make your day.' He could hear the triumph in her voice. She hung up before he could ask her what it was and he shook his head, amused. Even after what she had said last night, she couldn't help notching up a point.

There was next to no traffic at that hour and the ride from his flat to the office in Barnes took less than ten minutes. They shared the low-built seventies block with a branch of the Flying Squad and a child-protection unit. Parking spaces in the small car park at the back of the building were usually at a premium and hotly contested, but on a Saturday it was more than half empty. The only people working were those with a pressing case, on overtime. He parked the Ducati by the wall and jogged up the stairs to the first floor. Most of the team were already in, ready for the briefing in the main office at eight, but first he wanted to read what Gerachty had sent. He sat down at his computer, logged on and clicked open the email:

Hi there, hot shot, our guys found this on Paul Khan's computer. We thought it was spam at first. Not at all sure what it means but it's along the same lines as the one you gave me. The email address is the same too. Nice stuff, eh? They must be crazy, although you knew that already. BTW, we've just sent the scans of the phone records over to your constable. Let me know if you get a hit. No doubt we'll speak soon. Looks like I'll be handing this one over to you, if you're fool enough to want it. Kate.

From: alice-in-wonderland91@hotmail.com
Subject: Re: Catch up
Date: 15 July 2010 19:07:54 GMT
To: paulnkhan@me.com

gilded oars. Magdalen Coll. Oxford 1912. He raises the candle high so she can see. The coat of arms and faded letters shine in the guttering light, proclaiming the names of the dead and long-forgotten. To impress, He recites: 'When the white flame in us is gone, and we that lost the world's delight stiffen in darkness, left alone to crumble in our separate night. When your swift hair is quiet in death, and through the lips corruption thrust has stilled the labour of my breath. When we are dust. When we are dust.' She doesn't hear him. Stupidly, transfixed she imagines the glory of another age. The would-be poet pours another glass of wine and spreads his jacket on the damp wooden floor. The smell of decay rises up like incense in the

Like the previous email, it made little sense and began and ended in mid-sentence. He wondered what the point was, and read the lines over several times. But, apart from the obvious mention of oars and what seemed to be a boat-house and the link to where Paul Khan's body had been found, nothing else struck him. He gathered together the necessary papers for his meeting with Harper and left for the eight o'clock briefing.

Since he had last seen Angela Harper she had moved from Wimbledon to a small house in Putney. It was only ten minutes on foot from the office, across the common, and he set off in good time, enjoying the walk. The large expanse of dry, open grassland was punctuated with areas of dense wood-land and scrub. Avoiding the roads, he chose a path that cut through the middle, which was surprisingly busy at that time of day, being a popular route for joggers and dog-walkers. The grass on either side was long and had turned brown from the lack of rain. It was only a little after nine, but the sun was already strong and he could feel the sweat prickle the back of his neck.

Many of his colleagues viewed profiling as an arcane science, with profilers either held in awe or ridiculed, depending on their successes or failures. His own take on it was different. He was sceptical about profiling in general terms: it depended entirely on the quality of the individual. 'Rubbish in' equalled 'rubbish out' and profilers were not all born equal. As in every profession, there was a huge range of ability as well as experience and, in his view, only a small number were genuinely talented. In many ways, it was as much an art as a science and the truly gifted had a special insight or instinctive understanding that probably couldn't be taught. Harper was one of those few. He had worked with her before, both in an official and unofficial capacity, and each time she had managed to add a perspective that had been both different and invaluable. On top of everything, he liked her. While the basics of psychological profiling were not rocket science and any experienced detective could reach the same general conclusions, none of them could get under the skin of the mentally warped in the way that someone with Harper's background was used to doing.

By the time he arrived on her doorstep, his shirt was sticking to his back.

'Come in, Mark,' she said, giving him a quick peck on each cheek. 'I've just put the kettle on. Do you fancy a cup of tea?' She had a pleasant northern accent, although she had lived in London for years. She was dressed in jeans and a loose, sleeveless blue linen shirt. Judging from the pair of dirty rubber and canvas gloves in her hand, she had been gardening. Since he last saw her, she had cut her prematurely grey hair short, like a boy's. He decided that it suited her broad, strong-boned face, as did the slick of dark red lipstick, which she usually wore at all times of the day or night.

'A glass of water, please, with ice, if it's not too much trouble,' he replied, following her into the small, book-lined sitting room at the front. He had never understood the attraction of a cup of tea when it was so hot, but maybe that was his Italian blood coming out. 'I needed the walk, but it's boiling out there.' He wiped his brow with his hand and sat down on the sofa next to a large tabby cat, which was tightly curled up asleep on one of the cushions.

'Move Tigger if you want. He's the best hot-water bottle when it's cold, but not what you need on a day like this.'

He shook his head. 'I'm fine with cats and I don't think he'd like being disturbed.'

'You look very brown. Have you been away somewhere nice?'

'Sicily. It was over forty degrees, but at least I was in the water most of the time. You've caught the sun too.'

'Sadly, just in the back garden, I haven't had time to go away. I'll be back in a minute.'

He was just thinking that the room was a carbon copy of the one in her previous house, even down to the bright yellow paint and earthenware pots, which Harper liked to make in her spare time, when she reappeared with a mug of strong tea for herself and water for him.

'So what can I do for you this time?' she asked, sitting down in a large armchair opposite him and putting her sandalled feet up on a stool.

He explained about the two murders and showed her copies of the emails, photographs of Logan's and Khan's bodies as they had been found at the dumpsites, and the summary of the post-mortem report on Logan. He then ran through the key points that had come out of Khan's post mortem the night before. When he had finished, she drained her mug and put it down on the floor by her chair.

'I agree with you, it's not at all clear-cut, although it's far too early to come to any meaningful conclusions. However, I may be able to give you something that helps. Do you mind if I run through my thoughts out loud for a moment?'

'Please.'

'Chip in when you feel like it.' She stretched back and put her hands behind her head. 'Let's start with the first murder, as we know more about it. What's the crime telling us? The first thing is that the victim, Joe Logan, wasn't picked at random, he was selected. When was the CCTV camera at the cemetery knocked out?'

'A couple of days beforehand.'

'OK. The location was chosen in advance and I think it's very likely he'll have made some dummy runs. Have you checked the footage?'

'Yes, but the chip only has enough memory for fifteen days, then it re-writes. Apart from when he lets himself in and sprays the camera, there's nothing suspicious.'

'It's possible the killer knew how long the chip lasted and it's worth checking to see if anyone working there remembers someone asking about it. If not, I don't see him waiting fifteen days or more between the recce and taking out the camera. It's too long.'

'You mean, too risky?'

'Yes. This sort of person likes everything to run like a well-oiled machine. Too much can happen in fifteen days. To my mind, it will be more like two or three at most. I'd suggest you go back and look at the tape again. He'll probably have gone there in daylight, so as not to draw attention to himself. This guy is good at what he does. He may look quite innocent to one of your people watching the film.'

He nodded. Things were often missed and they would check again, although unless the killer had done anything outwardly suspicious, it would be difficult to spot him among the many people who used the cemetery. It would be more useful once they had a possible suspect.

'Next point, in no particular order, Joe Logan and Paul

Khan were tortured. But this is not somebody playing out their sadistic little fantasies, like the last individual you came to see me about. Here the torture is just a means to an end. The victims have something the killer wants. Going on what you've told me about Logan and Khan's backgrounds, I'm assuming it's more in the line of information, rather than something of physical value, like money or drugs.'

'That's what we assume.'

'OK. Let's also say you're right about the method of torture. We've all read about waterboarding in the papers, but we tend to forget why it's used. The main point is it's very effective, it leaves next to no physical trace and it gets results incredibly quickly. Apparently even the most hardened of individuals fall to pieces in a matter of seconds. So, the killer gets what he wants, the victims are now surplus to requirements, and he tops them in a quick and effective way. Single bullet to the head, point-blank range, no risk of Logan or Khan surviving and bearing witness.'

'It takes guts to look a man in the eye and pull the trigger like that,' Tartaglia said. 'There's no physical signs that he hesitated in any way, so it looks like he's done it before.'

Harper nodded. 'He did it cold. If you wanted to hire a killer, this is the sort of bloke you'd be looking for.'

'If you knew where to find him.'

'Yes. Which poses another question that we'll leave to one side for the moment. The killer knows his game, he's unfazed by it and is very unlikely to panic. So far, the behaviour is a hundred per cent consistent. The word that springs to mind to describe this individual is "efficient", like a machine. There's nothing spare or superfluous about his actions.'

'The way you describe it, he sounds like a pro.'

'Yes.'

'Then how does that tally with the rest of it? The emails, the dumpsites, etcetera, it's almost amateurishly theatrical.'

She smiled. 'I'm just about to come onto that. When he's done, you'd expect him to dispose of the body quickly and efficiently and make his getaway, right?'

Tartaglia nodded. 'Instead, he wants the bodies to be found and he mutilates both Logan and Khan.'

'Yes. The choice of sexual organs is significant, also the fact that he puts the man's penis in his mouth. He emasculates him first, then he ridicules him. It's highly symbolic and, in other circumstances, ritualistic. This is contradictory with what we know of our killer: both actions are unnecessary, they achieve nothing practical.'

'What about sending a message to others, some sort of a warning?'

'Surely killing him would have been enough, if that's the aim? No, it's a spiteful, petty action, and more than anything it reveals emotion. As you know, this sort of thing is incredibly rare in real life. Last time I saw that sort of thing was in a gangland killing many years ago. It was done as a form of post mortem humiliation of the victim. Anger and revenge were the driving forces. It turned out the victim had got a bit above himself and had been messing around with his boss's wife. Unfortunately, the boss was a well-known hoodlum with all the characteristics of a sociopath. What happened to the wife wasn't pleasant either, although we don't need to go into that. Going back to Logan's killer, we have another contradiction. The choice of dumpsite isn't efficient. We know it's not accidental, as it was selected in advance, so it must have some special significance, which warrants significant additional effort and risk. This again indicates some form of emotional engagement.'

'Unless he was just following orders.'

'That's very possible.'

'What about the way the bodies were positioned?'

'You mean, sitting?'

He nodded.

'Again it serves no practical purpose, but I can't read anything into it at the moment.'

'And the missing phones?'

'You said all the information was backed up elsewhere, so there's no reason to take them. It sounds like someone was having a bit of fun, which again doesn't ring true to character. Let's move onto the emails. Why send them? What's the point?'

'To frighten the victim in some way?'

She nodded. 'But how? It doesn't make me quake in my boots. We're not talking about a series of emails here, building to a climax.'

'There may have been others we don't know about, which were deleted.'

'Possibly. Even so, let's look at Joe Logan's actions. They may be able to tell us something. Imagine you're Logan for a minute. By all accounts he was intelligent and he must have been perceptive about life and human behaviour to be a writer. What would you do if you were in his shoes and you thought your life was in danger?'

'Come to us, or run away.'

'Yes. You wouldn't just stay put as though nothing had happened, would you? Clearly Logan didn't see the email or emails as life-threatening.'

Tartaglia frowned. 'It must have meant something to him, otherwise why bother sending it?'

'Maybe the message wasn't that clear to him either.'

'It's not exactly a bullet in an envelope or a dead horse's head on the pillow, I agree,' he said, still puzzled.

'Exactly. It's not straightforward or efficient at delivering its message. Again this doesn't fit. The person who put the bullet in his head wouldn't mess about with sending a message that's hard to interpret.'

'You're right,' he said, feeling that he had been a little slow. 'They wouldn't send one at all. They wouldn't want to risk Logan running away somewhere they couldn't find him.'

'Nor would they want him running to you lot and giving the game away. They just want something from him and then when they get it, bang, he's gone. Same with Khan. End of story.'

'You're absolutely right. I hadn't looked at it that way.'

Harper shrugged. 'You're so close to everything, it's sometimes difficult to see the wood for the trees. Going back to the email itself, the message warns of what's going to happen, or at least it points to the place where the body will be found. We know that now with the benefit of hindsight, but it does so obliquely. Have you thought that it may be more for your benefit than the victim's?'

'I wondered, but I still don't see the point of them. Maybe they have nothing to do with the killings.'

'Come on, Mark. Neither of us pays much heed to

coincidence. Things happen for a reason. I think we have to assume that the emails are linked. Have you spoken to any of Logan's friends? They might be able to shed some light on his reaction.'

'He was pretty much a recluse, from what we can tell. There's someone, but he's done a runner.'

'That's interesting.'

He nodded. Finding Alex Fleming had become the top priority, but he seemed as difficult to pin down as smoke. His flat was now under surveillance in case he came back, and they would have a warrant in the next hour or so to search it. But in the meantime, he seemed to have flown the coop.

'Whoever's doing this has a specific reason. You should concentrate all your efforts on finding the link between the two victims. There will *be* a link and it will lead you back to him.'

Tartaglia sighed. While some things were clearer, without any idea of the motivation, they were no further to finding the killer. 'Without having a clue to what he's after, it's impossible to know if he's likely to do it again.'

'I'm afraid so. The sort of person we're talking about won't stop until he's done, or he's dead . . .'

'Or we catch him.'

Harper gave him a sympathetic smile and inclined her head. He felt his phone vibrate in his pocket and took it out. It was Jane Downes' number. 'Excuse me a minute,' he said to Harper, as he took the call. 'What is it, Jane? I'm in a meeting.'

'I've been cross-checking Joe Logan's contacts with Paul

Khan's, and I've got a few hits, so it seems they knew some of the same people.'

'Good work.'

'There's more. I went through the phone records, starting with the last two months. One name pops up on both. It's a man called Tim Wade. Joe Logan rang him a couple of times before he died, as did Paul Khan.'

'Again, good work,' Tartaglia said, remembering the deep, resonant voice on the answer machine of the man called Tim who had also mentioned an 'Alex'. 'Have we got an address?'

'Yes. Both home and work.'

'Don't call him first, just get someone over there right away. And if you find him, take him straight over to Kensington and call me immediately.' As he hung up, he looked over at Harper and smiled. 'I think we may have found the link.'

22

'So you really know nothing about these emails?'

Tim stopped pacing the carpet and glared at Danny, who was gripping the arms of his chair as though he were in a boat on a rough sea. He stuck out his chin. 'I told you I didn't send them, and I don't know who did, so shut the fuck up about it.'

They were in Tim's study with the door firmly closed and Alex watching from the comfort of an armchair in the corner, feeling like the umpire in a tennis match as they batted around the arguments and accusations. Tim's desk and the floor near it were littered with papers and files from the case he was working on and there was barely room to move. The room was hot, claustrophobic, and Alex hoped he wasn't going to have another nosebleed. Danny was wearing the same clothes as the day before and looked as though he hadn't been to bed at all. He reeked of stale smoke and booze. The way Alex saw it, Danny seemed to be telling the truth, answering consistently and not slipping up however hard Tim tried to wrong-foot him. Tim clearly thought otherwise. Alex wondered why – was Tim trying to deflect the spotlight from himself for some reason . . . ?

He had knocked on Tim's front door just after two that morning and had found him still dressed. With barely a word, Tim had shown him straight to the spare room, provided him with an airline packet of toothbrush and paste and a clean towel, then said he was going back to work. Alex had slept soundly until the screaming of one of the children had woken him, but his dreams had been horribly vivid and he felt as though he hadn't slept at all.

'Sit down, will you, Tim?' he said. 'You're making my head spin and this isn't getting us anywhere. We need to work out what to do.'

Danny shrugged. 'What can we fucking do?'

'Don't you care?'

'Of course I care, but what do expect me to do about it? I'm all out of ideas.'

'Joe and Paul are dead, which leaves us three. If we're all telling the truth and none of us sent those emails, then somebody's talked.' Seeing Danny again now, he thought he was the most likely leak, although he probably had no recall of what he said when high.

As if reading his mind, Danny glared at him. 'If you're talking about Ashleigh, I never said a word. It's just as likely to be you or Tim from where I'm sitting. And anyway, it was all a long, long time ago. Even if someone did find out, what are they going to do now? I mean, what could they prove?'

Tim sighed and shook his head. 'You don't get it, do you?'

'Yeah, I get it. Just 'cause I'm not some fucking ponced-up QC, you think I've nothing to lose? Is that it?'

'Calm down,' Alex said. 'Tim didn't mean that.'

'Well, it sounded like it to me. Some people never change.'

Danny reached into his pocket and pulled out a pack of cigarettes.

'You can't smoke in here,' Tim said.

'Come on, I need a fucking fag.'

'No.'

'Just one. I can't concentrate.'

'I said no.'

Danny pulled a face and tucked the cigarettes away. It was true, Alex thought, some things never changed. They were all still obediently doing what Tim told them to do.

'What I don't understand is why Joe and Paul had to die,' Alex said. 'What happened was an accident, wasn't it?' He looked at Tim.

'You were there, for Christ's sake. You know it was.'

'I'm just asking the question.'

Danny was nodding slowly. 'Yeah, it was an accident. You know that, Alex. I don't know why you're being funny about it.'

'OK, then why are Joe and Paul dead? Answer me that. I think we need to look at every possible angle.'

'Keep your voice down,' Tim said forcefully. 'I don't want Milly to hear. Naturally she doesn't know about any of this and I don't want to worry her.'

'That's the least of your problems, surely. You may be next on the list.'

'I told you to stop being so bloody melodramatic.'

Alex held up his hands. 'Look, unless we can work out who's doing this and why, it could be you next, or Danny, or me.' Unless the killer is one of us, he thought. He heard the sound of the doorbell.

'There's something I still don't get,' Danny said, scratching his beard. 'Ashleigh was nearly twenty fucking years ago. If you're right and there's a connection, why's this happening now, after all this time?'

'I agree,' Tim said. 'It doesn't make sense.'

'Maybe it's got nothing to do with Ashleigh.'

Alex shook his head. 'There's something we're missing, something important.'

'Well, I'm buggered if I know what it is,' Tim replied, flopping down on the chair behind his desk. 'Let's try and look at it logically. Joe and Paul never met before Bristol, did they?'

'No,' Alex said. 'Definitely not.'

'And they weren't best buddies in the first couple of years, right?'

'Yeah. They only really got to know each other properly when we all moved in to Ashleigh.'

'I asked you to come and live with us and you insisted Joe had to come too. He was your mate. I'd only met him a few times before that.'

'Are you trying to blame me?'

'Of course not, Alex. Stop being so sensitive. I'm just trying to establish the facts. You said you wouldn't move without him.'

'That's right,' Alex said, not sure where he was going with this. 'We'd shared a flat together in the second year and we were really good mates by then. I didn't want to ditch him.'

'OK. So they got to know each other in year three. Then didn't he and Paul share a flat, or something when they moved to London?'

'What's the point of this?'

'You're a bit slow this morning. If it's not to do with Ashleigh, maybe it's something that happened in London.'

There was another ring, this time longer and more insistent.

'Shouldn't you answer the door?' Alex said.

Tim shook his head. 'It's probably the postman. Milly will get it.'

'Maybe you're right,' Alex said, 'although I can't think what either of them could have done to get themselves killed. But then explain the email sent to Joe. It talked about some sort of a crypt. It reminded me of the little church at Ashleigh.'

'Most churches have crypts.'

'Ones that flood?'

'Crypts are damp. They're underground.'

'I'm not stupid, you know.'

'Guys, guys, calm down,' Danny said, waving his hands. 'Just cool it. We've been coming at it all one way. I think Tim's got a point, Alex. Joe shared Paul's flat in London for a few months, before he moved in with Fi and Sally.'

Tim nodded. 'They had some sort of a row, which is why Joe left. Do you know what it was about?'

There was a loud knock at the door and Milly burst into the room. She was wearing a dressing gown over a long, trailing nightdress and she was barefoot. Her face was flushed and her eyes were red and puffy, as though she had been asleep. In the background, the wail of a small child started up like a siren. 'Tim, it's the police. They want to speak to you.'

'Me? Did you tell them I'm here?'

'Yes. I said you were busy but they won't go away.'

Tim gave a heavy sigh and glanced at Alex, then at Danny. 'I'll handle this. You both stay here. Keep the door shut and don't, for God's sake, make a sound.'

'I understand you know Alex Fleming,' Tartaglia said.

Tim Wade nodded. 'We were at university together.'

'Have you been in touch with him recently?'

'I spoke to him only yesterday. Naturally we were both very shaken up by what's happened to Joe.'

'And Paul Khan. You know him too?'

'Yes, of course. He was also at university with us. I assumed that was why I'm here.' He looked at Tartaglia enquiringly.

'I see,' Tartaglia said, thoughtfully. 'I was wondering what the connection was.'

Wade was a big man, a good six-foot-three or four, with broad shoulders, a powerful handshake and a deep, resonant voice that must have been a pleasure to listen to in the court-room and which carried with it a natural authority. Whether due to his size or his personality, he made the interview room at Kensington Station feel cramped. Minderedes sat beside Tartaglia taking notes. Wade had made no fuss about going with them, offering to assist in any way he could, although he had also made it clear that as a senior member of the Bar, he knew his rights. What he didn't know, and didn't need to know, was that Minderedes had just returned from searching Alex Fleming's flat. Fleming's flatmate had conveniently returned earlier that morning and given them access without the bother of a warrant, but the search had yielded nothing of interest. Fleming, like Joe Logan, seemed to be a man of few possessions, none of which seemed to relate to either Logan or Khan.

'That's what makes what's happened particularly odd,' Wade continued. 'When I spoke to Alex, we were wondering what exactly happened. There wasn't a lot of detail in the papers. And why them? One death, however sad, you can dismiss as bad luck, or something, but two, well, it looks like—'

Tartaglia stopped him. 'Were Joe Logan and Paul Khan close friends?'

'They used to be, a long time ago, but they had some sort of a falling-out soon after university and they never patched things up, as far as I know.'

'What was it about?'

'To be honest, I never quite got to the bottom of it. But they were oil and water. Reading between the lines, there was probably an element of jealousy. Coming from an immigrant family, Paul was very driven, almost to the exclusion of anything else. Joe, on the other hand, was less focused, a bit of a drifter and a dreamer, if truth be told. I think part of him admired Paul's energy, but I'm not sure he shared his values.'

'But you were friends with both of them?'

'Yes. I liked them both. There was no need to take sides.'

Tartaglia nodded. Wade's calm, open manner gave a ring of truth to everything he said, but it was something they would cross-check as soon as possible.

'Going back to Mr Fleming, we need to speak to him. Do you have any idea where he is?'

'I can give you his phone number and address, if you like.'

'We already have them, thank you. But he's not at home and he isn't answering his phone.'

Wade smiled. 'Knowing Alex, he's probably staying with some woman. Have you tried the restaurant where he works? He's there most days.'

'I thought he was an actor.'

'He is, but work's pretty slow at the moment. The restaurant's name is L'Angelo and it's in Notting Hill, near the Portobello Road, not far from here.'

Minderedes made a note then looked up at Wade. 'There's something that's puzzling me, sir,' he said. 'I bumped into your friend Mr Fleming on the canal, just along from Mr Logan's boat.'

'When was this?'

'Wednesday last week.'

'The day Joe's body was found?'

'Yes, sir. He was asking all sorts of questions about Mr Logan.'

'That's right. He mentioned it when we spoke. From what I remember, he'd gone over there to see Joe – they'd arranged to meet – and he found you lot there instead. You must have been the one who told him Joe had had an accident. Funny sort of accident, if you ask me, or maybe he was so shocked he didn't remember that bit clearly.' He gave Minderedes a hard look.

'Did he also mention the fact that when I asked for his name, he gave me yours?'

'Mine?'

Although he masked it well, Tartaglia saw that this was news to Wade and that he didn't look pleased.

Minderedes nodded. 'Any idea why he would do that, sir?'

'Absolutely not.'

'He gave a false phone number and address as well. You can understand how it looks, sir.'

'Of course. What a very silly thing to do. Maybe he panicked, for some reason.'

'What reason?' Tartaglia asked. 'Was he feeling guilty about something?'

'Come on, Inspector. What's happened has naturally unsettled him, and even the most sensible people behave like complete plonkers sometimes, particularly when dealing with the police. I see it all the time and I imagine you do too.'

'OK, let's say we give him the benefit of the doubt for giving my constable a false name, address and phone number. But he was one of the last people to see Joe Logan alive. He also called him several times in the week he died and those calls are logged. When we leave messages asking him to get in touch and he doesn't return any of our calls, it looks, well . . .'

'It looks bad, I agree.'

'I'm glad you see our point. And now it seems as though he's done a runner.'

'We don't know that, Inspector. I'm sure there's a simple, innocent explanation. As I said, he's probably playing away.' Wade leaned forwards across the table with an ingratiating expression and folded his large hands. 'Look, I've known Alex since we were boys. We were at school together, then university. I know him like the back of my hand and I can vouch for him. He may be a bit fey at times, but he's a decent, honest bloke and he wouldn't hurt anybody, particularly not

Joe. They were very close. When I spoke to him he was incredibly upset. I guess if he's deliberately avoiding you, which isn't proven, that may be the explanation. Perhaps he feels he has nothing to add.'

'We still need to talk to him,' Tartaglia said. Whatever Wade said, Fleming's behaviour was suspicious.

'Of course. If I speak to him again—'

'You mean *when*, surely?'

'OK, *when* I speak to him again, I will explain to him exactly why he's got to get in contact with you. But he's not a suspect, is he?'

'At the moment, no.'

'Good. I'm glad we've cleared that up, because there are absolutely no grounds for you to think he is.' He looked at Tartaglia meaningfully, then sat back in his chair. 'Naturally we all want to find whoever's done this horrific thing and we'll help you in any way we can.'

'So you have no idea who would want to kill your two friends, or why?'

Wade shook his head and put his hand to his chest. 'Hand on heart, Inspector, I haven't a clue and nor has Alex. It's the question we keep asking ourselves. Are the two deaths linked? Is that your thinking?'

'We're keeping an open mind for the moment. The fact that the two men knew each other may or may not be significant.'

'Well, neither Alex nor I can think of a reason why. I'm not a great believer in coincidence, Inspector, but sometimes it's the best explanation.'

23

Donovan waited in the car outside L'Angelo, while Chang went in to see if Alex Fleming was there. The road was clogged with shoppers and tourists visiting the nearby Portobello Market. The handful of cafés dotted along the street seemed to be doing a roaring trade, and through the glass frontage she could see that L'Angelo, too, was full. The restaurant was set back from the road under a heavy black awning and looked expensive, with huge vases of flowers, pale walls and subdued lighting. Chang was at the bar, talking to a young woman in a white apron. Donovan scanned the other waiters, who were rushing between tables, but she couldn't see anybody matching Fleming's description.

Part of her regretted saying that she would stay in the car and leave it to Chang, but she felt exhausted. She had been up half the night finishing Joe Logan's book, which she had been unable to put down. On a normal Saturday it wouldn't have mattered. She would have slept in, gone to the gym and would probably be meeting a friend for lunch, or doing some shopping with Claire. Instead, the alarm had gone off at six-thirty and she had struggled into the office, making the eight o'clock briefing by the skin of her teeth. What they had learned since from Tim Wade had been interesting background stuff, although hardly the breakthrough they had been looking for. But the picture he had painted jarred with what she had read in Logan's book, which seemed to have more than a passing element of autobiography about it. There were other elements of the book that were almost alarming. She knew it was supposedly fictional, but the gap between the two niggled her. She pulled out her phone and called home, waiting at least a dozen rings until Claire finally answered. Donovan heard the sound of running water in the background.

'It's me. Can you hear OK?'

'Hang on a sec,' Claire said. 'Let me turn this off.' The noise stopped. 'Sorry, Sam, what did you say?'

'It's about Joe Logan. We've just found out the names of some of his friends. Tim Wade, Alex Fleming and Paul Khan. They were all at Bristol, and Wade and Khan both did law. I wondered if you had ever come across either of them?'

'No. Sorry. Like Logan, they must have been there before my time.'

'Khan's been murdered too. I need to find somebody who was there at the same time who might have known them. Please can you have a think?'

'OK. I'll call you back in a minute.'

As Donovan hung up, she glanced over at the restaurant again, just in time to see the waitress Chang had been speaking to walk across the room and disappear through a door at the back. Maybe Fleming was somewhere out of sight. Chang was sitting on a stool, studying his BlackBerry in a relaxed fashion. A minute later, a woman in a black trouser suit appeared from the back with the waitress and came over to Chang. She saw them exchange words. Reading the body language and Chang's expression, it seemed that Fleming wasn't there, after all.

Chang came sauntering out of the restaurant, hands in pockets, looking pleased with himself. He opened the car door and slid into the driver's seat. 'Fleming's not there now, but he's working the evening shift later on today. The manager said he'll be there somewhere between four-thirty and five. Apparently, they come in early to get something to eat before the shift starts. It all smelled pretty good to me and I'm starving. Should we wait? We could grab a sandwich somewhere nearby.'

'No, we'll come back later. Let's pick up something to eat on the way. I need to get back to the office and speak to Mark.'

'What's up?' he asked, glancing over at her as he put the car into gear.

'It's Logan's book, that's all. Some things just don't add up.'

'I thought it was just a novel.'

'Maybe, maybe not.' She switched on Heart FM and turned it up loud to stop him asking any more questions. She wanted to be alone with her thoughts.

They had just stopped for sandwiches and coffee at a little café on the Barnes side of Hammersmith Bridge when Claire called back. 'I've found someone for you to talk to, don't know why I didn't think of it when I had you on the phone. Her name's Fi Marshall, or Fi Langford as was. She was in her final year when I was a fresher and she also read law, although I got to know her because we were both in the drama society and she produced a play I acted in. She was pretty social and she says she knew both Joe Logan and Paul Khan really well. She's obviously heard what's happened and she sounds really shocked. I've just spoken to her and she's happy to talk to you. She lives in the back end of Fulham and she'll be at home for the rest of the day if you want to go and see her. I'll text you her phone number.'

'I just can't get my head around what's happened,' Fi Marshall said, waving a large, paint-spattered hand in the air as she showed Donovan into the tiny sitting room of her flat. 'When Claire called and told me you were looking for someone who knew Paul and Joe, I said I was only too happy to help.' She flopped into an armchair, her feet up on the edge. 'Do sit down.' Fi was very tall, nearly six feet, Donovan reckoned, with shoulder-length brown hair and a broad, good-natured face, which was finely freckled with yellow paint.

'Thanks for seeing me at such short notice. I hope I'm not interrupting,' Donovan said, choosing the sofa. She had left Chang downstairs in the car, eating his lunch. The smell of paint was overpowering and she now wished that she hadn't bolted hers on the way there.

'No probs. Phil's hard at work in the spare room and it's great to have an excuse to take a break. I've been doing the ceiling and my neck's bloody killing me.'

'I'm trying to get some background,' Donovan said. 'I've just finished Joe Logan's book *Indian Summer* and I was wondering how much of it's actually true.'

Fi gave her a broad, toothy smile. 'The ten-million-dollar

question. I've had so many people ask me. As you'd expect, some bits are and some aren't. Joe obviously made up all the stuff about the funeral and the trip to Ypres, although that's really just the hook to hang the rest of it on, isn't it?'

'I was particularly curious about Jonah's death. Did he commit suicide, or did someone bump him off, do you think? The narrator says right from the start that he's the only person who knows what really happened but he never tells us.'

'You're wondering if maybe Joe had some dark and dangerous secrets.'

Donovan nodded. 'Exactly.'

'Well, I don't think you're supposed to know what happened to him or to Peter. I think Joe liked the ambiguity. Of course in real life Peter is Tim, so there is no actual mystery.'

'Tim Wade, you mean?'

'The one and only.'

Donovan hadn't seen Wade being interviewed. Minderedes had described him as an arrogant prick, although Minderedes was defensively chippy when he thought he was being patronised. The portrayal of Wade's – or Peter's – character in the book was much less black and white and more interesting.

'Were you all happy to find yourselves in Joe Logan's book?' she asked, wondering if Wade had been able to see elements of himself in the character.

'Tim was hopping mad, but then he's always taken himself very seriously. Now he's a QC, he doesn't want to be reminded of how many magic mushrooms and hash brownies he used to put away. God forbid you ever mention it to his face. You know that old Bill Clinton quote about not inhaling marijuana? Well, that's Tim all over. Clinton's quote about sex also applies. I'm very fond of Tim, but he's a bit of a hypocrite and always has been.'

'The book's quite true to life, then?'

'Let's say Joe had the measure of Tim better than anyone. Joe was very perceptive about people.'

'Tell me about the house. It seems an extraordinary place.'

'That bit was real enough. Even though it was falling to pieces, Ashleigh Grange was a fabulous place, like something preserved from another age.'

'Who owned it?'

'Paul's uncle. He was a property developer who'd made a packet out of dodgy student lets in Bristol and Bath. He bought the estate thinking he could get planning permission to turn it into a hotel, with a health club and golf course, but he bit off quite a lot more than he could chew. The planners were a nightmare, and the local ramblers association was up in arms because the whole place was criss-crossed by public rights of way. Most of that part went over my head at the time, but I've often wondered what happened.'

'Was the place anything like in the book?'

'The main house is Victorian Gothic, with turrets and towers and stuff, not lovely classical Palladian the way Joe painted it, but the rest is more or less the same.'

'So, there's a lake with an island . . .'

'Yes, and the most beautiful little church and graveyard for the family who once lived there. I used to love reading the inscriptions, although some of them were so sad. There were several babies and young children buried there and I used to wonder what had happened, what the stories were behind it all. There was even a little patch for all the beloved doggies. I'd often take a book and a drink and go and sit by the water to read. It was the most peaceful place when Paul didn't have the music on full.'

'Did they live in the main house?'

'No. We weren't supposed to go anywhere near it. Apparently, it was unsafe, although I think Paul's uncle just said that because he wanted to keep us out. He let Paul and the other guys have the head groom's cottage and part of the stable block in return for keeping an eye on it all. The main house was boarded up, although we found a way in, and Paul knew how to disable the alarm in case it ever went off by accident. It was extraordinary inside, like a time capsule. It reminded me of Miss Havisham's wedding banquet in *Great Expectations*. You know, everything decaying, all spread out on the table just as it was the day she was jilted. We used to roam all over it, from the cellars to the attics and we held séances, although everyone got so spooked out one time we had to stop. Think of *Turn of the Screw* and you'll get the picture. It was absolutely foul in winter, real bone-aching cold and damp, and endlessly muddy. Crashing there was a last resort, unless you were absolutely wasted or couldn't get a lift back to town, but in the summer it was the most fabulous place for parties.'

'So, who was actually living there full time?'

'There were five of them, the magnificent five, they called themselves, or something silly like that. Maybe it was the famous five. Paul, Joe, Tim, Danny . . .'

'Danny?'

'Danny Black. He was another lawyer. And Alex.'

'Alex Fleming?'

'Yes. He was an old friend of Tim's. They were all in their final year.'

'We know about Alex Fleming, but I didn't know about Danny Black. Do you have contact details for him?'

'I do indeed. It's funny – I had Tim on the phone only last night wanting his number.' She frowned. 'Why are you so interested in all of this? It's a heck of a long time ago.'

'As I said, we do a lot of background research. The last time Joe Logan and Paul Khan spent any real time together seems to have been at university.'

Fi nodded as though it made sense. 'Do you have any idea why they were killed?'

'It's not clear at the moment.'

'Were they killed by the same person, do you think?'

'We're treating them as two separate investigations, but the fact that they knew each other is obviously something that has to be looked into.'

Fi nodded slowly again. 'It's odd, the two of them . . .'

'Yes. Now what can you tell me about Mary?' Donovan asked quickly, wanting to get Fi off the subject of the two murders. 'What happens to her is another unsolved mystery – or at least why she drowns is.'

'Mary? She was supposed to be based on me.'

'On you? I didn't realise that.' She couldn't hide her surprise. Physically Fi, with her broad shoulders and long, muscular limbs, was nothing like the rather shadowy, ethereal Mary. The way Donovan had pictured the dead girl was almost pre-Raphaelite, floating in the lake like Millais' Ophelia. Also, Mary seemed quite a weak and vacillating character, whereas Fi struck her as down to earth and practical. She couldn't reconcile the two and wondered if Fi had got it wrong.

'Why would you? As you can see, I'm alive and kicking, larger than life in fact. I must have put on a good two stone since university. Comes of sitting behind a desk all day and taking next to no exercise. I used to have long hair down to my waist, you know.' She gave Donovan another wide grin as though she herself found it an odd idea. 'Anyway, Joe said he based her on me to start with, then the character sort of took over, like she developed a life of her own, if that's possible.'

'If Mary's you, why . . .'

'Kill me off? I don't know. Again, poetic licence, I guess. The whole guilt thing that runs through the book stems from what happens to her. I suppose he needed a device, and it works don't you think?'

'Yes, it's very powerful. Particularly the scene when she drowns.'

Fi sighed and hugged her knees tightly. 'Well, like me, Mary couldn't swim. He got that bit right, at least. They all used to go swimming in the lake and take boats out, even at night, with candles and stuff, but I'd never go. Water scares me, particularly when I can't see what's at the bottom. They used to make fun of me but I paid no notice. I suppose Joe just took parts of me, but gave me a fictionalised ending. I hope to God I never drown.'

She looked at Fi questioningly. 'Why does Mary decide to go to the lake? She tries to get Jonah to go with her but he doesn't want to, and in a fit of pique or something she goes off by herself. I got the impression she and Jonah were more than just friends, at least on his side.'

Fi shook her head and smiled. 'I'm not quite sure why Joe put that in. He never fancied me, I know.'

'OK ... In the book you see her walk out the door, leaving them all behind sitting around drinking, and next thing they know someone else goes out and finds Mary floating in the water – dead. She's fully dressed, so why is she in the water? There's no explanation. Did she hit her head, did she slip ... ?'

Fi shrugged. 'That's the detective in you coming out. It didn't bother me, not knowing precisely. It's just one of those sad, inexplicable things, like when a toddler drowns in a pond. It's just an accident. The point is the effect it has on everyone else, in particular Jonah. It's what tips him over the edge. I asked him why Mary had to die, but he told me it worked better that way.'

'I see.' Fi seemed to be a little short on imagination and clearly what happened to Mary had no significance for her beyond the written page. Donovan wondered if maybe she was reading too much into things, then she reminded herself of the emails. They pointed directly towards the book and Ashleigh Grange. 'You must have spent a lot of time with them all,' she said.

'Yeah. It was pretty much a free house, easy come, easy go. Sometimes the dinners and parties lasted for days.'

'Did you have a relationship with any of them? I'm afraid I have to ask.'

'A relationship?' Fi laughed, rocking back in her chair at the thought. 'That sounds so grown-up. We were really only kids. I had a bit of a snog and a grope with Tim in the first year, but that's about it. They were all great fun but they were a real bunch of lads, especially Paul and Danny. They actually used to keep score, if you know what I mean.' She raised her thick brows for emphasis.

'What about the others? I mean when they were living in the house together.'

'As I said, that was the final year. Tim had just started going out with Milly, I think, and if he played around at all, he didn't let on. As for Joe and Alex, they just went with the flow I suppose.'

'What happened to the house?'

'I haven't a clue. As soon as my finals were over, I went off home. I think Paul, and maybe a couple of the others, might have stuck around for part of the summer, but you should ask Tim. This was all at the beginning of the nineties and things were pretty tough economically. I think Paul's uncle ran out of money, or time – or both – and either he sold the house and estate on to someone else to develop or the bank repossessed it. It will still be there, though, in some shape or form. The house and buildings were listed so they can't have pulled them down.'

'Just one last question, just to make sure. You're saying there was no accident?'

Fi looked surprised and shook her head. 'God no. It was all harmless fun. Nobody got hurt. That was all down to Joe's wonderful imagination. Poor sod, may he rest in peace, wherever he is.'

'She says Logan made it up?' Tartaglia leaned back in his chair, hands behind his head.

Donovan moved aside an old mug of coffee and sat down on the corner of his desk. 'That's right.'

He looked at her quizzically. 'You think she's lying?'

'No. I watched her carefully and there wasn't a glimmer of hesitation. If she was lying, she's bloody good at it.'

'But she was good friends with all of them, right? If something happened, you'd think she'd know about it.'

'Possibly.'

He shook his head. 'More than possibly. At some point, someone would have said something. These sort of things have a habit of coming out. Maybe it means nothing happened. It could be as simple as that.' He could tell she wasn't pleased by what he said.

'I know it all sounds far-fetched,' she said a little irritably, 'but going back to the book, the five of them agree to keep quiet about it. They make a pact.'

'That was a book. As I said, in real life secrets have a habit of worming their way out over time. If nothing else, the book would have started tongues wagging and you'd think – being a good friend – she would have heard something.'

'I know.' Donovan sighed. 'It doesn't make sense, but I still think that if something did happen, she genuinely knows nothing about it. Maybe I wasn't hard enough on her, though, in a way, does it matter if she's lying? If it all happened the way Logan describes it, then a young girl died and she's at the bottom of a lake near Bristol.'

Unconvinced, he folded his arms and gazed at her for a moment. In the absence of any new information on Logan's second book, she was giving too much importance to the first one and what he saw in her eyes troubled him. The fact that she had not been herself for a while, that she seemed to have lost her usual spark, was more than just the general tiredness that affected them all through lack of sleep. He wondered what lay behind it. Sam's instincts were often good, but it was such a wild theory, he wondered if her judgement had been dulled by whatever was affecting her. He would be shot down in flames if he went to Steele with it, with nothing to back it up. He wished now that he had made time to read the book. It was almost impossible to argue from a position of ignorance.

'You honestly think there's something in it, Sam? You really think a girl died and Logan wrote a book about it? Why would he do such a thing?'

'Guilt. Something definitely happened, even if Fi Marshall knows nothing about it.'

'You have no proof.'

She slid off the desk and folded her arms. 'The way he described it all, it's so incredibly vivid and real that there has to be a grain of truth. Add to that what we know about Logan's character. He acted like a man with a secret.'

'Or a bit of a loner, someone dysfunctional.' Her expression tightened and he wished he hadn't spoken so dismissively.

'Maybe . . . I still wonder if writing the book was some sort of therapy.'

'OK. Let's say for the sake of argument that a girl drowned nearly eighteen years ago and the five decided to cover it up. Why wait until now to kill Joe Logan and Paul Khan?'

'I don't know.'

'And if her death was an accident, like in the book, why bother? And why torture Logan and Khan? Also, Logan's book

266

came out a while ago. I keep harping back to this, but why is it all happening *now*? What's triggered it?'

She looked down, kicking the carpet with the toe of her shoe. 'It sounds rather lame when you put it like that.'

He gazed at her for a moment, following the neat, pretty lines of her profile. 'I just wish we could find that second book.'

She turned on him fiercely. 'But where does Paul Khan's death fit in with that? Don't tell me *he* was writing another book about his university days?'

'You have a point. I was forgetting about that. The problem is, we're still missing such a huge chunk of the jigsaw. The fact that Logan and Khan knew each other is the only concrete thing we've got.' He stood up, deciding he needed to take a quick break and go outside for some fresh air and a coffee. His head was spinning and he wasn't thinking clearly. 'Maybe we should talk to Tim Wade again. It can't do any harm and we need to get to the bottom of this bloody book – if nothing else to rule it out. Take Nick with you. He knows what we went over with Wade earlier this morning. What worries me is that with two men already dead, will the killer stop there?'

24

Minderedes found a space on a yellow line outside Tim Wade's house and he and Donovan got out of the car. It was a mixed neighbourhood, downright seedy in places, but tucked well away from the main roads, the little criss-cross of streets in the immediate area where Wade lived had come up in the world. The row of spacious, redbrick Edwardian houses, with their shiny chrome door furniture and spanking new 4x4s on off-street parking bays, stood out like gleaming teeth in a mouth riddled with decay.

After all Donovan had heard about Wade – and had read about his fictional alter ego, Peter, the fixer among the five – she was curious to meet him face to face, although she wondered just how helpful he would be. They had already decided not to mention that they had spoken to Fi Marshall, although it was possible she had called ahead to warn Wade.

With Minderedes in tow, Donovan walked up the wide, tiled path to the front door and rang the bell. Almost immediately, a fair-haired woman answered the door. She wore jeans and a flowery pink shirt and was carrying a handbag, keys and a plastic shopping bag as though she was on her way out.

Donovan held up her ID. 'We're—'

'Police. Yes, I know.' She glanced at Minderedes. 'I suppose *you* want Tim again.'

'Yes,' Donovan replied. 'Is he in?'

The woman nodded. 'You'll find him in the back garden. Close the door behind you, will you?' She brushed past them and disappeared down the path. They went along the hall into a huge, open-plan kitchen that ran the width of the house, with a large conservatory-style extension. In a far corner of the garden beyond, three men were gathered around a table in the shade of a tall tree. Their voices carried across the lawn and they appeared to be in the middle of a heated discussion.

'Which one's Wade?' she asked Minderedes, as they stepped through the open French doors.

'The big chap on the left.' As he spoke, Wade looked around, stopped in mid-sentence and stood up. The other two men also turned their heads.

'Holy shit,' Minderedes muttered. 'Looks like Christmas has come early. That's Alex Fleming.'

'Which one?'

'On the right.'

'You'd better go and get him, then.'

She followed behind as Minderedes strode towards Fleming, who slowly got to his feet. He looked paralysed, like a rabbit caught in the headlights, although probably more with surprise than fear, his mouth slightly open, arms hanging limp at his sides. The garden walls weren't that high but she hoped he wouldn't be silly enough to try and run away. She felt in no mood for a chase.

'Alex Fleming, I need you to come with us now,' Minderedes said. 'You do not have to say anything, but it may harm your defence—'

'Hang on,' Wade said, marching over to Minderedes and towering above him. 'Keep your voice down. Why are you cautioning him?'

'But it may harm your defence if you do not mention ...' Minderedes continued as though he hadn't heard, still looking at Fleming.

'I said, enough,' Wade shouted.

Donovan held up her hand. 'We'll come to you in a minute, Mr Wade. As you well know, we've been looking for Mr Fleming. He's a possible suspect in a murder investigation and—'

'Alex is no suspect.'

'—and, as I'm sure you know, harbouring a suspect is a serious offence.'

'I'm not harbouring anyone. Alex has only just arrived. Tell them, Alex ...' He looked at Fleming, who sighed and shook his head.

'It's not going to wash, Tim. And it's time I spoke to them. I should have done it a lot sooner.'

'Yes, Mr Wade. Now, I suggest you keep quiet until DC Minderedes has finished.'

'... if you do not mention when questioned something which you later rely on in court. Anything you do say may be given in evidence.'

'I understand all of that,' Fleming said, spreading his hands and looking from Minderedes to Donovan. 'You really don't need to bother. I'm happy to go with you.'

'I'm coming too,' Wade said, taking hold of Fleming's arm. 'You don't have to answer any questions.'

'Thank you, Mr Wade. We'll need to speak to you too.'

'What about?'

'About what really went on at Ashleigh Grange.'

Wade folded his arms and compressed his lips into a hard line. She turned to the man in dark glasses and tight black jeans, who was still sitting in the shade, picking his teeth as though the rest of them weren't there. 'Are you Danny Black, by any chance?' The man seemed to consider the matter, then nodded slowly. 'Right. You'd better come too. Ring for backup, will you Nick? We're going to need two more cars.'

Several hours later, Tartaglia sat in an empty interview room in Kensington Police Station. Alex Fleming's signed statement lay on the table in front of him and it was dynamite. He had been trying to get hold of Carolyn Steele, but she was at a work conference somewhere out of London with her phone switched off. Fleming was cooling his heels in another interview room down the hall, while Donovan and Minderedes were finishing off with Tim Wade and Daniel Black. Drumming his fingers on the table, he glanced down at the statement again, although it was familiar by now:

STATEMENT GIVEN BY ALEXANDER CHRISTOPHER FLEMING – KENSINGTON POLICE STATION, July 17th, 2010

... We'd all just finished our finals and were letting off steam. Some people were staying at the house, kipping on the floor, and more people started arriving during the day. I don't know who they all were. Some were friends, some were friends of friends, plus there were some new-age types from the next-door farm who used to hang out with us. By evening there was quite a crowd and we decided to go over to the main house and set up the music there. We'd been drinking all day and I must have been pretty pissed. We'd also had a few joints and stuff. I remember dancing outside on the lawn with some girl. She was a first year who Paul had invited, but I don't know her name. It stays light until late at that time of year and there was this chapel. It's on an island in the lake, about ten feet off shore. You get to it via a little bridge. Someone, I think it might have been Danny, suggested going down into the crypt for a laugh. It was quite a spooky place with old coffins and stuff. We got candles from the house and a group of us went into the church and down into the crypt. Some of the girls got a bit scared and I went back to the house with them. When I saw the email someone had sent Joe I knew that's what they were talking about. Whoever sent it must have been there but I have no idea who it was. There were quite a few people in there at one point. The girl I was dancing with had gone off somewhere. I saw her later with Paul. I remember feeling a bit miffed about it. But there were lots of other people around. I have no idea what time this all was. I wasn't keeping track. But I remember hearing the clock at the stables strike midnight at one point. Later on, maybe an hour or so later, someone said they were going for a swim. Next thing, a whole load of us took off for the lake. It was pitch dark, but the moon was full and we could see quite easily. We took off our clothes and dived in. I can still remember it. There were screams and shouts – a lot of noise. The water wasn't that cold once you were in. We were all larking around, playing tag and stuff. Some people swam off to the pontoon in the middle and started diving off it. Suddenly the girl was there again. She swam up to me and prodded me. When I tried to catch her, she slipped away. She was a better swimmer than I was and she was laughing at me, teasing me, being really provocative. I thought I was in with a chance again. Then she disappeared under the water. I don't know where she went but she must have been holding her breath for a long time. Even in the moon-light, it was difficult to see. I thought I heard her call. I knew she was hiding somewhere and I swam towards the shore to look for her. I thought maybe if I hid, I could watch for her and surprise her. I swam under the branches of some trees and stopped, hoping I'd see her. It was very dark and quite shallow and I crouched down. I could hear splashing and voices coming from the far side of the lake. I waited for a bit, but I didn't see the girl. My head was spinning. I suppose I was pretty high and I needed to sit down somewhere. I started towards the bank. Then I fell over her. I couldn't really see much but I knew right away it was a person, a girl. She was naked, lying half in, half out of the water mixed up in some reeds. I thought it was a joke. I thought it was the other girl messing around. I grabbed her and tried tickling her, but she didn't move. She just lay there. I thought maybe she'd passed out, had too much to drink, or something, so I scooped her up in my arms and carried her up the bank. I laid her down on the grass. I must have been very stoned. I felt really giddy suddenly and I remember puking up. Then I went to sleep for a bit. When I woke, she was still there. She wasn't moving. I thought maybe something was wrong so I tried to shake her but she was out cold. I called out but everyone had swum over to the other side of the lake. Either they didn't hear me shouting over the music, or they didn't want to. I remember standing there wondering what the fuck to do. They were playing 'Suicide Blonde' just at that moment, which was rather ironic. I ran to where I'd left my clothes and got dressed. I was going to go back to the house and get help, when Tim appeared from somewhere or other. He'd fallen into the lake with his clothes on and was soaked. I tried telling him what had happened, but he just stood there, swaying, dripping on the grass, not really taking it in. He kept going on and on about feeling sick and wanting to get out of his clothes. He wasn't making much sense. When I finally did get through to him, he told me she'd be fine, that she'd probably had too much of something or other and passed out. He said she just needed to sleep it off. He then told me to go home and we'd see how she was in the morning. I didn't know what else to do and I was so tired. I suppose I wanted to believe what he said. So I walked back with him to the stables and we both went to bed. I don't know where the others were, if they were

ELENA FORBES

in their rooms or still up at the house. It was just getting
light when Tim came and woke me up. He had sobered
up and he had Paul and Danny with him. They couldn't
wake Joe, for some reason. I told them what had
happened, as far as I could remember it. I don't think
they believed me. They said they wanted to see for themselves, so we went down to the lake. Problem was, I'd
forgotten where I'd left her. While we were looking
around, I started to think I'd dreamt it all. I hoped she'd
just passed out, maybe needed to sleep it off, and that
she'd eventually got up and gone home. But after a bit
we found her. She was lying on the grass under the
trees, hidden behind some bushes. I was sure I'd left her
closer to the lake. I wondered if somebody had found
her and tried to move her. Or maybe she'd woken up
and moved herself. It was then that it hit me that she
was dead. I also realised that she wasn't the other girl.
It was a real shock. I'd never seen anyone dead before.
Someone, Paul, I think, said that he thought he'd seen
her earlier with some bloke and that they were heading
towards the boathouse. Danny said he thought he remembered her too, so it looked as though she had been at
the party. We decided to take a look in the boathouse,
although I'm not sure what we expected to find. When
we got there, we saw her bag on the floor, along with
some clothes and shoes. She'd obviously left them there
to go swimming. It was pathetic seeing them gathered
in a little pile, knowing that she wasn't coming back
for them. It brought it all home and I was sick again.
Then I had one of my nosebleeds. I remember Tim told

me to stop being so wet and get a grip. Someone went and got Joe and told him what had happened and he came down to the boathouse. Then Paul went off and found some rubbish bags and tape. I remember the bags were heavy-duty things, with the council's name stamped in white on the front. It's funny how you remember little details like that. I also remember thinking how surreal it was to be putting a girl in a bin bag. We wrapped her up, put her things in another one and used a few broken bits of stone from the graveyard to weigh her down. We were really worried someone would see us but everyone was still out for the count. We got one of the boats and Joe and Tim lifted her in and rowed her out into the middle somewhere. She must still be there, I guess. After we left, I never went back. I have no idea who she is or how she got in the water. I know what we did was stupid. It was wrong . . .

Tartaglia put Fleming's statement down on the table in front of him and stared out of the grimy little window for a moment. He checked his phone again, but there was still no message from Steele. There had been no need to exert any kind of pressure on Fleming. He seemed only too happy to unburden himself, and once he had started, his account of what had happened gushed out freely like water from a broken standpipe. Although it had the ring of truth, he was sure something was missing. In his mind, he again ran through certain parts of what had been said.

'Why didn't you tell somebody at the time?' he had asked. He had been standing at that point, as much to stretch his legs as to physically dominate Fleming, although there had been no need. Leaning his weight full on the back of a chair, he had looked Fleming in the eye.

Fleming didn't flinch. Flopped in his chair, with his short red hair standing in worried spikes, he looked physically drained, as though he were on his last legs. 'I told you. We thought we'd get into serious trouble. It was the last thing any of us needed. We all thought she'd either drowned or OD'd, or something. The last thing we wanted was police crawling all over the place. Anyway, there was nothing we could do for her.'

'What about her family? Didn't you think of them?'

'No. Nobody thought of that.' Fleming leaned forwards towards Tartaglia, hands spread palms up on the table. 'Look, you've got to understand how it was. This was nearly twenty years ago, right? We were just kids. You don't stop to think about other people's feelings when you're young. We'd just done our finals. We were over the moon. We'd had next to no sleep for days and we were all high as kites. Any form of rational thought was way beyond us.'

'Are you trying to excuse what you did?'

Fleming shook his head. 'No. Not in any way. I'm just telling you how it was. We acted on impulse, if you like. Later, when we had the time to think about it all properly, she was at the bottom of the lake and there was no going back. I often wondered about her out there somewhere.' He gave Tartaglia a rueful look and rubbed his face. 'Makes you think, doesn't it? I mean, some stupid thing you do on the spur of a moment can reach out and grab you far into the future. Or is it the long arm of the past, some cliché like that?'

He stared at Fleming, trying to see through the veneer of fecklessness. He was an actor, like Logan. How much was real, how much just a part he was playing? 'Do you have any idea how serious this is?'

Fleming nodded slowly. 'Of course. What we did was really wrong, but you have to put yourself in our shoes. It was getting light real quick. Someone was bound to come along and I guess we all just panicked.'

'You all?'

'Yes. All of us, together.'

'All for one and one for all? Was that how it was?'

'In a way.'

'So you'd cover up for one another?'

'No. That wasn't what I meant. We were mates, that's all, although we were pretty close. For that last year, I suppose we more or less lived in each other's pockets.'

'Did you think you'd get away with it?' he asked, wondering if there really had been such a consensus.

'I don't think any of us thought about it in a calculating way. We just reacted to the situation. But I do believe in karma. I had a feeling it would come out one day, one way or another. I'm only surprised it took this long.' He rubbed his face vigorously again, then looked up at Tartaglia. 'You know, I had a feeling someone saw us.'

'You think someone was watching?'

'I don't know. Tiredness and stuff can make you paranoid.'

'It's important.'

Fleming shrugged. 'It's just an impression, that's all. We were all tied up in what we were doing but I remember feeling sure that we weren't alone. Maybe it was the girl's ghost.'

'Come on, Mr Fleming. Are you sure there's nothing else?'

He shook his head. 'No. That's about it. I'm glad it's out in the open now. Joe wrote that book because he wanted it to come out.'

'You asked him?'

'Not directly, but I know he felt guilty. I think he found the writing cathartic and maybe he felt if he exposed it all, he'd done his bit.'

Tartaglia grimaced at such a strange form of morality. 'What about the others? How did they feel about it all?'

'I can't answer for them,' Fleming said simply.

It was not clear from his tone what he really thought. On the whole, he had spoken from the heart and what had happened all those years ago appeared to have affected him deeply. He had even put his face in his hands and wept when he described finding the girl. In trying to understand the dynamics of the group of five, Tartaglia saw him as weak and indecisive, a follower rather than a leader and easily dominated. He knew little about Logan or Khan, but from what he had seen, Wade was a strong personality, used to taking charge. Such things didn't change over time and he wondered what Wade's role in it all had been. He seemed practical, analytical and emotionally detached. As far as he was concerned, what they had done was down to the folly of youth. It was stupid and unthinking, but none of them was to blame for the girl's death. In Wade's view, it was clear the matter should end there. Even though he was well aware of the legal standpoint, he refused to accept any moral responsibility. As for Black, it was impossible to know what he felt deep down. He seemed in a poor physical and psychological state, his senses and responses dulled by lack of sleep or drink or drugs, or a combination. He could barely stay awake and his answers had been monosyllabic most of the time. Interviewing him and getting a coherent account had been a laborious task. Wanting to make sure that what he said tallied with what they had learned from the others, they had had to be particularly careful not to lead him in any way. When pressed, he had mumbled that he felt very sorry for what he had done, but the words had a hollow ring, as though he knew what was expected and was just going through the motions.

'Whose idea was it to get rid of the girl?' Tartaglia had asked Fleming.

Fleming shrugged. 'I honestly can't remember who suggested it first. But the only other options – by that I mean telling our parents or the police – weren't very appealing. I know it sounds callous, but we all had plans for the summer, which we were looking forward to. I guess we didn't want anything to put a dampener on things. I'd say there was no disagreement.'

'You're sure about that?'

'Positive.'

Tartaglia studied his face, but could read nothing from his expression. 'We're obviously going to have to try and trace the girl. No doubt someone reported her missing. Can you describe her? Can you remember what she looked like?'

Fleming scratched his head. 'I never saw her in proper daylight, you know. I remember standing over her, looking down. It was then I realised she wasn't the other girl, but it's funny, however hard I try, I can't see *her*. I mean, I can't see her face. It's as if I never really looked at her properly.'

'Really? You blocked it out because what you did was so terrible?'

Fleming looked horrified. 'That's not what I meant at all. This was nearly twenty years ago. Think of all the people you pass by on the street. Do you remember any of them?'

'But she wasn't on the street. She was dead.'

Fleming shrugged, as though it was pointless. 'I'm just telling you how it was and I'm not making it up. One thing I do remember, though, is how light she was. There was nothing to her. That's what strikes me most.'

Tartaglia studied Fleming for a moment. How could he recall so little about her? Was it important that she wasn't particularly heavy? Fleming was lean and muscular. Even in his late teens, allowing for physical immaturity, picking up a young woman in his arms would have been relatively easy. It was an odd detail to focus on. Maybe he was being deliberately misleading.

'Were there any marks on her?'

'Marks? What do you mean?'

'You know ... Any signs that someone might have hurt her.'

Fleming jerked his head back, looking genuinely shocked. 'No. Not that I was aware of.'

'No bruises, swellings, marks, signs of abuse of any kind ...'

'No. I tell you I didn't notice anything.'

'Could anybody have interfered with her in any—'

'Interfered with her? Of course not. Whatever happened to her was an accident. I'm absolutely sure of that.' He raised his voice in emphasis.

'When you remember so little about her, how can you be so sure?'

Fleming frowned and didn't answer for a moment, then he shook his head. 'Because I am. In my mind I've never questioned it.'

'And now?'

Fleming sighed. 'You're trying to put ideas in my head. At the time, as I said, I thought she'd just passed out. I didn't think of anything else. If there was anything suspicious, I'm sure I'd have noticed.'

'Even in the state you were in?'

'Yes,' he said, practically shouting. 'Talk to the others. They saw her too and they'll tell you the same. She looked normal, like she was asleep. When I left her, I thought she was still alive. I mean, she could have been, couldn't she? She could have died after I left her.'

Tartaglia said nothing. Fleming's insistence aroused his curiosity. Surely, it would have been morally more justifiable to leave her on the grass and go to bed if he knew she was beyond help. Why did it matter so much to Fleming that she had been alive?

'So, you don't know how long she'd been in the water?'

'No.'

'But she may have been one of the swimming group?'

'Maybe.'

'I can't believe you just left her there. She was already dead, or in a coma. Surely you should have gone for help.'

'Look, I was really out of it. I wasn't thinking clearly.'

Tartaglia shook his head. 'It doesn't add up. You say she was naked when you found her.'

'That's right.'

'And you were naked too.'

'Yes. We all were. What's your point?'

'You were drunk and you'd taken drugs, by your own admission.'

'I'm not trying to hide anything.'

'Did you have sex with her?'

The words seemed to take Fleming by surprise. He coughed and slapped the table with the palm of his hand. 'What? Are you joking?'

'Maybe she didn't want to. Was that it? Did you force her? Did she drown? Was that what happened?'

Fleming gasped and took a deep lungful of the stale air. His lips were wet with saliva and he wiped them quickly with the back of his hand. 'No. I tell you I didn't hurt her.'

'You raped her, didn't you? You wanted sex and she wouldn't play ball.'

'Stop saying that,' he shouted. Tears stood in his eyes and he was breathing fast.

'It all went horribly wrong and you tried to cover it up.'

'No. All I did was carry her out of the water. I didn't even notice she was naked, I swear.'

'You expect me to believe that?'

'She was well out of it when I found her. I left her exactly as I found her. I promise you.' Sweat was pouring down his face and he had turned red. Even though it might have been righteous indignation, Tartaglia wasn't convinced. But if he had killed her, accidentally or otherwise, proving it would be well nigh impossible. And if he hadn't killed her, was he covering for someone else?

'You have no idea who she was?'

'No, I tell you. I looked in the papers every day for the next few weeks but there was no mention of a missing girl. Maybe she wasn't local. She could have come from absolutely anywhere.'

'Was she a student?'

'I haven't a clue.'

Fleming had then had a nosebleed. He had been taken to the gent's and had cleaned himself up. When he returned, they had gone over and over the facts with him, but his story remained the same. Although it didn't add up in Tartaglia's eyes, they couldn't get him to change it. Tim Wade and Daniel Black both independently believed Fleming innocent of any crime. They had also separately corroborated the rest of his account, bar some minor discrepancies which could be explained by the passage of time and the state they had all been in that morning. Fleming was the only one of the three who had mentioned the possibility of someone watching. As to the other people who had been there that night, the field was wide open. All three men had struggled to give him more than twenty or so names. But several important questions remained unanswered. None of them had a clue who the girl was, who had brought her, indeed if she had been at the party at all or had arrived earlier in the day, or how or when she had died. Nor, more importantly, did they have any idea why Joe Logan and Paul Khan had been murdered. He began to wonder if maybe he was looking at everything the wrong way.

While he waited for Wade and Black's statements to be prepared and signed, he decided to go and stretch his legs.

As he stood up, the door burst open and Carolyn Steele swept into the room. 'I got your messages. I came as soon as I could.' She was a little out of breath as though she had run all the way up the stairs. She was dressed in a smart, pinstriped trouser suit and dark blouse. On closer inspection, he saw that she was wearing make-up for a change and a pair of very high red heels.

'Any chance of a coffee? I'm absolutely knackered.' As she dropped her bag on the floor and sat down at the table, he caught a whiff of perfume, something sweet and floral.

He was intrigued to know who she had been schmoozing. Whilst she was politically more astute than most he had worked with, he wasn't sure where the war paint and heels came in. She had never bothered with it before and although she looked good, in his view she didn't need it. 'I was just going to get one. What would you like?'

'Strong, with milk, no sugar, please. Any format will do.'

He left the room and went along the corridor to the machine. Unlike the ancient one in their office, it was state of the art and offered a perplexing variety of options. It took him a moment to work out how to order a cappuccino with an extra shot of coffee for Steele. As he punched in the code and waited, he thought of Anna Paget. It was now clear why her article had excited Logan's interest and he wondered if Logan had unburdened himself to her about what had happened at the lake. Instinct told him that he had and he felt angry at the thought of her withholding the information. Burning his fingers as he roughly extracted the first cup of coffee, he set it to one side and ordered up a large black for himself. While he waited, he took out his phone and dialled Anna's number, but it went straight to voicemail. He left a message asking her to call him, collected the two coffees and went back to the meeting room.

Steele had taken off her jacket and shoes and was rubbing her bare feet. The shoes lay discarded beside her on the carpet. 'These bloody shoes, they've crippled me,' she said, as he handed her the coffee.

'I'm not surprised,' he replied, amazed that anyone could walk in such things. She had always struck him as a sensible sort.

'I know. They're new. I should never have chanced it in this weather.'

He smiled and sat down. 'That wasn't what I meant.'

Without further comment, he filled her in on the main points of what had happened that morning and gave her the gist of Fleming's statement. She then insisted on reading the whole thing for herself. When she had finished, she looked up. 'Do you believe him?'

'I'm in two minds. Part of it rings true, but I feel it's an edited version. Reading between the lines, there was a lot of stuff going on there that night. It's difficult to know whether he's holding back just because we're the police and he doesn't want to get anyone into trouble, or if it's actually something more relevant.'

'Do you think he killed the girl?'

'I honestly don't know. My gut feel is that something went on between them, but if he did kill her, it was probably accidental. Whatever happened, unless he confesses, we've sweet FA to go on.'

'What about the others?'

'There's no indication that they had anything to do with her death. And as far as the rest of it goes, what they did with the body, etcetera, etcetera, all three stories more or less match.'

'You don't think they rehearsed it?'

'I'm sure they did, both at the time and since. But they weren't expecting us this morning and they had no opportunity to discuss anything together once Sam and Nick got there. They were brought here in separate cars and kept apart once they arrived. The accounts were quite detailed, particularly Fleming's and Wade's. It would have been near impossible to get everything right.'

'OK. What next?'

'We need to recover the girl's body. It's our only means of finding out what really went on.'

She nodded. 'I'll call Clive right away. Assuming the body hasn't already turned up at some point during the last eighteen years, we'll have to drag the lake. But he'll have to clear it first with Avon and Somerset. They may want to take charge of things at that end.'

'How long will it take?'

She glanced at her watch. 'If I can get hold of him now, hopefully we can get a search team over there tonight. Otherwise, it will have to be first thing tomorrow morning. What do you want to do with Alex Fleming and the others?'

'For the moment, we've got no real grounds to hold them.'

'But they've all potentially withheld evidence.'

'Do you really want to pursue it? We have no proof yet that what happened at the lake had a direct bearing on the two murders.'

'But the emails . . .'

'Obviously, whoever sent them knew about what went on there, but they could be a red herring, sent either as a wind-up or to confuse. The killings could be about something else altogether.'

'One of the three could have sent them.'

'Yes. Or, as Fleming said, maybe someone else was watching.'

Narrowing her eyes, she gave him a sideways glance. 'The key question is, if we'd known sooner, could we have saved Paul Khan?'

'I don't see how. I really don't think we can blame them for that. As I said, we still don't know why he and Logan are dead.'

She nodded as though she finally agreed. 'Do you think any of them could have killed Logan and Khan?'

'Yes. But again, there's no clear motive.'

'What about the girl? Maybe someone wanted to stop the truth coming out.'

'I don't think that's enough, do you?'

She shrugged. 'People have killed for a lot less, as you know. Have you checked their alibis?'

'It's being done as we speak. Fleming says he was at the restaurant the night Logan disappeared and didn't leave until after midnight. The night Khan was murdered, he had a drink with a woman who lives on the canal near Logan's boat. After that, according to him he went home, but there's nobody who can corroborate his story. If more than one person's involved in the killings, he can't be ruled out. As for Wade, he says he was either at his chambers or at home. Black is the only one of the three who doesn't seem to have any form of alibi for either of the murders.'

'And if they didn't do it, are they at risk, do you think?'

It was something that had been troubling him, but there was no easy answer. 'Nobody's asked for protection yet, but they're not stupid. It must have crossed their minds that they might be in danger too. You're not going to like it, but I think we should put them under surveillance.'

Steele shook her head. 'You know what that costs.'

'But there was hardly a gap between the two murders. If something else is going to happen, my gut feel is it'll be soon. Can we really run that risk?'

'Have any of them received emails?'

'No.'

'Well, then.' She sat back in her chair and studied him for a moment. 'Look, Mark. As you say yourself, we don't know why any of this is happening. Until we find out more, I just can't justify the expense.'

She was right, of course. To put twenty-four-hour surveillance teams on three people would cost an arm and a leg and there was nothing concrete to warrant it. But his gut was telling him otherwise. The five men, two dead and three alive, were inextricably connected. The answer had to lie there, if only they knew where to look.

She was tapping her fingers lightly on the table and gave him an enigmatic smile. 'I can see you're not convinced.'

He folded his arms. 'No. My worry is that by the time we have something tangible it will be too late. Another man will be dead and we might have been able to stop it happening. And there's another thing. Maybe if we put a watch on the three, it will lead us to whoever is doing this.'

She stared into space for a moment, then sighed. 'OK. Like you, the last thing I want is another murder. I'll go and talk to Clive. It has to be his call. Of course I can't promise anything, but you know how mindful of the press he is. They still don't know that the two murders are officially linked. With the threat of another death, well ... That may just focus his thoughts.'

25

Alex hadn't gone more than a few metres out of the police station when he heard his name being called. He looked around and saw Tim running up to him.

'How did it go?' Tim asked, briefly clasping an arm around his shoulders. His face was red and his shirt was marked with sweat. Alex wondered if it was just the heat or if he had found the police interview an ordeal, although he couldn't see Tim getting rattled by it. 'I asked, how did it go?' Tim repeated, when he didn't answer.

Alex kept walking. 'Fine.'

'What did you tell them?'

'What we said.'

'Which is?'

'You know. You wrote the bloody script.' Alex stopped at the pedestrian crossing. The light was red, the traffic streaming past, and he had no choice but to wait.

'That's not exactly fair, you know. We all agreed.'

'Did we?'

'Come on, now. You know we did. What's up?'

He glanced at Tim. 'What the fuck do you mean "what's up"? Isn't it obvious?'

'Keep your voice down,' Tim muttered, as several passers-by turned to stare at them. They probably thought he and Tim were having a lovers' tiff.

'I don't care who hears,' he said loudly, enjoying Tim's embarrassment. 'That's the least of my worries. I've just been practically arrested for something I didn't do nearly twenty years ago and now apparently I may also have killed Joe and Paul. Life's just sweet.' The pedestrian light turned green and he started out across the road as fast as he could, although he knew Tim wouldn't let it go that easily.

'Look, I'm not to blame for any of that,' Tim said, catching him up and keeping pace as he turned down Kensington High Street.

'No? You were the one who told me not to talk to them.'

'I didn't think there was any point.'

'Apparently, in their eyes, that looks very suspicious. But don't worry, I didn't tell them it was your idea or that I stayed with you last night.'

'You were the one who called at two in the morning saying you needed a bed for the night. I was only trying to help, as you know.'

'Yeah, well, your helpfulness just has a habit of getting other people into trouble.'

'Come on, Alex. You're being a tad unfair. Shall we go and have a drink somewhere and talk about this?'

He shook his head. A drink? That was always Tim's answer to every problem, as though it was a trivial matter that could be easily put to bed with a few kind words. He was struck by Tim's lack of emotion, as though being grilled by the police, let alone the memories of that fateful night, hadn't touched him in any way. By contrast, he felt shrivelled inside. He wondered now if he was the only one of the five to be so affected by what had happened, but then his connection with the girl had been on a different level. He knew things they didn't . . .

Alex waved Tim away with his hand. 'I don't want a drink. I'm due at work and I'm way late as it is.'

'Ring up and say you're sick.'

'Fuck off, Tim. They know I'm not. I had to call them from the station and tell them what was happening.'

'Come on. Just a quick one so we can sort this out. It won't take long.'

'No. You may not rate it, but my job's important to me and I can't afford to lose it.'

'OK, OK, I'm sorry. I didn't mean it to come out that way, but you're being over-sensitive, you know. We really ought to talk about what's gone on.'

'There's nothing to talk about.' He pushed himself faster, wishing that Tim would leave him alone, but he stayed right at his side.

'Look,' Tim said, trying to catch his eye. 'I'm sure the police don't seriously think you had anything to do with what happened to Joe and Paul. It's just a line. They're fishing. They tried it on me too. Naturally, I told them where to get off.'

'It seems I don't have a watertight alibi for the time of Paul's death.'

'I wouldn't pay much attention to that. They have to ask the question, of course, but even if you don't have an alibi, they really haven't a leg to stand on. They have no proof you did anything wrong. It would never get anywhere near a court.'

'That's not the way it came across to me.'

'They questioned me too, you know. It's what they do. Luckily, my clerk at chambers can vouch for me there. The rest of the time I was at home and they can talk to Milly about that. All I can say is that if they really thought you were in the frame they wouldn't be letting you go now.'

'That's very comforting,' Alex said acidly, although the sarcasm was lost on Tim. A posse of gossiping women with pushchairs carved a path between them, briefly separating them, but Tim skipped around them and caught up with him again. 'Believe me, Alex. I had no desire to make things difficult for you.'

Alex didn't reply. Barely aware of where he was, he carried on walking, head down, trying to blot out Tim's looming presence beside him. The pavement was busy with shoppers, and people on their way home from work. As they stopped again at another crossing, he caught the tail end of a conversation between two teenage girls next to him who were discussing some boy they both fancied. If only life was still so simple, he thought, although he wouldn't be a teenager again for anything in the world. It had been a painful, awkward, self-conscious time for him, if not for the others, and what had happened at Ashleigh Grange was the nadir. It had shadowed the following years, marking him permanently. The dirty little secret was always there, locked away deep inside like a tumour.

'Danny's still at the station,' Tim said in a matter-of-fact tone. 'They haven't quite finished with him yet, but when they let him go I thought the three of us should get together and have a post mortem.'

He glared at Tim for a second. 'That's a bloody unfortunate choice of words in the circumstances.'

'Yes, sorry. You know what I mean. I'll go back in a minute and see how he's doing. I just wanted to check you were OK.'

Tim's voice was full of concern and Alex glanced away. 'Well, I'm not OK. I don't want to talk about what's happened and I'd like you to leave me alone. I've got to go to work and I need to clear my head.'

Tim put a hand on Alex's shoulder. 'Come on, Alex. Look at me, will you?'

'No.'

'Please look at me. I'm not your enemy.'

He turned to face Tim. 'What the fuck do you want?'

'How long have you known me?'

'Too long, maybe.'

'Don't be silly, you're one of my oldest friends. I can see you're really upset and it's natural you want to lash out, but don't take it out on me. None of us had anything to do with what happened to that poor girl. None of us is to blame either for what happened to Joe and Paul. I'm sorry I stopped you going to the police earlier, but I thought it was best we didn't get embroiled. It was an honest mistake.'

Not trusting himself to speak, Alex stared down at his feet and shook his head.

'But don't worry,' Tim continued, oblivious. 'We're not in some third-world country. The police will sort it out.'

'They think I killed that girl,' Alex said quietly.

'You know that's ridiculous. You just need a good lawyer.

The police will work it all out eventually, then life can get back to normal. You'll see.'

Fighting back the tears, he met Tim's gaze. Tim was looking at him indulgently, as though he was a little child having a tantrum. As far as Tim was concerned, the whole episode was long ago and buried. Maybe it hadn't even affected him much at the time . . . As for the incident in the police station, it too could be quickly forgotten. Alex wanted to punch Tim, wipe the stupid, patronising expression off his face, but there was no point. Nothing he could say would ever make Tim understand. They were worlds apart. Always had been, if only he had had the sense to realise it.

'Normal?' he said to Tim. 'You just don't get it, do you?'

'What do you mean?'

'Just fuck off and leave me alone,' he shouted, ignoring the looks from the people around him. He saw a break in the line of cars and ran across the road, zigzagging through the crowd of waiting pedestrians on the other side. Tim called out something after him, but the words were lost in the noise of the traffic. Although the sweat was pouring down him, Alex kept running until he had put a safe distance between them.

Maybe he *was* over-reacting, but the questioning had been so intense. He had never found himself in such a position before and he hoped he never would again. He thought of the detective with the black hair and Italian name who had interviewed him. They were trained at interrogation, but Alex had never imagined anything as probing or as morally damning. The process had stripped him bare as thoughts and images bubbled up from the deep: so many things unconsciously stored and now released, he hadn't known what to make of them. For a moment, it had all seemed astonishingly clear again, but then he'd started to doubt himself. Like a magician conjuring visions out of the darkness, the detective had suggested things that hadn't been there before, foul ideas that took root in Alex's mind until he didn't know what was true or false.

The detective had sat motionless in his chair, his head resting lightly on his fingers, watching him, questioning him. Had Alex really just left her there by the lake and gone off home to bed? So he thought she was dead? No? Just unconscious? Had he tried to revive her, given her the kiss of life, maybe? Why not? What did he think had happened to her? Had someone hurt her? No? Was he sure? Were there any bruises, swellings, marks, signs of abuse of any kind . . . Abuse. The word shot through him. Nobody could possibly know what he'd done. In his fever, had he failed to notice the obvious? He pictured her before him, saw shadows spread like spilled ink over her skin, flesh discoloured and swelling, as though invisible hands were squeezing and pushing. Her thighs? Fuck. He hadn't looked at her thighs, or any other part of her. He hadn't looked at her at all. In his head, he had been somewhere else entirely, imagining that she was someone else. How the hell could he explain that? Blood? There was no blood. Not that he remembered. No, he hadn't touched her. No, he hadn't had sex with her. Nobody had interfered with her. Whatever had happened, it had been an accident, for Christ's sake. *An accident!*

For a moment, he was back there again, with her in the water. It was like a dream, the vision swirling around him as if he was the only thing that was still. He saw the black canopy of branches, the shimmering blur of the moon, stars wheeling pinpoints of light in the sky. The dull thud of the music reached out across the lake and filled his head. A breeze had come up from nowhere and he shivered as he stepped out with her onto the shore. She was limp in his arms, her head lolling over his shoulder, her long, muddy hair clinging to his back. He felt the chill of her skin pressed against his, the dry grass prickle as he walked up the bank and laid her on the ground. He forgot the others out in the lake, wherever they were. Their voices in the distance dimmed to nothing. He was alone with her, just the two of them. He stretched her limbs out on the grass and gazed at her for a moment, wanting her, wishing that she would open her eyes and look at him. But she didn't move. He knelt down and kissed her, then again, closer this time, feeling the clammy softness of her beneath him. Slowly, he ran his fingers over her skin, touching, caressing, exploring every part of her as though she was something new and strange. Still she didn't move. The fever stole upon him. The music exploded in his head, the beat clear and sharp, pulsing through his veins. Even the moon was humming. Everything was Technicolor and he was on fire. He closed his eyes and pulled her to him. Then he was inside her and he lost himself. He was somewhere else and she was the little first year, giggling, teasing, egging him on, wanting *him* – not Paul. It was like never before, like nothing he had ever even imagined. But it was all over too quickly. He rolled onto his back and lay on the grass looking up at the stars. They were spinning like motes of brightly coloured dust in a shaft of sunlight. When he shut his eyes, he could still see them, a kaleidoscope of colour turning round and round. The girl was gone and he was on his own.

Later, when he finally made it back to his room, tossing and turning in his bed as he tried and failed to fall asleep, it seemed surreal. He told himself, maybe it hadn't actually happened. Perhaps, fuelled by whatever crazy cocktail of stuff he had taken that night, he had been hallucinating. But a few hours later, in the washed-out early morning light, when he went back to the lake with Joe and the others and saw her spread-eagled on the ground, arms and legs at weird angles like something roughly discarded, the reality hit him. She was dead. What was even stranger, she looked nothing like the girl he remembered. Was it really her? It had to be. Christ, what had he done? Had he forced the last, dying breath from her with his madness? Or was she already dead when he found her? He didn't know which was worse . . .

The ringing of his phone cut through the nightmare. He shook his head and blinked, aware once more that he was outside in the middle of a bright, busy street. He pulled the phone out of his pocket and saw Maggie Thomas's name on the screen. He stared at it for a moment wondering what to do, then he ducked into a doorway and answered it.

Her voice was sweet and sunny, as though from another world. 'The police have just been by,' she said, after a brief greeting. 'They asked if you were with me the other night. I said you were. I hope that's OK.'

'Thanks. They're just checking my alibi.' He spoke slowly and deliberately, finding it difficult to form the words.

'Is everything all right?'

He took a deep breath. 'No. No, it's not.'

'What's happened? Is it about Joe? Is there any news?'

He hesitated. 'It must sound really odd, but another friend of mine has been murdered.'

'No,' she gasped. 'Oh, God, I'm so sorry to hear that. Where are you?'

'In Kensington. On my way to work.'

'Are you OK? Silly me, of course you're not.'

Leaning back against the wall, he squeezed his eyes tight shut. 'I feel like shit. It's all been too much.'

'You sound bad. Would you like to come over? It might help to talk to a friendly ear.'

He sighed. 'It's complicated.'

'Try me. I'm good at complicated.'

Her voice was soothing, her loneliness touching a chord in him. He pictured her lovely soft brown eyes, the kindness of her expression. Maybe he could talk to her. 'I've got to go to work. I can't let them down.'

'What about after? I never go to bed until really late.'

'It will be about one.'

'That's OK. This must seem strange, Alex. I mean, you don't know me from Adam, but I've good instincts about people and I've learned to trust them. Maybe I can help.'

The warmth in her voice reached out to him. He nodded, tears pricking his eyes. He knew what she was saying and he didn't find it strange at all. Sometimes there was that connection.

'I'm a night owl,' she continued cheerily. 'It's so lovely and quiet, it's my favourite time and there's going to be a full moon. We can sit outside if you like, and have a drink and a nice old chinwag. I'm sure it will do you the world of good.'

26

For a change, the sky was still light in places when Tartaglia arrived home that night. He parked the Ducati behind the front hedge and let himself in. He picked up a pile of post from the hall floor and went into his flat. It felt like an oven inside. He turned on a couple of lights then spent the next few minutes unlocking and opening all of the windows and the back door. Even so, there wasn't much of a breeze. He removed his jacket and tie and helped himself to a Peroni from the fridge. He lit a Marlboro and sat down at the kitchen table with the beer, listening to the buzz of music and voices from next door, finding the noise strangely soothing.

Cornish had vetoed the idea of putting Fleming, Wade and Black under surveillance on grounds of cost. He said that it wasn't clear that the three men were in danger. Steele had seemed surprised at his decision, but if she was annoyed she didn't show it and had gone back to the conference for the dinner without comment. Meanwhile, Cornish had spoken to his counterpart in Avon and Somerset police. After checking to make sure that no bodies had been found in the lake during the past eighteen years, a thorough search had been authorised. A specialist underwater team would be going out there to start work that night, as soon as the immediate area had been sealed off. According to Tim Wade, he and Logan had dumped the girl's body some way out in the middle of the lake. Although there was little current to contend with, the lake was apparently both large and quite deep. Based on past experience, Tartaglia expected the operation to take all night at the very least. He had spoken to a DI Graham Roberts in Bristol who had been put in charge of the operation at that end and said he would call if there was any news. So, from Tartaglia's point of view, there was nothing to be done until morning.

He took a long drag on the cigarette, enjoying the moment. Most detectives, and members of the forensic team, had their pet hates and his was dealing with bodies that had been in water for a while. It wasn't just the many practical difficulties posed by that type of decomposition, it was what water did to flesh. The visual images and the smell tended to stay with him for a long time after. He had been involved in many searches using dive teams, the most recent having been only a few months before, when the victim of a gangland contract killing had been thrown into the river off Chelsea Bridge. The body had been weighted down and they had had a job finding it and extracting it from the silt at the bottom. Rather than load the body into the boat, they had wrapped it up and attached a rope to one of the man's wrists to tow him in, but they hadn't gone far when they discovered that all they were towing was his arm . . .

Tartaglia enjoyed diving in hotter, sunnier climes, where the visibility was good and the water relatively warm. It was something he did for sheer pleasure and interest. In the few hundred or so dives he had done in his spare time since he first started, he had never needed a dry suit and had no intention of ever using one. He had the greatest respect for those that worked in the police dive unit, but he wouldn't have been capable of doing their job. Casting around for the sludgy remains of a human body in a cold, murky stretch of water, where visibility was zero and it made no difference if it was day or night, was the stuff of nightmares. At least the lake was a relatively confined area, although it wasn't so deep that the temperature of the water would have halted the natural process of decomposition.

According to Wade, they had wrapped the dead girl in plastic, which they then sealed with tape, but they had done it in a hurry and the package was unlikely to be airtight. Over time, the tape adhesive would degrade, helped by any snails, fish or crabs in the lake, and water would gradually start to seep in. After so long, he doubted whether there would be much left of her other than bone. Wade had told them that her clothing and shoes had been put into a separate bag and thrown into the lake with her but he was less clear as to the precise location. In their panic to get rid of her, they had forgotten about the other bag until they were back near the shore. Wade seemed to think Logan had hurled it away as far as he could towards the middle, somewhere near the boathouse, but he said he wasn't a hundred per cent sure. No doubt neither of them was thinking clearly at that point.

Now, once the police had found her, the next challenge would be to identify her – if only they knew where to start. They would check all missing person reports for that time in the area, of course, and then – assuming they found a match – they could use dental records, and possibly DNA, to identify her. It would be a slow process. Twenty years ago, record-keeping had been patchy and inconsistent. If she hadn't been reported missing locally, the chances of finding out who she was greatly diminished. Again he was reminded of Anna Paget's article and wondered why she hadn't returned his call.

He heard his mobile ringing from his jacket pocket in the sitting room. Thinking it might be Graham Roberts with some news, he jumped up and rushed to answer it. He was surprised to see Arabella Browne's name across the screen.

'Arabella. To what do I owe the pleasure on a Saturday night?'

'Are you in another bar? I'm not interrupting again, am I?'

'No, I'm at home.'

'What's that awful din?'

'The neighbours are having a barbeque.'

'Well, you won't be getting much sleep. Anyway, I've just had a call from someone in Bristol about a body in a lake. I hear it's one of yours.'

He smiled. 'That's right, but isn't that a bit far off the mark for you?'

'I get around. I had to go to Cornwall only a few weeks ago. Anyway, apparently there's been a spate of deaths in the Bristol area and the duty pathologist is tied up. Carolyn Steele gave them my name. Can you fill me in on what you're expecting to find?'

'The victim's a girl, or young woman. She's been at the

bottom of a lake since the early nineties. Apparently she was wrapped up in some plastic bags, so hopefully there's something left for you to see. We'll need to establish age, height, and so on, so we can try and ID her and, if at all possible, we need to find out what happened. It's not clear at the moment how she died or whether or not it was an accident.'

'Forgive the stupid question, but if you're not sure it's murder, why are you bothering with it?'

'There's a link to the last two murder victims.'

'I see. Have you got a forensic anthropologist lined up?'

'Not yet. Do you have someone in mind?'

'Yes. There's a woman at the university who may be able to help. We've worked together before.'

'It would be useful if she was there at the same time as you examine the body.'

'I'll see what I can do. I'll give her a call when we finish. Are you going to be visiting the scene, or are you leaving it to the locals?'

'I'm driving down early in the morning. Sam Donovan's collecting me. Do you want a lift?'

'No. I'm at the cottage near Frome. It's only about half an hour from the lake. I was in the middle of boning and stuffing a chicken for lunch tomorrow when I got the call. Jo and I have some friends coming over, but I guess they'll have to manage without me. I just hope she won't overcook it again.'

With that, she rang off.

He finished his beer and cigarette, wondering if it was odd or natural that a woman who cut up bodies for a living was also such a good cook, as he had discovered on a couple of occasions when she had invited him for dinner. Unable to make up his mind, he went into the bedroom where he undressed. Still thinking about the girl in the lake, he took a shower, closing his eyes under the hard jet of water as he ran through again in his mind what Alex Fleming had said and how he had behaved. It still didn't add up. He had just finished showering, when he heard what sounded like his doorbell. Quickly wrapping a towel around his middle, he went to check and opened the front door to find Anna Paget standing, hand on hip, in the middle of the garden path.

'May I come in?' she said, with a smile. She was wearing what looked like a short white slip, thigh-length black boots and not a lot else, as far as he could tell.

'No,' he said, wondering how she found his address, although any child could probably get it off the internet. There weren't that many Tartaglias in London. Why had she bothered, was the question. 'It's late. What are you doing here?'

'It's not that late. It's not even ten o'clock and I knew you'd still be up.'

'What is it you want?'

'Have you read my article?'

'Your article? What are you talking about?'

'I dropped a draft copy through the letterbox earlier. Didn't you find it?'

'No.'

'Well, it must be there somewhere.' She peered past him into the dark hall. 'It was in a plain white envelope. I definitely put it through this door on my way to dinner.'

'I picked up some post earlier. Maybe it's in there.'

'You said you wanted to see it as soon as possible,' she said a little sharply. 'And there are some things I need your help with in return. You also left a message saying you wanted to talk to me. I've just been to see a friend who lives nearby and thought we could kill two birds with one stone.' She made it seem the most natural thing in the world, as though he was the one being unreasonable. 'Now may I come in?'

He hesitated. He didn't like her arriving on his doorstep unannounced and he didn't like the idea of her being in his flat. But he needed to speak to her and short of making her wait outside in the front garden while he got dressed, he couldn't think what else to do.

'You can come in while I put some clothes on. Then we can go for a quick drink around the corner and discuss things there.'

'Are you sure you want to discuss it all in public?' She gave him a sceptical look as she brushed past him and went into the sitting room.

She had a point, but he still didn't feel comfortable with her there. He followed her inside and closed the door.

'Nice place,' she said, gazing around. 'Do you live here on your own?'

Ignoring her, he picked up the pile of post he had left on one of the chairs and leafed through it until he found an A4 envelope with the words BY HAND scrawled in one corner.

'Is this it?'

'That's the one.'

He tore it open and pulled out some typed sheets of paper headed 'Joe Logan article – draft.' As he quickly scanned it, he noticed that she had highlighted some of the paragraphs in the margin with fluorescent pen and marked them with

ELENA FORBES

a question mark. She had also scribbled in biro 'need more info' next to them. From what he could tell at a quick glance, they were to do with Logan's murder. The name 'Paul Khan' was written at the bottom of one of the pages with another question mark. He wondered how she had made the connection and how much she knew. Cursing the leakiness of the department, he glanced up at her. She had already made herself comfortable in the middle of the sofa, legs crossed, arms loosely extended along the back. The fabric of her dress clung to her like a second skin. She was watching him with an amused expression on her pretty face. In different circumstances he would have been only too happy for her to be there. In different circumstances, who knew what might have happened ... But for now, he wanted her out of his flat as quickly as possible.

'Aren't you going to offer me a drink?' she asked.

'No. As I said, I thought we'd go out.'

'I'm sorry if I'm disturbing you.'

'No, you're not. I doubt whether it even crossed your mind.'

She smiled. 'Is it awkward my being here? Do I make you uncomfortable? Is that it?'

'I don't mix business and pleasure. This is my home. You shouldn't have come.'

'I'm sorry. I work from home, so I don't get the distinction.'

He frowned. 'Well, you should. I remember your saying you didn't want Joe Logan in your flat because he was to do with your work.'

'That was different.'

'In what way?'

309

She shrugged. 'Let's say the situation was a little tricky. He wanted to blur the boundaries and I wanted to preserve them.'

'Then you'll understand why I want to go out.'

She looked surprised, as though nobody had ever spoken to her that way. Before she could say anything, he left the room. He dressed hurriedly, pulling on an old pair of jeans, a T-shirt and trainers, the first things that came to hand. He didn't want to leave her alone for too long. As far as he remembered, there was nothing lying about to do with the case, but he didn't want her nosing around.

Back in the sitting room, he was relieved to see that she was sitting exactly where he had left her.

'Please may I have a drink? I really don't want to go into all of this in some crowded bar with God only knows who listening. If you don't like my being here, we can go back to my place. It's not that far away and I trust you. You're a policeman, after all. I'm sure you wouldn't try and take advantage of the situation.' She gave him a pointed look.

He stared at her, bemused. Was that what she really thought? Being a policeman had nothing to do with it. Turning up at his flat at that hour, dressed like that . . . What man wouldn't be tempted? But the situation was an awkward one. However much he'd like to, he had no intention of taking advantage of anything. He had a good mind to tell her that they would do it another time, in a neutral location, but he would be in Bristol for all of the following day at least and he wanted to hear what she had to say in case it had any bearing on things.

'OK,' he sighed. 'We can stay here, but I can't talk long. I have an early start tomorrow. What can I get you?'

'A glass of wine will do.'

'I thought you didn't drink alcohol.'

'Occasionally, when I want to unwind.'

'You're not here to unwind.'

She smiled. 'I'm sorry. An unfortunate figure of speech. This is work, I know. I'm just tired, that's all. It's been a long day.'

'White or red?'

'I don't mind. Whatever's easiest.'

Wondering if it was a mistake allowing her to stay even for a short time, he went into the kitchen, opened a bottle of Gavi di Gavi from the fridge and poured a couple of glasses. Back in the sitting room, he handed her a glass, pulled up a chair and sat down opposite.

'Do you want to talk about the article?' she asked. 'If so, hadn't you better read it?'

'I'll read it later. I want to talk about the lake and what happened there. That's why I called you. You knew about the girl, didn't you?' She glanced away and took a sip of wine. 'Didn't you?' he repeated.

'Yes. Joe told me.'

'Why didn't you say anything?'

'I didn't think it was important.'

'Jesus! Not important! How could you possibly think that?'

She met his gaze. 'He told me it was a secret and he didn't want it known. *Is* it important?'

He stood up. 'Everything's important, as you well know. Just cut the crap and tell me what happened.'

For a moment she said nothing. He could see her mind whirring through things, no doubt working out how much she should give away. Then she shrugged. 'I don't see why it's important, but I'll tell you anyway. It was the article I wrote about missing people that got him started. He'd kept it quiet all those years and I guess he just needed to talk to someone. I think he felt I'd understand, that I was on the same wavelength, a kindred spirit, if you like.'

Logan must have been a fool, he thought. 'And what exactly did he tell you?'

'About what happened when he was a student, like in the book.'

'But it wasn't like the book, was it?'

'No. You know it wasn't.'

'I need to hear it from you.'

She gave an exasperated sigh. 'If you know it all already, why are you asking me?'

'Because I need to know exactly what Joe Logan said to you. As close as you can to his words, please.'

'I still don't see—'

'Just tell me what he said. And don't leave anything out.'

She sighed again. 'OK. But will you stop hovering over me? You're making me nervous.'

Reluctantly, he sat down again. 'Better?'

She nodded. 'He told me that there'd been a party at this place where he was living. The house was just like the one in the book. They went swimming in the lake and one of his friends came across a body. Can you imagine?' She looked up at him with large eyes. 'Apparently it was a dead girl.'

'Was it someone he knew?'

'No. He said he'd never seen her before, although he thought she must have been at the party.'

'What did he think had happened to her?'

'Oh, I don't know. I think he said it looked like she'd drowned.'

'He was there at the time?'

'No. I don't think he went swimming. This other guy found her. He was a mate of Joe's. Joe was somewhere else at the time and he only saw her later.'

'So he didn't actually see what went on?'

'No.'

'What happened after that?'

'He and some others decided to get rid of her. They were worried about getting into trouble, so they decided to put her back in the lake. This was in the morning, when everyone woke up. Joe was there. He was one of the ones who rowed her out into the middle of the lake and dumped her. He said it really haunted him, that he'd never stopped thinking about her, the way she looked, wondering who she was – somebody's daughter, sister, lover, who was missing her – that sort of stuff. It was why my article got to him. I really felt for him, you know?'

'I'm sure he appreciated your sympathy,' he said acidly. At least her account of what Logan had said tallied with that of the others. He put his feet up on the table and leaned back in his chair, hands behind his head gazing at her. He could see the outline of her breasts through the thin fabric of her dress.

A ghost of a smile lit up her features. 'I suppose she's still in the lake, isn't she? Are you going to try and find her?'

Was it a lucky guess, or did she know what was going on at the lake at that moment? She was amazingly well informed about a lot of things, but it was impossible to gauge anything from her expression. 'What else did he tell you?' he asked, finding it difficult to take his eyes off her. 'Did he have any idea who the girl was?'

She shook her head. 'If he did, he didn't say.'

'And he really thought she'd drowned?'

She shrugged and took another sip of wine. 'I asked him a couple of times. I mean, it's not every day you find someone dead like that, is it? But he said that she'd probably had too much to drink or taken some stuff and then gone swimming, so drowning was the most likely explanation.'

'Did he think his friend might have had anything to do with what happened to her?'

'No. Nothing like that. Weird, isn't it? I suppose we all watch too much crime stuff on TV, but I'd have been a bit more sceptical, wouldn't you? I remember Joe saying that if you couldn't trust your friends, who could you trust. He was like that. Straight up and down, that was Joe.'

From what he knew, Logan had been a lot more complex. According to Fleming, who knew him better than anyone, Logan had been pretty shrewd about other people, his friends included. Perhaps he had been naive where women were concerned, or at least a woman like Anna. He sat up and leaned towards her, clasping his hands. 'Did he trust you?'

'What do you mean?'

'Did Joe trust you. It's simple.'

She sighed. 'I suppose in the end, yes, I won his trust.'

He nodded. 'He told you his biggest, darkest secret. Did you have to sleep with him?'

'I didn't have to do anything. He just told me.'

'But did you sleep with him anyway?' he insisted, wondering how he could feel even remotely jealous of a dead man.

She shook her head wearily. 'Why does it have to be about sex?'

'Because it usually is.'

'That's not entirely true. I mean, you and I are having a perfectly normal conversation, aren't we?'

The disingenuousness of the remark brought a smile to his face. Did she think he was born yesterday? Maybe he had been a bit slow at the start, for a change. He'd had other things on his mind. Because of the case, because of what they had been talking about, he had been ignoring the signals. It was crystal clear now why she had come, but he still wasn't sure what he wanted to do about it. She was too closely entangled in the case and, more than anything, he didn't like the feeling that he was being manipulated. He frowned. 'You haven't answered the question.'

'Well, it's personal. I don't like talking about such things and you're not exactly making me feel very relaxed.' She dangled her empty glass in the air. 'I'm also not sure it's any of your business.'

'Everything to do with Joe Logan's my business.'

Frustrated, he got up and poured her some more wine, topping up his own before he sat down again. Whatever she told him, he felt he would never really get to the bottom of things with her. Like one of those Russian dolls, there would always be another layer. Perhaps he should tell her to go, so that he could get some sleep. It would be the sensible thing to do.

'I'll have a cigarette too, if it's not too much bother,' she added, with a fleeting glance at the box on the coffee table.

'You smoke?'

'Again, from time to time. I haven't had a Red in years, but I feel like one now.'

'They're strong,' he said, getting up and offering the pack. 'Are you sure?'

'They usually give me a lovely high, but at least it's legal, I suppose.'

Wondering whether she meant it literally, he bent down to give her a light. She slowly uncrossed her legs, leaned forwards and cupped his hand with hers. As she did so, she looked up into his eyes. It was a little thing, yet it jolted him. Without doubt she had used Logan, just as she was probably using him now, but it didn't matter any more. He could see from her expression that she was aware of the effect she was having on him and was enjoying it. He knew he was on the verge of doing something stupid, but as he held her gaze, so close that he could almost feel her breath on his face, he decided he didn't care.

'Tell me, just so I can tick the box. Did you sleep with Joe Logan?'

She smiled. She was still touching his hand as she threw back her head and blew out a plume of smoke. 'No. I didn't want to. That's the honest truth. Now I've come clean, you can give me something in return. It's about my article . . .'

'Later,' he said, tired of talking. He took hold of her hand and pulled her up towards him. 'There's something I need to do first.'

27

A tear dribbled down Alex's cheek as he stared up at the ceiling of the narrow-boat. Unable to sleep, he lay rigid, listening to the sound of Maggie's soft, rhythmic breathing. Exhausted, yet wired, he had gone to see her as suggested after he had finished his shift at the restaurant. They'd had several drinks up on deck, gazing at the moon and the stars while he tried to explain what was wrong. He told her about the police, about Paul, about Ashleigh Grange and the party. He also told her about finding the girl's body in the lake. It was more or less the same version he had given the police earlier. She had been warmly sympathetic and reassuring, but however much he wanted to, he couldn't bring himself to tell her what he had done to the girl. The words just wouldn't come. What woman would want him after knowing that? It was at the back of his mind as he described what had happened and he had broken down again, just as he had done at the police station. It was all still so vivid. He might as well have been guilty of holding the girl under the water with his bare hands. Maybe he had actually killed her and, if not, he was guilty of something almost as bad.

Maggie had comforted him, anaesthetised him with more

317

alcohol, then taken him downstairs to her bed. For a short while he had managed to blot out the image of the girl, but when he closed his eyes, he saw her again. He remembered the taste of her, the touch, the cold, gritty wateriness of her. The vision stopped him dead in his tracks and he couldn't go on after that. Maggie had put her arms around him and said that it didn't matter. He would get over it, she reassured him. Time was a great healer. But he wasn't so sure.

He heard the strange, rasping bark of a fox somewhere outside in the street. It was pointless trying to force things any longer. Sleep just wouldn't come. He sat up and carefully swung his legs onto the floor. As he did so, Maggie stirred beside him and he felt her hand reach out and caress the small of his back.

'Don't go yet, Alex,' she said drowsily. 'Please stay.'

'I can't sleep. I need to stretch my legs, but I won't be long.'

He quickly put on his trousers and shirt, slipped on his shoes and went upstairs. Out on deck, the air was fresh and heavy with damp, permeated with a faint rotting smell from the canal. He shivered and held his breath for a moment, but the taste in his mouth was sour. His glass was where he had left it on the deck beside a large pot of pink geraniums. It was still half full and he picked it up and took a gulp. The ice had melted and the tonic was flat, but the vodka still had a bit of a kick. Everything was quiet. The boats and houses along the canal were dark, curtains and blinds tightly closed. Although the streetlamps were still on, it would be light in another hour or so. Taking his glass, he stepped onto the towpath and walked along until he came to Joe's boat. He climbed over the police tape strung across the entrance and sat down at the small table where he and Joe had last had a drink. If anybody saw him, he was past caring. He put his feet up on the edge of the boat, jammed his hands in his pockets for warmth and stared unfocused down the line of boats into the distance, as he thought again about what had happened at the lake. He thought back to the conversation he had had there with Joe the other evening, trying to pin down in his mind exactly what Joe had said.

'Where were you that night?' he had asked Joe.

'I was well out of it, don't you remember?'

Alex nodded. At least that bit was clear. He'd seen him sitting under one of the trees, getting stoned with a couple of mates, although he couldn't remember who they were.

'What about Paul and Danny?'

'Off somewhere shagging for Britain, no doubt,' Joe had said, with a sideways glance and a little ironic smile. 'You and I were always crap at pulling. That's why I hated those effing parties, they made me feel so bloody useless.'

Me too, Alex thought, wondering again if Paul had got lucky with the little first year, although she looked barely out of school. After all those years it was amazing how it still niggled. 'What about the girl in the lake?' he had asked Joe. 'Do you remember her?'

'No, but then I was pretty wasted.' Us both, Alex thought. 'I'll bet she was with Paul or Danny at some point,' Joe had said thoughtfully. 'One of them must have asked her.'

'But they said they didn't know her.'

Joe had shaken his head. 'C'mon Alex. Call me cynical, but sometimes you're just too bloody naive for words. They couldn't get enough of the girls, particularly Paul. I told you, it's an addiction thing. He needs therapy, although he won't admit it. Anyway, they'd both lie like hell to save their skins.'

'Whose idea was it to get rid of her? Do you remember?'

'Good question, Alex. I know it wasn't me or you. We just listened to the others. I could barely speak, I was so shattered. You didn't say much either, I remember. You were in a right state, in shock, I guess. You just kept staring at her, as though she'd landed from Mars, and I made you sit down on the grass while the others took a look. I can still hear them bickering about what to do. In the end, maybe it was Tim who took charge and worked things out as he always did. But whoever initially suggested putting her back in the lake, Paul was pretty quick to run with it, like she was something dirty that should be swept quickly under the carpet. He went on and on about his effing uncle not finding out, like that was the worst thing that could happen.'

You were right, Joe, Alex thought, sipping some more of the diluted vodka. Memory was a funny thing and he'd forgotten some of the details until now. God, how he wished Joe was still sitting there with him. Questions multiplied in his head and he felt so alone. How could she have been there that evening and not one of them even noticed her? It was inconceivable. Why had she left her clothes in the boathouse? How had she got into the lake? She was naked, so she must have been swimming, but surely she wouldn't have gone there alone in the dark. And Tim . . . Where had Tim been? Safely with Milly somewhere, he supposed. The two of them were inseparable.

Try as he might to force them, the answers wouldn't come

and he shook his head. The detective had made him doubt his own recall, such as it was, but at least he had stirred things up. Maybe when everything settled again, the fragments perhaps falling into a new and different pattern, Alex would be able finally to make sense of it all. He was sure he had missed something important that night, something that was probably staring him in the face if only he could see it.

He drained his glass and was still sitting, half nodding off as it all swilled pointlessly around in his head, when he heard someone softly call his name. He looked up and saw Maggie walking along the towpath towards him. She was barefoot, a blue silk dressing gown wrapped around her.

She smiled. 'I thought I'd find you here. Why don't you come back to bed? You need some sleep, you know. Don't think about things now.'

He nodded, then yawned, and suddenly realised how tired he was. He struggled to his feet, but as he tried to climb over the tape, he stumbled. She caught his arm and helped him over.

'It will all be fine in the morning, you'll see,' she said, linking her arm through his and slowly walking him back along the towpath towards her boat.

28

Donovan parked the Golf a few houses along from Tartaglia's flat and switched off the engine. It was just before seven in the morning.

'You'd better climb in the back,' she said, nudging Chang, who was in the passenger seat beside her, listening to an iPod with his eyes half closed. 'I'll go and ring the bell.'

She was about to get out when she saw Tartaglia's front door open and a young woman appeared on the threshold. Sinking back in her seat, Donovan caught her breath and watched. Tartaglia had said that his upstairs neighbour was away, so she must have come from his flat. Pausing briefly to put on a pair of huge sunglasses, the woman stepped out into the sunshine and started walking towards them. She was small and skinny, with a mass of long, dark hair. She was wearing what looked like a simple white petticoat made of some sort of satiny fabric that clung to her in all the right places and was practically transparent in the light. The only other thing she appeared to have on was a pair of black, over-the-knee boots.

'Bloody hell,' Chang said, as he slid into the back and slammed the door. 'Who's that? Isn't that Mark's house?'

'Shut up,' Donovan said. 'Not a word about this to anyone.'

'Of course not. It's nobody's business and I don't gossip.'

Donovan said nothing. She didn't trust herself to speak. Her hands were trembling and she let go of the door handle. She wrapped her arms tightly across her chest. She was jealous – so jealous she could barely breathe. The force of the feeling took her by surprise. Did she really care that much? She wished Chang were a million miles away. She took a series of slow, deep breaths, trying to calm herself.

The woman came towards them. As she got close, Donovan could hear her humming something to herself. What with the hair and the glasses it was difficult to see much of her face, but she looked very pretty. From the easy sway of her hips and the way she held her head, she knew it, too. She pulled a phone from her bag, checked the screen and smiled. Still looking down at the phone, she passed their car, busy tapping out a text or email as she carried on along the street.

'Do you want me to go and get him?' Chang asked, once she was out of sight.

'No. I'll do it.'

Wondering if Chang had guessed how she felt or if he was just trying to be helpful, Donovan wrenched open the car door, strode across the street and up the path. The front door wasn't properly closed and she walked straight into the small, communal hall. Pausing briefly outside the door to Tartaglia's flat to wipe her eyes, she knocked. There was no answer. She knocked again, louder this time. She was about to go back outside and ring the bell when the door opened and Tartaglia peered out at her, frowning. He looked dazed. He was barefoot, wearing nothing but a pair of old jeans that he must have pulled on in a hurry; he hadn't even done the zip up properly.

'You told me to pick you up at seven,' she said. 'It's five to now.'

'Jesus, is it really?' He rubbed the thick stubble on his chin thoughtfully. 'I'm sorry, I must have overslept. I'll get dressed as quick as I can. Why don't you come in and make us some coffee while I take a shower.'

'No thanks, I'll wait in the car. I've got Justin with me.'

'I'm sure he can manage on his own. I could do with something good and strong to wake me up.'

'You certainly look like you need it. If you're desperate, you can get a coffee on the motorway. I'll be outside.' She couldn't keep the sharpness out of her voice, but she was past caring what he thought.

'Sam?'

She was already halfway down the path and didn't turn around. Her pulse was racing, every muscle tense. She had no desire to make small talk with Chang either and she sat down on the low wall of the next-door garden to wait, closing her eyes and letting the sun warm her face. Times like this, she wished she hadn't given up smoking. She felt sick and angry. Angry with herself, as much as him. She remembered the first day he was back in the office after his holiday, being struck by how fit he looked, the deep colour of his skin accentuated by the white of his shirt. He had never looked more handsome, she had thought. He had been diving off the coast of Sicily with his cousin Alessandro. There had been no mention of anyone else. Alessandro lived in Milan where he worked as a stockbroker. She had met him a few times, and although he was attractive and good fun, she had marked him down as a bit of a playboy. Although Tartaglia wasn't like that, she could picture the two of them on holiday together and it wasn't a comfortable thought. She had studied Tartaglia carefully on his return. As far as she could tell, there was nothing out of the ordinary about him, no air of inner excitement or something held back, no unusual texts or phone calls or other telltale signs. As far as she knew, there had been nobody important for a long while. So who was the woman? Maybe she was a friend of Nicoletta's and he had lied to her. Whoever she was, she hated herself for wanting to know.

There were times when she thought he looked at her a little differently, almost thought that something might happen between them. Occasionally, he even seemed a little jealous when someone else paid her attention. Then again, it could be her imagination, or wishful thinking. Why don't you tell him how you feel, Claire had said to her on more than one occasion. But what was the point? If he didn't see it, let alone feel the same way, there was nothing to be done. Saying something would only make things more awkward between them, particularly as they worked so closely together, and she couldn't bear the likely humiliation. It was best he had no idea. She inhaled a deep draught of the sweet morning air. She couldn't simply turn her feelings off like a tap, but nor could she carry on torturing herself every time he took a woman to bed. Friendship was no longer enough of a substitute. For a while she had been thinking that maybe she needed to put some distance between them. She needed something to give her a push and maybe that something had now come.

She heard the clunk of a car door and opened her eyes. Chang was strolling towards her, hands in pockets, whistling a tune that sounded familiar, although she couldn't place it.

'Lovely morning,' he said. 'Mind if I join you? It's too nice to stay in the car.'

She shrugged. 'He'll be out in a minute.'

He sat down next to her. 'Gum?' He held out a pack of Juicy Fruit.

'No thanks. What were you whistling?'

He unwrapped a stick and put it in his mouth. 'Mozart. *Marriage of Figaro*. I've been listening to it on my iPod.'

'It sounded nice. Cheerful.'

'In a way. It's about love.'

She stared steadfastly ahead, glad of her dark glasses. Was it an innocent remark or was she completely transparent?

'You look tired,' he said, glancing over at her after a moment. 'Were you up late last night?'

'No. I went to bed relatively early for a change, but I still feel worn out. I think it's this weather. It's difficult to sleep.'

'I know what you mean. I can share the driving with you, if you fancy a kip.'

'Thanks. I'll let you know.'

'What's the plan?'

'We drop Mark off at the hotel where the lake is,' she said, in what she hoped was a normal tone. 'He's meeting the DI from Avon and Somerset there. Then you and I go to Bristol and start checking with MisPer. Fingers crossed the girl was reported locally.'

'Sounds good.' He stretched and yawned. 'I feel knackered

too, but I only have myself to blame. I didn't go to bed until two.' He laced his fingers together and clicked his knuckles in a satisfied manner.

She said nothing. She had no idea what he did in his personal life and had no intention of asking.

'You know, I could really use a cigarette,' he said after a moment.

'You smoke?'

'Used to. I stopped when they brought in the ban. There didn't seem much point in carrying on when they made it all so difficult, but I still get the occasional craving.'

She looked at him, surprised. He always seemed so disciplined, so squeaky clean. He didn't seem the type to have vices. 'It's funny. I gave up last autumn, but I was just thinking a few minutes ago how I'd really like a smoke. Maybe it's the sunshine, or sitting here on the wall with time to kill.'

He nodded. 'There's definitely such a thing as a cigarette moment.'

'Only a smoker, or former smoker, would understand.'

'It's why I chew gum. I find it helps, stops me thinking about it. You should try it some time.'

'I don't think it would be the same.'

'You're probably right. Ah, here's Mark,' he said, getting to his feet as Tartaglia came out of his front door. 'We'd better be going.' As they started across the road towards the car, he glanced over at her and smiled. 'Shame, really. Nice moment, even without a cigarette.' He was still smiling as he slid into the back seat, leaving her wondering if she had heard correctly.

*

There was little traffic on the roads at that hour on a Sunday morning and they made it to Ashleigh Grange in just under two hours. Tartaglia sat in the passenger seat beside Donovan, with Chang asleep in the back for most of the time, headphones plugged in. Donovan seemed unusually silent, insisting on listening to Heart FM instead of talking, which suited him fine, the way he was feeling. Leaning his head against the window, he had dozed for most of the journey. In his more wakeful moments he thought back to the night before, images of Anna replaying in his mind. His last vague memory was of her getting out of his bed earlier that morning and moving around in the dark, no doubt looking for some of her things. He had glimpsed her momentarily silhouetted in the doorway as she went out into the hall. He remembered vaguely wishing that she would come back to bed again and that he could put off going to Bristol until later. Then he must have fallen asleep. Not long after that, or so it seemed, the sound of someone hammering on his door woke him. Wondering if it was Anna, he had struggled out of bed. The only traces of her were her article, still lying folded up on the coffee table where he had left it, and the wine glasses and the lipstick-marked cigarette butt in the ashtray.

He had found Donovan in the hall, looking tense for some reason. She had been in a strange mood all morning. Something was still eating her, although he had no idea what it was. He wondered if it was anything to do with a man, more specifically a DI called Simon Turner who had worked for one of the other teams. As he pictured Turner's big, bony face and arrogant, ice-blue stare, he felt the bile rise. As far as he was aware, he and Donovan were no longer in touch, but whatever was at the root of it, whether it was Turner or someone else, it would have to wait for another time. He had dressed quickly, made some instant black coffee for the sake of speed, and taken a cocktail of painkillers. Even so, he felt the dull throb of a headache that would only get worse over the course of the day, but the hangover was the least of it. Lack of sleep was doing his head in; his memory was fogged, his thought processes running in slow motion. Underneath it all, he had the uneasy feeling that he had done something seriously unwise.

When they reached junction 18 of the M4, he called Graham Roberts to let him know they would soon be arriving. They found Ashleigh Grange easily and Donovan dropped him in the main car park where Roberts was waiting as arranged, sitting in the driver's seat of a navy-blue Saab with the door wide open and reading the *Mail on Sunday*. Catching sight of Tartaglia, he put the paper away and got out of the car. He was a type of policeman that Tartaglia knew well: medium height, stocky build, with thinning, very short greying brown hair, and a tidy brush of a moustache. He must be near retirement age, but he looked trim and fit, dressed in a polo shirt, navy Nike tracksuit bottoms and trainers. He reminded Tartaglia of a Glaswegian rugby coach who had trained him at school.

They shook hands. 'Still no sign of anything, I'm afraid,' Roberts said in a London accent, which had surprised Tartaglia over the phone. He had been expecting some sort of a West Country burr. 'Do you want to go straight down to the lake now? The new search team has only just got started.'

'Please.'

'OK. We'll go via reception. It's probably easiest.' Roberts locked the Saab and they wove their way through the ranks of expensive-looking cars and started down the drive towards the house. It was bordered on either side by a high hedge of laurel and rhododendron and it was difficult to see much beyond it. 'I'd hoped for a quicker result,' Roberts said, 'but there's all kinds of rubbish in the water which is slowing down the search. It seems the lake was used as an unofficial tip by the locals until the hotel chain took it over. I'm surprised they didn't bother to clear it out, but I suppose it costs too much money and, as nobody really uses the lake anymore, what the eye doesn't see . . .' Tartaglia was silent, happy to let Roberts do the talking if he felt like it. 'The last time it was dragged,' Roberts continued, 'was back in the sixties. A young boy went missing from one of the cottages on the estate and they had everyone in the area out looking for him. The boy eventually turned up safe and sound at a friend's house, but in the meantime they found a vintage Rolls Royce in the lake. Back in the twenties or thereabouts, someone – drunk no doubt – had just driven it into the water and left it there. It must have been worth a packet, even after all those years covered in mud. Sadly, we haven't found anything interesting like that.'

Tartaglia yawned. 'Looks like the hotel's doing good business, if the car park's anything to go by.'

'Yes. Being so close to Bath, what with weddings and tourists and the like, it's packed most weekends until the autumn. We've cordoned off the grounds and the woods around the lake but we've had a job keeping the guests out of our hair. We've given them the run of the golf course to keep them quiet, and the spa, but that's all they're allowed for the moment. As you can imagine, there've been no end of complaints and they're all dying to know what's going on. After all the stuff on the telly, everyone fancies themselves an amateur detective these days.'

'If we find the body, how are you going to get it out of here discreetly?'

'Already thought of that. There's a private access road that goes right through the woods to the lake. I've had it sealed it off, for our use alone.'

'Which way are the stables?'

'Back the way we came, but it's a spa now. They turned the old stable yard into an indoor pool. They haven't done a bad job, I have to say.'

'You know this place quite well,' Tartaglia said, thinking that it was much bigger than he had imagined. To make any sense of what Wade and Fleming had said, he would have to try and familiarise himself with it, piece things together the way they had been eighteen years before.

Roberts nodded. 'I've lived here a long time.'

'But you don't sound as though you come from around here?'

'I'm originally from the Elephant and Castle. But we moved down here when I was fourteen, when my dad died and my mum remarried. By then, the damage was done.'

'I imagine this place has changed a lot in the last twenty years.'

'It certainly has. I know it like the back of my hand. My mum still lives in one of the nearby villages. I'm ashamed to say I used to come here with my stepdad to pot the odd rabbit or pheasant. That was before it was all redeveloped, of course. The colonel had died and his wife was living here on her own by then. She must have been in her eighties, blind as a bat and rattling around in the house like a dried pea in a tin can. When she died, the family sold it fast as they could.'

'When was this?'

'Must have been the mid-eighties. It was a right wreck by then and they hadn't the cash to keep it going, let alone do all the necessary repairs. It changed hands several times after that.'

'Do you remember it in the early nineties?'

Roberts shook his head. 'Sorry. I was working in Bristol by then, with a young family to keep me busy. All I know is Avondale Properties bought it about ten years ago and they've sunk an absolute fortune into it. I've played golf here a few times with friends and it's a good course, although personally I couldn't stretch to the membership. But the wife and I come here sometimes for a meal on special occasions. We were here for her fiftieth only last month. I also bought her a day at the spa as a special treat.'

'How far is it from the spa to the lake, or to the main house? I just want to get my bearings.'

'About a mile each way, I'd say, maybe a little more. It's a triangle.'

'Is there a map anywhere?'

'I'm sure we can pick one up at reception, if you want.'

'That would be useful.'

Roberts stuffed his hands in his pockets, looking thoughtful. 'Perhaps you can enlighten me. All I know is that there's a body in the lake and it's a young girl.'

Tartaglia nodded. He'd been wondering when Roberts would ask. 'We think she died during a party in the summer of 1991. There were some students living here at the time.'

'What happened?'

'We're not sure exactly, but one of them found her, then he and his friends decided to cover it up so as not to get into trouble. It's only come to light now.'

Roberts glanced over at him. 'Sounds fishy to me. You think the girl was murdered?'

'It's not clear. It may have been an accident. That's why we need to get her out of there if we can.'

'If it's just an accident, why are you here? I mean, you work for an MIT, right?'

Tartaglia nodded, picking up the suspicious, resentful edge in his voice. He had come across the attitude before. The Met was the only police force in the country to operate dedicated murder investigation teams. Outside the capital, the volume of murders was much lower and there was no need for special-isation. Roberts worked in CID where he handled a whole range of serious crimes. He was a bigger fish in a much smaller pond, but somehow that wasn't enough. His expres-sion said it all: 'Here's this flash, know-it-all Met Murder Squad DI, with his sharp suit and fancy foreign name, coming down from the smoke, muscling in on my turf.' Tartaglia had heard it before. It didn't help that he was a good fifteen years younger than Roberts. But life was tough and Roberts would have to learn to live with it.

'We've been told to pull out all the stops,' Roberts said, clearly not satisfied. 'I can't tell you the job I had getting the search team organised last night. Why the urgency, if she's been down there that long and you're not even sure if she was topped?' He looked at Tartaglia questioningly. He must resent being called out on a Sunday, particularly when he knew he was being given only part of the story, but it wasn't Tartaglia's job to enlighten him. Roberts would have read about the Logan and Khan murders in the papers but the cases were still not officially linked. Also, they were leaking badly enough as it was and there was no reason for Roberts to know more than the bare bones.

'What happened here might possibly be linked to an ongoing murder investigation,' Tartaglia said. 'I'm afraid I can't say any more at the moment.'

Roberts pursed his lips. 'I see. Can you tell me this much; if the girl was murdered, do you have a suspect?'

Tartaglia hesitated. He felt like telling Roberts to mind his own business. His head felt thick and he didn't like being cross-examined, but there was little to be gained from antagonising him. If the girl had been murdered, Fleming was the most likely candidate, but short of a confession there was no real evidence to nail him with. Nor, for the moment, was it clear who would handle the investigation. His only interest in the girl was in relation to the Logan and Khan cases and it would be logical for the inquiry to be handled locally. But it wasn't his call and there was no point stirring things up with Roberts until they knew exactly what had happened. He chose his words carefully.

'We have a statement from the man who originally found her in the lake, which is corroborated by others who were here at the time. There's no point in making assumptions or thinking about likely suspects until we have more information. As I said before, the first step is to get her out of the lake.' He hoped he had been emphatic enough and that Roberts would leave it there.

'I see,' Roberts said again.

They walked in silence for a few minutes, accompanied only by the rhythmic beat of their strides on the gravel. Eventually, the drive opened up into a wide turning circle in front of the main house. Although the honeyed colour of the stone was different, it reminded him of Abbotsford, Sir Walter Scott's house in the Borders, all pepper-pot towers, pointed gables and Gothic windows. If it had once been run-down, it didn't show. Everything was pristine and in good order, paint new, windows sparkling, lawns and flowerbeds as tidy as a municipal garden.

'Do you want to take a look around the house?' Roberts asked.

'Maybe later. All I need for now is the map, then let's go to the lake and see how they're getting on.'

The reception desk was in a small vestibule, just inside the front door. Tartaglia picked up a map and a glossy leaflet about the hotel and followed Roberts into an enormous, vaulted baronial-style banqueting hall. It was lit by two tall stained-glass windows, which cast a rainbow of colours onto the stone floor. He could smell fresh coffee and bacon. The buzz of voices and clink of china and cutlery were coming from a room off the hall, where breakfast was still in progress. It was only nine thirty, but he realised how hungry he was. He had picked up a couple of crois-sants and a Red Bull at a service station on the M4 but they had barely touched the sides and he had passed on the coffee from the vending machine, which looked undrinkable.

'Just need the gents,' Roberts said. 'Won't be a sec.'

As he disappeared back in the direction of reception, Tartaglia sat down in a comfortable armchair by the vast stone hearth. He still felt groggy and his head was beginning to ache with renewed vigour. He would give anything for a decent coffee but he didn't want to delay getting down to the lake. Shielding his eyes from the sun, which was streaming in through the windows, he took out the hotel leaflet from his pocket and started to read, hoping that he might learn something interesting about the place and that it might keep him awake. It gave a potted history of the house, which dated from the early 1800s. The land had originally been bought and eventually developed by Jeremiah Wilson, the son of a wealthy merchant from Bristol who had made a fortune importing tobacco and sugar in the late eighteenth century. Bristol had been a thriving port at the time and he wondered if slave-trade money had been involved too, although there was no mention of it. As Roberts had said, the Wilson family had continued to live in the house until the late 1980s. It had been turned into a hotel ten years later, well after Fleming and his friends had left. There was no mention of what had happened to it in the intervening period.

Roberts reappeared moments later and led the way out through a small door to one side of the huge, carved wood staircase. They walked down through a series of lawns and terraced gardens and came to a high yew hedge with a gate in the middle, which was manned by a uniformed officer. Beyond was an area of open parkland and woods. Roberts took a handkerchief out of his pocket and mopped his brow. 'The lake's just through the trees.'

They showed their IDs and once they had been signed in, they followed a path that had been recently cut through the long grass of the meadow. They had just entered the cool shade of the wood when Roberts's phone started to ring. 'Sorry about this,' he said, stopping to answer it. 'I'll catch you up. Just follow the path.'

The sky overhead was bright blue, and the air was filled with the buzzing of insects and birds, calling high up in the trees. A pair of young male pheasants were rooting among the dead leaves below, paying Tartaglia no notice. The path wound downhill through a dense mixture of deciduous trees and tall rhododendron. Within a minute he saw the lake in front of him. He stopped in the shade of a large beech tree and gazed down at the water. It stretched out smooth and dark, like a huge teardrop. He heard the muted sound of running water somewhere beneath him where, he assumed, the lake was fed by an underground stream. The leaflet had said it was man-made, excavated at the time the house was built, although it looked completely natural in its setting as though it had been there for a thousand years. The trees came right down the slope almost to the water's edge, some reaching far over, their branches scraping the surface.

He followed the path down to the water's edge to get a better view. Wondering how much longer Roberts would be, he lit a cigarette, enjoying the stillness. There was barely a ripple on the surface of the water, which shimmered in the morning sunshine. A small island lay just offshore, close to where he was standing. It was connected to the mainland by a narrow footbridge. A church stood in the middle, encircled by tombstones. On the far side of the lake, an impressive-looking building with pillars and gates opening onto the water nestled amongst the trees. He assumed it must be the boathouse. Several cars and a pickup truck and trailer were parked in a clearing nearby and a man in green track-suit bottoms was leaning on the bonnet of one of the cars, with what looked like a mobile phone clamped to his ear. Next to him were two uniformed police. The search team's RIB was moored beside what looked like a diving platform in the middle of the lake. One of the team sat in the boat keeping watch, in contact with the divers via a headset. They would be working in pairs, deep in the muddy water, the orange surface marker buoys the only indication of where they were.

The house was further away from the lake than he had imagined from Fleming's description and it must have been quite a hike at night, even under the light of a full moon. He tried to picture it all – Fleming kneeling down in the water under the trees, finding the girl's body. He wished now that he had asked Fleming to draw him a map to show exactly where he had been. But standing there, looking at the scene, Fleming's story sounded a little more plausible than it had done in the interview room, although he was still sure something important was missing from it.

He heard the cracking of branches in the undergrowth behind him and turned to see Roberts emerge at the top of the bank.

'Not much going on,' he said, as Roberts slid down and joined him.

'It's a bit like watching paint dry. That was my sergeant

on the phone. You can just see him over there on the far bank. He's the one in the green tracksuit. He thought I was still in the car park waiting for you and he was just ringing to say there was no news.'

'Shall we go over there?'

'Not much point at the moment, unless you just want to stand around staring at the water. I don't know how they'll find anything in there. It's as thick as soup. You're sure she's somewhere in the middle?'

'That's what we were told.'

Roberts shrugged. 'Well, they started right over there by that pontoon, or whatever it is. Apparently, they've been working their way outwards in some sort of formation, but I'm not holding my breath. At this rate, we'll be here all day. Do you want to go and grab a coffee and a snack back at the hotel? Maybe you can tell me a bit more about the case you're working on. They'll call me as soon as they find anything.'

He had no intention of giving Roberts anything further on the case, but the suggestion of coffee and a snack was something he couldn't turn down. 'Sounds a good idea. But before we head back, I'd like to take a look at that little church over there, and maybe also the boathouse.'

Roberts looked at him as though he were mad. 'Suit yourself. I'll just go around and have a word with the lads and tell them what we're doing. Let me know when you're ready.'

They parted company and Tartaglia started to walk towards the church. Sunlight shone through the trees onto the golden-coloured walls. Panes of glass were missing from some of the mullioned windows and a couple of sparrows flew out as he crossed the little bridge that linked the shore to the island. Surprisingly, the church door wasn't locked and he pushed it open. Light flooded in through the windows onto a bare interior that had been stripped of any furnishings. The stone floor was covered in a thick layer of dust, but he could still see where the handful of pews had once stood. A few memorial plaques were dotted around the walls, dedicated to members of the Wilson family, and a large, reclining statue of a young man in uniform lay on a plinth to one side of the altar. Briefly reading the inscription, it sounded as though he had been the only son, killed in battle during the First World War. Behind it, he found a low wooden door, which he assumed led down to the crypt. It, too, wasn't locked, and he carefully picked his way down the narrow stairs, using the little Maglite on his key ring to shed some light. The whole place reeked of damp. When he reached the bottom, which was flooded with an inch or so of murky water, he decided he had seen enough. The heavy metal gates in front of him, with their coat of arms, the decaying coffins on their shelves beyond; it all matched almost exactly the description in the email sent to Joe Logan. Whoever had written it, had to have stood there at some point. Was it one of the five, or someone else who had visited Ashleigh Grange?

Back outside in the sunshine, he breathed in the warm air and followed the narrow path that skirted the lake until he came to the boathouse. It too was built of stone, with gates and a landing stage on the water, and an upper storey above. A balcony spanned the width at the front, with two large windows and a door. The stone facing looked in a poor state of repair. As with the church, panes of glass were broken or missing and the large wooden gates sagged on their hinges, green with mould and rotting where they touched the water. A newish-looking sign had been fixed to one side of the stairs with the words 'DANGER KEEP OUT', no doubt put there by the hotel management, worried about public liability. He was surprised that they hadn't bothered to restore the building. He had never been keen on messing about in boats, even as a child, but it seemed such a shame to let everything decay. However, tastes had changed. The slow, quiet pleasure of taking a boat or a punt out on a lake on a summer's day was something rarely appreciated any longer. With the golf course and the spa to keep them occupied, the guests probably never bothered to venture this far from the hotel. Careful where he put his feet, he climbed the wooden stairs to the first floor. The small terrace was sheltered by the overhanging roof. It stood several metres above the water and commanded a clear view of the entire lake, as well as the chimneys and gables of the main house in the distance. It would have been easy to hide from view behind one of the pillars and he wondered if somebody had been there early on that long-ago morning. Fleming had said he had the impression someone was watching as the five men stood around the girl's body deciding what to do. Had they also seen Wade and Logan row out into the middle of the lake and dump her body?

The door was ajar and he pushed it open and went inside. The floor was covered in a thick carpet of dead leaves. An old-fashioned punt and a rowing boat lay under one of the windows, together with a jumble of wooden paddles, all beyond use. A few oars hung on the back wall, the blades inscribed with the names of school and university eights printed in faded gold lettering on the blades. All the inscriptions dated back to before the First World War and he felt for a moment as though he was in a time warp, as though nothing of consequence had happened to the house since. Perhaps all hope had died with the death of the only son.

Whoever had written the email to Paul Khan had stood right there too. He glanced out of the window across the lake and wondered how many people had known about the crypt and the boathouse. Given the sort of life Fleming and his friends had led, the field was an open one. He thought of the girl's clothing lying in a neat pile somewhere in the middle of the floor here. Why neat? Surely most teenagers didn't bother with tidiness, particularly not in that sort of situation. What had she been doing in the boathouse and why had she left her things there when everybody else had undressed beside the lake? Maybe she had been there for some reason before the party, but if so, why had nobody recognised her?

He heard a shout and looked out of the window. Roberts was jogging towards him, waving. Two of the divers had surfaced in the middle of the lake and were talking to the man in the RIB.

'We'll have to get that coffee later,' Roberts called out, as he came out onto the terrace. 'Looks like they've found something.'

29

Tartaglia stared down at the collection of discoloured bones laid out on the gurney. For all he could tell, the girl might have been in the lake for two hundred years rather than barely twenty. It was early evening and he was waiting for Arabella Browne in a small antechamber of the mortuary at Flax Bourton, just outside Bristol. She had left him to take an important call from London and had been gone a while. He was wondering how much longer he could last. The mortuary building was new and state-of-the-art, but the smell of the place was getting to him worse than usual. The small room was lined with fridges and he felt claustrophobic. An autopsy was in full swing in the adjoining theatre. Against the background of running water and the buzz of a saw, he could hear a woman's piping, nasal voice giving a detailed account of where she had been to dinner and what she had eaten the previous night. His head still felt thick and it was as if each sound was magnified.

They still had no idea who the girl was, but after a cursory examination the anthropologist had confirmed that the skeleton belonged to a female, between five-foot-two and five-foot-four, aged somewhere in her mid to late teens. A more detailed examination would follow, but it certainly seemed likely that she was the girl Fleming had originally discovered by the lake. The search team were still out combing the lake for the rest of her things, but in amongst the mess of mud and bone in the plastic wrapping, Browne had found a pair of gold earrings, each set with a dangling purple stone. Hopefully, they would help identify her. One thing they now knew for certain: her death was no accident. Browne had found a blunt trauma fracture at the back of her skull and her hyoid bone was also fractured. The girl had been strangled.

Alex Fleming said that he hadn't noticed any injuries when he found her, which was just plausible. If the blow to the head had happened more or less at the same time that she was strangled, there was unlikely to have been a great deal of blood. Also, the water in the lake could have washed any blood away. That was assuming Fleming was telling the truth. If not, the possibilities opened up. Wade and Black had both described her body as being muddy and said that her hair was matted with mud and waterweed, as though she had been lying in the shallows of the lake at some point. She could have gone swimming and been attacked when she came out. Or she could have been attacked and then dumped in the lake in an attempt to hide the body.

Tartaglia had seen many cases of manual strangulation, all bar one of them women. Although many were the result of domestic violence, there was often a sexual motive and he wondered if this had been true for the girl. Whatever had happened, unless the force of the blow to the back of the skull had knocked her out, she would have struggled. There

might have been physical signs – discoloration or possibly
bruising to her neck – as well as abrasions, cuts and scratches
either made by the killer, or by the victim as she tried to
defend herself. How could Fleming have noticed nothing?
The blow to the head had been straight on, not angled from
above. Given the girl's small stature, the most likely explanation was that she had fallen backwards with some force
and hit her head against something hard like a rock, although
he didn't remember seeing anything like that around the
lake. He pictured a scene, a man's large, strong hands around
the girl's slender neck, maybe he was on top of her, forcing
her down, throttling her, she hitting her head. In his mind,
she was being raped and the man on top of her was Alex
Fleming. They would arrest him straight away. Hopefully, now
that they had found her and had an idea what had happened,
they would be able to force a confession out of him.

The two women in the adjoining theatre had moved on
to speculating about the sexual attributes and abilities of a
male colleague. It was all getting too close to home and, even
though he had no choice, he felt like an eavesdropper. There
was still no sign of Browne and he decided to go outside and
call Steele with the news. He needed some fresh air to clear
his head and, more than anything, he needed a smoke. He
walked out of the room and through the front doors, looking
back briefly at the uninspiring modern building, recently
completed and tacked on like a prosthetic limb behind the
late-Victorian coroner's court. Browne had been extolling the
new facilities inside like a backpacker in a suite at the Ritz,
but he couldn't get excited. Outside, it was an unhappy archi-
tectural marriage. The new wing lacked any sort of vision

and was the usual compromise of the bureaucratic planning process. He wondered how the residents of rural Flax Bourton felt about it. In a way, it might have been better to bulldoze the whole thing and start from scratch.

He sat down on the front steps, lit a cigarette and dialled Steele's line. She picked up immediately.

'It's Mark. I—'

'I was just about to call you,' she cut in. There was urgency in her tone. 'Where are you?'

'At the mortuary in Bristol. Why?'

'You'd better get back here right away. Daniel Black has been murdered.'

The words hit him like a body blow and he closed his eyes. 'Shit,' he said. He put his forehead in his hand and took in a lungful of smoke. His fears had been realised and he felt the dull tug of remorse. If only they had put Black under surveillance or offered him protection. It wasn't his call but maybe he should have said more. He wondered how Steele was feeling. Panicked, he imagined. She wasn't the emotional type and it was difficult to tell much over the phone, but it was what every detective feared. Neither of them had felt much empathy for Black, but that wasn't the point. It was another senseless killing that, in his view, should have been prevented.

'What happened?'

'He was found floating face down in the lake in St James's Park. Same MO. Single shot to the head, point-blank range, castrated, just like the others. He was in the water, near the edge . . .'

'Like the girl.'

'That's right.' He heard a sigh before she added: 'Any more news your end?'

'Yes. That's why I was calling you. It looks like she was murdered.'

'God ... here was I hoping for some good news for a change.'

'Sorry. She was hit on the back of the head and the hyoid's fractured.'

'So, she was strangled.' There was a pause, followed by another deep, heart-felt sigh. 'Damn. That's all we need. You've told the locals to keep it quiet? The press are scenting blood and I don't want any link whatsoever with what's going on here.'

'I've spelled it out, don't worry. The DI down here doesn't seem to know much anyway.'

'Good. Where are Sam and Justin?'

'Last time we spoke, still going through the missing persons files.'

'Well, you'd better leave them to it and come back here. The girl's the least of our worries.'

'But we've got to find out who she is. She's the key to this whole thing.'

'You may be right, but I need you here now. Sam can look after things that end for the time being. I've got the Chief Super on my back asking why we didn't stop this from happening. The press are going to have a field day when they find out.'

He made no comment. It wasn't right to say I told you so, however much he'd like to. Even though he felt she should have pushed harder, the blame lay squarely at Clive Cornish's door. Hopefully, his boss, Detective Chief Superintendent John Manners, would work it out. If not, somebody, somehow, would have to tell him. Cornish was a liability.

'You're sure it's the girl's body?' she asked, almost as an after-thought.

'As far as we can be, at this point.'

'Right. We'll round up Fleming and Wade straight away. And you get yourself on a train to Paddington PDQ.'

It was half past seven in the evening. The sun was low in the sky, light filtering through the trees opposite into the front of the bar where Donovan was sitting. She could see Chang pacing up and down outside in the street, where it was quieter, using his BlackBerry to find them rooms for the night. She took a large sip of her margarita and sighed. It had been a while since she had had a cocktail and margaritas were her favourite. She loved the tang of the salt, coupled with the sharpness of the lime-juice, the kick of tequila just behind. The news of Daniel Black's murder had cast a pall over everything. Tartaglia had called her with the details on his way back to London by train. She could hear the anger and frustration in his voice and she couldn't blame him. In his view, sheer financial considerations had cost a man his life. Even more than before, the pressure was on to find out everything they could about the girl before something else happened. But there was nothing else she or Chang could do until the morning.

The bar was in the Mall, right in the heart of Clifton village. She had often gone there for a drink or a bite to eat when visiting Claire, all those years ago. The name had changed, probably many times since, as had the décor, but it still had a nice, airy atmosphere, with a high ceiling, old wooden floors and mirrors. The food chalked up on the board looked appetising and good value. Apart from a couple, holding hands across a table in one corner and a man on his own reading a book, the place was empty. Maybe it was always quiet on a Sunday night, but she was grateful for it. It was also good to have some space for a change. The music was loud, some sort of bland techno jazz that was not generally her thing, but for once she found the repetitiveness calming. Her thoughts turned momentarily to Tartaglia, wondering yet again who the dark-haired woman was. Then she stopped herself. What was the point? Luckily, she had been so busy all day she had barely had a second to think about him.

Being a Sunday, it had taken a while to get the old files sent over from storage. They had then spent the rest of the afternoon going through everything in a dark, airless office. The main problem was that nobody they had spoken to who had been at the party could remember exactly when it had taken place. There seemed to have been many parties at the house that summer. The only thing Fleming and the others had been sure about was that it had happened after their final exams. She had checked with the university and discovered that final exams for the many different faculties were staggered over several weeks, with the university breaking up for the summer towards the end of June. According to Wade, who seemed to have the best memory, the five had stayed on at the house until a week or so after the end of term, so the time window was quite wide. To complicate matters, people were often reported missing days or weeks after they had actually disappeared. It was also possible that the girl might have gone missing some time before she turned up at the party.

Using the physical description provided by the anthropologist, they had checked all open missing persons files for the whole of the Bristol area for a three-month period up until the end of July 1991 and had come up with two possible matches. The first was Cassandra Mayhew, a first year History student who had disappeared on the second of June, in the middle of her end-of-year exams. She had been living in a hall of residence in Clifton and had been reported missing by a friend, another girl on her course. She was just eighteen, five-foot-two, slender build, and described as having mid-length, slightly wavy brown hair. In the photo attached to the report, she had a fresh-faced, innocent quality, with dreamy eyes, and no make-up. The summary report mentioned the fact that, as a young teenager, she had been treated for depression and anorexia. Her friends had said that she was very worried about failing her exams and had recently broken up with a boyfriend.

The second possibility was Danielle Henderson, a fourteen-year-old who had last been seen on the morning of June twentieth chatting to a friend outside the school gates. She had been reported missing by her mother, Susan, when she didn't come home that afternoon. Although she wasn't at the university, Bristol Grammar School was situated on the edge of Clifton, right behind the main university buildings, so it was easily possible she might have come across one of the students at some point. She was described as being five-foot-four, with blue-grey eyes and longish, dark blonde hair.

There was no mention of her build. The photograph attached to the report showed her in school uniform, with her hair pulled back in a tight ponytail. Her face was pretty and childishly round, with dimples showing as she smiled sweetly for the camera. She looked young for her age, particularly given the way girls dressed now. The report mentioned the fact that her parents were divorced and that she had quarrelled with her mother shortly before she disappeared. She had also often talked about wanting to run away, some said to be with her father, and the friends who had been interviewed seemed less concerned about her whereabouts than her mother was. The view expressed by the officer writing the report was that there was a strong possibility that this is what she had done.

It was impossible to know if the photographs in the reports were recent at the time the girls went missing or, indeed, good likenesses that their peer groups would recognise. Families usually wanted to portray their loved ones in the best light possible and their choice of photographs could often be misleading. At first glance, either of the two might have fitted the basic description given by Fleming and the others, although Cassandra, or Caz as she had been known, seemed the more likely candidate, given her age and the fact that she was at the university where she might easily have come across one of the five men or their friends. Speaking to the girls' families was the next priority and she had tasked Jane Downes back in London with the job of tracking them down from the old information in the files.

She had just finished her drink when Chang reappeared. 'Good news,' he said, coming over to where she was sitting.

'I've got us two rooms a few minutes walk from here. Fifty quid each, including full breakfast. How's that? One of them even has a view of the Suspension Bridge.'

She smiled. 'Sounds good to me.' Luckily, following past experience, she had thought to bring a toothbrush and a change of clothes in case she had to stay over.

'We can go over there any time.'

'I wouldn't mind getting something to eat first. I'm hungry and the food here looks really good.'

'Sure. I'll order. What do you fancy?'

She glanced over at the board on the wall, trying to decide. 'Umm, I think I'll have the spiced aubergine tagine, with a side salad.'

'Do you want another one of those?' he asked, looking at her empty glass. 'Or shall I get some wine?'

'Another margarita, I think. It's doing me the world of good.'

Chang went up to the bar, where he ordered their food. He had removed his jacket and tie, rolled up his sleeves and undone a couple of buttons of his shirt. He was looking a lot more relaxed. For once she felt pleased to have his company, glad also not to be on her own. In fairness to him, he had been easy-going and cheerful all day, which was more than could be said for her. She felt a little guilty for having been quite so bad-tempered.

A few minutes later, he returned with two more margaritas, sat down opposite her and raised his glass. 'Here's to finding whoever's doing all of this.'

She raised hers in return. 'I'll definitely drink to that.'

'I was praying for something interesting for my first case,

but they say beware what you wish for.'

'Nothing like being thrown in at the deep end.'

'I suppose so. Did you manage to get hold of Mark again?'

'Yes. While you were outside. The signal kept cutting out, but he was nearly at Paddington. They're bringing Wade in for questioning as we speak, but so far there's no sign of Fleming.'

'Maybe he's done a runner.'

'But why?' She licked some salt from the rim of the glass, letting it dissolve on her tongue before washing it down with the drink. 'Even if he did kill the girl, he must know we can't prove it. And we're no nearer to finding out who killed the other three. I feel depressed just thinking about it. Let's talk about something else.'

'OK.' He was looking at her with an amused expression and she tried to think of something to say.

'I've never actually asked you what you did before you joined us.'

'That's easy. I was on secondment to the Chinese Intelligence Unit for eight months.'

'That sounds interesting.'

'Not really. Most of the time I was in some van or office listening to endless taped conversations. I was bored rigid, so I asked to be transferred to something more active. In the end they took me seriously.'

'This is certainly more cutting edge, if that's what you want.'

'It's exactly what I want.'

Feeling increasingly light-headed, she took another sip. 'You're a bit of a dark horse,' she said, after a moment, wondering if maybe she had misread him.

'How do you mean?'

'We've been working together for . . . how long is it?'

'Six weeks.'

'That's right. We sit next to each other. We've had the odd coffee, the odd drink and several car journeys. And yet I know nothing about you.'

'I thought you weren't interested.'

'Well, I am now,' she said, a little taken aback by his directness. 'Give me a thumbnail sketch.'

'OK. If that's what you want. I was born in Hong Kong and my parents still live there. My father's Chinese, my mother's English. My father's obsessed with this country and he sent me to school over here when I was thirteen.'

'Boarding school?' she said, surprised.

'Yes.'

'All that time walking around St Thomas's and you never said?'

'You never asked.'

'True. Still, you might have told me.'

'Why? I got the clear impression you didn't want the personal stuff.'

He spoke matter-of-factly, without any hint of bitterness. She had to admit it was a fair point. She hadn't really paid much attention to him before or wanted to know anything about him. He had been an inconvenience, just another newby who had to be shown the ropes when everyone was working flat out. But she was curious now.

'OK. What did you do next?'

'I went to Cambridge and read Oriental Studies. When I

graduated my father wanted me to become a lawyer, but I'd had enough of studying.' He paused.

'Then what?'

'I'd split up with the girl I'd been going out with for three years at university, so I had no ties. I took off and went around the world. It was only supposed to be for a year or so. But it ended up being seven.'

'What on earth did you do all that time?'

'I bummed around for a bit, first Europe, then the States. I started in Miami and then went over to the Turks and Caicos to stay with an old friend. One thing led to another and I decided to teach diving.'

'Diving?'

'Yes. I've been doing it since I was ten and I love it. It's also a great way to see the world. There are always endless job ads on the PADI website. Anyway, after the US, I moved on to Mexico, then South America. Eventually I ended up in the Far East. I'd work in a diving centre in some tourist resort for a while, earn some money, then when the season was over, or I got bored, I'd move on. Eventually, I worked my way up to instructor. I was out in Thailand by then, having a great time.'

'You should talk to Mark. He loves diving. He's just done some sort of underwater photography course.'

'Really? I didn't know that. He doesn't talk much about himself.'

She didn't reply. He was right. Tartaglia made a point of keeping himself to himself in the office, which only heightened the mystery for those that didn't know him well. She had thought he was a friend, even that they were close, but it looked as though she had made a mistake . . . Wanting to move the conversation away from Tartaglia, she was about to ask Chang another question, when the waiter appeared with their food. They ate in silence, letting the buzz of the music fill the gap.

'So, why did you stop?' she asked after a few minutes.

'I'd just turned twenty-seven. I suppose I was tired of being a nomad and I'd dived all the best sites around the world. I didn't fancy going back to Hong Kong and getting caught up in my father's business, so I came back to the UK. It's always been my second home.'

She took a sip of her drink, wishing that she had asked for a glass of wine instead. 'And why the Met? It's quite a change, isn't it?'

He shrugged. 'My father was still nagging me to be a lawyer, but it didn't float my boat, as they say.'

'Whereas the police did?'

'I thought it was worth a try. It was mainstream enough to shut him up, and yet completely different from what he wanted me to do. In the end, he gave up and left me alone, which is all I wanted. I was fast-tracked and spent the next few years being moved from one section to another. They wanted me to stay in the CIU, but I said I'd quit if they didn't move me to an MIT. Luckily I had a great boss who supported me and they could see my heart wasn't in it. In the end, they relented. For the record, I really like what I'm doing now.'

She sighed. 'Wish I could say the same.'

'You're not enjoying it?'

'I like the job. I certainly wouldn't want to do anything else in the police. I feel it's something worthwhile and I also feel I can make a contribution. But at the moment I'm a bit stale. I think I need a change of scene.'

He frowned. 'You want to move somewhere else? Join another team?'

'Maybe. Or maybe I need something totally different. I think I told you, my parents were both teachers. I was wondering if I should try it.'

'Are you sure?' he said, with obvious surprise. 'I know you can be dedicated, but you have a pretty short fuse.' He was smiling at her.

'You're perceptive. I suppose I haven't exactly been that nice to you, have I?'

'I didn't take it personally.'

'I'm glad. I've been a cow, yet you've put up with it. Why?'

'It's simple. I like you.'

She glanced away, embarrassed by his directness. There was more to him than she'd given him credit for and he was attractive, an interesting physical mix of East and West. She wondered why she hadn't noticed before, but maybe her mood had blinded her to everything. 'I don't know why I'm telling you all this,' she said, in between mouthfuls. 'I haven't mentioned it to anyone else.'

'What, not even Mark?'

'No.'

'I thought you two were pretty close.'

She felt herself colour. 'Not especially.'

'Well, you can trust me. I won't say a word, but I really hope you change your mind. It wouldn't be the same without you.'

'Thanks again. You're very good for my morale.'

'That's something, I suppose.'

She met his eye, then looked away and took a sip of her drink. 'Anyway, you haven't finished telling me about yourself. Do you have any brothers or sisters?'

'One sister, a year younger than me. She's a lawyer, or a barrister, I should say. So my father's happy. She lives in London too. Actually, we share a flat. You should meet her. She's the same age as you and I think you'd get on.'

She looked up at him, puzzled. 'Justin, how old are you, if you don't mind my asking?'

His smile widened. 'Older than I look.'

'Which is?'

'Thirty-three. I'll be thirty-four in October.'

'Oh.' She couldn't hide her surprise.

'I know, I know. Be honest, like everyone else, you assumed I was still wet behind the ears.'

'Well, not exactly. I thought you were probably mid-twenties, late twenties at most.'

He nodded. 'It's been the bane of my life. I've always had to carry ID to buy a drink or go and see a film. I suppose it will come in handy when I'm older, but it's a right pain for now.'

'Tell me about it,' she said, finishing the last bit of tagine. 'Just because I'm small, everyone assumes I'm barely out of my teens. Perhaps if I wore heels and make-up all the time they'd take me seriously, but I just can't be bothered to play the game.'

'You look very nice the way you are.'

She gave him a broad smile and drained her glass. 'Thanks.'

'Another margarita?' he asked.

'No. Maybe a glass of wine. Red. Something with a bit of body.'

30

Tim Wade leaned back in his chair until the frame cracked and rubbed his face slowly with his hands. 'I haven't lied to you,' he said quietly. 'I don't know who the girl was and I had nothing to do with her death. Are you sure she was murdered?'

Tartaglia nodded. 'Absolutely.'

'Can you tell me what happened to her?'

'I'm afraid not.'

'You think it was some sort of sexual encounter gone wrong?'

'Why do you say that?'

'Come on, Inspector. You and I both know what we're talking about. I've seen enough of that sort of thing in my time at the Bar, and I'm sure you have too, in your line of work. Why else would a young woman get herself killed at a party?' He fixed Tartaglia with a level stare. 'I'm right, aren't I? I'm surprised you found any evidence after all this time, but as far as Alex is concerned, he's not your man.'

Tartaglia held Wade's gaze. What he said was reasonable, although it was impossible to tell if it was what he really thought, or if he was hiding something. At face value, his words had the veneer of honesty and there wasn't a glimmer of anything less settled behind them. But he was a professional and far too experienced to be wrong-footed.

'How can you be so sure?'

'Easy. Alex and I have been friends for thirty years. He's honest, he's decent and he's always been absolutely hopeless with women. At one point I thought he might even be gay. Whether it's because he's lazy, or just hasn't the confidence, he never makes the first move. In a way, it's actually quite a successful strategy. The women all end up doing the work for him—'

Tartaglia held up his hand. 'Thank you, Mr Wade. But we're talking about murder, not whether or not he's capable of pulling women.'

'But that's the point. Alex is psychologically not the type. I've never seen him aggressive, or losing his temper in a serious way.'

'Aren't you jumping the gun a bit?'

Wade shook his head. 'I'm sure you've worked it out for yourself already, but why else would someone have killed her? I know you won't tell me anything, but my guess is it's unlikely to have been premeditated.' He looked at Tartaglia enquiringly. 'Do you agree?'

'Impossible to say.'

'You really think someone set out deliberately to kill her?' He shook his head dismissively. 'It was a party. Lots of people there, lots of drink and things going on. Things happen. Maybe someone got a bit carried away.'

'What's the point of speculating?'

'Just hear me out. The way I see it, based on my professional experience, there has to be some sort of emotion driving it. I'm thinking frustration, anger, jealousy, hatred, maybe sexual passion. Right?'

'Possibly.'

'Well, none of this fits with Alex. He's generally pretty placid. He doesn't get riled up and he wouldn't harm a fly.'

'People do strange things when they're high, particularly when they've taken a mixture of things, as Mr Fleming has admitted to.'

'Well, I disagree,' Wade said emphatically. 'And I'm very worried about him.'

'So are we. We're doing everything we can to find him. When did you two last speak?'

'Yesterday afternoon, after we finished here. He was in a pretty emotional state, I can tell you.'

'I thought you said he wasn't emotional.'

'I said he wasn't aggressive. He does self-pity very well and he was feeling extremely sorry for himself. It sounds like you gave him a pretty hard time. I tried to talk some sense into him, but he just gave me the brush-off.'

'Why was he so upset, do you think?' Tartaglia asked, wishing he could have been a fly on the wall during their conversation.

'Because he's not used to dealing with you lot. He doesn't know how you work and you scared him.'

'I don't see why, if he's innocent.'

'He said that you thought he'd killed the girl, that you thought he might have killed Paul and Joe too, and being a stupid fool, he actually believed you meant it. I told him it was a load of rubbish, that you were just trying to find out how much he knew and that you had no evidence whatsoever and that he shouldn't let it worry him.'

'That was helpful of you. We were just trying to get to the bottom of things.'

'As I said. Anyway, strong-arm tactics don't work with Alex. He was really upset about it and he wouldn't even listen to me, which is most unusual. Maybe he's run off somewhere to get away from all of this and bury his head in the sand.'

'Do you know where he went after that?'

'To the restaurant. He said he had to work.'

'We've spoken to the people at the restaurant and they confirmed that he worked his shift last night.'

'Was he there today?'

'No, and he's not due in again until Monday evening. We've checked with his flatmate and he didn't sleep there last night and he hasn't been back since. Does he have a girlfriend or partner?'

'No. Hasn't had one for ages, as far as I know.'

'Maybe he went home with someone from the restaurant?'

Wade shook his head. 'Alex isn't into casual sex. He's one of the world's last, genuine, old-fashioned romantics. It's why he's never married.'

'Really?' He found Wade's remark surprising and wondered what lay behind it. Was his view of married life cynical or merely pragmatic? Did he hanker after the single life? But there was no time to explore it. There were more important things to cover. 'Are you sure you don't know where he is?'

'Hand on heart, Inspector. If I did, even if he'd told me not to tell you, I would. As I said, I'm very worried about his safety.'

'What about Daniel Black? When did you last see him?'

'Again, it was after we both were finished here. I left Alex in Ken High Street, came back here and waited until Danny came out. We had a quick drink in the Scarsdale Arms around the corner, then he pushed off.'

'Do you know where he went?'

'He said he had to meet someone, but I've no idea who. Danny was always going off to meet some unsavoury type, so I didn't bother to ask.'

'You don't seem very upset by what happened to him.'

Wade stared at him and shook his head disapprovingly. 'Don't give me that. I've been around the block far too many times to allow myself to be provoked by some cheap remark. You have no idea what I feel and it's none of your business.'

'Still . . .'

'I'm here of my own free will. If you start trying to get at me, I'll stop cooperating.'

Tartaglia held his gaze for a moment, then inclined his head. It *was* a cheap remark. Wade had seemed visibly shaken by the news of Black's death and the discovery of the girl's body. He decided to play it straight. 'OK. Going back to the girl, in the statement you gave us yesterday, you said you met Mr Fleming that night after he had found her in the lake.'

'That's right.'

'Where exactly did you see him? I was there today and I'm just trying to get a picture of it all in my mind.'

'It was somewhere in the woods, but don't ask me precisely where. I was pretty pissed. All I know is I was trying to find my way back to the stables. Alex saw me and called out. He tried to tell me about her, but I'm afraid I really didn't pay much attention to what he was saying. I was shattered and all I could think about was bed. I know it sounds callous now, but he wasn't making much sense and it was really late. Is there any point in going over this again?'

'Please. Humour me for a minute. Was he agitated or upset?'

'Both, I suppose. But there's nothing suspicious in that. Even in the state he was in, he could see something wasn't right with her. He tried to get me to go back with him and take a look at her, but as you'll know if you've been there, it's all very spread out. I didn't fancy walking all the way back and I told him it would have to wait until morning.'

'But you believed what he said?'

'To be honest, I thought he was exaggerating. Alex is inclined to be a bit dramatic. People were crashed out all over the place by that time. I don't think anyone made it home that night. I just assumed that whoever she was, she'd had too much to drink, or something, and just needed to sleep it off.'

'If you didn't take what he said seriously, why did you bother to go back to find her the next day?'

Wade rubbed his chin thoughtfully. 'You know, I don't really remember. I'm not even sure if it was my idea. Maybe I thought we ought to check, just to make double sure.'

'But according to what Mr Fleming said, you came to find him and you had Paul Khan and Danny Black with you. So you must have taken it seriously.'

Wade shrugged. 'Maybe I said something to Paul and he said we should all check it out. He was very proprietorial about the place, as if the whole thing belonged to him, not his uncle. But I'm afraid it's all too long ago to remember the exact details. Anyway, why does it matter? What's important now is to find out who's doing this. Until you do, Alex and I aren't safe. We both need protection and you should have offered it to us before.'

'We're trying to sort something out now,' Tartaglia said, picking up the implicit threat in Wade's words. Hopefully, Steele would be able to square things with Cornish. If not, they would have to go up the food chain until they found someone with sufficient understanding and clout to do it.

Wade gave him a penetrating stare. 'Well, I'm not leaving here without it. I have no intention of becoming the next victim.'

'I promise you, Mr Wade, that's the last thing we want too.'

Wade shifted in his chair. 'Do you think this is all about that girl?'

'We're keeping an open mind for the moment.'

Wade shook his head as though he didn't buy it. 'It's got to be about her, hasn't it? The only problem is, there were any number of people at that party who could have done it. They got away with it until now, so why suddenly stir things up? She could have been there another twenty years without anyone knowing. And why kill Joe, and Paul, and now Danny? If it's someone close to the girl, say a member of her family, why start killing now, and why target us? I tell you, all we're guilty of is hiding her body. We didn't kill her.'

Tartaglia looked him in the eye but could read nothing. What Wade said made sense and it was something that had also been puzzling him. As soon as they had an ID, they would start tracing the girl's next of kin, but it still didn't get them much further towards finding out who had killed the three men. If it was a father, or a brother, how would they have known about what had happened that night? How would they know about the crypt, the boathouse and the lake, and about the five men, unless they were there? And if they had been there, why hadn't they done something about it sooner? On top of everything, even though the five had committed a criminal act in hiding the body, he agreed with Wade. It didn't seem sufficient motive for cold-blooded murder.

Nor did the theory that one of the five was behind what was happening hold water any longer. The post mortem hadn't yet been carried out, but it looked as though Black had been killed some time between six o'clock in the evening and the early hours of the next morning. The park was officially closed between midnight and five a.m., but it wasn't fenced in and access was easy. Although the area was riddled with security cameras, he held little hope of anything meaningful being found. The killer was far too organised. Black's body had been left face down in shallow water, hidden under the thick, overhanging branches of a willow tree. Tim Wade had been the last person they knew of to see Black alive. So far they had been unable to trace Danny's steps after that. It looked as though his body had been in the lake for at least twelve hours before it was discovered by an elderly Labrador, chasing a tennis ball, in the early afternoon. He wondered what the statistics were for bodies discovered by dogs; they deserved medals, as far as he was concerned. Fleming had been at the restaurant for the whole of Saturday evening until one o'clock Sunday morning, which probably ruled him out, although where he had gone afterwards was a mystery. It seemed that Wade, too, was in the clear. After his drink with Black, he had gone straight home and stayed in all evening. His wife would vouch for him, he said. He had left the house the next morning at nine o'clock and had arrived at his chambers by ten, where he had been seen working by two other members of chambers. He had then returned home for Sunday lunch with his in-laws just after one.

There was a knock and Steele put her head around the door. 'Mark, can I have a quick word?'

'I'll be right back,' Tartaglia said to Wade, getting to his feet. He joined Steele outside and they walked away down the hall. Once they were safely out of earshot, Steele turned to face him.

'Bad news. Either there's been one leak too many or the press have joined up the dots. The press office just emailed this over to me for comment.' She held up a sheet of paper with the headline **CENTRAL LONDON MURDERS LINKED**. He couldn't make out the details but he saw Anna Paget's by-line beneath the name of one of the regular hacks on the crime desk. His heart sank. What had he said to her the night before? He was sure he hadn't mentioned anything particularly sensitive . . .

'Isn't Anna Paget the woman who interviewed Joe Logan?' Steele asked. He nodded, hoping she couldn't read his internal confusion. 'There'll be a press conference first thing tomorrow,' she continued. 'I guess it was only a matter of time, but they'll all be on our backs now like a pack of hyenas and they'll whip the public up into a state of hysteria. You'd better tell your team to batten down the hatches. They are not to talk to anybody, and I mean anybody.'

'What about Wade? What shall I say to him?'

'Oh yes,' she nodded. 'I almost forgot. You can tell him he can have the protection he's asked for on the condition that he says absolutely nothing to the press. Hopefully his name won't come up anywhere, but tell him that if any journalists start sniffing around, he's to refer them to us and contact us immediately. In the meantime, we'll put someone in the house with him and his family twenty-four-seven and there will also be someone outside. There'll be a special alarm with a panic button that will come straight through to us in the event of an emergency.'

'He says he's in the middle of a case up in Oxford and he insists he can't abandon it.'

She sighed. 'That's very awkward. It would be easier if he stayed put, but if, as you say, he insists on going, tell him we can work something out. Given what happened to Danny Black, we must bend over backwards to keep *him* safe.'

'What about Wade's family? He has a wife and two children. He said he wanted protection for them as well.'

'When he's away, the alarm and the panic button will have to do. As far as I'm aware, they're not under threat.'

'He won't be happy with that. He seems to think the killer may use them to get at him.'

'I can't help what he thinks. They're not at risk as far as I can tell and we—'

'Haven't got the resources. I know. I'll explain it to him. I'm sure he knows how it works. Maybe he can send them away somewhere until this is all over.'

She nodded. 'What I don't want him to know is that we're also putting him under covert surveillance.'

He looked at her surprised. 'Don't you think it's a bit late for that?'

'No. We can't take any chances. It's possible the killer may be watching him. And if Fleming tries to contact Wade, we need to know about it immediately. I don't want to have to rely on Mr Wade's civic-mindedness to turn Fleming in. I also want to know what they talk about amongst themselves. They must have some idea who's doing this.'

'You really think so?' he said, again thinking back to the conversation Fleming and Wade had had the previous afternoon, wishing he knew exactly what had been said. If only they could find Fleming . . . 'Surely if they did, they'd say something?' he added. 'I mean they're clearly both in danger.'

'It depends what their role in all this has been. If Fleming did murder that girl, which seems highly likely, we have no way of proving it unless he owns up to it. We need a lever. If we could get him to admit to it on tape, maybe that would be enough.'

'What about Fleming's flat?'

'We're putting that under surveillance too and we'll be monitoring his phone, although it appears to be switched off at the moment.'

They started back along the corridor towards the interview room. They were almost at the door when Minderedes stepped out of the lift in front of them.

'There you are, sir,' he said to Tartaglia. 'I've been trying to reach you.'

'I've been in with Tim Wade and my phone's been off.'

'There's a message for you from Graham Roberts, in Bristol. He said they've found the girl's things in the lake. You're to call him as soon as you can.'

31

Donovan opened her eyes. Daylight filtered in at the edges of the blind but the room was dark and she couldn't see much. Her mouth felt dry and her head ached. She needed some water and some Hedex, which was in her bag, God knows where. She squinted at the luminous face of her watch. It was just before five in the morning, or six – she couldn't tell which. She felt a movement in the bed beside her and it all came flooding back. Was she in his room or hers? It took her a moment to work it out as she struggled to run through the sequence of what happened.

After more wine, they had paid the bill and left the restaurant. They had found their way easily to the hotel and checked in. She remembered going up in the lift with Chang and she remembered their going to her room first, where Chang said he wanted to look at the view. She had stood at the window with him in the dark, looking up at the Suspension Bridge, which was illuminated. She remembered that he had kissed her. She had no idea why they had then gone to his room after that, but they had had some more drinks from the mini-bar, put on some music from his iPod on the player, and one thing had inevitably led to another. She had no regrets about any of it, but she now wished she was back in her own room.

She could just make out the dark shape of his head on the pillow. From the quiet, easy breathing, she could tell he was asleep. She slid out of bed and felt around on the floor for her things, finding everything except one of her shoes. She had no idea where it had got to. She quickly put on her trousers and T-shirt and tucked the rest under her arm. She found her key card in one of her trouser pockets and quietly let herself out. Her own room was across the hall. When she opened the door, sunshine streamed in through the window. It was too bright and she drew the curtains. She found her bag and took a couple of Hedex, washed down with a glass of coke from the mini-bar. It was incredibly sweet but maybe the sugar would do her good. She undressed again and climbed into the shower, standing for several minutes under the hot water until her head started to clear. Apart from the hangover, she felt good; better than she had done for a long while. What had happened with Chang hadn't banished her confusion about Tartaglia but the distraction had made the pain recede a little – at least temporarily.

When she had finished showering, she put on a bathrobe and was about to get into bed when she heard her mobile ringing. She looked at her watch. It was later than she had thought, past seven o'clock. She got out of bed again, rummaged wearily in her bag until she found her phone and saw Tartaglia's name on the screen.

After a moment's hesitation, she sat back down on the bed and answered it. 'What is it?'

'I've been trying you all last night. Where've you been?'

He sounded tense. She couldn't tell if it was frustration or worry. She struggled to think of an excuse. 'My phone was on silent, sorry.' It sounded pretty lame given that she'd just answered it, but she didn't care. It was none of his business where she was. Nor did she want him to think he could call her at all hours of the day and night.

'I just wanted to talk to you. Are you OK?'

'Of course I'm OK,' she snapped. 'I'm in bed.'

'Shouldn't you be getting up?'

'I will in a minute. Is this why you called me?'

'No. They've found the girl's clothes, or what's left of them. They're not going to be much help, although we may get a shoe size, but there was a handbag. Luckily it was made of plastic. Although some water got in and ruined most of the contents, they found a bus pass in a little plastic wallet. It was inside a zipped pocket so it hasn't disintegrated. There's a name written on it in biro and it looks like Amber, surname Wiseman, and there's a Bristol address, which I'll send you in a minute.'

'There's no missing girl called Amber in the files that we pulled.'

'Maybe you missed the report.'

'No. We went through everything for those three months really carefully.'

'Well, I'm sure there's a simple explanation. Anyway, the main thing now is to talk to the family. I'm emailing you some photos that the lab has just sent me of the earrings that were found with the body. Hopefully they'll help identify her. See if the hotel can print them out.'

'OK.'

'If you need any help on the ground, let me know and I'll speak to Graham Roberts.'

'All right.'

'And Sam?'

'What is it?'

'Go carefully. Although I've no idea how it all links up, it's very possible that a member of her family is behind the killings.'

She took clean clothes from her overnight bag and got dressed. She had washed her hair but had forgotten to bring either a comb or a brush. She ran her fingers through it quickly. It would have to do. She packed up her few things and decided to go down to breakfast, hoping that nobody would either notice or care that she was barefoot. Downstairs, feeling suddenly very hungry, she ordered waffles with maple syrup and a pot of tea.

While she was waiting, Donovan helped herself to a slice of toast and marmalade from the buffet and had just sat down with it when she felt her phone vibrate in her pocket. She looked at the screen and saw it was Tartaglia's email. She flicked through it, then opened the attachments. Even though her phone screen was small, the photographs of the earrings were good, clear images and the first thing that struck her was that the earrings looked expensive and possibly antique. The pale purple stones, which she assumed were amethyst, were faceted and mounted in an old-fashioned gold setting. The hallmark meant nothing to her but they didn't look like the sort of things a student would be wearing. She was still looking at them when a text came through. It was a message from Chang.

Found shoe. Where is Cinderella?

She smiled and texted him back. A few minutes later, he appeared in the dining room.

'Why didn't you wake me?' he asked matter-of-factly, sitting down at the table.

She was pleased to find no awkwardness on his side. 'I thought you needed your sleep.'

He smiled. 'What's the plan for today?'

She told him what Tartaglia had said. 'We'll need to get going relatively soon. It's odd that we never found a file for an Amber Wiseman, but things were pretty haphazard back then.'

'I spotted this at the front desk.' He passed her a newspaper. 'Have you seen it?'

She stared at the headline for a moment. 'Jesus. Mark's going to be hopping mad.'

'Didn't he say anything about it?'

'No. But he sounded pretty rushed.'

'There's a longer piece inside with a whole lot of stuff about Logan and the others. I'll give you three guesses who wrote it.'

She flicked through the paper until she came to the article and squinted at the by-line. 'Isn't she the one who was interviewing Joe Logan?'

'Yes. But that's not what I meant.'

She looked up at him. 'What are you saying?'

He shook his head. 'It's nothing.'

'No it's not.'

They were interrupted as the waitress came over to their table with Donovan's waffles. 'That looks good,' he said. 'I'll have the same, please, with a black coffee.'

'Come on, Justin,' she said, once the waitress had gone away. 'What is it? I hate mysteries.'

'It's really not important.'

'Yes it is. Tell me what you were going to say.'

'OK. If you really want to know . . .'

'I do.'

'Well, you know the woman we saw coming out of Mark's yesterday morning?'

'Yes.'

'That was Anna Paget.'

She stared at him. She felt her cheeks burn, sure now that he knew the cause of her confusion. At least he had the tact not to refer to it openly.

'How do you know what she looks like?'

'Nick googled her and showed me some photos. He thought she was really hot.'

'Bloody Nick. That's all he thinks about.'

'In a way, it's a good thing he did. She writes for one of the dailies. Sometimes they use a photograph of her.'

'Can't say I've noticed her.'

'That's because you're a woman, plus you rarely pick up a newspaper from what I've seen.'

'I'd love to spend all day reading the paper,' she said irritably, 'but I don't get the time.' Mechanically, she started to eat her waffles. She still found it difficult to believe. Getting involved with anybody who was a potential witness in a case was serious enough, but the fact that she was a journalist made it ten times worse. She was amazed that Tartaglia could be so foolish, but then the sanest of men were sometimes driven to do the stupidest things where sex was involved. Anna Paget also looked like a woman who knew how to handle herself. She wondered if Tartaglia had been indiscreet, as well as stupid. She looked up at Chang. 'Are you quite sure?'

'Yes.'

'Why didn't you say something yesterday?'

He shrugged. 'You told me to shut up, if you remember. Anyway, I thought you probably knew.'

She avoided his eye. It wasn't the truth. He had tried to spare her feelings, but she decided to let it go.

The address on Amber Wiseman's bus pass was only a five-minute walk up the hill from the hotel. The house was in the middle of an impressive Georgian terrace, overlooking the Downs. Donovan rang the doorbell and, within a minute, it was answered by a stout, middle-aged woman, with short, fluffy grey hair and glasses.

'I'm sorry to bother you,' Donovan said, showing her ID. 'We're with the Met Police. We're trying to trace a girl called Amber Wiseman. All we know is that she was living here in 1991. She would have been somewhere in her teens.'

'I've never heard of her,' the woman said, peering over the rim of her spectacles. 'My name's Nicola Bradshaw. My husband and I bought the house a couple of years later.'

'Do you remember who from?'

'Not really. The woman who owned it was rarely there and the agent showed us around. From what I remember, she was getting divorced. It used to be some sort of a commune, I think. Or at least she had lots of people staying. I remember going to see it one lunchtime and walking in on two people going at it hammer and tongs on one of the sofas. The house was painted all these dreadful dark colours and it was a real throwback to the seventies.'

'Do you still have her solicitor's name?'

'We must do somewhere. If you come in, I'll go and have a look. Luckily, I'm very hot on filing. My husband always teases me about it, but it comes in useful.'

She ushered them in and they waited in the wide, high-ceilinged hall while she went upstairs.

'Nice place,' Chang said, gazing around.

'I prefer cosy,' Donovan replied. 'I wouldn't know what to do with myself somewhere this big.' She caught sight of her reflection in the huge gilt mirror that hung over a marble-topped console table. 'God, I look a sight,' she said, running her fingers through her hair, which was standing in thick tufts and rubbing her cheeks hard to generate a bit of colour. There was nothing she could do about the bloodshot eyes.

'You look fine.'

'Don't lie. I look bloody awful.'

'OK. You look bloody awful.' He bent forwards and kissed the top of her head.

'Don't,' she said, ducking away.

'Nobody's looking.'

'That's not the point.'

He held up his hands, smiling. 'Whatever you say, Sarge.'

Mrs Bradshaw returned a few minutes later with a folded sheet of writing paper. 'Here you are,' she said, handing it to Donovan. 'The woman's name is Devereux. Her solicitor's in Queen's Square, just down the road.'

'Can we walk or should we drive?'

'I'd walk. Parking is a nightmare around there. It won't take you more than ten minutes and it's downhill most of the way. I've written down all the details. Hopefully, they'll be able to help.'

They thanked her and walked out into the sunshine. As Mrs Bradshaw had said, the walk was easy and it was good to be outside in the fresh air. Queen's Square was just off the main thoroughfare, close to the university, and the solicitor's office was in the middle of a terrace of eighteenth-century houses, overlooking a small park. Explaining that they were from the police, they asked for Nigel Smith and the receptionist showed them into a small waiting room at the front. Minutes later a tall, youngish-looking man in a suit and a loud red and green spotted tie came in.

'I'm Simon Grigson,' he said, holding out his hand to each of them in turn. 'I understand you're from the Metropolitan Police and that you were asking for Nigel Smith?'

Donovan showed him her ID. 'That's right.'

'Unfortunately, Nigel retired about a year ago, but maybe I can help.'

'We're trying to trace a girl called Amber Wiseman. All we know is that in 1991 she was living in a house on Sion Hill in Clifton that was owned by a client of your firm, a Mrs Devereux. Mr Smith dealt with the sale of the house. The woman who's living there now gave us your details.' She showed him the piece of paper. 'It's urgent we trace the girl's next of kin.'

Grigson glanced at the paper, then nodded. 'Are you saying she's dead?'

'Yes.'

'When did this happen?'

'If we're right, in 1991. I can't give you any more details, but we have a body which we need to ID and all we have to go on is the name and that address.'

'I'm sure you'll appreciate it's tricky . . .'

'It's really urgent, Mr Grigson. Someone out there's been missing their daughter all this time. They need to know what happened to her and it's a murder enquiry. I don't have to tell you—'

He held up his hand. 'OK. I understand. Give me a moment and I'll try and find the file. The originals were all sent to archive ages ago but we hold most of the summary documentation on the system in PDF format.'

'Thank you.'

A coffee machine sat on a table in one corner with a pot of what looked like fresh coffee. As Grigson left the room, she and Chang helped themselves. As usual, he seemed to be coping well on little sleep, but her head was still hurting and she couldn't take any more pills for a few hours. She sat down with her cup in a large leather armchair and massaged the bridge of her nose and around her eyes, trying to relieve the pain. Chang took his coffee to the window, where he stood looking out for a moment. Then he turned to her.

'What if we can't trace the girl?'

'Trust me, we will, one way or another. It may just take time.'

Just as Donovan had got to her feet to pour herself a second cup of coffee, Grigson returned.

'The woman we acted for, who owned the house, is now called Frances Neville. She lives in a cottage in a village called

Chelwood, just south of Bristol. It's about a twenty-minute drive. I've just spoken to her and told her you're on your way. Apparently, she's had an operation on her foot a couple of weeks ago and can't go out. I'll leave you to explain what it's all about.'

An elderly woman opened the door of Frances Neville's cottage and showed them into a small, open-plan sitting room, filled with an eclectic and colourful mix of furniture and objects that looked as though they had come from the four corners of the world. Frances lay stretched out on the sofa, listening to *Woman's Hour*, her heavily bandaged foot resting on a large tapestry cushion. She was very slim, wore jeans and a plain, fitted white shirt and looked to be in her late fifties, with olive skin and frizzy, iron-grey hair, which was clipped up untidily on top of her head. Her dark eyebrows were well-defined and arched and her eyes were heavily rimmed with black eye-liner giving her an almost surprised expression.

'I'm glad you got here so quickly,' she said interrupting, as Donovan started to introduce herself and Chang. She bent forward and turned off the radio. 'That silly solicitor seems to be in quite a muddle. He tells me you think Amber's dead, or at least that's what it sounded like. And he said it happened a long while ago.'

'You know who Amber Wiseman is?'

'Of course I do. She's my daughter, more's the pity, and as far as I know she's very much alive. You'd better sit down and explain what this is all about. I do love a good mystery.' She rubbed her hands together and gestured Donovan and

Chang to the chairs opposite, her heavy silver bracelets jingling at both wrists.

'I'm sorry, Mrs Neville, but—'

'It's *Miss* Neville. I've been married four times but I've gone back to my maiden name. It's simpler that way. Wiseman was Amber's father's name, not that he stuck around for long. Now what's all this about Amber being dead?'

'I'm very sorry about the confusion, Miss Neville. We found a girl's skeleton in a lake near Bristol. She's apparently been in the water since the early summer of 1991. We found some of her things along with a handbag. The name Amber Wiseman and your old address in Clifton were written on a bus pass inside. Naturally we—'

'How wonderfully intriguing. Well, it's definitely not Amber, I can assure you. I haven't spoken to Amber for years – we don't get on, you see – but I can assure you it isn't her.'

'If you're not in touch . . .'

Frances waved her hand dismissively. 'She came to my mother's funeral, which was two years ago, although she didn't say a word to me, so it definitely can't be her.'

'OK. Why then would this girl have her bag?'

'Maybe she knew Amber. When did you say this was?'

'June or July 1991.'

She stared into space for a moment, then nodded slowly. 'Amber would have been fourteen, going on fifteen in 1991. That's the year I split up with Mike, which is why I had to sell the house when we eventually got divorced. I can't remember what I was doing in June or July but I certainly spent a couple of months out in India. I used to have an interior-design business, with shops in London and Bath, and a lot of our furnishings and needlework pieces came from there. When I got back, I took Amber off to stay with friends in America for the summer to get away from Mike.'

'What about the girl?'

She frowned, as though thinking back. 'There was a group of them that used to hang around together. They were always swapping clothes and make-up and things. She must have taken Amber's bag.'

'She? Do you have any idea who it might be?'

'What's that?' She peered up at Donovan, as though she hadn't been listening.

'Do you know who the girl is?'

'Yes. I'm sorry, it's all coming back to me now. It must be Danielle.'

'Danielle Henderson?' Chang asked.

She looked over at him and nodded. 'I can't remember her surname, nor can I remember when it happened, but she disappeared one day. Everyone thought she'd run off to the bright lights. Danielle was always borrowing Amber's things. If it isn't her, I can't think who else it could be.'

Chang opened his rucksack and took out one of the files. 'Is this Danielle?' He held up a photograph for Frances to see.

Frances put on a pair of reading glasses, which were hanging on a beaded chain around her neck. She examined the photograph and frowned. 'How sweet. She looks about twelve in that photo, but that's Danielle. She and Amber were thick as thieves for a time. They were both usually plastered in make-up with skirts up to here.' She put her hand on her hip. 'But then, what girls aren't these days?

Danielle's mother was very silly, though. She was way too overprotective and gave her no freedom at all. Danielle would come over after school sometimes and occasionally she'd stay the night, but the mother was constantly on the phone, fussing about whether she'd done her homework, what time she was coming home, whether she'd eaten properly and that sort of thing. Poor Danielle had to scrub her face and change out of her clothes into something sensible every time she went home. It's enough to make anyone rebel, don't you think?' She peered over her glasses at Donovan for confirmation.

'What about her father?' Donovan asked, thinking that Danielle's mother sounded like most parents she had come across, her own included.

'From what I remember, he'd had the sense to bugger off long ago and that was part of the problem. Danielle was an only child. She was her mother's sole focus, with all her mother's hopes and dreams riding on her. When she went missing, I had the mother on the phone crying her eyes out as if I'd hidden her somewhere, or somehow we were to blame. I never understood why she was so hostile. The local police came to interview Amber, but of course she had no idea where Danielle was. I think they'd had some sort of a falling out, as girls do at that age.'

'You said everyone thought she'd gone off to London. Why was that?'

Frances shrugged. 'She often talked about it. When she disappeared, the police interviewed all of Danielle's classmates at school, including Amber. Everyone just assumed she'd run off.'

'If she and Danielle quarrelled, why would Danielle have had her bag?'

'Heaven knows. I suppose she must have borrowed it and forgotten to give it back.'

'You didn't think it was strange when Danielle disappeared?'

'No, not really. I got the impression Danielle wasn't at all happy at home. She also had a well-developed sense of fantasy.'

'What do you mean by that?'

'Well, if you want the truth, she could be quite devious. It's quite possible she stole Amber's bag.'

'Really?'

'She certainly told the most terrible lies, like children do when they're desperate to impress. She used to pretend she was friends with all sorts of famous people and that she was going to go and stay with them in London. As I said, she often told Amber she was going to run away, but I thought it was just another one of her little stories. When I heard she hadn't come home, I just imagined she'd finally gone and done it.'

32

It was nearly eleven o'clock in the morning when Alex put his key in the lock and opened the door to his flat. He had spent the whole of Sunday at Maggie's as well as the night, although he had opted for the sofa, not wanting to risk further humiliation. Amazingly, she seemed to understand and had been happy just to have him there. He had been so tired that he had enjoyed a deep and dreamless sleep. At least for a while he had managed to banish the demons from the lake. Maggie had gone out early that morning to drive to an old rectory near Northampton, which was a potential new property for her books. He had been so deeply asleep he hadn't heard her go, but she had left him breakfast and a note telling him to make himself at home. He wasn't due at the restaurant until late afternoon, but rather than stay on the boat on his own with nothing to do, he had decided to go back to the flat for a change of clothes.

The hall lights were still on and the first thing he noticed was a sheet of paper on the floor, held down by an empty whisky bottle. *BIG BROTHER'S WATCHING YOU ALEX!!!* was scrawled across the page in thick, black marker. He picked it up, turned it over and found a message in Paddy's familiar illegible writing:

Hi Alex, if you're seeing this, you've probably come home from wherever you've been hiding yourself. Hope it was fun!!!! The fuzz have been all over the flat. They're after you, mate! What have you been up to? I don't know for certain, but I think they're keeping a beady eye on this place so WATCH YOUR BACK!

P.S. Woman called Anna says please call and it's urgent!!!!! Says you have the number.

He went into the kitchen. Taking care not to be seen, he peered out of the window. The road below was busy with cars and pedestrians. It was impossible to tell if any of them were plainclothes police, but if they were watching the flat, they were bound to have seen him come in. Why they were still after him, he had no idea, but he had no wish to be hauled in for more unpleasant questioning, accusations and threats if he could help it. He grabbed a plastic bag from under the sink, threw in his phone charger and a change of clothes and went into the bathroom, which overlooked the rear. He glanced quickly out of the window. He had a clear view over the patchwork of gardens to the backs of the houses on the next street, but as far as he could tell there was nobody out there. Maybe they weren't watching, or maybe they were concentrating their efforts on the front. From the road, the house appeared to be hemmed in by other buildings, but appearances were deceptive. The dry-cleaners' below extended out into most of the garden at ground level. Beyond was a wall, no more than six feet high, with a small alleyway on the other side that led along between the gardens and stopped at the back of a newsagent's. During business hours, particularly in the summer, the newsagent's door was kept permanently open. He had twice managed to climb out of Paddy's flat this way, when Paddy in a rush had accidentally locked him inside. Luckily the owner of the newsagent didn't seem to mind.

He went into the sitting room, turned on some music loud, so that if anyone came to the door, they would assume he was still there, then went back into the bathroom and climbed out of the window. He edged onto the boundary wall that separated the property from the house next door, pulled the window shut, then dropped down onto the flat roof of the dry-cleaners'. Within minutes he was walking through the newsagent's and out into a nearby road. Cutting through the network of small streets, he rejoined Chamberlayne Road further along and jumped on a bus that had just pulled up at a stop. It was heading south towards Ladbroke Grove. He was the only person to get on and, as the doors closed behind him and the bus accelerated away, he scanned the road. As far as he could tell, nobody was following him.

He got off the bus halfway along Ladbroke Grove and went into a café just past the Westway. It was owned by an old Greek Cypriot called Harry and was a nice enough place to while away a few hours. He had often stopped there for something to eat when walking to work for the lunchtime shift and it was one of the few places he knew that still did a decent fried breakfast. Harry came over and he ordered coffee and a full English, with fried bread. He debated about charging up his phone, then decided against it. From the little he knew from the TV, the police might be able to track him if he switched it on.

'Do you have a phone I could use?' he asked, as Harry returned with a brimming cappuccino, thick with a coating of chocolate, just the way he liked it.

Harry gave him an easy smile. 'Sure. The landline's on the blink, but you can use my mobile.' He took a small, green Nokia out of his pocket and handed it to Alex.

Alex found Anna's card in his wallet and dialled her mobile. She picked up right away.

'Anna Paget.'

'It's Alex. Alex Fleming. You asked me to call.'

'Have you seen the papers?'

'No. Why?'

'You'd better take a look. The shit's hit the proverbial fan and I really need to speak to you. Can we meet?'

'What's it about?'

'Just look at the paper and you'll see.'

'This is to do with Joe, right?'

'And Paul Khan, and now Danny Black.'

'Danny?'

'Didn't you know? Alex, I'm *so* sorry. I thought you would know.'

'No. Oh God, I . . .' He put the phone down for a moment and stared into space. He felt numb. So Danny was dead too. Another one of the five. He had never been that close to Danny, unlike to Tim and Joe, but it was still a shock. Only he and Tim were left. Which one would be next? He felt sick. He heard the tinny sound of her voice coming from the phone's microphone and put it back to his ear. 'When did this happen?' he whispered.

'Yesterday. I'm really, really sorry, Alex. I didn't mean to shock you like that. I'm really sorry. Please can we meet? It's really urgent I speak to you. Where are you?'

He took a moment to answer. 'In a café in Ladbroke Grove.'

'Shall I come to you?'

'I don't know, I can't think. What happened to Danny?'

'He was found dead in St James's Park. Again, I'm so sorry. The police as usual aren't saying much, but I'll tell you everything I know when I see you. Why don't you come to my flat? That way we can talk in private.' She gave him the address, which he memorised, having no pen or paper. 'If you're coming by tube, it's about a ten-minute walk from either Earl's Court or Fulham Broadway. How long do you think you'll be?'

'Half an hour or so. Maybe a bit more.' He found it difficult to focus.

As he hung up, Harry came over with his breakfast. Still in a daze, Alex thanked him and handed him back his phone.

'Are you OK?' Harry asked, peering at him.

He shook his head. 'I've just had some very bad news. Do you have a newspaper I could borrow?'

'Of course. Hey, Sonia,' he called out to the young woman who was busy making sandwiches behind the counter. 'Pass me the paper, will you? It's somewhere over there by the toaster.' She slid a copy of the *Daily Mail* across to him, which he passed to Alex. The headline said it all:

BRUTAL LONDON MURDERS LINKED

He gazed down at the steaming plate of food in front of him, then pushed it away. He was no longer hungry.

Tartaglia sat at his desk staring fixedly at the computer screen. The surveillance team had called in to say that Alex Fleming had been back to his flat but had somehow managed to give them the slip. How it had happened, he wasn't sure, but Fleming was acting very much like a guilty man and efforts were being redoubled to find him. He had checked with the team minding Tim Wade up in Oxford, but at least that end appeared to be secure and there was no sign of Fleming having tried to contact Wade. For the moment it was a waiting game, but he didn't feel in a patient mood. He had spent the last few hours trying to catch up on paperwork, but he couldn't concentrate. His head was buzzing. All he could think of was the headline in the morning paper and Anna's name beneath it. What a fool he'd been. At one point he remembered their talking a little about the case in bed. She had asked him how it was going and if they were close to finding Joe's killer. She had seemed interested to know about the psychological motivation of someone who could do such a thing and he had given her his view, couching it in very general terms that might have applied to a number of cases he had worked. At no point had he mentioned Paul Khan or Danny Black. Nor had he mentioned Ashleigh Grange or the lake. However distracted by her, however temporarily off guard, he couldn't believe that any of it had come from him.

But where had she got it from? In a way, it didn't matter. He knew how it would look if anybody found out what had happened between them. He started to wonder if he could trust his memory. Although it was a bitter pill to swallow, he now knew why she had come to see him at his flat and why her behaviour had been so overt and like an idiot, he had fallen for it. In many ways, he was no better than Nick Minderedes, and the thought stung him.

He was on the point of calling her, then decided against it. He would get more out of her face to face. The files were still sitting on his desk and he made a note of her address. He changed out of his jacket and trousers into leathers and boots and went downstairs and out the back to where the Ducati was parked. He drove fast, weaving in and out of the heavy traffic along the Lower Richmond Road. Once over Putney Bridge, he cut through the side streets until he came to Edith Grove. It struck him again how close she lived to Brompton Cemetery. Edith Grove was one way, with traffic flowing fast in the direction of the embankment, and there was nowhere to park. He drove the bike up over the pavement and into the front garden of the house, where he dismounted behind an ancient-looking Lancia. He took off his helmet and checked his watch. It had taken him just seven minutes.

According to the file, Anna lived on the first floor. Looking up, he saw that the window was open wide and he assumed she was in. He chained his helmet to the bike and went up the stairs to the front door. None of the bells were labelled and he pressed them all repeatedly until finally he heard her voice over the crackle of the intercom.

'Who's that?'

'It's Mark Tartaglia. We need to talk.'

There was a pause. 'Now's not a good time.'

'I don't care. May I come up?'

'No. I'm on my way out to meet someone.'

'I need to talk to you.'

There was another pause then she said: 'OK. Wait there. I'll be down in a minute.'

He went back to the front garden and stood by the bike, his mind still spinning. He lit a cigarette and looked up at the window. He saw her pull it shut, talking on the phone to someone, the handset cradled against her ear. A few minutes later the front door opened and she came down the steps towards him. She was wearing shorts and a tight-fitting black vest, the way she was dressed when he first met her.

'I'm really sorry but I can't talk now. I've got to go and see someone. Can't you come back later?' She gave him a pleasant enough smile but her sunglasses hid her eyes and he couldn't read her expression.

'I've seen the paper.'

'It's good, isn't it?'

'No, it's not good. You used what I told you.'

'Ah, that's what this is all about. Don't worry. It wasn't earth-shattering. What you told me, I mean. You just helped confirm a few things.'

'That's not the point. What I said was between us. I didn't expect to see it in print with your name under it.'

'Mark, sweetheart, I knew most of it already. Hand on heart. What you said was just helpful background stuff.'

'I'm glad you got something out of it, then.'

The smile disappeared and she put her hand on her hip. 'Look, I didn't come to see you to get information out of you. I'm not that cheap.'

'Don't give me that crap. There's all sorts of information in that article you're not supposed to know, let alone publish. What about all that stuff about Paul Khan and Danny Black . . . Where the hell did it come from?'

She tapped the side of her nose. 'Ways and means. But don't worry. You may have been a little pissed, but interesting though it all was, you didn't give away anything vital. Anyway, none of it can be traced back to you and, as I said, I knew it all before.'

He shook his head disbelievingly. He still couldn't work it out. Had he left her alone at any point? Apart from when she first came in and he had gone to get dressed, he didn't think so. When he came back, she had been sitting in the same place, as though she hadn't moved. Even if she had got up and snooped around, there hadn't been much time, nor anything to see. There were no files or important documents or anything else of a sensitive nature lying around in the flat and his phone was password protected. Then it dawned on him. His notebook had been in his jacket pocket, hanging over the back of a chair where he had left it when he came home. She would have needed a while to decipher its contents. The only opportunity had been in the morning, when she got up, leaving him in bed. He'd been heavily asleep, even for him. Apart from vaguely glimpsing her as she left the bedroom, he hadn't been aware of anything. He certainly had no recollection of her leaving the flat. Then another thought struck him. Had she drugged him? It would explain the blinding hangover the next morning and his unusually befuddled state of mind. The thought shocked him. It was too late to go for a blood test and even if he knew for certain, it would do no good. He could hardly arrest her and have to admit to Steele and the rest what had happened.

He stared into the black mirrors of her glasses. 'You put something in my wine, didn't you?'

'That's ridiculous.'

'Is it? Did you go through my notebook while I was asleep? Jesus Christ, I can't believe I was so stupid.'

'Is it your ego you're worried about, or your job?'

He shook his head in disgust. 'I should never have let you in the door.'

She sighed. 'Stop being so paranoid, will you? I came over to see you because I wanted to. It seemed like a good idea at the time. End of story. It had nothing to do with your job or mine.' She held up her hand before he could get a word in. 'And no, I didn't snoop around your flat and no, I certainly didn't look in your notebook. Whatever we did and said is between the two of us.'

Instinctively, he knew she was lying. 'That's not good enough and you know it. What we both did was wrong. The only difference is that my job's on the line if anyone finds out.'

'Trust me, they won't. Now, I've really got to get a move on. I'll catch up with you later.'

The address given for Danielle Henderson in the missing-person report was half way down York Road, in the Montpelier area of Bristol. Like many of the older parts of the city, the street was narrow and on a hill, with a mixture of modest, multi-coloured Georgian terraced houses, Victorian buildings and modern council housing. The house was on three floors, the front painted a faded, damp-stained peach, with a weather-beaten eighteenth-century porch and sash windows. Cars were tightly parked along both sides of the street and there were no gaps anywhere. Leaving Chang to find a space in one of the neighbouring streets, Donovan got out and rang the bell. It was answered moments later by a small, bird-like woman with greasy, dyed blonde hair scraped loosely back in a short ponytail.

'Yes?' She eyed Donovan suspiciously, a lit cigarette clamped between bony fingers. At first glance, she looked far too old to be Danielle's mother, with a deeply lined face and the papery grey skin of a heavy smoker.

Donovan held up her ID. 'I'm from the Metropolitan Police. I'm trying to locate Susan Henderson.'

'What do you want with her?'

'It's to do with her daughter, Danielle.'

Her watery eyes widened. 'It's Danni. We called her Danni. So you've found her, then?'

'Are you Susan?'

'No. I'm Reenie. I'm Susan's mother. Susan passed away two years ago.' She spoke with a throaty, West Country accent. 'Danni's dead, isn't she?' Her expression was resigned, as if bad news was something she was accustomed to.

'I'm afraid so. May I come in?'

'I knew all along Danni hadn't run off, like they said,' she muttered, moving aside to let Donovan pass. She closed the front door and shuffled away along the narrow corridor. The house was airless and smelled strongly of stale cigarette smoke, as though nobody had opened a window in years. Reenie was wearing fluffy pink slippers in the shape of Garfield and looked painfully thin under her loose-fitting tracksuit bottoms and T-shirt. Donovan followed her into a small kitchen at the back, which looked out onto a sloping strip of overgrown garden. The room was painted a pastel shade of blue, with a border of flying seagulls pasted around the top. In a corner by the sink was a cage. Inside, a sparrow sat puffed up on a perch asleep.

Reenie stubbed out the butt of her cigarette in a saucer on the counter and turned to Donovan. 'Have a seat.' She gestured vaguely towards a couple of chairs and a small, yellow Formica table that was pushed up against the wall. 'Do you want a cup of tea?'

Donovan pulled up a chair and sat down. 'Thanks. If you're having one.'

'Yes. I need one, after what you just told me.' Reenie switched on the kettle and took down a couple of mugs from a shelf, which she wiped methodically with a tea towel.

'Sugar?' she asked, as the kettle pinged.

'One, please.'

'And milk?'

'Just a drop.'

As Reenie prepared the tea, the sparrow started to make harsh chirruping sounds from the cage. Donovan turned round to look at him. It was almost as though he was shouting for attention and he was standing up on his perch, looking straight at her, his head cocked to one side, black eyes glittering in the light from the window.

'Don't mind Steve,' Reenie said, coming over to the table with the tea. 'He's just a nosy parker. Won't mind his own business and he wants to know who you are. It's not often we get company.' She sat down opposite Donovan and passed her a mug. It looked well-used, the side decorated with one of the signs of the Zodiac printed in dull gold. Reenie's had a picture of Sagittarius, Donovan noticed, while hers was Pisces. She wondered if it had belonged to Susan or Danielle. The tea looked good and strong, but it was too hot to drink and she put it down on the table to cool.

'You're sure it's Danni?' Reenie asked, taking a sip of hers.

'As far as we can be, at this stage. We'll need to take a DNA swab from you to see if there's a match. If you had the name of her dentist that would also help. In the meantime, I wonder if you recognise these?'

She took the colour photocopies of the earrings out of her bag and handed them to Reenie, who stared at the images for a moment, then closed her eyes. 'Those are my earrings. At least, they belonged to my mother. She gave them to me just before she died. I thought I'd lost them. Trust Danni to have taken them.'

'I'm sorry.'

Reenie shook her head. 'Where did you say you found her?'

'Her remains were in a lake in between Bristol and Bath. From what we know, she went to a party given by some students who were living near the lake and died there. This would have been in June, or possibly early July, 1991. I'm afraid we're treating her death as murder.'

Reenie met her gaze with burning eyes. 'Murder?' She sank back against her chair. 'Dear Lord. I suppose it had to be, didn't it? I mean, if she'd had an accident or something, she'd have turned up sooner. What happened?'

'It looks as though she was strangled.'

She swallowed hard. 'Sweet Jesus! Do you know who did it?'

'We have a suspect, but that's all I can say for the moment. I need to ask you some questions, if you don't mind.'

Reenie nodded and hunched over her tea, her hand clamped tightly around the mug. Donovan saw tears in her eyes. After a moment, she got up, grabbed a tissue from a box by the sink and blew her nose loudly. She wiped her eyes with the back of her hand, then, fumbling, helped herself to a Silk Cut from a packet on the counter. Her fingers were trembling as she lit up. She took a long, deep pull as though struggling for air, then leaned back against the cupboards. 'I've been hanging on waiting for this day for so long. I can't tell you what it's been like. I couldn't say nothing to Susan, but I knew Danni was dead. I just wish my Susan was still here. She'd have given anything just to know what happened.'

'You said Susan died.'

She nodded. 'She was only fifty. It was cancer, they said, but I know it was Danni's going missing. It cracked her up and she went to pieces after that. She wouldn't get out of bed, wouldn't go to work, wouldn't see her friends or anyone, really. The pills the doctor gave her only made it worse. Right through it all, she was always so sure Danni was still alive. She tried everything she could to find her and she spent all her savings on some psychic who said he'd help her find Danni. But he was just a charlatan. Even I could see that, but she was so desperate I said nothing. You can't imagine what it's like, losing your child, not knowing all this time what'd happened to her. No parent should have to outlive a child, let alone a grandchild. I hope you find whoever did this.'

'We will,' Donovan said with as much conviction as she could muster.

'I've never thought the death penalty was the answer, but whoever did this deserves to be strung up. They've ruined three lives.'

'I'm very sorry,' Donovan said.

Reenie gave a wheezy sigh. 'Thank you. I can see you mean it, which is more than I can say for the police what come here when Danni disappeared. They was worse than useless.'

'We'll need to contact Danni's father,' Donovan said. 'Do you have an address for him?'

'Colin? I haven't a clue where the sod is. There's no love lost between him and me, I can tell you.'

'We'll still need to contact him.'

'How I hate that man. They were childhood sweethearts, him and Susan. When he ran off with that little teenage whore while he was out in Northern Ireland, it broke Susan's heart, it did.'

'He was in the army?'

'That's right. Upped and left Susan and Danni high and dry, without a penny or a roof over their heads. That's why they had to come live with me. When he tried to wheedle his way back in, I saw him off. I told him exactly where he could go. They were both so soft, they'd have had him back at the drop of a hat, but I was having none of it. I gave him what I had in my savings account and told him to bugger off. He was one of those . . . what do they call 'em . . . ?' She waved her frail hand vaguely in the air. 'Serial adulterer. Isn't that it? Never could resist a short skirt and a pretty face, he couldn't, and the younger the better. He'd only've broken Susan's heart all over again.'

'What about Danni? Was he close to her?'

She nodded. 'He doted on Danni, I'll say that for him. She could do no wrong in his eyes. He used to call her his little princess and he'd heap presents on her whenever he came home. It was difficult for Susan to see how close they was. But it didn't stop him messing around, though, did it? When Danni went missing, my first thought was she'd run off to him. It's what the police thought too. But then they told me he'd gone straight back to Northern Ireland after the Gulf War ended, so I knew for sure something must've happened to her. However silly she was, she'd never run off on her own and leave us with no word. At heart, she was a good, sweet girl, however they tried to paint her. When he come home and found out about her being missing, he was round here straight away, threatening to kill us both like we'd had something to do with it. It was truly frightening.'

'Do you know where he is now?'

Reenie stubbed out her cigarette. 'Abroad. Last I heard, he was out in the Middle East somewhere, working for some security company. Your best bet's to try the army. They should know how to find him.'

'Which regiment was he in?'

'The Light Infantry, although he left a while ago. Maybe they'll have an address or something on file.'

'Do you have a photograph of him, by any chance?'

'There's one up in Danni's room. He sent it to her just before she went missing. I remember the fuss I had trying to get a frame she liked. Nothing was good enough. I'd have chucked it long ago but Susan wouldn't let me. She wanted it all kept just the way Danni left it. Before she died, she made me promise again not to touch it, in case Danni'd come home. I told her Danni'd be a woman by now and she wouldn't want it like that no more, but she wouldn't hear a word of it. Danni was still her little girl. I go up there sometimes to dust and hoover. Maybe now Danni's dead, I'll have a clearout. Perhaps Susan wouldn't mind now.'

'Would it be OK if I took a look?'

'Help yourself,' she said, lighting another Silk Cut. 'It's the room on the top floor. Why don't you go ahead while I tidy up here, then I'll follow you.'

33

Danielle's room was right at the top of the house. Listening to make sure that Reenie was still safely downstairs, Donovan called Tartaglia to tell him about Colin Henderson. His mobile rang, then went through to voicemail. Not bothering to leave a message, she called Steele, who was at her desk, and explained what she had learned. Hopefully, it wouldn't take long for them to trace Henderson and find out if he was still abroad.

As soon as they were finished, she tucked her phone away in her pocket and gazed around the small room. An old Japanese paper lantern hung from the centre of the ceiling like an enormous white moon. The furnishings were makeshift, but the room was clean and tidy. Light flooded in through the window and it must have been a pleasant place to be, with a nice view of the little Georgian houses opposite, one periwinkle blue, one yellow and one a soft pink. Like many teenage girls' rooms, the walls were plastered with posters and torn-out pages from magazines of actors and pop stars. She recognised a young Jason Donovan, Michael Keaton as Batman and Kevin Costner in *No Way Out*. A small collection of CDs were stacked by the player. The

Bangles, Cure, R.E.M., Guns N' Roses, Sinead O'Connor, B52s. It took her straight back and it struck her for the first time that she and Danielle were the same vintage. She wondered why it hadn't occurred to her before. In her mind, and no doubt in that of everyone who had known her apart from her grandmother, Danielle would be forever frozen at the age she had been when she disappeared.

The bed under the window looked freshly made, the duvet cover a girlish riot of pink and purple peonies, with a moth-eaten, one-eyed teddy bear lying against the pillow. Fourteen: that awkward transitional period between girl and woman-hood. She noticed a hairbrush lying on top of the small chest of drawers. Like everything else in the room, it too had been thoroughly cleaned, but there were still a few strands of pale blonde hair caught amongst the bristles, maybe left for senti-mental reasons. It might still hold some DNA that could be matched with the body, if needed, although with the earrings there no longer seemed any room for doubt. A shelf unit above the desk held a small collection of books and a framed photo-graph of a man who Donovan assumed was Colin Henderson. He was wearing uniform and was attractive in a rugged sort of way, with short black hair and blue eyes. He looked to be in his late twenties or early thirties at the time. She took it down from the shelf and, turning it over, found a small colour photo of two young girls sellotaped to the back. It had been roughly cut from a strip taken in a photo booth. They were squeezed into the small cubicle, heavily made up, grinning at the camera, their arms locked around each other. It took her a moment to realise that the blonde one was Danielle. She looked nothing like the girl in the photograph in the missing person report. Wondering what had happened to the other photos and if they had been hidden to escape Susan's censorship, she heard Reenie's hacking cough on the stairs behind her.

'Is this Colin?' Donovan asked, turning around with the photo as she entered the room.

Reenie nodded, steadying herself against the doorframe for a moment. 'Handsome devil, isn't he? Give me a plain man any day. They're much less worry.'

'What about this? Is this Danni?' She held up the small photograph.

Reenie shuffled over to where she was standing and took it, holding it up to the light and peering at it short-sightedly. Then she nodded. 'Where'd you find it?'

'It was taped to the back of this frame.'

'Danni must have put it there. Fancy nobody noticing. Susan hated her dressing up like that and wearing make-up.'

'Who's the girl with her?'

'That's Amber. Amber Wiseman.' Donovan picked up a sharpness in her tone.

'I gather you didn't like her.'

'Amber was trouble.'

'I went to see her mother this morning . . .'

'Frances? I wouldn't pay no heed to her. I doubt she's changed much, although age is a humbling thing for a woman like that. I often wonder what would've happened if Danni hadn't met Amber. Maybe she'd still be here now.'

'You really think that?' Donovan asked, trying to marry this up with what she had learned from Frances that morning.

ELENA FORBES

'I do. And if you want the honest truth, I'd say the rot started with the mother. She had no morals.'

Donovan looked at her surprised. She hadn't particularly warmed to Frances, but she seemed quite harmless, although it was difficult to imagine how she had been twenty years before. 'Isn't that a bit strong?' she said, curious, hoping to provoke Reenie into saying more.

'I'm telling you, that woman was no better than she should be. The permissive society, isn't that what they used to call it? She'd leave Amber on her own far more than is good for a young girl and it gave Amber ideas. She'd come and go as she pleased, any time of the day or night, just like a bloomin' adult. From what I know, Frances'd be off out somewhere most nights. According to Amber, she'd been getting her own supper and putting herself to bed since she was six. Can you believe it? It's no wonder Amber turned out the way she did. Susan once went round their place to get Danni after she'd stayed over. It was past midday, but Frances was still in bed with some man she'd picked up. Of course Amber had no idea who he was. Susan said the place looked like a bomb'd hit it, with bottles and stuff everywhere. I had half a mind to call social services when Susan told me. Danni wasn't allowed to see Amber after that, apart from at school.'

'But Danni liked Amber, didn't she?'

'Danni knew no better. Like her mum, Amber could turn on the charm when she wanted. She certainly knew more than most girls twice her age, I can tell you, and she had a mouth on her that'd make your hair curl. When I heard through one of the mums at Danni's school that Amber'd run off to live in London with Frances's boyfriend, I didn't

407

half laugh. It'd all been going on in secret for a while, so they said. Getting her own back in spades, she was, and Frances was hopping mad. She and Amber didn't speak for years after that.'

'I hear Danni and Amber quarrelled just before Danni disappeared.'

Reenie shook her head knowingly. 'Don't you believe it. That was just their little story so's Susan would think they weren't friends any more. It fooled Susan but it never fooled me. They were thick as thieves, those two. Just after Danni disappeared, Amber come looking for her. When I told her Danni'd gone missing, she smiled, like she thought she'd an idea where Danni was. I was so angry, I slapped her hard, I did, and I cut her cheek with my ring. I grabbed hold of her and I tried to make her tell me where Danni had gone but she wasn't saying nothing. I just remember the look in her eye, real angry like, as though nobody'd ever dared do that to her before. She didn't cry or nothing, she just turned and walked out the door cool as a cucumber. I'm sure whatever she told the police, it was a pack of lies.'

'I see. Do you mind if I borrow these photos?'

'You can have them. I'll only put them both straight in the bin otherwise. I don't want to be reminded of him and I certainly don't want to think of Danni that way either, particularly not with Amber.'

Alex got off the bus at Fulham Broadway and walked along the Fulham Road until he came to the address Anna had given him, which was at the end of a parade of bric-a-brac shops. The window was dirty, with the blinds drawn down against the heat of the sun and a notice on the door said 'closed'. From the little he could see, peering in through a gap into the dark interior, it looked like another junk shop and he wondered if he had come to the right address. But he was sure he had remembered the number correctly. Maybe she lived above the shop, although it looked equally derelict from what he could see from the street. He pressed the buzzer and a moment later, the blind on the door was pulled back. A man peered out at him.

'I'm looking for Anna Paget,' Alex mouthed.

The man nodded, undid the lock and opened the door. 'You must be Alex.'

'Is she here?'

'Yes. She's expecting you.' A bell tinkled as he closed the door behind Alex. 'She's just finishing off a piece. She won't be long. She said for you to wait here.' His manner was abrupt, as though he had better things to do. His face was tanned like leather and he was lean and wiry, maybe five-eight or nine, with very short, thinning grey hair and deep-set blue eyes. He was wearing black tracksuit bottoms, trainers and a black T-shirt with some sort of logo on the front. Alex wondered if he was Anna's partner, although he looked quite a bit older.

The shop was furnished as a living area, with the front and back rooms knocked into one. An old piece of carpet covered part of the bare boards and an ancient-looking sofa and chairs were grouped around a makeshift coffee table, with a TV next to the fireplace. Someone had recently been having a fire, in spite of the hot weather, and the room smelled of smoke. At the far end was a small, open-plan kitchen, with a bar dividing it from the sitting area. The man turned on a lamp and looked over at Alex.

'Can I get you a drink or something while you wait?'

'Do you have anything cold?' he asked.

'There may be some coke in the fridge, or there's white wine. I've just opened a bottle for Anna.' He gestured towards the coffee table where the bottle was sitting temptingly in a cooler. 'She likes a glass when she's working and she said you and she might have a drink together.'

Alex nodded. 'A glass of wine would be great, thanks.' Even though he had to go to work later on, a glass or so wouldn't hurt and it might help to oil the wheels. There was something about Anna that made him feel awkward and he wanted to take the edge off his nerves. The man went over to kitchen area, took a glass from the shelf and came back to the table where he poured out the wine, which he handed to Alex.

'There you go. Sit down and make yourself at home. There's a paper somewhere over by the sofa, if you want to look at something while you wait. Anna will be with you when she can.'

Alex sat down and, taking a sip of wine, opened the early edition of the *Standard*, which was lying on the floor on the far side. It was difficult to read in the half-light and he had to move closer to the lamp to see. The front page was filled with copy about the three murders, following on from a police press briefing held that morning, but it was all a re-hash of what had been in Anna's article, with nothing new. No doubt there was a lot she had kept back. He had been sitting there a while and had started to wonder when Anna was going to appear, when the man came back into the room. 'She's ready for you,' he said. 'I've got to go out, but you'll find her through there and down the stairs. Door's at the bottom.'

The man went out, slamming the door behind him. Alex knocked back the rest of his wine and got to his feet. The door at the back of the room opened onto a landing, with stairs going up to what he assumed was the bedroom area and another narrow flight leading to the basement. The dull throb of music was coming from below. It was dark and he couldn't see very well, nor could he find a light switch anywhere and he more or less had to feel his way down. A door faced him at the bottom. It was a funny place to work, he thought, but creative types liked their own space and maybe it was more private. He pushed open the door and went inside. It was some sort of a darkroom, painted black, with a naked red bulb hanging from the middle of the low ceiling. Akon's *Sexy Bitch* thudded from a player sitting on a chair in the middle of the floor, but there was no sign of Anna anywhere. Wondering if he was in the wrong room, he switched off the music and called out her name but there was no answer. The room was stiflingly hot and airless and he felt suddenly a little dizzy. He was about to leave when he noticed a row of black and white prints hanging above some cupboards along the wall. The faces of two girls had been superimposed on a grainy background. They were heavily made up and were hugging each other, grinning, the same image repeated over and over again. He gazed at them for a moment, finding it difficult to focus in the poor light. He blinked and shook his head but it made no difference. There

was something about the faces ... something familiar ...
He pulled one of the photos off the line. He didn't recognise
the blonde, but the other one ... He felt a draught behind
him and heard the door close. As he turned, the lock clicked
into place and the light went out.

Donovan thanked Reenie for her time and the photographs
and went downstairs. Chang was waiting on a yellow line at
the end of the road. She climbed in and told him about Colin
Henderson. 'She's given me a photo of him, although it was
taken about twenty years ago. I've spoken to Carolyn and
they're going to try and trace him. But if he's behind this,
there's still a lot of stuff that doesn't add up. I mean, how
did he know what happened out at the lake and why start
this only now? And why those men?'

Chang nodded. 'It's not clear. Who's that?' he asked,
noticing the photo of Danni and Amber.

'The blonde one's the dead girl, the way she didn't want
her mother to see her.'

'May I?' She passed him the photo. 'She certainly doesn't
look anything like the schoolgirl in the missing-person report,'
he said, after studying it.

'Amazing what a bit of slap and attitude can do for a girl.'

'I've always thought so. Who's the other girl?'

'That's Amber Wiseman, the daughter of the lady we saw
in Chelwood and owner of the handbag.'

'Are you sure?'

'That's what Danielle's grandmother said.'

He stared at it for a moment, then said, 'Well, if I didn't
know any better, I'd say that looks like a young Anna Paget.'

34

Tartaglia watched Anna walk along Edith Grove and turn the corner. She had been keen to cut their conversation short, which wasn't surprising. But the urgency in her tone made him suspicious and he decided to follow her and see where she was going. Leaving the bike in her front garden, he ran down the street and into the Fulham Road. He caught sight of her a little way ahead on the far side of the road, walking quickly as though in a hurry. She passed the entrance to Brompton Cemetery and Stamford Bridge and Chelsea Football stadium, and seemed to be heading towards Fulham Broadway and the tube. A little further along, she stopped outside a shop and he ducked into a doorway, watching as she felt in her bag for keys, unlocked the door and went inside. The shop looked disused, the window dirty and shielded from the street by blinds. It was impossible to see inside. He was wondering what to do, if he should go and take a closer look, when he felt his phone vibrate in his pocket and saw Donovan's name on the screen.

'Oh Mark, I've been trying to call you,' she said breathlessly when he answered. 'Where have you been?'

'On my bike. I can't talk now.'

'You've *got* to listen.' In a rushed tone, she proceeded to tell him about her visit to Danielle's grandmother. 'But don't worry. When I couldn't get hold of you, I called Carolyn. She'll put someone onto tracing the father right away.'

'Good,' he said distractedly.

'There's something else, something you should know. It's about that journalist, Anna Paget . . .'

'What is it?'

'I don't know how to put this, Mark . . .'

His stomach clenched. She was trying to go carefully with him and he realised at once that she knew. How, he had no idea, but it was enough that she knew. 'Say whatever you've got to say,' he said softly.

'Well, her name's not Anna—'

'What do you mean?'

'Her real name's Amber. She was Danielle Henderson's best friend.'

She said something else but he didn't take it in. He clicked off his phone and leaned back against the wall feeling sick; images, thoughts, fragments of conversations from the last couple of days streaming through his mind. How stupid he had been in so many ways, but there was no point worrying about that now. There was still so much he didn't understand. Blindly he walked into the light and crossed the road, oblivious to the oncoming traffic. He rang the bell then hammered on the door. 'Anna, open up. I know you're in there.'

He continued to bludgeon the door with his fist until finally he saw the blind flutter and heard the turn of the lock. The door opened a fraction and she peered out. He shoved his boot in the gap and pushed it open.

'What the fuck do you think you're doing,' she shouted. 'You can't just force your way in here.'

'Yes I can.' He slammed the door behind him, blocking the exit. He looked around, but there was nobody else there.

'Get out.'

'Not until you tell me about Danielle Henderson. And I hear your real name's Amber, not Anna. Is everything you've told me a lie?'

Her eyes widened a fraction and she swallowed hard, backing away from him as though she was afraid he was going to hit her. 'What's it to you?' she said quietly. 'Nobody's called me that in a long time.'

'Was it all a lie?'

'No. Now, please can you go.'

'Not until I know the truth.'

'Can we do this somewhere else? We can go back to my flat, if you like.'

'It's too late for that. I'm calling for a car.'

As he put his hand in his pocket, she grabbed his arm. 'Wait, Mark. Please. I'll tell you what you want. Just the two of us, now. Danni was my best friend. When she disappeared, I had to find out what had happened to her. That's all.'

He hesitated. He knew he should take her to the station, but what if she decided not to cooperate? He needed to get the full story out of her now otherwise they might lose precious time.

'You'd better make it quick. Tell me about the party. You were there, weren't you?'

She let go of his arm and walked over to the sofa, where she sat down, hugging her knees into her chest. 'Paul asked me. He told me to come along and bring anyone I wanted. It was a Friday, I remember, and Danni and I decided to bunk off from school. My mum was in London and there was nobody home, so we went back to my place to change. We then hitched a lift together. To cut a long story short, I was dancing with some guy when Danni came over to say she was going off to the lake to have a swim. She tried to persuade me to go too, but I didn't fancy it at the time. She had some bloke in tow but I never saw him properly. I guess I wasn't paying much attention. I went swimming in the lake later on with some other people but I didn't see her. Much, much later I went to sleep on an old sofa in the house. Next thing I knew it was light. I went back down to the lake where I'd left some of my clothes and that's when I saw the five of them gathered around talking. I didn't know their names then, but they had a rowing boat and they were all arguing about something. None of it made any sense at the time. I left them to it and went to look for Danni, but I couldn't find her. I just assumed she'd gone home and I cadged a lift back to Bristol with some bloke. To be honest, I thought she'd gone off with someone.'

He stared at her, wondering how much she had left out, how much she had distorted. 'So the last time you saw her was when?'

'I can't remember. Quite early on, I think.'

'But I thought you went there together?'

'And your point is?'

'You don't think you should have looked after her? She was fourteen, for Christ's sake.'

'Nearly fifteen. And so was I. Anyway, I was her friend, not

ELENA FORBES

her keeper. Besides, there were so many people coming and
going, it was impossible to know what was going on. How
was I to know that something had happened?'

Callous though it seemed, her version tallied with what
he had learned from Wade and Fleming and he decided to
let it go for the moment. 'Didn't you think something was
wrong when she didn't go home?'

'No. It wasn't until I went to school on Monday that I
found out she was missing.'

'You didn't think something might have happened at the
party?'

'No. I just thought she'd gone off to be with her dad. She
often talked about wanting to live with him and not her
mum. She'd even said something about it that day. She told
me she'd saved some money and was going to run off.'

'Didn't you think it was strange when she didn't get in
touch?'

She shrugged. 'I did wonder, but I assumed they were
abroad somewhere. Then I went off to London to get away
from my dreadful mother and I moved in with Brian. Danni
wouldn't have known how to contact me. That bit was more
or less as I told you, except I knew Brian before.' He shook
his head angrily. It didn't matter any longer. 'He was a friend
of my mother's,' she continued. 'Paget was his surname. Even
though we weren't married, I used it. I didn't want to
remember what I'd left behind and I changed my name to
Anna. He preferred it too. He said my old name reminded
him of my mother.'

'How did you make the connection?'

'I bumped into Colin, Danni's dad, in a bar one day. I

hadn't seen him for years, but I recognised him immediately. He was back in London for a short while and when I learned that Danni wasn't with him, that she was still missing, I worked it all back and realised something bad must have happened to her, either at the party or on her way home. Around about the same time, I read Joe's book. There was so much that was similar about the setting and the friends, I had to find out what he knew. When I read the bit about the girl drowning and remembered the five of them by the lake that morning, it all started to make sense. I'm a journalist, you know. It's what I do, put two and two together . . .'

'Go on,' he said sharply.

'I then wrote to Joe, as I told you, and asked him if he would let me interview him. You know the rest.' She got up, as though the conversation was over, and moved towards a small kitchen area at the back.

He grabbed hold of her arm. 'Did you tell Colin Henderson what you'd learned?'

'Maybe.' She tried to pull away but he held her tight.

'Did you tell him?'

'OK. Yes, I did. He had a right to know.'

'Jesus. You started all of this,' he shouted, realising how it had all been set in motion. 'Where's he now?'

'You're hurting,' she said, trying again to shake herself free.

'You're not going anywhere until I have some more answers. Where's Colin Henderson?'

'I've no idea.'

'Yes, you do.'

'I swear I had nothing to do with what he did.'

'But you knew—'

She shook her head vigorously. 'No. Not at first. But when Paul died, I realised there must be a connection, that it had to be him. But I've no idea where he is. Please believe me.'

She looked up at him with tears in her eyes. As he held her gaze, wondering how he had ever been crazy enough to have anything to do with her, he thought back again to what Angela Harper had said, the contradictions, all the things that didn't add up. The expression 'cut and shunt' came to mind. Two separate things joined awkwardly together. It finally made sense and he saw her for what she was. Rage filled him.

'You've been in all this together,' he shouted, his face inches away from hers. 'The emails, the choice of the dumpsites, it had to be two people. It's the only explanation. Whether you pulled the trigger or not, you're just as guilty.' He pushed her away and she fell hard against a chair. He pulled his phone out of his pocket.

'No,' she shouted, getting up and grabbing hold of him. 'Don't call. I promise I had nothing to do with it. Please let me explain.'

He shook her off. 'There's nothing more to explain. Where's Colin Henderson?' As he said the name, he thought he heard a noise.

'I swear I've no idea,' she shouted. 'I'm telling the truth.'

Again another sound, this time louder. He grabbed hold of her and clamped his hand over her mouth. 'Shut up.' She struggled and he pushed her down to the floor, holding her in an arm-lock with one hand, the other still tightly over her mouth. 'If you move, I'll break your arm.' He was listening. He was sure he had heard something. The noise had come from somewhere in the house. Maybe below. Someone else was there.

35

'Wake up,' the voice shouted.

The blow knocked Alex's head sideways, jolting him out of his stupor. He tried to call out but something was crammed tight in his mouth. Next thing he knew, he was sitting upright in a chair, hands pinned together behind his back, ankles clamped together. He felt someone's breath on his face. He stayed still. He was blindfolded, that much he could tell. Even though his eyes were squeezed shut, he was aware of a light beyond, a source of heat shining at him.

'If you're ready to listen, nod your head.' It was a man's voice, deep and authoritative.

He was wondering whether to respond, when he heard a distant banging followed by shouting somewhere nearby. A minute later he heard voices, more clearly now, a man's and a woman's, coming from directly above him. The footsteps beside him moved away. He felt a draught as though a door had been opened. Through the thick fog in his mind, he struggled to make out what the voices were saying. His mind drifted back to the lake and to the girl. It was because of her, because of what someone had done to her that he was going to die.

He knew now that he wasn't to blame. He hadn't killed her. Somehow that part was finally clear. She was already dead when he found her in the water. Then he thought about the others, Joe, Paul, Danny and Tim. Had he missed something? Had one of them played a part in her death? As though on the outside looking in, he again pictured the five of them by the lake arguing about what to do, about going to fetch her clothes from the boathouse. How had the discussion gone? He saw Joe sitting on the ground beside him, his face in his hands, wanting none of it; and Danny, standing close by and staring vacantly out across the lake as though on another planet, not saying a word. He saw himself, passively watching as Tim and Paul battled it out, with Joe lobbing in the occasional weary comment about calling the police. Where exactly had everyone been the night before? What had they been doing? And who was it who first had the idea of going to the boathouse to look for her things? It now seemed such an odd thing to suggest.

He felt as though he was grasping at something just out of reach – something that had been there all along. Then the answer came to him: there was one person who should have been there but was absent. At first it didn't seem important, then he realised it was. As he sat in darkness thinking it all through, running through the implications of what was now clear, he heard more footsteps overhead and shouting, this time the woman's voice, then the man's again. He had no idea who they were but somehow he had to get help. He felt weak and numb. Using all the strength he could muster, he started to rock the chair backwards and forwards. He heard it creak, felt it give, then with a thud he fell sideways onto the floor, his shoulder taking his full weight. The lamp, or whatever it was that had been shining in his face, smashed to the floor beside him. He felt a sudden movement of air in the room. As the footsteps rushed towards him, he clenched in antici-pation. A hand came down over his face, squeezing his mouth and nose until he thought he would suffocate. Something cold and hard was pressed against his temple.

'Who's down there?' Tartaglia whispered, his face against hers.

With a squeal, she shook her head. Her eyes were wild and he saw tears.

'Let's go and find out, shall we?'

She shook her head even more violently, but he held her tight and marched her to the door. He kicked it open. The stairwell was dark and narrow. Leaning back against the wall for support, he held her tightly against him and started side-ways down the stairs. She was still struggling, lashing out with her feet and trying to bite him. He knocked her head hard against the banisters. She gave a muffled moan and stopped fighting for a moment. At the bottom was a door. It was slightly ajar, with a faint red light coming through the gap.

'What's in there?' he hissed into her ear, a few steps from the bottom. 'Who's there? Is it Henderson?'

She started to struggle again, trying to wrench herself free. Tired of her, curious to know what was in the room, he lifted her up and threw her towards the door. As she fell into the room, a single shot rang out. He dropped to the floor and flattened himself against the wall. He heard the sound of a door slamming somewhere in the room and a heavy bolt being drawn. Then there was silence.

He waited for a few moments, wondering what to do. He could see Anna lying on the ground just inside the room. She didn't appear to be moving. Slowly, keeping as close to the wall as he could, he peered into the room. Henderson, or whoever it was, had gone. Anna was on the floor, face down. He knelt beside her and turned her over, feeling her pulse. She was alive, although she appeared to be unconscious. As far as he could tell, she wasn't bleeding anywhere and he assumed she had been knocked out by her fall. She looked so small, so fragile, and for a moment his thoughts drifted back to the few hours they'd spent together. But such thoughts were pointless. The hideousness of what she had done was all that counted. He heard a noise from the far corner of the room, half sigh, half moan. He looked up, and in the strange red light saw a man, stripped to the waist, lying on his side on the floor, tied to a chair. He was groaning and straining against his ties as though in pain. Tartaglia took his keys out of his pocket and shone the little key ring torch at the man's face. He was blindfolded and gagged and his face was covered in blood, but Tartaglia recognised the deep, unmistakable copper of Alex Fleming's hair.

'It's Mark Tartaglia, Alex. The other man's gone. Stay still and I'll try and sort you out.'

Fleming stopped wriggling and after a couple of attempts, Tartaglia managed to heave him into an upright position. He undid the blindfold and the gag and Fleming gave a sigh of relief.

'Are you OK?' Tartaglia asked.

Coughing and clearing his throat, Fleming nodded.

Tartaglia took out a small pocket knife and sawed at the cable ties holding Fleming's hands and feet until he was free. Fleming tried to stand up, but his legs wouldn't hold him and he slid to the ground where he sat huddled against the wall.

'Stay there,' Tartaglia said. 'I'm just going upstairs to call for help.'

Fleming gave him a lop-sided smile. 'I'm not moving.'

'Can I get you anything?'

'A glass of water. And a fag, if you have one.'

Two hours later, Tartaglia stood outside the shop with Steele. She had just been dropped off and was walking up and down distractedly, talking on her phone. Fleming had been taken off to the Chelsea and Westminster Hospital up the road, to be patched up. Anna, too, had been taken to hospital, suffering from concussion. She had regained consciousness but was being kept in overnight for observation, under guard. The entire shop, which apparently had been leased by Colin Henderson, was now sealed off and being treated as a crime scene, with Tracy Jamieson and her team busy inside. The bullet that Henderson had fired into the air as he made his escape, as well as its casing, had been recovered and sent off to the lab for analysis, but nobody doubted that it had come from the same gun that killed Logan, Khan and Black. As for Henderson, there was no trace of him anywhere.

Steele finished her call and tucked her phone away in her bag. 'That was Colonel Wykeham, Henderson's former commanding officer,' she said. 'He's just given me some very useful background on Henderson. He wasn't just in the army. He was in the SAS and he served both in Northern Ireland and briefly out in Iraq during the first Gulf War. From what Wykeham said, he wasn't a leading light.'

Tartaglia looked at her quizzically. 'How do you mean?'

'It's bizarre, given everything he seems to have done, but the picture that comes across is one of failure, particularly in his eyes, which is what's important. Apparently, ever since he joined the army straight out of school, his goal was to get into the SAS, but it wasn't an easy ride for him once he was in. Wykeham described him as a loner, an outsider . . .'

'I thought they're all like that.'

'I suppose it's a matter of degree. He said Henderson wasn't an aggressive natural leader. Both his colleagues and his superiors saw him as not tough enough, and it didn't help that he came from the Light Infantry when most of them were paras. I don't understand the culture, but it sounds as though he was treated as a second-class citizen and bullied. There's also a history of Henderson having been bullied and abused both at home and at school. What is important is that he saw himself as a failure.'

'But he made it into the SAS. That's more than most men would ever be capable of.'

She nodded. 'He failed against a very high benchmark, but the point is it really got to him. It seems to have coloured everything he did, including what he's doing now.'

'But I thought you said he was out in Northern Ireland during the troubles. You don't survive that unless you're pretty tough.'

'Apparently he was in a passive surveillance role, never

front line. He didn't shine in the first Gulf War, either. When he went back to Northern Ireland, he hooked up with a twenty-year-old Irish girl and his marriage fell apart. After that, when he came back to the UK, he worked as a staff instructor until he retired. Since then he's been out in Africa and the Middle East, employed by a security company. He's had a string of girlfriends over the years, he drinks a lot and he's suffered from depression. His whole life has been blighted by the fact that in his eyes he's never, until now, had a chance to prove himself. Wykeham said that he's never killed anybody before and that the challenge would be for him to keep his head. Wykeham said he'd expect him to screw up sooner or later.'

'Well, he hasn't so far. Until now. How the hell are we going to catch him?'

'We're watching the ports and airports, but from what Wykeham says, he will have worked out his escape route well in advance and he may be long gone. With his surveillance background, he knows how to blend in and with his contacts overseas, he may easily be travelling on a false passport.'

'How do they think he's going to react now? Will he try and come after Fleming or Wade?'

'They think not. Wykeham's view is that now his cover's blown, he'll see it all as too risky and he'll abort the mission.'

'Abort the mission? That sounds very cold-blooded. Are you sure?' He couldn't hide his scepticism. Henderson was a man, not a robot and, more than anything, he was a father – a father bent on finding out the truth and exacting revenge. Surely emotion would still be the driving factor.

'That's what Wykeham says and he was adamant about it.

In Colin Henderson's eyes, the operation he's been running has gone pear-shaped and his training and everything he's learnt over the years will tell him to get out.'

36

Alex walked out of the hospital and crossed the Fulham Road. He had been there for several hours and it was now late afternoon. He felt as though he had been hit by a truck, but apart from some broken ribs where Henderson had punched him, and needing stitches to his cheek and above his left eye, where he had been pistol-whipped, there was nothing seriously wrong that a few stiff drinks and some decent sleep wouldn't fix. He considered himself very lucky indeed that he hadn't spent long in the darkroom. He had given a blood sample and they would find out soon enough what drug he had been given, but it was academic. He was alive, and that was all that mattered.

Brompton Cemetery was only a few minutes away along Fulham Road. He had arranged to meet Tim there at six. When he had called him earlier to tell him what had happened, Tim was on his way back from Oxford after his case had been adjourned. Tim had tried to coax him back to his house for a drink to hear the full story, but Alex had refused, saying that he wanted to go to the cemetery and see the place where Joe's body had been found. In the end, curiosity had got the better of Tim. Alex checked his watch and saw that it was already well past six. He turned in through the gates and walked past the lodge and the chapel. The air felt strangely close and as he started down the path towards the colonnades, he heard the distant rumble of thunder.

The cemetery was much as he remembered, although he had forgotten the sheer size of it and how the tombs were so densely spaced. The first and only time he had been there before had been one summer about ten years back, when he had gone there for a picnic with some actress he had been working with. Sheltering from the rain, which had started suddenly to pelt down, they had climbed into one of the mausoleums. The family had been Russian, he remembered, and it had been built like a small, ornate chapel, although the inside was a bare shell with only a little round stained-glass window for decoration. They had eaten their sandwiches and drunk the best part of a bottle of cheap red wine sitting on the dusty floor, then the woman had insisted they have sex. He had been all fingers and thumbs as he desperately tried to please her, but the thought that anyone might come along had been almost paralysing. He had seen her once or twice after that but he had forgotten her name, although he still vividly remembered the place and what had happened. He was looking around for the exact mausoleum when he spotted Tim looking down at him from the open arch of one of the colonnades.

'You're late,' Tim called out.

'Sorry,' he said, walking slowly and awkwardly up the steps to where Tim was standing. The painkillers they had given him at the hospital seemed to be wearing off.

Tim looked him up and down. 'God, you look a fright. Does it hurt?'

'Yes, but it's nothing serious. I just have to take it easy for a few days.'

'Well, I'm glad you're here,' Tim said, as they started along the covered walkway together. 'I've had two young boys offering me their services already and there are some very odd types hanging around. I wouldn't want anyone I know to see me here, in case they got the wrong idea. What kept you?'

'I had to talk to someone else from the police before they would let me go. They're offering me counselling, although I think I'll be OK.'

Tim gave him a gentle pat on the back. 'Not wishing to be cynical, it's probably because they're worried you'll sue them for not giving you protection. But if they're offering, I'd take it. These sort of things take an age to iron out in the mind. You're bloody lucky to be alive, you know.'

'Don't rub it in.'

'What you told me sounds horrendous. Something like that can mess with your brain, not least the fact that you survived, while Joe and the others didn't.'

He nodded. Sometimes, for all his thick-skinned single-mindedness, Tim could be surprisingly sensitive. Survivor's guilt hadn't yet kicked in, but he was sure it would when he had time to think about things. For the moment, there was so much already messing with his brain that he felt strangely numb and detached about what had happened to him that morning, almost as though it had happened to someone else. Maybe it would hit him later, or maybe he was already in shock and just not aware of it, but things would just have to run their course. Until guilt or whatever stopped him in his tracks, he had to keep going. Besides, there were other ways to deal with guilt. There was something he still needed to do to make amends to Joe and the rest. 'You know, I've been thinking about it all again,' he said, as they passed a young man leaning casually against one of the pillars watching them. 'I'm talking about what happened at the lake.'

Tim looked over at him. 'Why won't you let it rest? You've got enough to deal with and they'll catch the man who's doing this. Then it will all be over.'

Alex shook his head. 'It won't be over until they find out who killed the girl. She was murdered, you know.'

'So they told me.'

'The man who killed Joe, Paul and Danny was her father. It's funny, I don't blame him for what he tried to do to me. I don't feel any anger towards him and I understand now how he had to find out who killed her.'

'Stop worrying. They can't pin anything on you. After all this time, well, the evidence will be long gone . . . if there ever was any.'

'I'm not worried any longer. After what happened this morning, it's all clear. I was sitting in that chair in that foul darkroom waiting. I know it's a cliché, but maybe because I thought I was going to die, I suddenly saw it all so clearly.' He stopped and turned to face Tim, who looked puzzled.

'What's that?'

'I didn't do it. I didn't kill her.'

Tim sighed. 'Alex, nobody ever thought you had. It was just the police playing games, trying to scare you.'

'But I wondered, I really did. When that policeman started throwing all that stuff at me, I thought maybe, somehow, I had. And that I'd blanked it out. I mean you read about people doing terrible things that they then forget. It's the mind's way of coping, I suppose. And I was pretty high. I might have done anything. But I now know that I didn't. I didn't kill her.' He said it again, loudly this time, feeling the sudden joy and power of those words.

Tim smiled. 'I'm glad you've finally got that through your thick skull. Now do you feel like a drink? There are a couple of good pubs in the area and we could go and celebrate your new-found wisdom.'

'In a minute. I just want to take a look at the crypt.'

'All right, then. But let's make it quick. This place is giving me the creeps.'

They walked to the end of the colonnade, passing another man who was standing in the shadows with his back to them, hands in pockets looking out through one of the arches as though admiring the view.

'Wouldn't fancy coming here after dark,' Tim whispered.

Each to his own, Alex thought, momentarily amused that it made Tim uncomfortable.

'As I told you,' he said, glancing over at Tim as they turned down the stairs at the end of the walkway. 'I've been thinking about the night of the party. I wanted to ask you a few things, just to get it all straight in my head. There are just a few bits and pieces I seem to be missing.'

'Fire away, although I'm afraid I don't recall much about that evening.'

'Where was Milly? She wasn't there, was she?'

Tim sighed. 'No. She'd gone home to her parents for the weekend. We'd had a row, quite a serious one in fact. Can't even remember what it was all about, but I thought it was all over between us at the time. Seems so silly now, whatever it was.'

'That makes sense.'

'What do you mean?'

For a moment Alex said nothing. They came to the steps leading down to the crypt and he turned to face Tim. There was no point stringing it out any further. 'You and she were practically joined at the hip, you did everything together. Yet when I saw you in the woods, you were on your own.'

Tim looked baffled. 'Your point is?'

'You went to bed on your own and the next morning you were still on your own.'

'And?'

'What I mean is, you had to be on your own. What happened doesn't make sense otherwise.'

'You're the one who's not making sense, Alex. Let's go and get that drink and you'll feel better.' He put his hand sympathetically on Alex's shoulder, but Alex shrugged it off.

'There's something else. You know I told the police that Paul had seen her going off towards the boathouse with someone. But I remember now it was you who said that.'

'Me?'

'Yes. That's why we all went trooping off there and found her clothes in the boathouse and bagged them up. That was your idea too. Tidying up, I think you called it.'

'Your memory's better than mine.'

'Maybe. None of us were thinking clearly that morning so we didn't stop to ask questions, but how did you know they'd be in there?'

'I suppose I must have seen her going in.'

'But you didn't see who she was with?'

'I really don't remember. Must we re-hash all of this now?'

'Yes. That's why we're here. I need to square the circle. There's one more thing that's come back to me. You were also the one who persuaded us to put her in the lake.'

'No I didn't. It was Paul's idea, or maybe Joe's.'

'No, it was yours,' he said insistently. 'Paul was against it to start with, then finally he went along with what you wanted to do. Joe wanted to go to the police, don't you remember? But you convinced us all we had to do it, like you've been convincing us to do things all these years. It's why you're so bloody good at your job.'

Tim frowned. 'What if it *was* my idea? So what? I'm sure I was just thinking of protecting us all.'

'No Tim, that won't wash any more. You were protecting yourself.'

Tim was staring at him. 'Alex, you've gone mad. Given what you've been through, it's not surprising but—'

'Look,' Alex shouted, pointing down the stairs that led to the crypt. 'That's where Joe's body was dumped. He was in there. In that horrible dark hole. It's not a good place to end up, is it? And all because of something you did and made us all lie to cover up. I don't know how you've lived with yourself.'

Tim rubbed his face, which had turned bright red. 'Keep your bloody voice down.'

'You killed her, Tim.'

'Shut up.'

'Tell me what happened. It's just you and me.'

For a moment Tim said nothing, then he sighed heavily, his broad shoulders sagging as though he was letting out the strain and tension of all those years. 'It was an accident,' he said quietly. 'Just an accident.'

'She had a fractured skull . . .'

'She fell against one of the boats in the boathouse and hit her head. OK?'

'You raped her, didn't you? That's what the police think happened.'

'I said shut up! It wasn't rape. She wanted it, she wanted me. I'd had too much to drink and I got carried away, that's all.'

'That's all? She was strangled, Tim. Why?'

'Look, one minute she's fine and loving it, telling me to keep going and it's OK, the next she's screaming, saying she's going to tell her dad. I just tried to shut her up. As I said, I got carried away, in the heat of the moment. I never meant to kill her . . .'

'You stripped her and put her in the lake—'

'I didn't know what else to do. I panicked.'

'But all those years, I've been thinking that somehow I—'

'I didn't expect you to bloody find her.'

'Get down,' a voice shouted from the distance. 'Get down.'

As Tim wheeled around, a shot rang out. Alex felt something wet and warm hit him in the face, but he felt no pain. He touched his cheek and found blood. He looked up and saw people zigzagging towards them between the gravestones. He thought he caught sight of Mark Tartaglia. 'Get down,' someone shouted again, but he was unable to move. He noticed a man walking slowly down the steps from the colonnade. He was dressed in black and had a gun at his side. Alex recognised Colin Henderson. He heard a strange sound beside him and looked around. Tim was clutching his neck. Blood spurted in bright jets between his fingers and he sank to his knees, then fell forwards on the ground.

Alex knelt down, pushed Tim over onto his back and cradled his head in his lap. 'It'll be all right, Tim. Don't try and speak. We'll get an ambulance.' Tim's lips were moving slightly but he had become very pale.

A shadow fell across them and Alex looked up to see Henderson staring down at Tim. Then he turned to Alex and held out his gun by the barrel.

'Here, you take it,' he said, his face expressionless. 'I'm done. I heard what he said and I know now you didn't kill her.'

From behind the tall gravestone where he had taken cover, Tartaglia saw Alex hesitantly take the gun, holding it gingerly like someone who had never touched one before and was afraid of it. Colin Henderson held his hands up high in the air and turned towards Tartaglia. 'I'm unarmed,' he shouted. 'You can come and take me.'

Tartaglia stepped out into the open. 'Keep your hands up high where we can see them,' he shouted back. He ran towards them and grabbed the gun from Fleming, as two members of the surveillance team rushed to cuff Henderson. Fleming's face was spattered with Wade's blood, some of which had run down his neck, otherwise he seemed unharmed. 'Are you OK?' Tartaglia asked, as Henderson was taken away.

'As much as I can be,' Alex replied quietly, tears running down his face as he stared at Wade.

'We have it all recorded, crystal clear. Thank you.'

Fleming said nothing. Tartaglia followed his gaze to where Wade lay glassy-eyed in a pool of blood outside the crypt where Joe Logan's body had been found. The irony didn't escape him. Wade had started the whole thing nearly twenty years before and his actions had cost several people their lives.

'I know it's probably the last thing on your mind,' he said, meeting Fleming's eye, 'but we'll need a statement from you when you feel up to it. Shall I send someone over to fetch you in the morning?'

Alex shook his head wearily. 'No. Let's get it over and done with.'

37

'Where do you want me to drop you?' Tartaglia said to Fleming as they walked out of Kensington Police station together several hours later.

'On the canal, where Joe's boat is. I'm going to see a friend of his who lives a couple of boats along.'

'You mean Maggie Thomas?'

'That's right.'

Something about the set of Fleming's jaw didn't invite further questioning.

It was raining, the first time in weeks, and the pavement was slick underfoot. Donovan was waiting for them just outside in her Golf. Fleming climbed awkwardly into the back, while Tartaglia took the passenger seat and explained where they were going. He had spent the best part of the evening sorting out Fleming's statement and felt exhausted. Colin Henderson was still being interviewed elsewhere by Steele and a detective from DCI Grainger's team who were still officially handling Paul Khan's murder. It was a lengthy process and would continue the following day, but they already had the gist of what had happened. He had watched part of it on a screen in another room and had been struck by Henderson's composure. Slim and wiry, he sat upright in his chair, his surprisingly sensitive, weatherbeaten face unmoved as he described the sequence of events; about how he'd known Anna since she was twelve; about his meeting her again after all those years, and how he had desperately grabbed the opportunity to find out what had happened to his daughter. Genuine love, so difficult for him to express in words, showed in his eyes as he talked about Danni and about his longing to know what had happened; how the uncertainty had hung over him like a cloud, colouring everything he did.

His quiet desperation and strength of feeling had impressed Tartaglia, particularly coming from someone so unemotional and shut down, and he respected the man for his honesty, even if at times, when describing what he had done, it was also brutal. He had shown no mercy for his victims. In his view, they were all guilty for hiding what had happened, even if only one of them had actually killed her. The only time he had hesitated was when he talked about Anna. But whatever he felt for her, he refused to discuss it. Some of what he said corroborated the bare version Anna had given Tartaglia that morning. He was amazed to find that she had told him the truth, or at least an edited version of it, about the accidental meeting between her and Henderson, her reading Joe's book and her piecing together what had happened. Apart from the obvious, Tartaglia wondered if part of the attraction for Henderson had been the connection with his daughter, although Anna would have used anything to get what she wanted. However, Henderson clearly cared about her, refusing to implicate her in any way in the actual killings, saying that he had been acting alone. Although Tartaglia didn't believe him, so far Henderson was sticking to his story.

As for Anna, she would be properly interviewed when she was released from hospital, but based on the few things she had said so far, it was clear she intended to deny any knowledge of or involvement in the murders. So long as Henderson stuck to his story, with a good brief she might even get away with it. Everything she had said, even down to the misleading information she had given them about the second book, could be given an innocent spin by a good barrister. She must have had fun planting that red herring, he thought, although she would deny that too. He had been through every detail in his mind and although he had no doubt of her complicity in the killings, there was no hard evidence yet to back it up. The task of the next few days would be to find something to prove her guilt and he wouldn't stop until he had.

As for her real motivation, he was none the wiser. Had she really cared about Danielle that deeply? He thought back to their brief drink together in the Scarsdale Arms when she had asked him if he believed in the justice system. 'I just want to know for myself,' she had said. 'Do you think you deliver justice to the victims and their families?' He remembered the way she had looked at him, like a young girl who wanted to believe. Was there some softness and genuine feeling there that he had missed? Something sweet and tender left over from her youth that hadn't entirely shrivelled? He hoped so. Or perhaps the whole thing had just been a game, like so much of her life. Either way, she had to find out the truth. She would have got Joe to tell her everything, as far as his knowledge went. He would have been putty in her hands, and Henderson too, probably. She would have got a kick out of pulling his strings, sending the emails, planning the bizarre dumpsites, getting him to add the last dramatic touches to the bodies of his victims. She was behind all the things that didn't fit psychologically with everything else Henderson had done. Thinking of her, thinking of what had happened between them that night at his flat, he felt no lingering connection, just revulsion. He hoped he would never have to see her face to face again. Whatever her motivation, he felt no remorse for her, however damaged she was. He had seen it so often before, the bullied becoming the bullies, the abused becoming the next generation of abusers. The depressing but inevitable knock-on chain reaction of evil. But it was no excuse.

Henderson was a different matter. However hideous his actions, there was no sign that he had derived any sadistic pleasure from what he had done. Coming from a background and training where violence was the norm, a means to an end, he had simply wanted to find out who had killed his daughter. A part of Tartaglia felt a glimmer of sympathy for him and he understood the pain that had driven him. His former colleagues had dismissed what the man had done as a cold-blooded mission designed to prove himself, but they had underestimated him and missed the point. It had been about Danielle and nothing else. She had been the one light in his darkness. In Henderson's shoes, what father would not have wished to do the same? The only difference was that Henderson had seen it through in reality.

He was still musing about it all when Fleming leaned forwards.

'Hey, can you stop for sec?' he said. They were in the Edgware Road, not far from the canal.

'Do you want to walk?' Tartaglia asked, surprised. Fleming seemed physically drained as well as badly bruised from what had happened.

'No. I just want to get something from a shop.'

'OK, but don't be long.'

Donovan stopped the car and Fleming got out. Tartaglia watched as he walked slowly back along the pavement, shoulders hunched against the rain, to a brightly lit supermarket and went inside. A minute later, he reappeared holding several bunches of flowers.

'He's one of the world's last, genuine, old-fashioned romantics,' was how Wade had described Fleming the day before. The thought made Tartaglia smile.

Two minutes later, Donovan pulled up alongside the canal and Fleming got out. He was about to walk away, when he turned and bent down as though he wanted to say something. Tartaglia opened the window.

'Just one final thing,' Fleming said, leaning in, 'so's it's clear in my mind. When you asked me to meet Tim at the cemetery and wear a wire, were you using me as bait?'

'You agreed it was the only way to trap Tim Wade,' Tartaglia said.

'That's not what I meant. Did you know that man would come after me, come after us?'

It seemed an honest question, as though Fleming hadn't yet made up his mind. 'No,' he said firmly, hoping to convince him. 'I assumed he'd gone.' Never in a million years would he admit to anyone his true thought processes, that he had suspected that Henderson might show. With his surveillance background it would have been child's play to keep watch without being observed. He would have seen Fleming carted off by ambulance to the hospital just a few minutes down the road. He would also have known that there wasn't anything seriously wrong with him. He would have found out exactly where in the hospital Fleming had been taken and when he was due to be released. Again, child's play to follow him the short distance to Brompton Cemetery. But should there ever be an inquiry, Tartaglia would deny all of it. He had no idea what Steele thought; it was not something either of them had brought up, but he knew she would back him. Her head would be as much on the block as would Clive Cornish's, who had sanctioned the whole operation. 'We had a full debrief from his superiors,' he said to Fleming. 'Their assessment was that he would abandon what he was doing to save himself, and that he would try to leave the country. A man matching his description, travelling on what turned out to be a false passport, caught a flight to Paris. We didn't think you or Wade were at risk any longer.'

Fleming shook his head. 'You honestly believed that?'

'Look, we have to work with what we're given,' he said noncommittally. 'Everything happened so fast, there wasn't much time for analysis. They told us they knew Henderson inside out. They gave us a full psychological profile and they said he'd abort the mission, that that's how he'd see what he was doing.'

'Jesus, you really believe that? I'm no amateur psychologist, but that's crap. He was her dad; he had to find out who killed her, whatever happened to him. He wouldn't have stopped until we were all dead, or he was.' Tartaglia said nothing. That had been his assessment too, but however much he found himself reluctantly warming to Fleming, he had no intention of agreeing. 'Why don't you tell me the truth?' Fleming continued. Rain was running down his face and he was getting soaked but he seemed oblivious. 'You set me up, didn't you? You used me as bait and you knew he'd come.'

He met Fleming's eye. 'Listen, I'll tell you the truth when you tell me exactly what you did with Danielle by the lake.' He didn't expect an answer, but it was the last piece of the puzzle, the one final thing he needed to satisfy his curiosity. All along Fleming had acted like a guilty man, guilty of something even worse than finding and hiding a young girl's body, and he wanted to understand why.

For a moment Fleming said nothing. Then a half-smile flickered across his battered face. 'That's something nobody ever needs to know but me, but I'm comfortable with it now. Her ghost has finally left me.' Slowly and awkwardly he stood up. He wiped his mouth with his sleeve and, with one final glance at Tartaglia, turned and walked away, the flowers carefully cradled in the crook of his arm. For a man who had been to hell and back again, there was a surprising lightness to his step as though nothing in the past mattered any longer and the future was a brighter place. Almost envious, Tartaglia watched him go, saw him disappear down the steps to the canal and Maggie's boat. Fleming was right. He had baited the trap knowing that Henderson would come. Back in the hospital, when Fleming had told him of his suspicions about Wade, the ethics of risking Fleming's life were the last thing on his mind.

He had had qualms about using Fleming but there had been no other choice. Anyway, Fleming was hardly innocent. He had been caught up in the evil deed since the beginning. They had to nail Wade and if they netted Henderson too, it was worth the gamble. All that mattered to Henderson was finding out the truth of what had happened to Danielle. Given the opportunity, he would want to hear what the two of them had to say before finishing them off. If Fleming protested his innocence, as they had carefully rehearsed, then accused Wade of her murder, he might leave Fleming alone. He had also gambled that Wade, thinking himself and Fleming alone, would confess. However outwardly resilient he appeared, it must have been a weight off his shoulders to finally unburden himself. Whether his account was entirely honest was another matter, although it had sounded plausible. His death was unfortunate, but after the destruction and misery he had caused, Tartaglia couldn't feel too much pity for him, although he felt sorry for the collateral damage to his wife and children. Wade had directly, or indirectly brought about the deaths of several innocent people.

As Donovan accelerated away down the street, he took one last look at the canal, his mind turning again to the murdered young girl whose body had been pulled out of that stretch of water only a few months before. It was a dark world in which they lived. He turned to Donovan.

'Have you got time for a drink? You and I need to talk.'

'So, what's up?' he asked, passing Donovan a diet coke and sitting down opposite with a double vodka and soda. He wasn't driving and had decided he needed something strong to buoy him up in what was going to be a difficult conversation.

She sipped the coke and said nothing, avoiding his eye. They were in a bar he knew on the Goldhawk Road, close to where he lived, that stayed open late. It was half full even at that time of night and the music was loud, which gave him some cover. He had no desire to make a scene but he was determined to have it out with her. He couldn't let things go any longer.

In the middle of all the mayhem earlier, Steele had pulled him into an empty meeting room and closed the door behind them. 'What's all this I hear about Sam wanting to leave?' she had asked hurriedly. They were standing just inside the room, Steele with her back to the door, hands on her hips as though she meant business. He had stared at her dumbfounded. 'Are you serious?'

'Perfectly. I have her letter of resignation in my bag.'

He had struggled to take it in, thinking that there must

be some sort of a misunderstanding. 'Have you spoken to her?'

'Not yet. I wanted to talk to you first.'

'But you say she wants to leave?'

'That's right. So you know nothing about this, no reason why?'

He had shaken his head.

'Anything going on in her personal life? Her family OK?'

'As far as I know.'

'What about a boyfriend?'

'There's nobody around at the moment, from what she's said.'

'That figures. And you haven't done something to upset her?'

'Me?'

'I mean, this isn't something personal between the two of you, something I need to know about? So long as I know, I can deal with it. Maybe . . .'

He held up his hand. 'Hang on. Stop right there. Are you asking if Sam and I are . . . well . . .'

She folded her arms. 'That's exactly what I'm asking. Whatever you get up to in private is your business, but when it affects a member of my team, I have to know.'

'Whatever I get up to? Jesus, I can't believe this. What do you think I am? Some sort of cheap office Don Giovanni?'

'I wasn't thinking cheap and you haven't answered my question.'

He took a deep breath, trying to hold back his anger. 'Nothing has happened between Sam and me. OK? Nothing has *ever* happened.'

She nodded slowly. 'OK. I'm sorry, but I had to ask. I mean it's obvious to everyone the girl's in love with you.'

'What?' he shouted. 'That's rubbish.'

'No, Mark, it's not. I thought maybe you'd finally . . .' She spread her hands in a woman of the world fashion as though whatever it was he was supposed to have done would have been the most natural thing in the world. 'I mean, these things happen. After all, we're . . .'

She said something about their being only human, which would have been an interesting comment coming from her in another context. He sank down on the edge of a nearby table, tuning out the rest of what she was saying, and rubbed his face slowly with his hands. In love with him? Did she really feel that strongly? Nobody apart from Nicoletta, whose opinion he had discounted, had ever said anything to him on the subject, let alone spelled it out so bluntly. But he recognised the truth of it now. Perhaps he had known instinctively all along. He had just chosen to ignore it out of convenience. He felt guilty, thoughts flashing through everything he had ever said and done, wondering if he should have acted differently. Even though he might have given mixed signals, he hadn't done so deliberately. His feelings just weren't consistent. And they were both adults. He cared about her more than words could say, but love? Was it really love? A brother's love, maybe, but more than that he didn't think so. He looked up and met Steele's eye.

'OK,' she said matter-of-factly. 'I can see this is all news to you. I suggest you have a think, then speak to her. You know her better than anyone here, or so I thought. You sort out this mess, try and convince her to stop being so silly, and let me know. Until then, I won't do anything with her letter.'

The music changed to a song by Jay Sean he knew Donovan liked but there was no sign that she had even heard it. She stared vacantly into the middle distance, lost in her thoughts. He took a slug of vodka, then put the glass down. In normal circumstances, he would have taken hold of her hand and made her look at him, but he knew it wasn't a good idea.

'Sam, there's no point pretending things are OK. I hear you want to leave. Why didn't you tell me?'

She shrugged. 'I was going to.'

'But Carolyn knew first. What's going on? I thought you and I were close.'

She shifted in her seat, still avoiding his eye. 'It's lots of little things. I've just had enough, that's all. No big deal.'

'No big deal? How can you say that? What sort of little things?' She said nothing. 'Come on, after everything we've been through together, at least you can tell me.'

She wrapped her arms tightly around herself as though cold and shifted her gaze to a far corner of the room. 'Let's say I'm just feeling a little disillusioned.'

'Disillusioned? Can't you be more specific? This is all so sudden. I just want to try and understand.'

She wasn't usually the judgemental sort, but at the back of his mind was the nagging certainty that she had guessed what had gone on between him and Anna Paget. Not that she would tell anyone. He knew he could trust her, but what must she think of him? He also wondered what her view was of the conversation she had overheard in the car between him and Alex Fleming and all the moral issues it raised. She would know intuitively what had really gone on, the version that nobody would ever hear. They usually saw things as one, but now he wasn't sure. Perhaps he had crossed too many lines.

'Come on, Sam. Talk to me. I'm your friend, remember?'

She looked up at him. He saw the emotion in her eyes, the awkward tightening of her mouth, and realised he had said the wrong thing. For a moment she didn't speak. Then she sighed, as though tired of the whole conversation, letting her arms fall limply to her sides.

'Yes, you're my friend, Mark. But why can't you understand? I've just come to the end of the line. I've had enough and I need a fresh start. It's nothing personal.' She stood up. 'I'd better be going.'

'Don't you want to finish your drink?'

'No, I'm tired. I want to go home. Do you want a lift? It's still raining.'

Seeing she meant it, he got to his feet. Nothing personal. It was the opposite of what it was, he realised. She had come to the end of the line with him and he felt shaken.

'It's OK. I'll walk. I could do with the fresh air and I don't mind a bit of rain.'

On impulse, he grabbed hold of her hand and looked deep into her eyes, wishing that he could say something to persuade her to stay. 'Sam, I'm sorry. I'm truly sorry.'

Holding his gaze, she nodded. 'I know you are.'

He wondered if she understood what he really meant. He let go of her hand. There was so much unsaid between them, where should he start? She gave a little wave, then turned and walked away, picking her way through the crowded room to the door. She didn't look around. He watched her go, feeling as though he had lost something precious. But there was nothing he could do, he couldn't solve the problem. He sank back down in his chair and drained his glass in one, letting the buzz of the room envelop him as he enjoyed the kick of the alcohol. He felt sadder than he had done in a very long time. A part of him still couldn't believe that she could just cut loose like that and he waited a few minutes, hoping that maybe she'd return. But she didn't. He stared down at his empty glass. He put it to his lips and sucked it dry, crunching the last fragments of ice. Maybe he would find a way.

What to do now? He'd better go home, put on some music and get slaughtered. If nothing else, it would block things out temporarily. To hell with the hangover.

As he got to his feet, he felt a light tap on his shoulder. 'Hi there, Mark,' a chirpy female voice said in his ear. He turned around. It wasn't Donovan but a blonde-haired girl in a short, figure-hugging black dress. 'Remember me? Christy, from next door?'

He nodded vaguely, struggling to recognise her. Dressed as she was, with make-up, and her hair miraculously poker-straight, she looked transformed from the other morning, somehow older and more sophisticated. He wasn't sure which version he preferred. 'I hope the coffee helped.'

'Like magic. I couldn't trouble you for another ciggie could I? None of them smoke.' She jerked her head towards a large table near the window where he saw his neighbours, Janelle and Becs, amongst a group of women. They seemed to be having a good time, talking and laughing, with a table full of glasses in front of them. They must have been sitting there all along, he just hadn't noticed, he'd been so wrapped up in the conversation with Donovan.

'Of course. Here you are.' He felt in his jacket pocket for his cigarettes and lighter.

'Why don't you come and have one too?' she said with a smile. 'You look like you need cheering up and I'm dying to hear about what you do. Janelle tells me you're a detective.'

He hesitated. He really ought to go home, but the thought of sheltering under the awning outside for a smoke and a chat with her wasn't unappealing.

'You're on your own, aren't you?' she added, before he had thought of an excuse. 'I mean, your friend's gone, hasn't she?'

Was it that obvious? Although anyone glancing over at him and Donovan would probably have seen that something was amiss. He was about to say that he was on his way out but, feeling churlish, changed his mind. He noticed that the glass dangling from her hand was almost empty. 'I'll join you for a smoke, but can I get you another drink first?'

'Thanks. I'll have a Snakie.'

'A Snakie?'

'A Snake Bite. Fosters, cider and grenadine. They'll know what it is at the bar.'

'That sounds a pretty lethal combination.'

She grinned. 'It is.'

'I'll see you outside in a minute, then.' He handed her the cigarettes and lighter, still wondering if he was doing the right thing. As he made his way towards the bar, he decided to stick with vodka, maybe another double for good measure. It was already having a pleasant, numbing effect. There was nothing he could do for the moment about Sam and perhaps there were better ways of blotting out what had happened than going home on his own and getting pissed.

ACKNOWLEDGEMENTS

Thanks are due to a number of people for their time and expert advice, as well as apologies for my having wilfully ignored it on occasion in the interest of fiction. Any errors are entirely mine. Consultant Senior Investigating Officer David Niccol, from the Metropolitan Police, and Forensic Consultant Tracy Alexander deserve particular mention, not least for their patience, good humour and excellent company. I would also like to thank DI Mike Christensen and Dr Peter Jerreat, Accredited Home Office Pathologist, for their invaluable help. Thanks also go to Henry Worsley and Tuggy Meyer for furthering the story with some very useful and thought-provoking insights, as well as to Lisanne Radice, Louise Heyes, Jay Roos, of the Brompton Cemetery, Richard Williams, and the real Mark Tartaglia. As ever, I am grateful for the support of my fellow writers and crime aficionados Cass Bonner, Gerry O'Donovan, Richard Holt, Keith Mullins, Kathryn Skoyles, Nicola Williams and Margaret Kinsman. Lastly, special thanks go to my fabulous agent Sarah Lutyens and her team, to my wonderful editor Jane Wood and everyone at Quercus, and to Stephen Georgiadis, a great copy editor manqué.